Wilderness WIFE

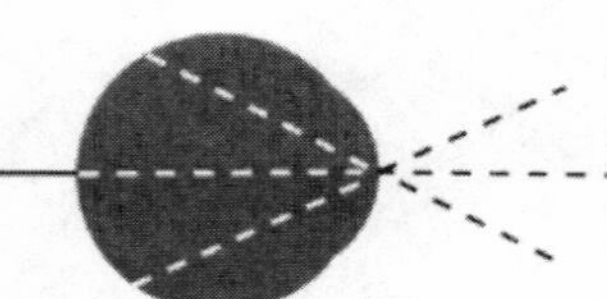

This Large Print Book carries the Seal of Approval of N.A.V.H.

Wilderness WIFE

DELORES TOPLIFF

CENTER POINT LARGE PRINT
THORNDIKE, MAINE

This Center Point Large Print edition
is published in the year 2022 by arrangement with
Scrivenings Press.

All Scriptures are taken from the KING JAMES VERSION (KJV): KING JAMES VERSION, public domain.

Wilderness Wife is Historical Fiction. The author researched the lives of Marguerite and John McLoughlin, their children, Marguerite's first husband, Alex MacKay, Lord Selkirk, Governor Semple, and many other prominent figures and events extensively. More minor characters and events are fictional but represent the history and society of that time.

The text of this Large Print edition is unabridged.
In other aspects, this book may vary
from the original edition.
Printed in the United States of America
on permanent paper sourced using
environmentally responsible foresting methods.
Set in 16-point Times New Roman type.

ISBN: 978-1-63808-451-8

The Library of Congress has cataloged this record
under Library of Congress Control Number: 2022938360

To Jesus who put love for story in my heart,
gave me amazing teachers,
and stories worth telling.

Acknowledgments

I loved growing up in the shadow of Fort Vancouver built by Dr. John & Marguerite McLoughlin. John's influence is widely known. His half-native wife, Marguerite's, courage and example are inspiring. Together they changed North America. I'm privileged to tell her story. I'm thankful for the wonderful friends and family I will always have in the area and for great teachers along the way, especially incredible Jane Weber who launched me into creative writing and showed me the kind of teacher I wanted to be.

Thanks to editors Erin Howard and Kim Vogel Sawyer for telling me which elements didn't work when I got too bogged in history and suggesting paths that did. You've made this a better book and me a better writer.

Thank you, readers, for embracing my first two books, *Books Afloat* and *Christmas Tree Wars*. I hope you enjoy this as much and welcome *Strong Currents*, next in the *Columbia River Undercurrents* series.

Thank you Linda Fulkerson, Scrivenings Press, for believing in my books, and agent Julie Gwinn for wisdom and encouragement along the way.

Many say writing is a lonely journey. I don't find it so. I've met some of my best life friends at

Christian Writing Retreats, Conferences, and in mentoring groups.

I benefitted from (and now own) many fine books about the McLoughlins and have loved visits and conversations that triggered further research. Visits to Fort William Historical Park in Thunder Bay, Ontario, Canada and surrounding areas helped set Marguerite's scenes in my heart along with frequent times at Fort Vancouver National Historic Site, Vancouver, Washington and the final McLoughlin home in Oregon City, Oregon, both part of the U.S. National Park Service. Other important locations are the Minnesota Historical Society's North West Company Fur Post now the Snake River Fur Post in Pine City, Minnesota, and beautiful Grand Portage National Monument, Grand Portage, Minnesota, also part of the U.S. National Park Service. Those visits and discussions with staff made this book richer.

Chapter 1

Indian Country, Central Canada, 1810

I kneel at the river cleaning the fish our Tom catches for our winter supply. For weeks the children and I have listened for the musket shots my husband will fire from the river bend to signal his return. Icy weather will come soon. Each day our children ask, "Is Father all right, Mama?"

"Of course," I say, trying to sound confident. "Few men have his skills."

But then, although I hear no sound except the river's music and see no shadow on my path, I sense human eyes. My hand flies to my throat as Alex MacKay stands before me, his arms crossed, his bearded face intense under his shaggy blond hair.

After ten months of being away, my explorer husband is back.

"Alex! You're home." I plunge my tanned hands into the river's icy current to rinse them, then rub them dry on my rough skirt as I scramble to my feet. He stands unsmiling and unmoving as I rush forward and fling my arms around him in case he's an apparition that may vanish if I don't take hold.

"Hello, Marguerite."

I reach up and smother him with kisses. "Why didn't you send word? Or fire your musket from the river bend for your hero's welcome?"

"I wanted to surprise you."

"Tom ran to the river bend twice this morning and offered to go farther. I'll call the children." As I lift a hand to my mouth, Alex grips my wrist.

"Not yet. We must talk. You *are* beautiful. I wish to remember you as you are."

"Remember me? Must you leave again? Does Mackenzie require another journey?"

"Not Mackenzie." He stomps one boot against a stone, freeing a dirt clod from his heel. "Helping him makes me famous too. He brags that no one possesses my wilderness skills. We've done what no other man achieved and proved it by carving our names and date on a boulder by the Pacific." His eyes gleam. "It doesn't hurt that he's my cousin either."

"We're so proud." I hug him again, but seeing his expressionless face, I release him. Success with Mackenzie has changed him. I easily read the woodland around me—today's frost-touched crimson foliage announces winter soon—but can't read my husband's face. "Alex, what's wrong?"

"With Mackenzie knighted, I'm also sought after. I must go to Montréal."

"So far?" I glance toward our cabin. "Then we must prepare."

"No. I can't take you or the girls—only Thomas."

"For how long?"

"As long as it takes. This is my chance for fame."

"Tom's only eleven. Do your parents need support? Is that it? We'll all go. I'll care for them." I have heard of my husband's parents but am not sure they know of me.

Alex bristles, pushing a hand through the shaggy hair I love to caress. "Marguerite, you don't understand."

My clenched hands fall to my side. "Then help me."

"I must secure my fortune. And his."

I tremble, like I am seven again seeing Father shot to death by a trading partner as Mother and I stand helpless. Except this death is happening now.

"What of our daughters? And me?"

He shrugs, his face impatient.

"You and they belong here in Indian Country. When they are older, I'll try to arrange good marriages for all three."

My lips form words, but my heart is stone. "Alex, what are you saying?"

The light in his blue eyes dims, as if he sinks beneath ocean waves. The right half of his mouth lifts in the crooked smile he uses when he knows his words will hurt. "It's plain enough. You're lovely but of mixed race. Tom has your father's and my lighter coloring and European features. He will be accepted."

"By people who are not family?" I tug his unyielding arm.

"Each man gets one chance in life to be something. I won't waste mine."

I release him to barricade my arms across my chest. "They are your daughters, and I—I am your wife."

He barks a hollow laugh. "My wilderness wife—a *façon du nord* frontier marriage recognized in this wilderness, but not legal in Montréal. Most North West Company men, including your father, left families behind to come west. I was young and unmarried when I came. I love you, Marguerite, but it's time to choose my society wife."

"Do I not matter to you?" His words attack like diving ravens. I tug my hair as my head pounds with confusion.

"Ours was a trading post contract, not the binding vows of a clergyman or priest."

I mask my emotions, but tears wet my cheeks. "There was none, only the fort clerk, but our vows meant much to me. As you said they did to you."

"They were enough then, and you've done me much good." He speaks with his detached voice that can drive me almost mad. "Mackenzie being knighted makes my fortunes rise."

He pulls me into the crook of his arm, but I resist.

"You're the best thing I've known, but this part of my life is over."

Alex has always been ambitious, but this sinks in. He is leaving us as completely as Father did. I cannot breathe. I see and hear Father dying again, smell the blood, taste the horror that he's never coming back.

No. There must be something I can do to keep him. "Why, Alex? Our girls love you."

"And I love them. Perhaps one day you can visit me in Montréal, although I could not acknowledge you. Thomas will find better prospects there than he could have here."

Fire scorches my breast as his hand strokes my coppery arm. He steadies me as I stagger. "Marguerite, it is sad. If only society were kinder."

"If only *you* were kinder." I shake off his hand. "I've seen you free screaming rabbits from snares because you felt sorry for them. Won't you spare us?"

"I wish I could. Please don't make this hard." His eyes warm with approval at seeing the new moose hide stretched nearby. "That's a fine animal. You're as good a shot as ever."

Alex is fortunate I do not aim my musket at him.

He surveys the rainbow trout Tom brought from the creek. "Those are large fish."

"He's downstream catching more." I point that direction. "Every morning he has searched for you—twice today." I gesture to a tall grove of evergreens. "Our girls are there picking cranberries and chirping like birds. Give your special call."

He shakes his head. "Not yet. First, walk with me to the house. Cook these splendid fish while I explain the generous arrangements I've made."

"Without you." I search his eyes, trying to recognize the man I married.

He cups my chin and studies my face. "You often speak of Sault Sainte Marie, your favorite childhood home. I've arranged for canoes to take you there. Your old friend, Peter Arndt, is in charge of the fort. I'll send enough funds for you to start over. You won't be destitute. Please make our parting sweet. Don't be sad in front of the children. I'm doing what I must."

I try to rush ahead to our cabin, but he holds me back with his hand on my waist.

"Is my travel trunk still in the attic? Tom and I will leave in the morning."

I almost stumble. "You will take my son from me that fast?"

"Snow will come soon." He kicks dirt free from his other boot and points its toe at crimson bushes by our cabin door, their leaves curling with frost.

"Yes, your trunk is stored there." I spit the words, sounding like the hoarse woodland spirits my Cree mother described.

He shakes his head. "Don't take this so hard. I'll call the children now. We'll talk more tonight." He lifts a hand to his mouth and gives the sharp cry of a hawk.

"Father's home!" our girls shriek. They come running, bringing heaped baskets of wine-colored berries.

Tom rushes to us carrying a bigger stringer of fish. As the children embrace their father, I try to calm myself. Perhaps Alex did not explain himself well but has a plan that will not destroy our family.

After enjoying his favorite braised trout and fried crispy potatoes, Alex pushes back from the table and pats his stomach. "Wonderful! As tasty as always. We don't get food like this while exploring."

"Mama is a good cook." Tom's pleased smile tears my heart.

Alex gazes fondly at our children. Soon he climbs the ladder near our fireplace and lowers down his trunk, then digs through its layers. He reaches in and removes woodland treasures he once gathered—a cunning whistle, a reed flute, the beaded belt my mother made him. He gives those to our girls. The city clothes he has not used for years are at the bottom. He lifts them now and shakes them free of dust.

"Girls, Thomas and I go to Montréal tomorrow."

"On an adventure?" Tom's face brightens.

"A grand adventure. We will have fun." Alex flashes his winning smile. "Take your best clothes but leave everything else. We'll buy new things there."

"When will we return?" Thomas asks.

"I'm not sure. We have much to pursue."

As night settles and all four children go upstairs to their beds, I linger in our living room rubbing imaginary dust from the silver wedding candlestick that gleams on our fireplace mantel.

Alex stands in our doorway. "Come to bed, Marguerite."

When I follow, he closes the door behind us. As he reaches for me, I whisper, "What about our marriage contract?"

He sighs, his forehead scar vivid. "Please understand. These have been good years. You've given me much. Don't be sad." He kisses my cold cheek as one comforts a crying child. "I'll never forget and always wish my future could include you, but I can't have two families, now can I?" He strokes my arm. "I ache for you when I'm away."

"And I for you, but how can you ask such a thing?" I must not let my hunger for him betray me now. I bite my lip and taste hot coppery salt.

A frown unites his eyebrows. "Because I am your wilderness husband."

My heart pounds. I pull away before my emotions unravel. "Seventeen years is payment enough. Besides, the time of women is upon me." God, forgive my lie.

"I didn't want it to be like this." His hand drops, and his voice carries disappointment.

As he climbs into bed and pulls the blanket to his chin, I flee to our living room, taking refuge in the maple rocking chair he carved for me to soothe our babies. My mind wars until I fall into a restless sleep.

In my dream, a fully rigged sailing ship races to escape a massive storm on tossing seas. It struggles to reach shore but flounders and breaks apart on jagged rocks. The man at the wheel turns my way, and I see Alex, the zigzag scar on his forehead white with strain. His blue eyes flash a desperate message I cannot read.

"Jump, Alex. Jump!"

He throws his shoulder against the wheel to change course, but wild waves splinter the deck and swallow ship, crew, and Alex, the last man to go down. Debris and oil stains ripple the water that calms at last. White seagulls circle and cry overhead.

Bolting upright, my breath comes in labored pants. I add a log to the fire and begin this morning's tasks. I cook a hearty breakfast before rousing Alex and Tom. While they eat, I mend Tom's coat and pack food for their journey. We say little. Miraculously, our girls still sleep.

"*Au revoir*, Marguerite. I'll send word when I can." Alex pecks my cheek and heads off without looking back. I hug Tom fiercely until he pulls free to catch his long-legged father, not realizing there's no promise we will see each other again.

Everything in me aches like a bird whose nest is robbed of its young. Can nothing end my pain? As a half-breed woman, I have no rights apart from my husband. *Dear God—fight for me!*

In our bedroom, I take our marriage contract from the wooden box Alex carved as my wedding gift. Worthless paper? I had believed it to be so much more. Now I want to tear it to shreds. But what if he changes his mind and returns? Instead, I slide the paper back into its box.

Perhaps I should have expected problems, knowing how poorly many North West Company men treat their wilderness wives. Many left families behind in eastern Canada when coming here. Most never returned, yet Montréal is where men must go for promotion and advancement.

Alex had been young and single when he chose me. He said he was happy with me, and I believed him. Kneeling by the bed still warm from his body, prayer spills from my lips. "Lord, my father taught me to trust You. You knew when I married that this day would come. Give me wisdom and help me understand the dream You gave. Keep Alex and Tom safe. Keep me strong for our girls. Don't let me fail them."

Tears prickle my eyes. I choke back sobs our girls must not hear. My jaws clench as heat blisters my heart. My hands fist until my fingernails cut my palms.

Lord, never leave us—like Alex, like Father . . .

My father had no choice. I will not let Alex's decision destroy us. Although my married life has ended, our daughters born of this failed marriage must not feel abandoned. My mind recalls this morning's vivid dream that seems more real than this gray day. I repeat my prayer, proclaiming my trust in God. Even if hungry rocks beneath the ocean's tossing surface devour our family, surely God will show a way to survive.

When at last I rise, a stronger woman gazes back from my mirror. She resembles my mother, but greater resolve shines from her eyes. I think she is a woman who will not easily give up.

Chapter 2

Songbirds greet this morning as they do each day, unaware that there is no cause to sing. The sun follows its familiar arc above the horizon. *Lord, give me the right words for the girls. Hold our hearts in Your hands. I cannot fail.*

Our eldest wakes first. Marie's face puckers when she descends the stairs and sees Alex and Tom are gone.

"How can they have left when I heard nothing? I wanted to hug them. It might be months before they're home—maybe summer."

"Or even longer, dear." I slide my arm around her waist. "There is much Father hopes to accomplish."

Her green agate eyes narrow. "He didn't say when he'd return, did he? What aren't you telling me?"

"He wants us to leave here and winter at Sault Sainte Marie."

"What? Leave our home? Why can't we stay here?" Her nose wrinkles as if she smells spoiled food.

"He prefers it. I loved it there and it will be a joy to show you that place. Your father is gifted. After his great success with Mackenzie, many doors are open."

Understanding pinches her face. "Those doors are open for Tom but not us? Not for you?" With an intake of breath, she hurls herself against me, and her tears soak the front of my dress. Finally, she leans back and studies my face. "Did he make any promises?"

As a knife twists my heart, I can't hold back tears. I won't lie but may soften the truth. "It is too soon to know his future, so he didn't promise. If he stays in Montréal, he will try to have you girls visit."

"But not you? Nothing will be the same, will it?" She grips my hand. "I am sorry, Mother. No wonder you looked sad last night."

"I hoped you wouldn't see." I stroke her chestnut hair and use my thumb to wipe the last tears trailing her cheeks. "With his plans uncertain, I don't know how much to tell your sisters."

She sighs. "Maybe he wants us closer to populated areas while he's away. And then if he returns, the girls are spared grief. If not—time will make things clear."

I hold this girl-woman in my arms and tuck her head under my chin like a mother bird shelters the young in her nest. God has given my girl wisdom beyond her fourteen years. Marie and I cling until we hear little Catherine fuss in her sleep. Soon Nancy comes downstairs carrying five-year-old Catherine wrapped in her yellow-

and-blue patchwork quilt. Catherine's almost blonde curls are so much like Alex, I catch my breath and grasp the table to steady myself. Nancy's auburn coloring matches the gleam in her eye. Sturdy and always craving excitement, she'll take this change in stride. Both girls yawn and stretch, neither expressing surprise to see their father and brother gone so early.

Marie is the most like me and the nearest grown, a little mother to her sisters. Her expressive eyes watch me silently with concern. She starts a pot of oatmeal while I explain that we'll spend this winter elsewhere. Then, to remove the worry from their faces, I say, "I saved some chocolate for a Christmas treat. Since Father begins a new adventure now, and we do, too, we will enjoy this today."

"Hurray!" Nancy shouts.

Catherine echoes, "Hurray!"

The promise of hot chocolate makes Marie smile. She looks up from stirring our porridge and rests the hand-carved wooden spoon across the pot's rim. "That sounds wonderful, Mother, a perfect start to our day."

"Yes, and I'll make plenty." I serve fragrant steaming cups and tell the younger girls we will visit my parents' best friend, Peter Arndt, at Sault Sainte Marie until Father and Tom return. That's enough truth for now. "We will leave most supplies here for travelers who pass through and face emergencies, but we'll take the essentials we will need through the winter. Finding food and shelter can save lives you know. You've heard your father's and my survival stories."

"We love them." Marie lifts her eyebrows, and her eyes glint green. "Maybe this trip will help our courage grow too."

"But not too much. We'll have our own small adventure but I want our travel to go well. Your father is suited to high adventure." Even as I say those words, I wonder how I ever believed our life here would be enough to hold Alex. I should have known from the beginning he would pursue greater things. I force a smile.

"You're brave, too, Mama." My lively Nancy's look of admiration warms my cheeks. "You shot that big moose and saved us when our canoe capsized."

"Thank you, love. That's what mothers do. I'm assigning tasks to prepare for our travel. Marie, please collect the bedding and school supplies. Nancy, please pack enough winter and summer clothes for you and Catherine in case we're away that long. Please also help her choose a few favorite toys while I pack pans and dishes."

"How will we travel?" Nancy's eyes grow bright with excitement. Of my three girls, she's my adventurer.

"Father made arrangements as he passed the fort west of us. Freight canoes carrying beaver pelts east before winter have saved space for us." I scan our living room and frown. "Probably very little space. That's why we can only take basics plus a few treasures to remind us of home." I'm thankful that my daughters show excitement for what lies ahead instead of sorrow for what we leave behind. Their cheerful hearts make our tasks easier.

The next morning, as mist still rises from the river, we hear singing before we see voyageurs swing into view in two large canoes bearing North West Company insignia. With joyful cries, the men sweep off their red caps and bend low in greeting. The tall one in charge says, "Madame Marguerite, I doubt you remember, but I am Marcel Dubois. Long ago I worked with your father one season. What a fine man. I am sorry for his terrible death and will help you in all ways I can."

"*Merci*." His kindness makes my eyes dampen. I don't recall him, but his manner reminds me so much of Father that I feel sweet sadness. He helps select a few traps and tools to take while I cook up our remaining food.

Dubois surveys our piled bundles and says, "Be sure to include your medical supplies. Your skill is badly needed."

The afternoon sun sinks fast this time of year. The men dig into my hearty servings of moose roast and Indian bread topped with cranberry jam or maple syrup. Later, they sing voyageur songs that give my girls glimpses of my childhood. I join in.

Suddenly birds hush, the sun sets, and it is night.

"If we may spread our bedrolls by your fire, we will rest well and load your goods for travel early tomorrow."

"*Mais oui*, *Monsieur.* And we'll take this extra food for our journey."

He tips his cap and pats his stomach. "*Merci*, Madame MacKay. You are as gracious as your mother."

"I hope so. Call me Marguerite."

"As you wish." His eyes light. "Carrying food will speed our travels. The wise ones in the villages warn that bitter cold comes soon. We must go before ice chokes the channels."

The next morning as we load canoes, the last skeins of geese fly southward, honking through pale skies as dense gray clouds pile up in the north. I point them out.

Dubois nods. "*Alors*, I see them too. We must start."

Every day we wear more layers of clothes to stay warm. Our daily routine sees the men bend horizontal over their paddles, digging deep in the current where the water has enough depth to thrust canoes forward. Where it is shallow, our canoes sometimes scrape stones in stream beds. Then, if we risk getting stuck on rocks or bogged in mud, we draw canoes and bundles out of the water. The men lift our vessels over their heads and with heavy loads walk along deer trails parallel to stream edges until the water deepens again. They call this *portage*.

One settlement on Lake Superior is named Grand Portage. It is rich in game and has many navigable channels to the interior. We spend a day near the settlement to rest and gather fresh meat—fish, frogs, snared rabbits, a deer. That evening a fat, lazy bear pads past us on its way to hibernation. The tall man lifts his musket and fires as fast as ever my father did. We enjoy sweet, tasty flesh that night with its nourishing fat. All through the night, we roast meat strips over fires to carry with us.

When my girls shiver in the cold, Dubois shakes out the bear's thick, hairy hide. "Spread this over your laps. This will be better once it dries and cures, but the hair gives warmth even now."

On our thirteenth travel day, the river tumbles fast between high rock cliffs that almost block the sun. We are nearly to where the current shoots forward fast again to a wider place when a boulder tumbles down. It narrowly misses the front canoe but slaps the river near us into a frenzy of frothing waves that bring us close to capsizing. Several bundles tip out. As we grab for them, little Catherine slips over the gunwale and disappears beneath the water.

"*Secours*! Help!" I scream and dive in. I clutch her dress and pull her close despite the shocking cold, but I cannot reach our canoe or shore. "*Secours*!" I cry again as my head pops up for a single breath of air. Will our lives end here? Has God brought us this far to be lost?

Somehow our steersman paddles our canoe to the last massive rock before the river shoots forward into a whirlpool guarding the lake. How he did it, I will never know. He had God's help. Soon, Catherine and I wash up against the canoe and see concerned faces cry out and hands grapple for us until we are caught. We are tossed up onto a wonderful soft bank of green moss, water streaming from us. We are like drowned rats, but we thank God for our lives.

We stop early that night because all are exhausted and several of us need dry clothes. We linger contentedly over our meal and find our bedrolls early.

"Thank you for saving me, Mama," Catherine says, her trusting blue eyes fixed on me. "I knew you would."

I say the same to our Lord above and to those who helped us. Although I wanted to save her with all of my heart, I didn't have the strength to rescue her alone.

I hold her close, inhaling her little girl smell as she sleeps, feeling her soft breath on my neck. I feel guilty enjoying her sweetness when Alex cannot, but the Lord reminds me that parents who steadfastly go through hard times with children deserve to enjoy the good times too. Where is Alex tonight? Does he know his flesh and blood nearly perished today? Or has he put aside thought of us like discarding a worn coat for a new one? Unable to sleep, I gaze long at the glittering stars overhead for a long time, giving thanks.

After fifteen days of exhausting travel, familiar log buildings swing into view along the river that joins Lake Superior with Huron. In some ways, coming to Sault Sainte Marie means returning home. Yet no married woman wants to be sent back home by her husband like damaged goods. As paddlers guide our freight canoes through boiling rapids, their paddles splash, making my daughters shriek and grab their skirts. I consider screaming, too, but with shame at being shipped here like unclaimed baggage.

Peter Arndt, the kindly old factor who manages this fort, begins slicing away my shame from the instant he sees us. “Marguerite! Girls! God be praised. I’d do a welcome dance if these old legs would permit it.”

He pushes the log stockade gates wide open,

then limps forward, shouting orders to buckskin-clad men. “Ring our church bell. Fire both cannons.” The heavy bronze bell clangs out deep tones followed by two four-pounder cannons booming twice across the water, and I picture St. Peter himself throwing open heaven’s gates to make our entrance wonderful. This good man makes my three girls laugh and brings a smile to my face too—my first since Catherine and I were pulled from the river.

Peter kisses my cheeks and clasps me in a warm hug. “Marguerite, angel of God, how the years have flown. And now you bring these lovely daughters, such precious beauties.”

I tower above him. Have I grown so tall, or has age diminished him? “Peter, thank you for—”

“For receiving a great gift? Nonsense.” He waves me quiet, sending workers to help the voyageurs carry our luggage and bundles. His weathered face glows as he ushers us through the fort’s entrance, although moisture shines in his eyes. “How wonderful you’re here. I’ve talked of nothing else for days. Have I, Jules?”

A mountain of a man grunts under my largest trunk. “*C’est vrai*. That’s true. Of nothing else.”

“Take them to our guest quarters tonight. Tomorrow I’ll show Marguerite and the girls around so they can choose which rooms best please them.” He turns to me. “Remember when you and your parents first came? You were a charming child the size of your youngest." He places one hand on Catherine's head, while his other grasps his cane. "I was young and strong then." He sighs so sadly, we all laugh.

"Those years were paradise, Peter. I wish we had never left."

"Your father did what he believed right." His chin trembles. "But his death was a tragic blow to all of us."

I shudder, and my voice drops as I recall that horrid scene. "Mother began dying the moment she lost him."

"Of course." His tongue gives a comforting cluck. "Our priests promise eternal fire to men like those who betrayed and struck down your father. By the saints, I pray it's true. Now I'm blessed you're here with your lovely daughters, exquisite dolls with flashing eyes." He bends and studies their faces. "Do you girls sing like your beautiful mama? *Alors*, she could sing like an angel from heaven! I hope you still do, Marguerite."

My daughters smile shyly. Nancy says, "She does, she does."

Peter's joy warms the winter in my heart. "God bless you, Peter. You could make dead stones live."

His eyes sparkle. "Then God be praised, for that is my hope. And your youngest? The very image of you at that age." He pats her honey-brown hair, nearly as light as Tom's. If Alex had noticed her complexion, he might have taken Catherine, too, unless he didn't want to bother with a girl.

"Let me introduce them. My oldest is Marie." I urge her forward and note she surpasses him in height. "At fourteen, she is nearly grown."

"A true beauty," he says, gallantly kissing her hand in an old-world gesture.

"And this is Nancy, age twelve."

"*Enchantée*." He clicks his heels together.

Nancy's eyes widen in ecstasy. "Mama, is he a king?"

"Almost," I say.

Peter roars with laughter. "No, child. But I recognize royalty when I see it and have planned a welcome you won't forget. Cook prepares a feast—roast ducks with savory rice and cranberries. And a surprise dessert with candied nuts and apples."

All three daughters nearly swoon.

I urge my baby forward. "The baby, Catherine—"

"Me not a baby, Mama." She frowns and shakes her tawny curls above her golden-bronze complexion.

I smile. "—is five years old and growing up entirely too fast."

Peter lifts her in the air, converting her frown to delight, and then lowers her and reaches for me. "Marguerite, having you come restores these tired bones. And your daughters—there is so much of you in them, how could they not be wonderful?"

"You praise me too much." I duck my head.

"No, not enough." He gestures to a nearby alcove. "You girls may wash here, and I'll show you a room where you may rest until dinner if you wish."

"We'll wash," Marie says, "but show us the room later. We're too excited to rest and want to explore."

As they step to the alcove, he leans closer, his voice sober. "I know Alex has gone and taken Tom."

"That's true." I turn to hide my sudden sheen of tears.

"Then God be merciful. I find it hard to forgive any man who leaves you and takes your son."

"I pray and hope one day he—"

There's sudden loud confusion outside. Two workmen rush forward, supporting a third man who sags between them with blood gushing through his split pant leg. One calls, "Where's the good doctor? Is he here? Gaston has chopped himself."

"Doctor McLoughlin left for the river to go to his next post." Peter gestures to his helper. "Jules, run fast and try to catch him. You two, take Gaston to the dispensary."

Apparently having heard the excitement, my

girls return. The girls and I follow the helpers carrying the injured man. We enter a treatment room, and they lift him onto a table. I get a good look at his injury and wince.

I whip my shawl from my shoulders. “He needs a tourniquet. Girls, go outside and pray.” They’ve seen many wilderness crises, but I will spare them seeing this much blood.

A tall man with a lion’s mane of hair bursts into the room carrying a black doctor’s bag. He grabs a knife and slits open more of Gaston’s pant leg, revealing a deep, nasty gash.

“The log was hollow, and I struck a wasp nest.” Gaston grimaces in pain. “Their sudden stings made me lose aim. Save me, Doctor. I can’t be an invalid.”

“Of course you can’t, but first I must stop your blood loss.” He twists my shawl tighter, pressing hard until the bleeding slows. “Now, I need fresh water, alcohol, and clean bandages.”

Peter scurries and gives orders while McLoughlin probes, Gaston clutches the table with both hands and groans, “*Mon Dieu*, my God, have mercy.”

“I know it hurts but lie still, man. I must work fast. Remember, pain proves you are alive.”

“Then that is good.” The poor man grunts louder still.

“Swallow this,” Peter says, offering Gaston an evil-smelling jug of alcohol.

He greedily swallows, his face ghastly white.

"Thank God it's a clean wound." McLoughlin dips his needle and thread in cleansing iodine. "Keep him still. These straps will secure his arms. Jules, you're strong enough to anchor his good leg and restrain his injured one so I can work." The doctor begins stitching muscle and flesh together while Jules holds Gaston down. "Peter, grip the wound flaps together while I suture."

Peter backs away. "I cannot. My hands are palsied."

"Let me help." I step forward.

The doctor pauses, and his dove-gray eyes appraise me. "Are you sure? Many women faint."

"I do not." I soap my hands in water and press the wound's cleansed edges together firmly as the doctor resumes stitching.

He studies me more closely. "You've assisted medical men before?"

"Not trained medical men, just wilderness people."

"Ah, you are Madame MacKay. Peter announced your coming. All of Canada praises your husband."

Perhaps the doctor makes small talk to keep me calm, but his words wound. I incline my head. "As he deserves."

"When does he return?"

"He . . . Uh . . ." My eyes burn, and I cannot breathe. I fan the sliced area with one hand to prevent two large black flies buzzing overhead from landing and then grip the wound edges tighter.

The good doctor looks my way and then re-threads his needle, but he lacks enough suture to close the gash. "Have you more, Peter? This cut is long, and I'm out of material. Do you have silk? Any kind of thread? Next season's supplies hadn't reached Fort William when I came through."

Peter grimaced. "I'm sorry, John. Nothing."

I always carry split moose sinew in my supplies for that purpose. I call to Marie through the doorway, "Bring my red sewing bag. And witch hazel leaves to slow the bleeding."

Minutes later, she rushes in with my kit, offering its packet of strong glistening sinew as thin as catgut.

McLoughlin stares open-mouthed at the smooth white coil.

"It's something I improvised," I explain.

"Improvised? Perfect, Madame." His luminous eyes are thoughtful as he closes the wound, the smooth thin cord following his needle in and out before he ties off each knot. I hand him scissors as he clips and then repeats the process each time. As he finishes stitching, when there is little skin left for me to grasp, his hand brushes mine. The smell of him is clean and fresh, like the split heart of a pine log in winter when its resin knot explodes in flame in the fireplace. Something frozen in me yearns for the comfort of home and a fireplace. I shake myself. Those days are over for me.

He removes the tourniquet, reaching for bandages.

"May I offer a leaf poultice for Gaston?"

The doctor looks up. "What kind?"

"Witch hazel helps the blood to clot."

He nods, then watches as I crush the ribbed leaves in my hand and moisten them into a green herbal skin to cover the wound. I hold it in place as the seepage slows. Next, the doctor applies bandages. After that, he fills a wash basin with clean hot water and rinses his hands before refilling it and offering it to me.

"Madame?"

I feel calmer than I have in days. Helping save someone's life restores order to the fragments of mine. My stress rinses away with our patient's blood.

McLoughlin pats Gaston's shoulder. "You were lucky today, man. You'll survive more adventures thanks to Madame MacKay's cleverness. Her tourniquet and suture saved you more than my skill. Keep the wound clean and dry. Perhaps she will check you tomorrow."

His eyes ask me that favor, and I nod. "Of course."

"Above all, Gaston, from now on"—

McLoughlin's mouth lifts in an easy smile—"promise you'll only chop trees, not your leg."

Gaston grips his hand. "*Mais oui*. I am chief of wooden-headed idiots, am I not?"

"No." The caregiver's voice soothes. "It was an accident. You're not the first man I've stitched for that. I fear you won't be the last."

"Peter," Gaston says, "please give the doctor a bottle of rum charged to my account." His friends help him stand and support him as he leaves, still expressing great thanks.

McLoughlin turns to me and bows at the waist. "You haven't had professional training, Madame MacKay? Then you are gifted."

Heat climbs my cheeks. "I'm a simple frontier woman glad to help."

"The finest I know," Peter adds. "And a marvel at raising daughters as lovely as herself."

"So I see." The doctor views my three daughters as they enter the room and glance at the bloody signs of surgery with no sign of discomfort at all. In truth, they've seen such signs often.

I retrieve my stained shawl and rush to leave. "The girls and I will find our quarters where I will launder this."

"Jules will guide you," Peter insists. "I'll call you soon for dinner."

As I smooth out my rumpled traveling skirt and shepherd my three girls along the path, I hear

McLoughlin ask Peter, “Why have I not heard of this remarkable woman before?”

“Because much is made of her husband. Not enough of her.”

My face reddens knowing Peter continues explaining more. Their voices fade as I answer my daughters’ questions, but my mind wonders what McLoughlin will think of me now.

It doesn’t matter. He travels to a new post. While it has been pleasant to meet and work with this man, I am relieved knowing we will not meet again. It would be embarrassing to spend time in his presence now that he knows the circumstances of Alex’s departure. I am happy with the memory of today’s successful medical care.

Chapter 3

At dinner, Peter Arndt stands at the head of the long plank table and turns toward an aged priest. "Thank you, Father Laurier, for blessing our meal. It is good to have you stop on your way to your other parishes. And thank You, blessed Savior, for safely bringing Marguerite and her girls to us. We welcome them with this toast and wish them joy and blessings every day."

The moisture brimming his eyes brings tears to mine.

"Hear, hear. All rise." Jules lifts his glass high in my direction and drains the contents. His lips smack, and his cheeks redden.

"Don't worry, Marguerite," Peter says with a wink. "Your girls have apple cider to drink while we have harder stuff."

"Apple spider! Where's an apple spider?" Young Catherine's blue eyes widen in horror. Marie has braided a circlet of dried blossoms for Catherine's hair, making her look like a real princess.

"No, child. It's a treat Uncle Peter makes from pressed apples. Something delicious in your glass for children to enjoy."

She bends and tastes, sipping daintily, but then gulps it all.

"You care for us too well, Peter." Happiness lightens my voice.

"No. I wish to do more."

When our stomachs cannot hold more, Peter calls Catherine to him. "Child, sit with me while I flame brandy for our dessert."

"May I, Mama?"

"Of course." She rushes past me, skirts rustling, and settles on his lap, trailing the fragrance of dried flowers behind.

"Watch, child. This liquid flames blue when I hold fire near and makes our dessert taste better. Marie and Nancy, you may also come and watch." He tips a little more brandy over the top of the large bowl. When he strikes a flint, tongues of blue fire dance like Northern Lights before burning out.

"That is beautiful," Marie says. "May we taste some?"

"Of course." Peter serves us. "Marie, did you know this fort is named for you?"

She flushes with pleasure. "Is that true, Mama?"

"For you and our Lord's mother, for whom you are named. Peter, my girls have never seen such treats. They will love you forever."

"As I hope." He slaps his other knee and turns to the priest. "Father, forgive me, but I can think of no better way to become immortal."

Father Laurier spreads his arms wide, his lips

widening in an inviting smile. “Jesus gave the example of welcoming little children to Him.”

Across the table, Doctor McLoughlin leans toward me. “Your tourniquet and sinew saved Gaston today, you know. The way he was bleeding . . .” He flinches. “I hate to think how it could have ended.”

I shake my head. “It was your skill, Doctor. Wilderness women simply do what we must when there are no doctors near.”

“And are knowledgeable and stay calm in crisis. You are remarkable. My uncle, Simon Fraser, is also a physician, but when his dear wife helps, she often becomes dizzy at the sight of blood and requires attention herself.” He indulges a fond laugh.

“Simon Fraser?” Jules asks. “The famous explorer? Then surely, he and your husband know each other, Madame MacKay.”

“Yes, Jules, they do,” Peter answers quickly, sparing me. “I can’t thank Alex enough for sending Marguerite and the girls here while he has to be away.”

“But Mama,” Nancy speaks candidly, “Father said he won’t—”

“Never mind. Let the grownups talk.”

As Peter turns the conversation to winter trapping, McLoughlin’s eyes meet mine with compassion. When Catherine’s napkin slips and drops under the table, McLoughlin dives for it.

"Allow me," he says, but I've already bent, too, and our hands brush, shooting pleasant tingles through me. Am I so starved for affection that a stranger's kindness unnerves me?

"Thank God you hadn't left when we needed you today, Doctor," Peter says again at the meal's end. "Where do you travel next?"

"To Rainy River for personal reasons." Sadness lines his face. "And west from there to see if the Hudson's Bay Company truly plans to import Scottish farmers to confiscate our lands, as rumors say."

Peter gasps. "Surely not."

"They wouldn't dare," Marie interjects. "Father says if they do, it means war."

"It could," Peter answers sternly. "We've heard the stories, too, but pray they're untrue." He turns to my daughters. "Let's discuss more pleasant things. Your mother says you girls love school, so I offer my services." He dips his head politely and sweeps his hands to include all those around the table. "You'll find many fascinating people here willing to help. Not all have book learning, but they all have practical skills."

"Wonderful," Nancy says, eyes shining.

"Do you enjoy learning?" McLoughlin studies their faces.

"More than anything," Marie answers. Her sisters nod.

"When I travel, I carry extra books besides

my Bible. And when I leave, I often find homes for them." His eyes gleam. "Perhaps I can repay your mother's kindness by giving you a gift." He turns to me. "With your permission, Madame, my best European history is yours—in honor of your Swiss father who is revered by all North West Company employees. Anyone who knew him remembers and speaks highly of him. His integrity and courage are legendary."

"Thank you, Doctor." Warmth heats my neck. "Your words bring joy. My daughters know little of my father. I don't have a wealth of memories since I was so young, but those I have are strong." Sadness clogs my voice.

"Only memories? Nothing more?" His eyebrows lift. "I've read excellent written accounts. I'll find copies to bring you next time." He glances at my daughters. "And more books if you like."

I lift my hands. "That would be heaven."

"Return soon, Doctor," Peter urges. "You don't come often enough. If only Headquarters would assign you here permanently."

"Every fort wants physicians, but you know company strategy. They rotate us to give token coverage while reducing costs. Still, I find God often has me at the right place at the right time."

"As He did today," Peter agrees, "or we might be arranging Gaston's funeral."

Gaston flinches, his bandaged leg propped beside him on a rough bench.

McLoughlin's eyes twinkle. "But once they hear of Madame MacKay's skill, they will send for her instead of me or any other physician."

"Nonsense," I sputter.

"We won't tell them." Peter's voice is conspiratorial.

The doctor's joyful laugh surprises me, and I feel myself blush. Laugh lines I had not noticed earlier make his face and eyes fascinating. He is younger than I first thought—and highly skilled for such a young man.

"Madame MacKay," he says, "it may interest you to know that if Fort William becomes the new interior headquarters as many expect, they will establish a real school with trained teachers from back east."

"Truly?" One hand flies to my face. "In these wilds?"

"So they say. If that proves true, I will send you word."

Hope springs in my heart like a bird leaving a temporary nest to migrate home. "That would be a great kindness."

"But if that means these precious ones leave," Peter fusses, "I won't thank you, Doctor. I'll become a deaf old man incapable of hearing any word that means they might go."

I place my hand on his arm. "Peter, you are

ageless. Wherever we travel from now on, you must retire and come with us."

"Thank you, child, I will consider that." His face glows like the harvest moon climbing the dark sky outside these windows. "You are as gracious as your saintly mother. How proud she would be of you, Marguerite. I am proud for her." His eyes blink. "But look, Catherine falls asleep in her plate."

Her chin drops dangerously near her dessert.

Peter starts to rise. "You need rest, and morning comes early. Let me carry her."

McLoughlin is already on his feet, scooping her up in his strong arms. "I have her, Peter. She's no trouble. Their guest room is near where I sleep, so I'll take her." He shifts Catherine's slight weight and looks my way. "I leave at first light, Madame MacKay. It has been a pleasure to meet you. May God grant that we meet again."

"In His time," I say, and turn to acknowledge the others. "Thank you for this wonderful evening. Father Laurier—Jules—especially you, Peter."

He points heavenward. "How can we do less when God sends angels to us?"

"Then I thank our Lord most of all. *Bon soir*. Rest well, all."

Marie, Nancy, and I follow the tall doctor as he leaves the dining room and strides confidently down the path. I marvel that in one-half day's time, our family's heartache has been lessened in this safe place where we enjoy the first warm welcoming touches of a new home.

Soon, my daughters' breathing finds the soft patterns of sleep. Where are Alex and Tom tonight? Will I see them again? I press sobs into my pillow, dreading many empty days ahead. Yet as I think of God's kindness even today, my tears slow. My last thought before sleep is to wonder if we will ever see Doctor John McLoughlin again.

Chapter 4

This chill morning makes me reach for Alex's warmth, but his side of the bed is empty. He must be away on another trip. I squint one eye open. Above me, yellow morning light streams through a window of wavy pressed glass. Our wilderness cabin has no bedroom window. This room is very large. I hear my three girls breathing softly nearby. As last week's crushing events clang into my consciousness, my stomach sickens.

This is not my marriage bed in our wilderness home. Alex won't be coming back. He's on his way to Montréal, taking Tom, our only son, with him, but not our daughters. The girls and I have rushed to Sault Sainte Marie before winter, this fort where my parents and I lived several seasons when I was young. My stomach calms a bit as I recall arriving yesterday. Peter Arndt, the fort's aging factor, welcomed us so sweetly it salved my heart with a pleasant new memory. Further kindness from a doctor I met and assisted here gave me more distance from my troubles and made me feel like I'd received medical aid along with his patient.

"Doctor McLoughlin," Peter had introduced him. A Scottish name, although his accent sounds French. Now as I throw my blanket back, the sun climbs above the horizon, and I hear morning sounds on the river. Canoe paddles splash, probably McLoughlin—a fine man who showed me more kindness in a single day than my husband Alex had for months.

I think of Alex and Tom. Where are they? I pray our Lord will protect them despite Alex's choice to leave us behind so he may advance in Montréal. I hear again the pledge he freely gave at our wilderness marriage long ago. He had sounded sincere as a young bridegroom when he spoke his vow, professing undying love in his eagerness to have and hold.

"You lost your father young, Marguerite." He kissed me tenderly. "As your husband, I shall always love and protect you." What mockery those words became when he reminded me our marriage was only a *façon du nord* contract, the unofficial common law convenience of Indian Country. How could he speak his vows then, but abandon the girls and me now? What kind of man breaks promises so easily? I watch our sleeping daughters—Catherine, warm and breathing softly, curled at the edge of my bed, Marie and Nancy sharing the bunk across the room. Harsh circumstances make women mature early. My daughters don't yet realize I am husbandless and they are fatherless, but they will survive as Mother and I did, though it took determined skill and constant daily choices.

Sometimes, I hear the comforting Bible verse Father frequently spoke or sang—"I will never leave you nor forsake you." Eyes welling, I cling to those words, because life teaches that only God, not man, keeps such promises.

A black-capped chickadee trills its song in the maple tree mostly bare of its golden leaves outside our window. This bird sings although it surely understands it will soon face winter and fierce enemies. Its melody carries one of David's Psalms to my heart. "Our soul is escaped as a bird out of the snare of the fowlers." *That's true, Lord.*

I hear Him saying, *I've been faithful every day of your life. Trust Me for coming days.*

My hand traces Catherine's cheek, my fingers brushing back her tresses. Her curls come from Alex's side of the family, a gift our children appreciate. Mother's hair, closer to the color of a running deer than a raven, hung straight like a waterfall. Mine is lighter, thicker, more like my father's with his red glints. Thomas has my father's and his father's coloring, ruddy cheeks and an upturned nose below sparkling blue eyes—plus plenty of mischief to go with it. But missing him brings pain.

Marie blinks awake. When she sees my eyes open, she speaks quietly to not waken her sisters. "Will Uncle Peter really hold school for us?"

Dear Peter Arndt, more grandfather than uncle,

eager to ease our disappointments. "He is a man who keeps his word. If he says he will hold school, he will do it."

She gives a contented sigh. "And that wonderful book of European history? May I read it today?"

"Of course, *ma petite*. I peeked inside. It has color plates—something you have not seen before. You may show your sisters."

Her eyes glow. "With pleasure, Mama." She glances around the room and then her eyes look through the window at the growing light. "This is a good place. Can you be happy here?"

She seeks a reassuring answer, so I give it. "Yes. It may take time, but you girls bring me joy."

"And Thomas?" Her face crumples. "It's hard having him gone, isn't it? He's so young."

She is not many years older. My heart pains, but I try to lighten her mood. "In spite of his tricks? The dead mice he hides in your shoes?"

She chuckles. "And live frogs in my apron pocket. Yes, even his tricks, for that's how he shows love."

We laugh together. "You are wise to know that. One day he will return—our love will draw him. As for being happy here, how can I not with everyone so kind. Happiness grows in small ways, like spring's green shoots after winter's long cold."

"Yes, Mother. That's why spring is my favorite

season." And with that, my almost grown girl ducks under her blanket and sleeps again.

True to his word, after breakfast Peter leads us upstairs and down, stomping through all parts of the fort to give us our choice of rooms. Near the end of one corridor we see a large upstairs room showing glorious views of the river below.

Nancy tugs my arm. "Mother, please. May we choose these rooms? The scenes are gorgeous and the river's song is music."

Pleasure warms my breast. "Yes, if Uncle Peter agrees."

"I do most heartily. I'd give you the moon if you asked." He sweeps his arms wide. "I have this same view from my rooms below. If you need anything, just pound on the floor for my attention. I might rig a pulley to hoist anything you wish."

"And for us to ride?" Nancy's eyes flash and I think she might try! She adds impishly, "Holler when you need anything, Uncle Peter. We'll serve you."

He laughs, and we join him.

I place my rocking chair, in which I held and rocked each of my babies and sang, near the fireplace. Peter's men bring a plank table with benches, two chairs, several wooden chests, and another bed. I stroke the thick wool coverlets and quilts. "Thank you, Peter. What luxury."

"No, truly necessities, but I'll give you the best

I have. Here comes Jules with tea, bread, and jam to further celebrate your coming. You need to have little treats around your rooms." As Jules places the plate on the table, delicious smells tantalize us.

Young Catherine pokes her finger in the raspberry jam and licks it clean before I can stop her. "Not as good as yours, Mama."

"Child, mind your manners."

"But it's true."

Peter interrupts. "Let her be, Marguerite. I'm sure the jam is not as good as yours. Join us, Jules."

"Thank you." Expecting Peter's cordiality, Jules has already sat and opened a napkin he pulled from his pocket. He spreads it across his ample lap.

"Peter, you spoil us." I sort through an armful of crimson autumn leaves my girls have gathered and arranged them in a vase for the table.

"Not true." He shakes his head fiercely, making his bushy eyebrows waggle. "You could receive a lifetime of tender care with no ill effect."

"Did you really know our Mama when she was little?" Nancy asks, taking an unladylike bite of bread.

"Yes."

"What was she like?"

"Like the angel she is now." He leans back. "And nearly as lovely. Wonderful in so many ways." He lifts his fingers and counts. "First, sweet and beautiful, like you girls. Second, when she sang, birds in the trees listened." He turns to his friend. "Didn't they, Jules?"

"Always." Jules inhales a third piece of bread and jam before brushing crumbs away. "Excuse me," he says, "I must resume work before my employer fusses."

Peter winks and waves Jules away before he continues counting. "Third, your mother sang in French, English, and two native languages, besides reciting poems."

"So many ways, Mr. Arndt?" Marie asks. "Are you teasing?"

He gasps in mock horror. "I am not. It's God's truth. But call me Uncle Peter, as I count you part of my family. Even as a child, your dear mother carried a battered doll wrapped in slings and bandages to care for, the same way she helped Doctor McLoughlin yesterday with Gaston."

I look at him in surprise. "Really? I don't remember the doll."

"You don't?" He gives a mock gasp of horror. "But you took her everywhere until she fell apart and your mother refilled and re-stitched her each time, so afterward you added more bandages and more blankets. No wonder you are a skilled nurse and mother now to these three beauties." He twines one of Catherine's soft ringlets around his finger.

"Don't you have a little girl of your own?" Catherine asks in innocence.

His face clouds with such pain that I wince. "I almost did," he says. He turns to me. "You may not remember, Marguerite, but after your parents moved west, I married Monique, a sweet French and Métis woman."

His sorrowful tone warns me his story is sad. "Mother mentioned her."

"After two happy years, we expected a child. Nothing dampened our joy until Monique had complications at the birth. We tried everything, but no solution helped. The weather turned bitterly cold, impossible for anyone to come assist, and no one here had medical skill. I offered my life to God for theirs if, if only . . ." He lowers his head. "I couldn't stop the hemorrhaging. Or save our precious infant. I think little Claire would have been like your Catherine. They await me in heaven, which makes me eager to go." Tears roll down Peter's cheeks, and we also dab our eyes.

"Our grandpa and grandma are in heaven," Catherine says, her sweet face scrunched. "May I be your little girl?" She slides her hand into Peter's.

"We all will be," Marie adds.

Peter nods but does not speak. When I do, my voice sounds strangled. "Peter, how did I not know? I'm thankful God did not take you—

you're needed here for many more reasons than the fur trade."

"You think so?" His voice quavers.

"I know so. Do you not see your value? You maintain peace and order through this entire region and show kindness to everyone."

"I try, and I have since learned some medical skills. However, I don't do well with these unsteady hands." He holds them out in front of him and we note their shaking. "That's why we're glad whenever Doctor McLoughlin comes. We need more talented men like him in this wild country." He tousles Catherine's hair and, after retrieving a handkerchief with his free hand, loudly blows his nose. "I miss my wife and child, yet sometimes it seems they are near." He squares his shoulders. "I seldom discuss their loss, but I know you understand pain, Marguerite."

"Yes," I whisper. "But I'm sorry for yours."

Deep lines etch his face. "My girls lie surrounded by flowerbeds under that large elm by the main gate. I've provided them with the woodland flowers Monique loved most."

"May I help garden next spring, Uncle Peter?" Marie asks. "Or anything else that will help you?"

Little Catherine squeezes his hand. "I'll water your plants."

"Of course." He blows his nose again. "You girls are as sweet as hollow trees full of honey that drive bears mad." He folds his handkerchief and tucks it away.

Marie's face puzzles. "It's been a long time since they passed. Why didn't you remarry?"

I flinch at her question, but he hesitates.

"Your mother may know." He studies me. "Do you, Marguerite?"

"I'm not sure. I was young."

Now he addresses me, not Marie. "I wrote your parents of my loss and heard from them. But it took nearly two years for word to reach me of your father's death. Eventually, I wrote your mother suggesting we share companionship, promising to love and care for you both."

"You did?"

"Yes, with all my heart. I've always admired her."

His loving gaze pierces me. I finger his frayed jacket cuff, as if my caring touch might mend his heart. And then I recall Mother's searching looks the times we visited here after Father's death. And Peter's, as well, that I didn't understand at the time.

"I didn't know—but wondered. She missed Father dreadfully, but always spoke highly of you."

He sighs. "I am glad."

"Did she not answer?"

"We exchanged notes, although it is difficult sending messages in this vast land. She assured me of deep friendship but said it was too soon." His shoulders slump, and he swallows before saying more. "She said we must both heal first and then consider."

"She would have been honored." And then I guess her real reason for hesitating. "Peter, she was so conscious of her native blood and felt undeserving of Father, let alone a man leading a larger trading post!"

"Pah, blood and status is nothing." His voice rises to a wail. "She was a treasure I would have always cherished—both of you. Monique's origins were similar. Only love matters, not heritage." He wipes his leaky nose on his sleeve.

"Not all feel that way." I picture Alex's face as he explained why he would leave me.

My daughters' eyes widen at Peter's words. When Catherine grasps the hem of his wool coat and tugs, he again rests a trembling hand on her curls. "God bless you, child. You heal an old man's heart." His other hand grasps mine tight again, but he says nothing more.

"That's why Mother called you Uncle Peter," I say. "We are family. When she lay dying, she wished to write you, but her strength failed. She made me promise to send word, which I did, and—better yet—to see you. I understand now that she wished to say more." I lean my head on his shoulder. "I'm so sorry."

"Many things are healed in heaven." He gazes

through the window. "Her last message before the diphtheria outbreak said perhaps it was time to move forward. She promised to attend the Fur Rendezvous here after you and Alex married."

"But the sickness came, and she became ill and then was gone."

"Exactly. *Quelle douleur*, what sadness!" His eyes blaze with such intensity, I imagine him young, eager, and strong again. "How good to have you and your girls here now," he says.

I fling my arms around him. "We love you, Peter. We thank God for you."

"And I thank Him for you."

Astonishment bursts inside me. "Did Alex know? Is that why he sent us here? For you to care for us?" For an instant, I think kindlier of Alex.

"No, not from me. But I thought perhaps you knew and told him."

"No, I did not." I see my husband's face again. He is brave but not sensitive. "Perhaps God nudged him, and for once Alex listened."

"Then God be praised." Peter bends and speaks to me alone. "Never worry, Marguerite. My funds are small, but won't run out—even if Alex sends nothing."

"I don't worry. I know how to trap, hunt, and forage."

"Of course, you do."

Little Catherine hugs his leg. "I'll help."

He bends and kisses the top of her head, and she twines her soft arms around his neck. My other girls soon join that embrace until his face shines. "At times, I've thought God did not feel human pain, but now I know that, despite delays, He cares and brings comfort." He pats my youngest girl's cheek as he releases her and pushes to his feet with his cane. "Come, let's find curtains for your windows, and . . ." He looks around. "Whatever else do you need?"

"Nothing, Peter. We are fine."

Marie looks up shyly. "Tell me, why the fort is built here?"

"*Mais oui*, that is easy, *Ma Chérie*. The boiling rapids make this spot a natural toll gate for those who pass—every boat going through must stop. Long ago, a Frenchmen married a native woman here and built the first post. Next, his assistant married the chief's daughter. They brought cows, bulls, oxen, and horses here from Fort Michilimackinac. This place has flourished ever since."

"We love farm animals," Nancy says. "We only have wild creatures in our woods."

"These do work and give us food," he says. "Early settlers built our strong blockhouse." He slaps the stout log wall supporting the room where we stay, and then gestures beyond. "Later, managers expanded the fort to what you see now."

"I love history," Marie says. "I want to learn and teach others. But . . ." She squirms. "May I ask something more?"

"Of course."

"Are there tasks I can do to free you, so you can teach us school sooner?"

"*Alors*." He snaps his fingers and laughs heartily. "There's no need to wait. Everything is easily ready. Come to my library one hour before dinner. You, too, please, Marguerite. We will start today."

Chapter 5

Doctor McLoughlin's handsome leather-bound European history volume releases its pleasing scent as Marie opens and explores its pages. I happily sit nearby. Besides color plates of Canada, it contains maps and engravings of European nations including Father's birth country of Switzerland. Peter's library also has shelves filled with maps marking all North West Company posts. On one, he shows us other places where I lived as a girl plus the wilderness site we just left. Next, he traces Mackenzie's route north along the river named for him years before Alex joined him on their successful journey west to find a route to the Pacific.

"Mackenzie is your father's cousin," Peter remarks, "so you are kin. He is a fine example of someone who explored possible routes until he found one that worked."

As he unrolls more maps and shares more details, all three girls and I pay rapt attention. Alex owns many of these same charts. I recall Father poring over similar maps too.

"Imagine being an early explorer of unknown areas, like Mackenzie. There had been rumors of a river leading west, but the first one he pursued turned north. He found seams of coal and rich resources, but no route to the Pacific. He proved that the Peace River enters Slave Lake, joins the Mackenzie, and empties into the Arctic Ocean—not the Pacific. He couldn't carry many rock samples back—mostly maps and small fossils—but here are a few." Peter takes several down from a shelf and sets them before us.

"We love rocks," I say.

My daughters squeal with delight and run their fingers over these specimens, checking their weight and structure as if they are silver or gold.

Nancy is so excited, she trembles. "Show us the route Father and McKenzie followed to the Pacific." She reverently touches the triangle signs marking high mountains on the map. "How did they find their way between so many steep places?"

"They almost didn't but paid attention to the stories of natives which, apparently, earlier explorers overlooked. Watch." As his gnarled fingers trace the route Alex and Mackenzie found to the Pacific, we lean close.

"Their accomplishment is celebrated because it wasn't a single river but a complex puzzle of rivers that got them there. First, they crossed this high mountain range that men call the Great Divide." He points out triangular peaks marching north to south on the map. "These are so tall, they wear snowy caps all year long."

"I'd love to see those." I shiver.

"Me too," Nancy says. "Brrrr. Imagine snow in summer. How did they climb so high?"

"Mackenzie and your father are brave," Peter says. "First they traveled the Peace River until they found a river flowing west. Locals warned them not to stay on it when that one turned south because its canyons hold boiling rapids. Instead, they crossed mountains farther west, passed warring tribes, and descended waters the Bella Coola people use to reach the Pacific. They carved Mackenzie's name on a huge boulder there, 'From Canada by land July 22nd, 1793, in two months and eleven days.' "

"Amazing," Marie says.

"Yes. That is why Mackenzie is now knighted and writes books and gives lectures on both sides of the ocean. Your father may do the same. You must be very proud."

"We are," Nancy says.

Few children have such a parent. I am a wilderness woman. How could I have believed that life with me would be enough to hold Alex? I will be strong and raise my three daughters well. I say, "Your father will be pleased that you want to study and that you have opportunity."

"He said girls don't need education." Nancy pouts.

"Maybe because he thought there was little use for it in our wilderness," Marie answers.

Nancy folds her arms. "Well, Tom's lucky he's

a boy. He can travel anywhere for adventures or have education or anything he chooses."

"And you can't?" Peter asks. "Your mother has proven brave many times. You girls will too. She lets nothing stop her. There's no reason you cannot all travel someday if you wish, and keeping learning as much as you want."

"Travel isn't always glorious," I say. "My father told dreadful stories of hunger, making them eat terrible things."

"Yes," Marie says. "Our father did too. Bugs, worms—even nuts from animal waste—but only when their lives depended on it."

"Ewwww!" Nancy says.

"Even explorers have good and bad days," Peter says. "I'll save my worst stories for another time but give you assignments now." His eyes dance. "You're to each choose a different river, including their surrounding land, to trace on these big sheets of paper. When you finish, we'll paste the sheets together and make one large map of Western Canada. If you don't mind extra work, I'll give you enough paper to make sets for yourselves."

"I will!" Nancy's fingers flex.

I can picture her traveling every continent plus all seven seas.

Marie's cheeks flush. "We'll gladly make extra copies. I'll never tire of work like this."

Catherine is too young to draw maps, so

my older girls have her color in blue water.

Peter smiles. "I have work for you, too, Marguerite, if you don't mind. After seeing your skill with McLoughlin, I hope you'll inventory our medical supplies and make a list of replacement items needed for our dispensary. After losing Monique and Claire, I know having correct medications on hand can make the difference between life and death."

My burning face makes me confess, "I want to help with all my heart, but I can scarcely read and write. I try, but my words look like chickens scratching in dirt. Father began teaching me but was killed before we got far. Mother lacked his skill, and there wasn't opportunity. Alex lacked the patience to teach me." I hang my head. "I am ignorant but determined my daughters will not be."

"Ignorant?" He snorts like a raging bull. "Never say that. You lack formal opportunity, but you are a wise, gifted woman. Few are your equal."

His intensity fans smoldering coals into flames in me, raising my confidence. "God bless you, Peter, but my girls' handwriting already surpasses mine." I gulp a breath. "But if you let them help—"

He claps his hands. "Of course, that's the perfect answer." He beams with all the kindness in the world. "You shall have all the help you need."

That evening, after another amazing supper meal in the main hall, my daughters and I retire to our pleasant room.

"Mama," Marie pleads, "Uncle Peter tells stories about when you were young. Please tell us more."

"Yes," Nancy adds. "He says you were always brave, but you haven't told us much. How old were you when your parents took you to Athabasca? Why did bad men kill Grandpa?"

They begin releasing an avalanche of questions. "I hoped to spare you that ugliness." My mouth tastes bitter bile. "But perhaps you are old enough to hear. Only God knows what cripples men's hearts, like Cain killing his brother Abel. A trader named Peter Pond and his partner from another company asked to meet Father to discuss business. After Mother served a nice meal, Pond and his friend pretended to start a fight with each other. When Father intervened, Pond's musket fired twice, shattering Father's thigh. The men claimed it was an accident, but Mother and I saw it wasn't. And Father's helper heard them plan murder because the Indians preferred trading with Father." Wiping my cheeks does not stop my tears.

"Nothing could stop his bleeding although Mother tried many remedies. Mother wanted to grab the musket and shoot the men herself but realized if they killed her or she went to prison, it would leave me an orphan. I won't forget her anguish though as she ordered them away. It took Father two full days to die from blood loss, but he spoke forgiveness over those men and loving prayers over us." I check my daughters' faces. "Am I sharing too much?"

"No. We want to know," Marie says.

"It's good that you tell us." Nancy rests her cheek against my knee.

I lean back in my maple rocker as my mind relives that horror, hearing Mother's screams—and mine—and then terrible silence when my good, strong father lies dead. Alexander MacKay was not the first man to abandon me. Father did not wish to, but his life was ripped away. Catherine, nearly the age I was then, climbs into my lap. And now her father is also gone but by his own choice.

I wrap Catherine in my arms. "Until I was seven, Mother and I basked in Father's love, a love as strong and steady as sunlight heating the earth and the moon brightening the nighttime sky. But even our love could not save him. The men tried to hide their deed, but Mother and witnesses told what we had seen and heard." I close my eyes, remembering. "A year earlier, a rabid wolf had run into our camp snarling and foaming. Its eyes held hate, and it ran straight at us even after Father's bullet pierced its heart. It dropped just feet from us, fangs open. Pond's face looked like that. Father tried to calm him despite seeing his crazed rage."

I open my eyes, bitterness flooding my tongue. "After Pond shot Father, Mother and I screamed and clawed both men, but they flung us off like dolls." My hands shake. "It's been almost thirty years ago, and I still tremble. We hated seeing Father suffer, but if any man was ready for heaven, Jean-Étienne Wadin was."

"We'll see him again, Mama. He knows how good you are to us and everyone." Marie's arms clasp my neck. "What happened to those evil men?" Her face is deathly pale, her voice breaking. "I hope they hung them."

I stroke Catherine's hair. "There were no constables in Athabasca. The North West Company sent your father's cousin, Alexander Mackenzie, to investigate. Employees said Father's only weakness was being too kind and trusting. They wanted his killers hung."

"Me too." Nancy's face purples. "What did the Company do?"

"It's hard determining justice from far away. Montréal's Crown magistrates were in charge. Despite eyewitnesses, Pond and his companion insisted it was an accident. It took two years for a verdict. The court judged Quebec to be too far away to prove the facts or enforce a sentence. Both men were acquitted and walked free."

"No!" Nancy and Marie make strangling sounds.

"Yes. That next year Pond returned to a different part of Athabasca. Mother made sure we didn't see him, but he and his men repeated a similar crime. They robbed fort manager Ross of furs in broad daylight. Ross was shot and killed by one of Pond's men, but Pond was held responsible."

"As he should be." Gentle Marie gives an unladylike snort. "Employers lead by example. The assistant understood Pond's desire."

"That's exactly what the jury decided." I'm amazed at my oldest girl's wisdom. "My father led by example, as Uncle Peter does. That time Pond and his men went to jail for a period while magistrates spent half a year determining how far west their authority ruled. Somehow Pond escaped and fled to the United States. They couldn't arrest him there. He wasn't hired to supervise men again in Canada, but he continues to explore and make maps out west, for which he is loudly praised."

"He still lives? Then may God be his judge. I would almost like to meet him someday." Now my Marie's voice is honed to a sharp edge. "What is wrong when leaders won't uphold justice?"

I sigh and rest a hand on her shoulder. "Much, yet sometimes men's hands are tied."

"Did the Company help your mother and you

with finances after your father's death?" Nancy asks.

"Neither the crown nor the Company will pay for unproven crimes. We had nothing. Mother and I joined her people and lived by the woodland skills I have taught you. Later your father came to the wilderness and found me. You know the rest."

"Thank you for telling us, Mother." Nancy leans against me, twining a curl around her fingers. "We're doing well."

"I have my father's Protestant prayer book and legacy of songs," I say. "In addition, I have a treasured paper in fine handwriting showing that his mother's name, Marguerite Wadin, is also mine—not the scratched picture writing on birch bark that Mother's Cree people use. Mother was wise and brave, famous for her skills with plants. She taught me much, but she never learned writing skills. I wish I could write like my father. But here we are today, warm and safe, lacking nothing really. That's enough for now." I rise and draw the curtains across the window, then turn down the quilt on Catherine's bed. "Off to bed now, girls. Sleep well!"

The girls ready themselves for bed, but the line between Marie's brows deepens. "Mama, you've had too much sorrow." She hugs me again. Nancy and Catherine come join until we end our evening wrapped in a sweet four-way hug.

"With such blessed love, we will thrive, girls. I've known happiness too. You three and Tom are my joy." Tears thicken my throat.

"Not Father?" Nancy asks.

Marie gives her sister a withering look. "Don't cry, Mother. We'll be the best daughters in the land," she says.

"I'm crying with happiness because you already are." I fight for control so they won't see that sorrow and weakness still lives in me.

The next day, while busy at the fort, I recall more stories to tell my girls. They need to know the heartache of past years but also the victory times. My heart lightens as I decide to tell them happier tales. As sunshine follows rain, they will see the Lord also leads our lives in pleasant places. That evening as we gather in our rooms before sleep, I share one of the best times of my childhood.

"Tonight you will hear good things. Before Father's death, our family had happy years. Mother and I listened for his homecoming along the river as he and his voyageurs in their red caps paddled loaded canoes home singing as they came."

"Like we waited for Father?" Nancy smiles.

"Yes, like that. Until Father's death, nothing shadowed our world. Remember this song my father taught?" I lift Catherine in my arms. " '*Auprès de ma blonde, qu'il fait bon, fait bon, fait bon. Auprès de ma blonde, qu'il fait bon dormir.*'

"Since my hair had Father's light coloring, like Catherine's now, he patted my head and called me his girl. The words mean, 'With my blonde one, life is good, is good, is good. With my blonde one, it is good to rest.' And he'd pick me up and stomp and whirl until Mother joined in. It wasn't only his happy words we loved, but his total joy as he and his men dipped their paddles in unison, racing home after their summer trading and exploring. Those songs still bring me much happiness. We'd be wise to sing them often."

"Yes." Nancy nods. "And one day we will teach them to our children."

That makes me smile. "Sometimes I dream Father is alive and well. He taught me to know and follow animal signs, to set snares and shoot better than most men. On his last birthday with us, he laughed with Mother as they danced and he whirled me high calling me *la petite chou*, his little sweetheart."

"Sing it now!" Nancy urges. She leads us in joining hands, and we prance around our room. We twirl in circles until we finally collapse in a happy, breathless heap. My whole body feels younger and stronger after such joy.

The next day as they study with Peter, I open my prayer journal for the first time since our arrival and write how we lost our husband and father in a single day. But on the next page, in my scratchy writing, I record how God brought us to a good place in the care of a loving protector and friend.

The Bible is true. God does see every sparrow fall. I breathe more easily and enter pleasant sleep without tears.

"Tomorrow, I send out men to harvest wild rice," Peter announces at dinner. "Jules will carry a musket in case he sees a moose. Do you and your girls wish to go?"

"With pleasure!" I answer at once. My girls' eyes shine. I cannot resist boasting, "We're good rice gatherers."

We leave in pre-dawn mists. Jules pushes forward Indian style, his paddle barely breaking the water's surface as he strokes. The river's quiet murmur is the only sound besides water drops falling from the paddles as they stroke. We reach the rice paddy, and the men and I cut the stalks free with machetes. My daughters then bend ripe rice stalks over our canoe and beat them rhythmically with wooden rods to loosen grains in a symphony of movement older than Mother's people.

Suddenly, a monstrous shape rises from the river's edge—a massive bull moose bearded with green river weeds, flings water far and wide.

"*Seigneur*." Jules drops his paddle and grabs

his musket. But he moves so fast, his shot goes wide. Rushing to re-load, he fumbles, and the bellowing, near-sighted moose begins striding away.

"*S'il vous plait*?" I ask. Without waiting for Jules' answer, I grab his musket and swing it into position in one fluid motion. *Crack!* the fire piece roars, discharging thunder, and with a surprised cough the massive bull staggers and drops heavily into willows on the bank.

"*Sacré bleu*!" Jules looks at me, rubs his eyes, stares at the moose, and looks at me again. "What a miracle shot."

"No, that's our mama." Nancy's face glows.

At the end of the afternoon, we return to the fort and tell Peter we have rice with us and meat waiting at the rice paddy. Jules spreads his hands wide to describe the scene. "Maybe it was beginner's luck, but Marguerite's lightning bolt entered that monster's heart and dropped him with one blow." He shakes his head, his eyebrows knit. "We must have her shoot again to see if she can repeat such a shot."

My daughters giggle while Peter shouts, "God be praised," and hops in his stork-like dance. "Send two canoes with men—*rapidement*. We feast on fresh moose tonight. Wonderful, Marguerite. Let the others do the work now."

As men load knives, baskets, and kettles to retrieve the animal, a large freight canoe reaches our shore. A scarlet North West Company banner flutters from its bow.

Peter sighs. “There’s always more business to tend to.”

Chapter 6

New arrivals don't come every day. My daughters and I watch Peter approach the large canoe and greet its occupants. As he waves them inside our stockade, one man lingers and draws Peter aside. After conversation, Peter brings him toward us. "Marguerite, this is Jarvis. Jarvis, meet Madame MacKay and her daughters."

The small, fit man in buckskins removes his red voyageur cap and bends from the waist. "I am pleased to meet you, Madame and girls."

"Thank you, *Monsieur*," I say. We curtsy.

Peter steps closer. "Marguerite, he has news for your ears alone."

My glance instructs Marie to take her sisters inside.

"Jarvis comes from Company headquarters and warns of more dishonest competitor activities," Peter says. "But he also brings word of Alex."

As Peter and I walk with Jarvis through the stockade's gate, I put my hand to my throat. The man hesitates as if he knows his report will bring pain. "Madame, your husband is celebrated across Canada and has influential friends, but the truth is, he also has enemies. When our Company told him to watch DeLorme, the independent trader diverting business to himself at Grand

Portage, Alex exceeded Company policy by felling trees across DeLorme's trails. DeLorme finally closed his fort and left that area. Company officials label Alex's actions extreme, but have done nothing. That trader now counts Alex a bitter enemy and threatens his life."

My heart squeezes. "And our son's?"

"Tom is a minor so DeLorme blames Alex alone. The reports do not mention your son, so he seems safe for the present. As a result of censure, Alex has left our Company but been hired by John Jacob Astor, an ambitious American businessman. They plan to start a new venture in faraway Oregon, which promises to make them richer still. Alex is to build a fort there and establish Astor's trading empire. Tom will help."

"That far away?" I exhale, unaware I'd held my breath.

"Yes. If they reach there, they'll at least be safe from DeLorme."

"Thank you, Jarvis." Peter claps the man's shoulder. "You and your men will enjoy fresh moose steaks tonight from the animal Madame MacKay just dropped."

"Excellent, Madame MacKay? *Très bien*."

He turns away but won't meet my eyes. What else isn't he saying? "Please, Monsieur. Is there more I should hear?"

"It's not clear. There's some confusion." He folds his arms across his chest and stares somewhere above me. "You are Madame Alex MacKay, are you not? With one son, Tom? I gave Peter an envelope the Company sent with small funds due you after your husband's termination. But I have a second envelope for a Madame Alex MacKay with a son named Alexander. Do you have two sons? Or is your son's name listed wrong on the second envelope?"

Peter steps forward, his lips white. "Let me speak with Marguerite alone. Please bring me the second envelope at dinner."

As Jarvis leaves, Peter moves his hand to my shoulder. "I'm terribly sorry, Marguerite. I'd heard rumors and asked questions, but I didn't want to believe. It now seems clear Alex took another wife farther west and fathered another son." He grips my hand.

"I sometimes wondered." I swallow tears. "Alex expects comfort." My blood turns to ice. I whisper, "Please don't tell our girls."

"I will not. You deserve better, Marguerite. I believe on my visits west I saw a woman with a child who looks remarkably like Alex."

"Where?"

"Far, but twice they have attended our Fur Rendezvous."

"Then I will not stay for the next. How old is the child?"

"Younger than Tom but older than Catherine."

"*Mon Dieu.*" A dagger twists in my heart.

"Until now, I had hoped Alex might return. But now, even if he has not yet claimed a society wife, how could I accept him?"

"I pity him." Anguish fills Peter's eyes. "He has lost great treasure."

"I am as much a widow as my mother."

"I know Alex loves you. I expected more from him. I think greed has run away with him."

Truth blazes through me. "Alex loves what and when he pleases, especially himself. What of this other woman? Who cares for her and her child? Did he sign a *façon du nord* marriage contract with her too?"

"Perhaps, but I'm not sure. It is terrible. Probably the Company sends her separate funds in the second envelope. Beyond that, I only know that God cares for widows and orphans."

"Thank you. I know that too." I kiss his cheek. "Tell Jarvis my girls must not know."

"I promise he is skilled in keeping confidences." He links my arm through his as we stroll inside to join the others.

Through dinner I respond to small talk but cannot eat. I notice little else besides hearing the men call the moose delicious as they devour it. After the girls and I reach our room, there's a rap on our door. I answer.

"I bring more candles," Peter says, "so yours don't burn out and leave you in darkness." The concern in his eyes speaks louder than words.

"Thank you again for our magnificent moose dinner, Madame Marksman." He pats his small paunch and turns to my girls. "It cheers me to hear children's voices in our fort again."

"You should bring more families here," Marie says, moving past me and taking the fragrant hand-dipped tapers from him.

"That is my plan once we make conditions safer. Company upheaval still needs to calm. I bid you all good night with blessed sleep." The kind man lightly kisses my girls' foreheads and beams fatherly affection my way. He climbed these stairs solely to check that we are well—and helps make it so.

Although the candles we're using burn low, we save his gift for longer winter nights.

"Can I learn to make candles like these, Mama?" Nancy says.

"I'm sure you may. These are better than mine since they have proper molds." My fingers trace the smooth texture. "And real beeswax, the color of honey. Smell the sweet scent." We all inhale.

Nancy sniffs twice. "They smell wonderful, but we don't need candles to hear your stories. We see well enough and listen by firelight."

That night, we include Alex, Tom, and Peter in our prayers. After climbing into bed, my girls beg me to share another memory. As I begin, Marie, resting her head near the wall, says, "Listen,

Mama. Downstairs Uncle Peter is praying and names each of us."

"Indeed, he does." My voice breaks. "God bless him forever."

I share happy tales of my father until sleep claims all three daughters. Then I lie awake, wondering about another Madame MacKay and her son. How will they manage? Has Alex sent them somewhere else also? Or will they live alone in western wilds? I wish them well but do not want to meet them. Where is Alex? Does he miss me as much as my arms have ached for him? Does he feel remorse when he thinks of us? Not if he lives a lie.

To reach Oregon, he will not travel overland as Lewis and Clark did to the south of us. Peter says Alex and Tom will transport supplies by sailing ship from New York around South America, a trip that will take six months. Our son will experience more adventures and dangers than my mother's heart could wish. Will I recognize him the next time we meet? Will he recognize me? God grant that we do see each other again in this lifetime.

And then my thoughts turn to that good man, young Doctor McLoughlin. Has he reached Rainy River and resolved the problem taking him there? He sees patients wherever he goes. Has he gone farther west to the newer Red River settlement?

There is word of treachery there with Hudson's

Bay people invading our Company holdings. Indeed, Father believed us safe at distant Lac La Ronge until Pond struck him down. There's recent talk of Hudson's Bay and our Company finding ways to consolidate and end the rivalry, but that seems impossible.

God be with the good doctor too. I end my prayers as my mother did, reciting the Lord's Prayer. Instead of God's kingdom on earth, ours is a fallen one. Alex must learn it's not his will, nor John Jacob Astor's will, but God alone who decides men's achievements and rewards on earth.

The next morning, I count out my small currency and thrust it into Peter's hand. "Here is payment to help your care of us."

"What are you doing?" He closes my fingers around the bills and pushes my hand back, almost angrily. "You and your girls bring me great joy. Do not rob me now. And as for Company benevolence, it's seldom equal to what people deserve. Promise you'll leave these matters to me, Marguerite."

"If it matters so much, I will for now."

After Jarvis's visit, Peter becomes more attentive, opening his trading supplies to outfit the girls and me with heavy coats, hats, and boots before winter. We sew moose hide mitts and fur-lined boots for ourselves and others at the fort, but we indulge Peter by accepting the Company goods he pours upon us. "Please add these to our account," I say. "The funds Alex sent cannot last long. I will gladly work to supplement them."

"You will not." His brow darkens to thunder. "I have told you not to worry about funds. With all the good you do collecting and dispensing medicines, harvesting food, and teaching marksmanship here"—his mouth quirks—"you more than pay your way. I'm sure you are also a skilled trapper."

"We all are, more than skilled," Nancy boasts.

Peter smiles. "What would you need to run traplines from this fort? I wager no animal could be safe. You girls and your mother will be as rich as kings."

My daughters chuckle while Nancy strikes a dramatic pose and counts on her fingers. "We would need more traps, and skinning knives, plus animal scents. We make our own stretching boards and snowshoes. If you issue store credit for us at first, we'll make extra snowshoes and footwear you can sell." Suddenly, realizing she may have been too bold, she lowers her gaze. "That is, if you wish."

"Of course, I wish," he practically roars, "and I will pay handsomely. Items shipped here from back east are of inconsistent quality. I will be glad to have your good supplies."

"You'll like our craftsmanship." Nancy gains confidence again. I see a shrewd businesswoman emerging.

"You've convinced me." Peter's smile deepens to a rumbling laugh.

Nancy doesn't slow down. "For math practice, will you let us manage your trade accounts when people come? You're too busy. Father taught us how."

"Indeed, I am too busy. And old." He clasps his hands. "I'm sure your father taught you well, and I do need help. How did I survive before you came? We shall all prosper." He winks and his joyful laugh rumbles again.

Later, as my daughters color their maps at our table, I share more of Father's story, tenting my hands like a proper story teller. "Young Jean-Étienne Wadin sailed here from beautiful faraway Switzerland. Its name means *White Land.* He described a vast ocean between Europe and Canada that Mother and I could not imagine. It took him weeks to cross. I would love to stand at an ocean shore one day and see big waves rolling in. He showed courage to come alone, don't you think?"

"Yes," Marie answers. "I could not."

"But I could." Nancy scoots closer. "And I will one day. You were brave, too, Mother, to come here, although you were sure of Uncle Peter's warm welcome."

"Coming here was easy in comparison." I settle young Catherine against me. "In 1759, when Father arrived, England was fighting France to own Canada. He helped the British win victory on Quebec's Plains of Abraham and used his payment to travel west and begin trading furs in the Athabasca region."

"I think this is the river he followed." Nancy's finger traces a squiggly blue line stretching from the prairies west to high mountains.

"Most traders left wives and children in Montréal, and after years in Indian Country, took new ones. When my father and mother met, they signed a *façon du nord* marriage contract and birthed me. I inherited Father's songs and love for adventure, but will have no more adventures now. I am old. Gray begins to streak my hair."

"Mama, no!" Marie insists. "You'll never be old."

My heart warms at her words. "You're sweet. Mother taught me wilderness hunting and medicine skills. Your father offered me a marriage contract before I turned sixteen." I wave a hand. "A lifetime ago, but I don't want you to marry that young."

"Does Father have a family in Montréal?" Marie's eyebrows pucker.

I bite my cheek. "Only parents and brothers there." I avoid her knowing glance as I settle in my chair. "Sometimes, Mother and I journeyed with Father in his freight canoe. He carried trade goods west to Rainy River and other posts. He brought metal cooking pots, axes, knives, guns, mirrors, cloth, beads, and blankets. He refused to carry alcohol because it causes trouble. Some say that's the other reason his competing trading partner killed him. Peter Pond loved profits and drank much himself. Even the night he shot my father."

"How terrible. Couldn't Pond see that alcohol ruins people?" Nancy's face mirrors the same concern Father's face often wore. "Traders should help people, not harm them."

Marie chimes in. "It's wrong to only consider profit."

"I think so too." My pride swells. How do children become so wise? "For that reason, your father seldom trades for firewater. It's easy to make enough profit trading the furs Europeans crave for useful items. Isn't it strange that ships filled with beaver pelts cross the ocean where people pay fortunes for hats?"

Nancy makes a face. "I wouldn't wear one. Are your father's parents in Switzerland alive? Would they want to see us?"

"I'm not sure if they still live. If they are, they are very old. There should be other family members. I'm sure they would be happy to meet you."

Marie's eyes brighten. "I want to meet them.

We could hide inside bundles of fur and journey there."

I press my hands together. "Squished this flat."

Nancy sucks in her cheeks to look thin. "One day, I will cross the Atlantic to see more parts of the world."

"I want to go too," Catherine says. She scoots away from me and watches Marie's careful hand sketching mountains.

I sigh. "That would be grand. Our dreams sound as big as the ocean."

Nancy angles a grin at me. "You always say God has good things in store for people who love Him, Mama."

Nancy uses my scripture reminders against me. "Yes, He does. If you recall nothing else, remember that."

"We will." Marie brushes Catherine's hair. "Seeing you live helps us believe too."

"Thank you." I blink away tears. "When Mother and I couldn't go with Father, he brought home surprises—a carved wooden doll for my fifth birthday, a painted wooden bird that flapped its wings for my sixth. That year, I surprised him by wiggling my loose front tooth back and forth until it came out. I gave it to him.

" 'Treasure from my princess,' he said. Each summer he taught more songs. Mother prepared his favorite foods or mended his leather jacket and leggings. By watching her, I learned those skills too."

"And now you teach us," Marie says.

"Yes. Most tasks stay the same. Do you remember my father's favorite song?" I sing it for them.

"*Alouette, gentille Alouette, Alouette, je te plumerai, Je te plumerai la tête, Je te plumerai la tête, Et la tête, Et la tête, Alouette, Alouette, O-o-o-oh.*"

I smile. "Do you know why it was his favorite?"

Catherine's eyes sparkle. "Because the words sound like happy birds."

"That's right. First, we'll sing in English. 'Lark, little Lark, I shall pluck you, I shall pluck you, I shall pluck *your head.*' " I touch her ear to show the action. "Each time he finished a verse, Father nuzzled me with his golden whiskers, or tossed me high and caught me again, making me guess which body part he would sing about next by tickling me—like this!" I nuzzle Catherine's ribs with my chin until she giggles and squirms.

"And your beak, and your neck, and your back, and your wings, and your feet, and your tail, *je te plumerai*," I sing. Then I sigh, remembering. "But my favorite part was when he put my name in the song—the same name as his beloved mother's in faraway Geneva, where his father taught university. *Marguerite, gentille Marguerite, Marguerite, je te plumerai.*

We sang until we collapsed with laughter."

Nancy props her feet on the bench and cradles her knees. "Sing with our names."

So I do, including theirs and Tom's, until there's a knock at our door. I open it and find Peter beaming, which makes me beam too. "I'm sorry. Have we been too loud?"

"*Au contraire*, I love your singing. As bees go to flowers, I'm drawn to your voices. May I join?"

"Of course." Marie waves him in, and we sing for him.

After he leaves, I tell my girls, "I need to save the memories of my childhood, like you girls press and save beautiful flower blossoms, so I don't lose them."

"Yes, Mother." Marie's eyes shine. "We love books, but there aren't enough in the world. Since handwriting is easy for me, as you share memories, I'll copy them in my best hand. You'll share them all with us, won't you? So we can always remember too? And then, if we see your father's people on this earth one day, they'll cherish the gift."

"We'll also make our own copies and add maps," Nancy says.

"Lovely," I say, touched by their interest. "Even if we never cross the ocean to find my father's people, having such a book would be a wonderful treasure. With your help, I'll do it."

At that moment, the years fade away. I recall Father teaching me, asking me to keep daily tallies of items when he returns from his trading trips, and telling me stories. I must capture those moments along with our journeys and blessings now.

And so we begin recording family memories in a handsome portfolio Peter provides. He also gives us special paper and sharp quills with his best ink, capturing my life story. With every portion, I see more and more of God's guiding hand.

Yet in coming days, I am restless. Alex has sent Peter some funds for receiving us, but no matter what Peter says, I'm sure they aren't enough. Though that good man loves us, we won't live here at his expense. I rouse my girls early and escort them through the pre-dawn to the fort's kitchen to prepare breakfast as a treat for everyone and give the cooks a morning off.

I assign Marie to toasting bread on the massive wood stove's surface. Nancy and Catherine gather plates to set the tables. "It's our privilege to do more than required to earn our keep here, girls," I tell them as we work, "when we receive such loving care."

Busy at the stove stirring porridge, I am startled by a sad voice.

"Marguerite, don't pain me."

I turn and find Peter, his hands holding a mug.

I pour him a cup of tea. "Peter, I wouldn't for the world. But I'm a woman who has had her own home. We'll feel more fully part if you let us help more here."

"Preposterous. Who measures such things? You and these girls bring joy and already do more than enough." He frowns. "But if you feel strongly, we could use your wisdom and help with winter preparations."

"Gladly. Name anything you like." I stir the big pot of porridge again before it burns and then pull it safely to the cooler side of the fire box. "Your hunters have asked my help making pemmican. I can demonstrate my method of combining meat, lard, and berries that lasts well if you like. You also wanted a list of dispensary supplies which we've started." I pull a partial list from my pocket. "We want to be blessings here."

He sets his cup on a counter and captures me in a brief embrace. "*Magnifique*!"

"We'd also like to scour the forest for roots, leaves, and herbs before winter fully sets in to replace your medicines that didn't arrive."

"*Mon Dieu*—a perfect answer to prayer. My people know animals but little about plants in the woods." He lifts his cup and takes a satisfied swallow. "Tell me where and when you go, and I'll send a marksman each time for your safety."

Nancy scurries to us, laughing. "Did you forget

Mama getting the moose? If you hold a shooting contest, she will win."

He cups his ear. "Eh? A shooting competition? We have one each Christmas."

"Good. Let Mother show her skill. She's trained us girls to be good shots too." Nancy makes no effort to hide her boast.

Peter's laugh is sheer joy. "Then this fort is safe forever!"

Through late fall and even occasional warm days as winter starts, we harvest woodland bounty. Already the ground is frozen hard most mornings. I teach my girls to know which medicinal plants grow near harmful ones, like foxglove or dock leaves for nettles, or jewel-weed for poison ivy. I teach them more secrets too. To steam plants to split their skins open and discard the bad but keep the useful parts. To use absorbent moss for diapers and bandages. To know when plants are the most beneficial judging by their color, odor, or taste. To make salves, ointments, powders, tinctures, and teas to fight infections, relieve fevers, staunch bleeding, heal wounds, strengthen blood, assist childbirth, and far more. My daughters confidently roam the woods, reading its signs.

"My mother would be proud," I tell them. "She lived by more than most people see and hear."

"I wish we'd known her, Mama, but we're glad

you're teaching us." Marie's words warm me.

Each evening we sit around the table in our room, and I share more stories of Father's wisdom and adventures. Marie writes them down. As the flames in our fireplace crackle, I tell them another story, marveling at how God helped Mother and me survive times even harder than those He guides my precious daughters and me through now.

"The year after Father died saw our worst smallpox outbreak in Indian Country, making death wails rise in villages for months. Still, we wished Father had died of some terrible sickness rather than at the hands of fellow traders. Pestilence stalked our land like the fearful monster Mother's people call *Majimanidoo*, 'he who has no soul,' who is always hungry yet never gets his fill of death."

All three girls shiver.

"Nearly half of our people died, and death's stench clung like rotting garments. It seemed the ground shook from the monster's tread. We heard howls that raised the hair on our necks, so we hid from his passing—unless it was only our knees shaking with fear.

"Mother became fearless, her forest remedies bringing much good. She missed Father badly and did not fear death. Together we treated raging coughs, burning fevers, and drained pus-filled lesions. She brought infected folks inside our home, yet we stayed well. She said God decided we'd had enough loss that year."

Marie leaned forward. "Mama, I'm glad you helped people, but tell happy stories too."

"You're right." And then I recall a blessing Mother gave that I will pass on to my girls. "I've shared challenging times that made us strong, but God also brought joys. I will share a lesson my mother taught, and her mother before her." I move to my rocking chair, then point to the little rug at my feet. "Marie, come here. Mother filled even simple tasks with lasting meaning. Marie, you are the oldest and the most like me. I'll bless you first." I brush my fingers through her long, lustrous hair with smooth strokes, and she relaxes against my knees.

"Grandma taught you by fixing hair?" Nancy asks, observing me.

I send her a smile. "Not by fixing it, but by braids showing our heritage. She said God weaves a special design in lives and shapes our paths like we weave strands together. Watch." I use my fingers and divide Marie's hair into three parts. I hold one section in each hand while the middle portion drops straight down.

"Mother said my first strand was my Swiss father coming from across the ocean, finding her in Indian Country, and birthing me. Like this." I cross the first strand over the second. "Except your first strand is your brave father, who now travels to the world's far side."

Marie glances at my face, her eyes concerned.

I assure her, "Yes, tonight I am happy." I take another strand of her hair. "Next, Mother crossed my second strand over the first, showing how Father's and her lives blended. But two strands alone cannot make a lasting braid. That takes three." I cross the strand and curl my fingers around the third. "This strand shows the new life that came from her and Father's joining, like God blended my life with your father's for your heritage. All three strands braided together show your divine destinies. I will speak your individual blessings."

Catherine tugs my skirt. "Do me next."

"You must wait your turn. You are the youngest."

She pops her thumb in her mouth and leans against Nancy's shoulder.

I deftly weave a thick braid in Marie's hair as I speak. "Mother braided my hair and said, 'You are much like your father, sensitive and joyful, yet rushing forward in many directions at once like spring's singing rivers. It surprises me that you walk woodland trails quietly enough to catch creatures. You are also like your father in that. He was big and strong, yet when he wished to be silent, he could approach mature deer like whispering wind.' I laughed with her, happy inside, for I was my father's child, and his exuberance and energy lives in me."

Marie's eyelashes glisten. "Your words are beautiful and true. Is my design like yours?"

"In many ways." I ask God for good words to bless. "Marie, your first strand is your good father, handsome and brave, exploring many directions, and now taking Tom to the far coast."

She nods. "What of my strand through you?"

"You know my heritage. Father had European learning and feared nothing, yet in the end I wished he was less trusting. His learning and courage, blended with Mother's woodland skills, is also yours."

I near the end of the braid. "God adds unique gifts in you girls. Marie, you are my eldest with the alertness and gentleness of a deer, watchful but wise to guide others when needed. You are already an astute leader. As you hear God's voice and directions, many shall follow you." I pull a bit of string from my pocket and tie the braid. I drape it over Marie's shoulder.

Marie rises on her knees and faces me. "Thank you, Mama. That was beautiful." Tears glimmer. When we hug, she swipes her eyes. So do I.

Marie returns to the table, and Nancy takes her place on the little rug.

Catherine taps my arm. "Mama, don't forget me."

"Be patient, child. I'm doing this in the birth order God gave."

Nancy's slightly curly auburn hair glints with a touch of red in the firelight as I divide it into three strands. "From your father's side and mine you have European spark. You are feisty—not wanting to wait to see how things turn out but taking charge."

She slaps a hand over her mouth. "Like I did pursuing business with Uncle Peter. Sometime that gets me in trouble. Was I too bold?"

"Lively, but it turned out well. Even when your boldness gets you in trouble, your humor usually gets you out." I begin her braid. "You girls have less native heritage than I, but enough to love woodland scenes, read the forest well, and find God's patterns in earth and sky. You have a keen sense of justice, which makes you bolder than Marie. You will not stop until right is accomplished."

"That's good, isn't it?" Her uncertain voice seeks assurance.

I chuckle. "Usually. You are like the Bible widow who pounded on the sleeping judge's door until he awoke to give what she needed. In that same way, you won't stop until justice happens, no matter the cost."

"Then I am like you." Now she sounds smug.

My heart warms. "Braver." My fingers weave, weave. "God made you our lovely middle girl, our peacemaker. You hate conflict and invent tricks or jokes to chase away troubles and make us laugh. Maybe that's also from this red in your hair."

"I love to laugh."

"You're perfect for our family."

I tie the end of her braid. There are no tears as I release her. Her eyes spark and her dimples flash. We laugh, hug, and I playfully swat her bottom as she steps away.

Catherine slips in. "I waited long, Mama." She sighs so deeply, her lips tremble.

I settle her against my knees. "Little Catherine, our youngest. The Lord sent you to complete our family."

"You needed me."

"Yes, except babies get spoiled."

"I'm not spoiled." She sounds so shocked, we all laugh.

"A little, but you're growing up."

I divide her fine hair into three strands. Her hair shows hints of Alex's blond curls. "Look at you, adding another hair color to make our family interesting. Remember the Bible's story of Queen Esther? I think God says you are a young Esther. He's training you to be a queen. You will have seasons of sweet spices and others with myrrh and bitter herbs."

"She saved her people, Mama." Catherine's little shoulders square with pride.

"Yes. I don't know what that means in your life, but there is a connection. Your destiny may be to win a king's favor and help your people."

"A real king?" She turns her head and gapes at me with blue eyes so much like her father's.

"I'm not sure, but my heart says you will see wonderful things."

"What else?" She faces forward.

"Your second and third strands interweave with the first and bind them together in beauty. You bring joy and also give others joy." I tie her much shorter braid.

"That's good." She turns and flings her arms around my neck. "What does your hair mean?"

"Mine?" I touch my hair's coiled braids, which show their first streaks of gray. "I'm older now than when my mother taught me these things."

"You will never be old," Nancy says. "You stay young and beautiful."

"You're kind, but my mirror shows the truth."

"What about Tom?" Nancy's eyes snap with curiosity. "Can you tell us his?"

My eyes blink away tears as I picture him on chubby legs, arms reaching forward, running into life. His tousled haystack hair invites any bird to nest until I tame it with my scissors. I keep a lock of each child's hair in the wooden box Alex carved, where I store special things. I took Tom's from the box after he and Alex left and placed it in a small bag. I wear it on a cord around my neck, and the bag rests between my breasts. I grasp it now.

"He will face hardships, yet God is making him strong. I pray every day he will be a *believing* Thomas, not a *doubting* one."

Marie places her hand on my knee. "Thank you for our blessings, Mama. We will pray, too, until Tom and Father come home."

I dare to dream. "Or we join them there. Wouldn't that be fun? I would love that to happen someday."

"That sounds wonderful." Nancy looks ready to pack and leave for the West Coast right now.

Gazing at my daughters, my heart is full. Although we face uncertainty in this distant fort, we are together and are rich beyond measure. In all things that matter most, we are as wealthy as those living in royal houses.

Chapter 7

Sault Sainte Marie, Indian Country, 1810-1811

Tonight when we enter the fort's great room for dinner, Peter holds furry green leaves in one hand, his eyes dancing.

"It's nearly Christmas, and I have mistletoe to hang over our doorway."

I frown at the snip of green. "Mistletoe? I've heard of it, but never seen it. How did you get it in these wilds?"

"I didn't." Peter teases me by holding it briefly over my head and then hiding it behind his back. The girls step close and he shows it to them. "Ships in eastern ports sometimes bring us unusual goods from far south. Near Christmas, voyageurs sometimes tuck surprises into their packs. I won't let my workers harass you or your sweet girls. But since this comes from far away and is interesting, I'll hang it here for people to see but insist that no one demands kisses."

He adopts a severe look. "I'm sure you girls know warm affection is only exchanged between two people properly committed to each other and promised in marriage."

"Oh, yes," Marie says. "Mother has taught us well."

I rest a hand on his arm. “Thanks for your reinforcement, Peter. You’re like a loving grandfather.”

“And that is how I feel.” He hands me the bunch of small dry green leaves and we study their leathery surface. “With your help, we will make this a festive place. I hope you and your girls will suggest entertainment and perhaps sing songs.” He waits expectantly.

“We would be glad to, Peter. You must also tell us which men sing well, which do bird whistles, juggling, and things like that.”

His mouth crinkles upward. “Besides using spoons to eat, Jules is a master at playing spoons for music on his knee. He makes them sound like the castanets Spanish ladies click when they dance.” His eyes grow dreamy. “Yes, together we will make this the best Christmas yet.”

“Wonderful. My girls and I will love to help.”

Winter arrives with full ferocity of deep snow and swirling storms, which means Christmas is almost upon us. Christmas means gift-giving and special treats, and we spend time each day preparing. The cooks bake special things they hide away. Every laborer and those caring for barn animals are seen whittling, building, polishing stones, or fashioning things from interesting bits of fur, leather, bone, antlers, stones, or wood.

Catherine shivers with excitement. “How can

there be so many secrets? Do we have to wait until Christmas Day to know them all?"

"Yes, little one." I pull her close. "But it will be worth it."

There's little outside activity as snow piles deep into drifts. Canoe travel isn't possible on the frozen rivers. Instead, men and dog teams mush its surface or snowshoe or ski to check traps and deliver goods. Two days before Christmas we are surprised when Jarvis again trudges through our gate wearing many layers of leather and furs with a pack on his back as big as people say Saint Nicholas carries.

"Welcome. What brings you in such weather?" Peter claps the man's shoulder and has Jules remove the heavy burden.

"Company news and merchandise for your store, if you're interested."

"You have a good eye. Show me," Peter says. "But first, give news of the outside world. What's happening at Fort William? What is our Company doing about the Hudson's Bay Company threat? Are they still inserting men into our trapping grounds?"

"One question at a time, Arndt. Get me inside to thaw out and I shall answer all." Seated in the fort's dining room near a roaring fire, Jarvis pulls off his boots and stretches his feet toward hot flames. I hand him toasted bread and a mug of hot tea.

"Thank you, Madame MacKay. You are sweetness itself. I bring letters." After finishing his refreshment and wiping his mouth, he gives letters to Peter, one to Jules, and then to several others, before holding up one last sealed white envelope and looking my way. His glance shows that he recalls my request not to disclose my family's personal news in public. He simply says, "This last is for you, Madame," and hands it to me with a flourish.

"Is it from Father?" Marie asks, reaching out.

"I don't think so. Only my name shows outside, and the writing is not his." I fumble with the envelope until Peter hands me his pen knife to slit it open. Inside is an elegant, handwritten script I don't recognize.

Dear Madame MacKay, it begins, *I pray this finds you and your daughters well. I write keeping my promise to share the good news that a school will begin at Fort William this next fall.*

I give a sharp intake of breath. The writer is Doctor McLoughlin. "Excuse me, I must read this alone." I rush upstairs to our rooms, sit at the table, and continue reading.

> Now that Fort William is Company headquarters for Central Canada, quality education is a priority. Two teachers from Quebec will arrive by canoe sometime next summer when Lake Superior

> is navigable. The first school term starts next fall. Don't be concerned that Alex MacKay is no longer in Company employ. Girouard, our present fort factor, says that your family receives privilege through your father's faithful service.

I clutch the letter to my breast, then open it flat again to finish reading.

> In closing, let me say how much I valued your assistance and knowledge of remedies last late fall as you helped me repair Gaston. I hope he has mended well to enjoy many more years of health.
>
> If you do come to Fort William, I will aid your transition. Assure Peter that I don't wish to pain him by luring you here. He must retire and come along.
>
> Finally, do not think me insensitive regarding personal matters. Without saying more than that your husband travels for new business ventures, I asked Girouard what housing could be provided for you and your girls. He assures me that he will gladly make your family a priority. Yet, if for any reason suitable space is not available when you come, I will vacate my

bachelor quarters, as I am gone more often than I am here, and can live comfortably in my dispensary rooms. I told him it would be helpful to have someone of your skill help me on occasion and to be a valuable resource when I am not. He agrees.

As you consider this news, please be assured of my friendship and continuing prayers for you and your family. I hope to hear your favorable response. Greet your daughters during this blessed Christmas season.

I remain your humble servant and friend,
Doctor John (Jean-Baptiste) McLoughlin.

By the time I finish reading, my fingers flutter so badly I nearly drop the letter. So much blood in my head has rushed elsewhere, I'm lightheaded.

Marie enters the room and hurries near. "Mother, have you finished? Is it from Father?"

"No, but it is good news I must consider. I'll share more later." I return the letter to its envelope and tuck it into the folds of my dress.

Peter appears, looking alarmed as he peers through our doorway. "Is all well?"

"Yes. I received an unexpected letter I must absorb."

"You're sure?"

"Yes, truly."

He nods, then departs, taking Marie with him. I sit in my chair rocking, thinking. My biggest surprise is not news of a hoped-for school, nor the hand-written invitation inviting us to Fort William. The greatest impact is that my heart feels warm and cared for by receiving the kindness of this cordial letter from Doctor McLoughlin's own hand. I remind myself that McLoughlin acts from gratitude, for I am an aging woman. I am not even of sufficient social class to be his friend.

How should I answer? Attending school would be wonderful for my girls. Shall I reply with a letter Jarvis can carry on his return? Or wait? My head throbs with overthinking. My only news of Alex is that he journeys farther still, which now troubles me much less except for Tom's welfare.

Another thought intrudes. Are there more Madame Alex MacKays scattered across Canada? I will manage the best I can to plan wisely for my girls. If there is one clear thread through our situation, I have not yet found it. But then, in my mind's eye, I again see Mother braiding hair to teach me my heritage and destiny. I feel her soothing hands pull me against her until I relax—as I've held my own daughters while braiding their hair and speaking their divine destinies.

Lord, You are my loving father. Help me see the design You're braiding into our lives, confident that You securely hold the strands in Your hands.

Two days after receiving Doctor McLoughlin's letter, while I remove fresh-washed clothes from the line behind the dispensary, Peter approaches with a look of determination steeling his gaze.

"Marguerite, may I surmise the letter you received is happier than news of Alex?"

I lower a blanket into my laundry basket. "Yes, that is true." When I share its contents, including mention that a school will be established at Fort William, he nods.

"That makes me sad and glad, but you must go."

I regard his sad face. "If we do, we will always return to visit you. Or, as Doctor McLoughlin suggests, you must retire and come with us."

He sighs. "I can't yet. I must labor one more year until events calm. Then possibly . . ." He sticks his pipe in his mouth and chews its stem. "Jarvis also brought next year's fur prices," he says. "Payment for beaver, martin, and mink has tripled, exactly the furs you and your girls trap most. You shall leave here rich."

"Show me the records," I insist. "I fear you exaggerate in our favor."

He glares at me. "*Alors*, how can you say such a thing? I will show you later."

By now my girls have run to join us. They fold and carry our laundry while I tell them everything McLoughlin put in his letter.

"The nice doctor wrote us?" Marie asks. "They

are opening a school we can attend? Hurray!" Her fingers flutter as if her hands are eager to take literal hold of her education.

Back in our rooms, placing clothing into bureau drawers, Nancy bubbles with joy. "It's so nice he remembered us. Please thank him when you write."

I nod. "I will. I'll scratch out a draft which I hope Marie will put into fine writing."

She beams at me. "With pleasure."

That evening, while my girls help the cooks in the fort kitchen, I'm alone and chew my quill, ready to begin. First I speak the words aloud as I place them on the page.

"Dear Doctor McLoughlin, Your welcome letter cheers us. We appreciate your interest and efforts on our behalf. We will not overlook such an opportunity, and God-willing, will come to Fort William before the school year begins. I would be honored to assist you in giving medical care. All three girls and I will also willingly do other tasks at the fort. We all thank you for remembering us this Christmas season. We commend you to God's care and blessings through the coming year. Yours gratefully, Marguerite, Marie, Nancy, and Catherine MacKay."

When the girls return, Marie reads my draft. "Good, Mama." She lays it aside. "You've been to Fort William. Please tell us what it is like."

I lift Catherine to my lap, where she snuggles

against my heart. My other two sit on the floor nearby, arms around their knees. "In early days, Grand Portage was where trails and streams led to western Canada from Lake Superior. It is beautiful. I look forward to showing you."

"I'm glad, Mama. We want to see *many* places," Nancy says.

"After my father helped England defeat France to win Canada, the North West Company formed a fur-trade base at Grand Portage. My father joined them there. Later, they bought land from the Ojibway where the Kaministiquia River flows into Lake Superior and built Fort William."

"Why is it named William?" Nancy, my curious one, asks.

"William McGillivray was the chief partner directing the Company."

Nancy's eyes sparkle. "When people are famous, are places named for them?"

"Not always, but often. Fort William connects eastern and western Canada, so interesting people visit all year long. Their Fur Rendezvous each early fall is wonderful with trappers and native people bringing crafts and furs. They have dances, canoe races, and contests, plus wonderful foods. We will try to arrive in time."

"Yes!" My girls' voices soar.

Nancy retrieves a copy of a map and circles Fort William. Her eyes trace a trail on the paper.

I clear my throat, and she looks at me. "Uncle Peter won't let us travel alone," I say.

"Will he come with us?" Marie asks.

"He says he must work here another year before retiring. By then, he hopes there will be calm between the two fur companies."

"How likely is that?" Marie sounds skeptical.

"I think we have to wait and see."

Nancy sits next to Marie. "Will we travel there in freight canoes too?" she asks.

"Probably."

"Then Uncle Peter must come along, because he gets the best trade prices," she declares boldly. "Then, once he's there, we won't let him leave."

I stroke her cheek. "That's a good plan. You're a dear schemer."

"Make lists so we can help you pack," Nancy says.

"Yes, I'll make lists for each of us, and the time will pass quickly."

Yet even I'm shocked at how the days fly as we mark them off on the calendar. Along with the promised blessing of school, I prepare my heart for the adjustment we will probably face where there is more non-native population. At the Company's headquarters in Central Canada, we will almost certainly find prejudice between people of white skin and brown. As a child, I heard Europeans scorn marriages between whites with natives.

Métis, they called us, half-breeds, in unpleasant tones, as if the children born are defects, carrying a disease to be avoided, not the blessed, blended heritage of two peoples. When I married Alex, I thought he would be like Father, bringing home songs and gifts from far places. But people can seem alike outwardly, yet have different hearts. They say love is blind and I fear it's true. From the beginning, Alex never sang as Father did. "A waste of time," he called it. But he was so strong and handsome, I kept songs alive in our home while he focused on adventures to build fame and fortune.

Before we married, Mother touched her heart and said, "I feel sadness here. Alex seeks greatness, but I don't sense your father's goodness." Her eyes held mine. "My people say that a lack of peace is a hungry animal that devours the happiness of those around them. I don't want your happiness eaten."

I bristled. "Alex is smart and ambitious. He will be fine once we marry."

She answered, "It's hard to teach someone happiness if they do not wish to learn."

I did not listen. If Mother were alive, I would confess she spoke truth. Diphtheria, that merciless sickness, stole her and many others as its ghost stalked our forests. It did not come during the years Alex and I had our first children. We were spared that horror. Like Father, Alex traveled constantly. The difference was, when Father came home, he gave us his delighted attention while Alex only planned more trips.

I convinced myself that he would change as our children grew older, but his ambition ravaged us like the packs of starving wolves lurking in winter snow banks beyond each home's firelight. The only way to keep them at bay is to build big fires that burn through the night until daylight comes. Then, the animals fade away.

No matter what, I will do what I must to keep our home fires burning bright and hot to keep enemies away.

It seems we wait forever for Christmas, and then suddenly, it is on us. To knit a warm scarf for Peter, my girls collect raw wool from sheep in the barn and comb and dye it lovely colors from nuts, roots, and berries. They argue about whether beet root, red autumn leaves, or sumac fruit makes the truest red. We test them all and sumac wins. When powdered, it's also a tasty spice. Nancy adds a note reminding Peter to wear it around his neck constantly after we leave until he comes to us at Fort William.

Secret intrigue happens each night as people carrying bundles walk through the dark.

Catherine and I join Marie and Nancy in volunteering to help serve the Christmas dinner. "What is our main course?" Nancy asks several days ahead, always ready to enjoy a good time.

"That is a secret you can't know until Christmas day." The chief cook turns to Jules and speaks slyly. "Make sure you bring it to the back door and have it here by midnight. It will take that long to cook it to perfection. We will use the back fireplace—not one any helpers can see."

"But they will smell the deliciousness," Jules says.

"That can't be helped," the head cook answers.

"Can't see what?" Nancy cajoles.

Jules and the head cook refuse to answer.

Night comes early on these shortest days of the year. In late afternoon of Christmas Eve, when it's almost dark, we hear a strange sound—a cry or squeal or grunt—from the barn.

We stand still and listen. "What is that?" Nancy asks Jules as he passes.

"Nothing at all. You're imagining things. Stay inside. Sometimes when it's very cold, even the snow squeaks underfoot." He opens the back door and steps outside to demonstrate, sliding his feet and spinning to demonstrate how noisy dry snow can be. He proves it is very noisy.

Early Christmas morning, as we're cozy and warm in our beds, delicious smells drift up from the kitchen. My stomach rumbles to taste whatever that wonderful food is.

Catherine clutches her stomach. "When can we eat, Mama? I'm hungry. It hurts to wait. Can we please go to the kitchen now?"

"No, dear. Cook let us prepare several dishes yesterday, but he won't allow any of us in there today. We must wait until noon when Uncle Peter or Jules rings the big church bell to gather us together."

"But that is too long!" she cries as if in pain.

Nancy and Marie nod in agreement.

Even my stomach growls. I lay out biscuits and jam. "Come and eat breakfast now. Peter also gave us a bit of chocolate. We need this morning time to finish wrapping gifts and little surprises for each other."

We're wrapping our last items when the church bell tolls its powerful notes. Catherine leaps from her chair. "It's time!"

"Almost," I say. "Uncle Peter said he'd give a first warning bell when things are almost ready, and then ring it loud and long when it's time to come."

"Will we have church too?" Nancy asks.

"Not today. Father Laurier can't travel here until New Year's, but Peter will read the Christmas Story in Luke, the way my father used to do."

"That's nice," Marie says. "And don't forget, there will be songs and skits from many others besides the special solo Mother has prepared,"

I smile, thinking of Christmases long ago. "Uncle Peter's favorite Christmas carol is *O Come, All Ye Faithful*. In memory I see his face as it shone years ago when Father sang it for him. With effort, the Lord helps me recall all the words so Marie can write them down for me now."

"Will he be surprised?" Nancy asks.

"Probably, but he'll remember that night long ago."

"May we help you sing the chorus?" Now that Marie sees all the inspired words, her voice rings with awe.

"Yes, please do join with me."

Within minutes, they sound like angels.

When at last the church bell rings long and merrily and we all gather together, the mysterious squeal and nighttime activities are explained. Recovered well from his axe cut, Gaston and Jules stroll in carrying a massive roasted pig on an iron spit on their shoulders. They hook the spit onto two giant hooks in the main hall's main fireplace. The succulent aroma is wonderful. Voices groan with oohs and ahhs.

"What is in its mouth?" Catherine asks.

"An apple," Peter says. "In royal palaces in Europe, fat Christmas pigs are roasted with apples in their mouths to show they were fed well in their last days. German cooks often serve applesauce with roast pork. I don't know if you've tasted it before, but you will love it. First, let me read the Bible story and pray, and then it's my pleasure to serve each of you, from the oldest person here to the youngest."

He does, and manages to remember everyone's name and age. The meat is so tender, it falls from its bones on our plates. Conversation stills while we savor each bite.

Nancy swallows her last bit and sighs. "Moose and bear are nourishing and put flesh on our bones, but this is the most delicious meat I've ever tasted." She looks around to everyone at the table. "Thank you to all who helped prepare it."

The cook tilts his head in acknowledgement. "You're welcome."

Peter smiles and waves for us to get more servings. "Come eat all of it," he says. "It will be a year before we feast this well again."

After dinner, we're still groaning, but we enjoy the presented skits and songs. I'm amazed this fort is so gifted with talented people. Older men sing voyageur songs just like my father did. Jules is a master at playing spoons, as Peter stated, and Gaston has recovered well enough to dance to the rhythm.

"Look," Nancy says. "We must learn those songs and dances."

"Yes!" Catherine shouts.

Peter leans near. "Your moose sinew did wonders for Gaston. We should always use it for stitching."

Shadows lengthen outside and the blazing candles begin to burn low. At last it's my turn to stand near Peter to sing my gift. I clasp my hands together and gaze at him as I sing. "O come, all ye faithful, joyful and triumphant. O come ye, o come ye to Bethlehem. Come and behold Him, born the King of Angels . . ."

His face lifts in ecstasy.

"How wonderful!" he says.

My girls join on the chorus, "O come, let us adore Him, O come, let us adore Him, O come, let us adore Him, Christ the Lord!"

Peter can't hold back his tears. They squeeze from his eyes and drip down his cheeks.

"Such blessings," he says. "The years roll back and our loved ones are with us again."

Those words make my voice wobble on the closing notes. I feel the presence of our loved ones too.

"Your gift blesses me," he says. "I also made something special for you." He lifts his plate and reveals a piece of white cloth the same color as the tablecloth beneath it. It covers something flat. We can't see what it is until his trembling hands lift and extend his gift.

"What is it?" Catherine asks.

I lift the covering gauzelike cloth and find absolute treasure. He or someone has rubbed a birchbark surface soft and clean and inscribed in black ink an almost perfect likeness of my father, mother, and me at the time we celebrated Christmas here with Peter many years ago.

I cannot breathe. Tears thicken my throat. "Peter, who made this so perfectly?"

"My memory is clear of those days. I asked God to help me capture your faces, for they are too precious to forget. I knew it would bless you to have a likeness. My hands shake, but God helped me make a few short strokes or lines each time until I was done." His face shines brighter than the candles lighting this room. "It turned out well despite my limitations."

I hold it against my chest and bow my head. Only God can give back something lost. "Peter, it's a masterpiece I'll cherish forever. I love you even more for thinking of this."

My girls press close and gaze, tracing their fingers around my father's noble brow and strong jaw and touching Mother's braids, which Peter has drawn piled in a crown of braids in the Swedish way Father loved her to wear it. Mother's tender doe-like eyes smile at us in peace. Peter has captured us perfectly and made this a holy night almost like the first in Bethlehem, with the Christ child Himself present with us.

When my tears stop, the girls and I push back our chairs and rise quietly. Without speaking, we all work together and clear away the food items before we return to our rooms. The fort and the landscape around us bask in a holy hush.

Chapter 8

Fort William on Lake Superior, 1811

Days lengthen after New Year's, and months fly until it's time to load freight canoes with our family's goods packed between bales of furs. My girls have trapped many of their own pelts and are rich with Peter's payment.

"What is our route?" I ask him as Jules helps other men add our pelts to those already on the canoes. Jules will travel with us, and I am grateful for his kind attention. "I've only approached Fort William from the west."

"The shortest distance from here is straight west across Lake Superior." Peter's arm waves a direct line. "It's seldom possible to canoe straight across, but in this exceptionally good weather, you might."

Chills prickle my neck. "Coming to you, our canoe capsized and we nearly lost Catherine. Can you assure me that won't happen if we paddle straight across?"

"No one can promise, but the pelts of fur-bearing animals are thin this summer and the moss on trees less thick. Nature's signs suggest this warm, dry weather will continue. You should be able to paddle directly across without a problem. Compared to traveling the northern coastline around the lake, it will cut travel time in half." He takes my hand. "I have prayed, and I have peace. Still, you must have peace too."

The love in his eyes warms me. "Peter, I've also prayed much. I'll keep on as we go, but I have enough peace too."

Jules strides to us. "Everything is ready. Time to go."

Making the decision to go and preparing for our departure proves to be the easy part. I find it very difficult to bid Peter goodbye. I swallow tears. "It's hard to part from you, Peter."

"For me too. I promise I will come as soon as I can."

"See that you do."

The girls and I give him final hugs, and then we settle into a well-packed canoe. The rowers push us away from the bank, and Peter stands near the water and waves. We crane our necks backward and wave too. We don't face forward until we can't see him or Sault Sainte Marie at all.

A steady east wind at our backs speeds us on our way. We and our canoes are small floating leaves on Lake Superior's vastness. We travel by day and make camp at night on some of the lake's islands. Finally, near noon on our twelfth day, I look ahead and recognize the forested hills and boulder-filled shore of the western edge of Lake Superior south of Fort William. Rugged domed mountains and cliffs rise like castles.

"This scenery is wonderful!" I look here and there, trying to take it all in.

Jules looks around too. "Magnificent. As if shaped by giants."

I shake my head. "No, by God himself."

"Of course, that is what I meant." He lifts a hand and points. "Look, girls. They say all this is created by fire and ice, that glaciers grinding the land dropped heavy loads to form the Great Lakes. This lake, Superior, is the largest and deepest. And that high mountain"—he points again—"stood above the glaciers, so the upper slopes did not get scoured. The Ojibway call it Thunder Mountain."

"A perfect name." I shiver not from cold, but from seeing this inspiring majesty. The mountains seem to form a giant cup. There is a sense of mystery, and I've heard stories about my mother's people holding sacred ceremonies here.

The rippling crystalline-blue waters carry us to shore. In my wilderness home with Alex, news of visitors sometimes came by startled birds rising suddenly, or forest animals falling silent. On the beach, apparently alerted by some invisible signal, a crowd gathers for our arrival. Behind them on low hills above Superior's cold waters, stockade buildings stand tall and strong.

I don't expect to know any members of the welcoming crowd, but when hands reach out to steady us and beach our canoes, Doctor John McLoughlin is one of those offering a smile and guiding us to shore. He towers above the rest.

"Welcome," his hearty voice booms. He lifts Catherine from me and holds my arm as I step to the gritty beach, then helps Marie and Nancy to land. After sitting in our canoe so many days, it takes time for my legs to stop quivering. I'm dizzy with excitement, but my girls are worse. They are spring fawns finding their legs and wanting to bound along this shore. Their eyes dart here and there, they giggle and chatter, naming many different parts of this new world they want to see at once.

I interrupt. "Girls, I'm as happy to be here as you, and I will allow you to explore, but first we must claim our belongings and find where we'll stay."

"True," Doctor McLoughlin says. "Show me your baggage. I'll carry all I can. After that I'll give you a good tour." He scans the canoes. "Where is Peter? Don't tell me he let you come without him."

"It was hard, but he stayed behind for now." I lean against a tall tree's solid trunk and rest my wobbly legs. I break off green pine needles and pop them into my mouth, enjoying their spicy flavor. "There's talk of uprisings, which he felt compelled to address, but he says nothing will stop him from coming next season."

The doctor grimaces. "There's *always* talk of uprisings. When my assignments take me to him next, I'll do my best to bring him back."

"Thank you." I'm less wobbly now, and my girls seem calmer. But our heads still swerve, wanting to take in all we can of this busy place at once.

"Mama?" Marie points to carpenters sawing and hammering, frontiersmen in fringed leather unloading fur bales as if they weigh nothing, and soldiers guarding the fort's main entrance with flintlocks and muskets. "You said this place would be exciting, but it's even better."

"It's much bigger now," I say, "and with far more people."

Nancy trembles with excitement. "I don't know what I want to see or do first."

The doctor laughs. "Let me help you decide. I'm glad you're eager to take it all in. I'll do my best to show you everything after we take care of several tasks." He hoists two heavy cartons onto his back. "Fort William's Chief Factor, Girouard, wants to greet you, and then I'll show you your new home. After that, we can explore everything. Come." His teeth gleam in his tanned face.

The girls pick up their loads and cheerfully follow, chattering like magpies.

I regard this professional man about whom I know little, although Peter praises him to the skies. The doctor has a bushy mane of lion-colored hair and ruddy complexion. I'm tall but he towers above me. We race to match his long strides.

"Do you know Girouard?" he asks as we enter the fort's main gate.

I shake my head.

"You will like him. He's a Québécois who traveled with your father in early days to choose fort locations." He stops before an impressive white two-story home occupying the central location in the stockade. Matching flower beds in protective netting line both sides of the long porch next to green lawns struggling to grow. "Here we are."

A smiling, rotund middle-aged man descends the steps and clasps my hand in his chubby one. "Madame MacKay, a hearty welcome! I feel I've always known you through my great regard for your father." He bends over my hand and kisses my fingers in the French fashion before taking my daughters' hands also.

He turns to me. "You and your lovely girls bring beauty and civility to this rough-hewn place. I was to be your father's junior partner at Lac La Ronge that ill-fated winter, but Montréal promoted Peter Pond instead. How I wish things had been otherwise. I so respected your dear father." He gives a deep sigh. "But welcome now. I'll do my best to make you happy."

Raucous bleats from three milk goats staked

at the corner of the house rend the air. Girouard shakes a fist. “They are demons, hooved demons! We need milk for the babies, so what is a man to do? But I swear, if they pull loose again and devour more grass and roses, we’ll add roast goat to our menu.”

Hiding smiles, my daughters hurry forward and pet the animals.

“Ah, you feel sympathy,” Girouard says. “I admit they are cute.” After several more minutes of chatting, Girouard allows us to go see our new home.

The good doctor rushes us across the square. “The previous residents planted a garden—corn, squash, beans, and sunflowers. But they couldn’t stay to harvest. If we can keep the goats away, it should give a good crop.”

The plot of healthy, upright, waving green plants is cleanly weeded. “You or someone labored much.”

He shrugs, but his cheeks flush. “It was nothing. A small welcome.”

He escorts us inside the house, which has four good-sized rooms. My daughters scurry from room to room, eagerly claiming their spaces. Nancy peeks from a doorway. “Mama, this is nice.”

The house is more than I expected, and I am delighted with the accommodations. I turn an appreciative smile on McLoughlin. “Thank you,

Doctor. We are indebted to your kindness."

"Not at all. We're privileged to have you here." He flushes again.

I ponder the reaction. It's a bit hot in the house, but not extremely. Perhaps he flushes easily.

He moves to the door. "I'll leave you to settle in. Please let me know if you find anything lacking." I assure him I will, and he hurries off.

The girls and I unpack and then write notes to Peter, urging him to come soon. I pray he heeds our bidding. I miss him already, but my daughters and I enter this new season of our new lives with relative ease.

Sault Sainte Marie was wonderfully welcoming, but school and daily life here are everything we hoped for. My happy girls absorb learning like thirsty flowers drinking rain after a drought. They settle in as though this has been their home for years. With people being so kind, we don't feel like strangers. It warms my heart when old-timers speak of my parents. I am thankful not to find the prejudice I expected.

However, when I see whole families together, I sometimes feel pangs of unhappiness. I wish that for us too, but that time is over for us. Seeing my daughters truly happy soothes my twinges of loneliness. And truthfully, I'm so busy, I hardly have time to notice.

I discover that Doctor McLoughlin is a joy to work with. I help in the dispensary daily and wherever else I can be effective. Its log structure is near our home. Someone covered its flat roof with sod. Girouard often threatens to tether the goats to graze so they leave his lawn and roses alone.

After one such blustering tirade, the doctor tells him, "They might slip off the roof and hang by their necks until dead. That would break the hearts of every child here, plus end your milk supply."

"True, doctor. I suppose that is worse than losing my flowers," the chief factor says. "Still, you're a bright man. Help me find a solution that saves the goats and my flowers."

McLoughlin laughs. "I doubt we'll solve that today. The challenge could stump the best minds leading this world's capitals."

My girls sneak carrots and beans to the goats from our garden whenever they pass. Our harvest is abundant, and our days fall into a pleasant rhythm.

"You spoil me," Doctor McLoughlin surprises me by saying one afternoon when we organize the dispensary shelves.

"How so?"

"When you assist, I quickly have all I need. Without you, my bumbling fingers prick myself or my patients with needles." He waits until I look up. "Some days when I'm working here alone, patients ask for you. They value your calmness and knowledge of natural remedies." His eyebrows lift. "Sometimes they ask when you'll return, and then they leave until you've come back."

"I think you're exaggerating," I tell him, hiding my smile, but he assures me it's true. I'm happy he's pleased, and when he's away, I stay busy tending wounds and distributing remedies. I also teach my daughters to distill and compound herbal extracts and infusions.

"With you here, my skills are multiplied," the doctor says, his gaze boring steadily into mine. "With you here, my dispensary is the best it's ever been."

I blush under his praise. "You're a busy man, and you deserve the help."

"The people at Fort William will never let you go elsewhere, Marguerite, even if you wish."

I am more determined than ever to be a help and deserve his glowing words.

The next time he's away, the girls and I check his dwindling inventory. He has ordered supplies from Toronto and Montréal, but they may not arrive before freeze-up. We replenish his salves and ointments, also adding as many tinctures and teas as the season allows. In addition, I've begged large amounts of moose sinew from the butcher shop, which I clean for sturdy thread as well as bones for needles of varied sizes.

He is astounded when he sees what we've done.

"I don't want to overwork you, but whenever you wish to gather such materials, you bless us all. I've never been so well-supplied, even when our yearly orders do arrive on schooners in time." He stands with his hands on his hips, scanning his loaded shelves and shaking his head in wonder. "You make me think the entire forest is a living apothecary filled with medicines and cures."

"That's almost true. We will teach you."

"You'll find me a grateful, faithful student."

Through autumn, he's busy taking as many trips to distant outposts as he can fit in before winter stops travel. This time when he's away, we make a huge effort to prepare so many medical supplies, his cupboards overflow. I request a fort carpenter to build a new set for more storage.

On his return, Doctor McLoughlin stands open-mouthed. "How amazing." His smile embraces us. "You and your girls are more industrious than the beavers I've seen preparing for winter all along my way. I'm happy I purchased these small gifts for you from my journey."

My heart flutters. He has brought mementos in the same way my father used to. My girls gather close. He kneels first before little Catherine and opens his pack.

"A lovely doll for you. You will like her embroidered deerskin dress and ribboned braids. Her hair is darker than yours, but she reminds me of you."

"Oooohh, thank you." My youngest flings her arms around his neck and squeezes before clasping the doll to herself.

"This beaded belt is yours, Nancy. I have not seen this cunning design of rivers and mountains before, but it seems right for you as you love speaking of distant places."

"And one day I will do more than talk of it. This is wonderful. I may never take it off."

His smile widens. "And for Marie, a trapper cured these soft ermine pelts and fashioned a collar for the neckline of any garment. It will keep you warm."

Marie gazes at the collar in wonder. "It's lovely, Doctor McLoughlin. The Queen of England doesn't have finer furs. Thank you from my heart. My sisters and I will cook delicious treats and stuff you until you grow fat."

"Mercy, no." But his eyes twinkle. "And for you, Marguerite."

I hold up my hands. "It is enough to bring my daughters gifts. There's no need to bring me something."

"I wish to. You have been wonderful help and turned this rugged bachelor dispensary into a well-ordered clinic where people heal." He lays an intricate chain carved from birch in my hands. Its length reaches from my index fingertip to my elbow. There is a clever way to fasten it into a complete circle if I wish. "I've seen nothing like this. Where did you get it? Who is the maker?"

His handsome face reddens. His bold gray eyes meet mine. "I had not seen one like it either. One night as I rested, the idea to carve a multi-linked chain from a solid piece of birch came to mind. Flickering fires gave too little light to read, but enough to carve as I thought of you."

"How nice that you thought of us." My cheeks warm and my heart pounds at such kindness freely given from someone who had no obligation. I hold his marvelous chain in my hands, turning it this way and that, its polished links glowing like honey. "It's lovely, Doctor. What does it mean? What is it to be used for?"

I study him. Above his beard, his cheeks redden as though he has just come in from the cold. He shrugs. "It's just a pretty gift I carved that means whatever you wish. It could be a necklace, or you could rest it on a table to surround a bouquet of flowers. To me, it means that great beauty comes from simple things when time and care are given."

I cannot stop tears from springing to my eyes. I can guess the amount of time and care that went into such a gift. "W-what a lovely thought," I stammer. "We are honored to receive such beauty." My fingers stroke its gleaming links. I slip it over my head for a moment but soon remove it. "It's too beautiful to wear."

"Not at all!" He shakes his head strongly.

"Besides, it looks wonderful on you. Please wear it."

"I cannot. I'm not used to being fussed over."

"Then it's time you were."

Marie touches the gift with gentle fingers. "He's right, Mama. A gift made so carefully is meant to be displayed and enjoyed. Do you think we girls might borrow it sometimes for special occasions?"

I don't hesitate. "I don't see why not. Such beauty is too great to be owned by one person, especially someone old and plain."

"Old and plain?" The doctor nearly explodes, his words almost harsh. "It is made for you, Marguerite. Some plague has damaged your eyesight, for no one near matches you."

My eyes widen. He is more grateful for my help than I imagine to craft so fine a gift. My cheeks heat, and I hardly trust my mouth to speak. It seems a personal gift, but he is far above my station. For an instant, I picture Alex who, in recent years, would never spend time making such a gift, and my eyes return to the doctor. "Thank you. It's exquisite. I appreciate it."

His expression gentles. "You are welcome. I did everything but carve your name on it, and perhaps I should have done so. I did carve an *M* just here." He leans close and shows me the tiny initial worked inside the first link.

"Ah, I see it. Near the top. How cunning. That could stand for Marguerite or Marie."

"Yes, I suppose so. Your names are similar. Even if I had carved 'Ma' or 'Mar,' your names begin the same."

"You're right. I had not thought of that."

"Next time, I will carve your full name so there is no doubt. Good night, Marguerite. Sleep well." He turns and goes to his quarters.

I should bid him goodnight, but I find myself struggling for words. Why does he feel such immense gratitude to me? If he were older, I might think he offers this sweet gift like a young man wishing to woo a young woman, but I am nine years his senior. All I know is, after returning from his long, wearying journey, he took time to bless my girls and me before seeking rest.

I slip the exquisite hand-carved chain through my hands again. I will long remember his kindness to my girls and me.

Chapter 9

Two days later, plunging temperatures bring us a first snowfall. Thankfully, it melts quickly and we are blessed by a stretch of Indian summer with temperatures so balmy, we harvest plentiful cranberries and the grouse that eat them.

The girls and I are picking berries when a native youth comes running from a nearby village, calling as he runs.

"Help! Where is the doctor? We need him at our village."

I step into his path. "Who's hurt? What do you need?"

Bending over, hands on knees, he fights for breath. "My brother . . . rolled into fire. Bad!"

Doctor McLoughlin is at the dispensary so I take the boy to him. The doctor grabs his medical kit and insists I come along. I exchange my basket of berries for my red sewing bag and ask if my daughters may follow. He has begun running but waves for them to come.

As we near the village, the young man points to a crumbling cabin. "We just moved here," he says. "Much to fix."

My two older daughters gather firewood while Catherine grabs a pine branch and sweeps the debris-filled yard.

“Here.” The young man ushers us inside. The stench of burned flesh assaults us as we enter. The worried parents greet us, eyes wide with hope. The father grips the doctor’s hand and hoarsely whispers, “*Miigwech*. Thank you.”

I stare at a boy, perhaps nine or ten years old, who lies uncovered on a mat on the floor. He bites his lips against pain, his face screwed up tight. The burns on his leg look angry. Part of his leggings also burned, leaving leather bits stuck to his skin. The mother sits on the floor close to her son. She holds one of his hands and croons a simple melody while gently rocking.

Doctor McLoughlin crouches next to the boy. Anguish darkens his eyes. “Bring fresh water, please.” The boy’s father fills an earthenware bowl and brings it.

“Thank you.” The doctor dips a clean cloth from his pack into the water and gently brushes away the loose shriveled skin. He frequently rinses the cloth and removes beginning signs of pus. “It will scar,” he tells the boy’s parents. “But if this inner part can heal, your son should walk and run again.”

The parents sigh as if they’ve held their breath a long time.

“May that be true.” My words are a whispered prayer.

My daughters stand at the door, their hopeful eyes seeking permission to slip inside. I nod, and the boy's father and older brother take a step back and make room for them.

Doctor McLoughlin frowns at me. "Marguerite, there is nothing in my supplies for burns this deep. Do you carry any honey?"

"Honey? I'm sorry, no."

"What can honey do?" Marie stares with compassion at the injured boy.

"Medical books say it's been used for centuries to soothe damaged skin and reduce infection and inflammation. I can't explain how it works, but many healers claim good results. I'd like to try."

"These woods have honey," Nancy says, her green eyes ablaze. "We will search and find it." She runs out the door, and Marie hurries after. Catherine hunkers in the corner, tears filling her eyes as she watches the boy.

As Doctor McLoughlin gently washes more burned flesh, the boy's eyes roll and he moans. His mother fetches more fresh water and lays a moistened rag on his forehead. His body violently shakes, and his brother brings a deerskin. I take it and lay it across the boy's torso, careful to avoid the area where the doctor is working.

Doctor McLoughlin puts a pinch of my powdered willow bark in a cup of water and lifts it to the boy's lips. Soon, the boy's eyes are less wild, and the parents' faces show flickers of hope that he may recover. The mother serves us a bit of pemmican along with maple sugar lumps she has prepared herself. Catherine reaches eagerly when the mother offers her a second piece. Finally, we hear my older girls whoop and holler. They scramble inside the cabin with triumphant smiles. They carry a stout tree branch with amber honey oozing from a hollow place inside.

The doctor gives a pleased grin. "You girls are to be praised. This will make a wonderful difference in this young man's healing." He gently applies the honey and says a prayer. I can't tell if the parents understand his Christian prayer or not, but they do not object. The boy's breathing deepens, and he yields to sleep. His mother rests a gentle hand on his chest, her eyes pinned on his face.

Doctor McLoughlin sits back on his heels. "Marguerite, are there plants in these woods that can speed his healing?"

"Yes, many." I name several, but the boy's parents shake their heads. People of this tribe seem unaware of the woodland remedies Mother's Cree people use so freely, or they're not familiar with local names. Plus, as the brother said, this family is new here. It would be of great benefit to know how to make poultices from certain leaves and steep well-chosen roots long enough to make healing waters. Perhaps I can teach them.

I turn to the doctor. "What if you spread more honey on that clean deerskin to protect the boy's leg and we search the woods for local remedies? It's very late in the season, but that brings its own gifts. I'm sure we'll find something." I look at the boy's father. "Would you like to come?"

He nods. I indicate he should bring a basket.

The doctor makes a protective covering for the boy's leg. Then my older girls, the boy's father, the doctor, and I venture into the woods together. As he promised, Doctor McLoughlin is a quick learner. The father also recognizes a number of plants quickly. We're all astonished that in less than an hour we return to the family's home bearing comfrey leaves for healing poultices and many plant parts and roots for teas and tonics to cleanse the blood and build up the boy's strength to fight fever and infections.

I give the mother simple instructions. Her smiles and nods say she understands.

The parents and older brother thank us repeatedly in their dialect for coming. We may not catch every word, but their meaning is clear. We return safely to the fort by dark. Before the girls and I part ways with the doctor, he takes my hand.

"Thank you, Marguerite. With your help, I am a better equipped healer than ever. These treatments must become better known. I'm convinced of their effectiveness. My brother, David, in medical school in Scotland, needs to know if these or similar remedies grow near him."

"I suspect they do," I say. "I keep my ears open for information. Sometimes people in foreign lands know the same plant by a different name but have knowledge of its benefits. If the exact plant does not grow near your brother, I'm sure our Lord has created something for a treatment or cure. If we walk the woods and listen, the Lord directs our eyes to the remedies He wishes to teach us. I'll ask Nancy to draw pictures of the best plants and flowers for easy identification and Marie to label them with simple instructions."

"Both would be priceless gifts. I can never thank you enough."

"There's no need for thanks. The Lord gives them as free gifts." I bid him a good evening, and his gratitude continues to echo in my heart as I drift to sleep that night.

The final three full weeks of Indian summer pass pleasantly. Autumn's last red and gold leaves fall from the trees like rain until only bare branches point to the sky. One early afternoon, the burned native boy and his brother come to the fort. The boy walks slowly but strongly, leaning on a walking stick. His leg is badly scarred, but clearly its strength is returning. His shining eyes express greater thanks than his halting words. His brother gives me a leg of fresh venison. A bond formed. These are friends we hope to see again.

Incredibly, days fly faster instead of more slowly, and Christmas is upon us again. The fort's Christmas dinner is simple, but Girouard gives each child their own reading book plus hair ribbons for girls and small jackknives for the boys. He approaches me, smiling broadly, and bows at the waist. "For you, Madame MacKay, this smocked garment to guard your clothing as you help us, and this leather satchel for your remedies."

The satchel is handsome with multiple interior compartments. In fact, it looks nicer than the doctor's battered one. I stammer, "You are very kind. Both are wonderful. I will always do my best to help everyone here."

"That we know. Thank you."

Days later, in January, a sudden diphtheria outbreak threatens everyone. The good doctor is a human whirlwind, visiting homes within the fort and the native settlements far beyond. He will not let me go with him, insisting I stay home for my daughters' sake. He begs Girouard to supply nourishing broth, even if it means slaughtering the goats. To save his noisy pets, Girouard sends hunters out through deep snow, and we rejoice when they bring back a big bull moose. Doctor McLoughlin tells the people to boil the water they use and burn or bury waste to stop the spread of disease.

Despite precautions, I am stricken. I try to hide my fevers and tremors, but he sees and comes to our home twice daily to assume my care.

"I will manage . . . on my own," I insist but can scarcely speak. "Help others. I know . . . what to do."

"You lack strength, Marguerite." His words are gentle, kind. "Now you are the patient and must do as I say."

I wave him away. "You can't become ill. Marie . . . will care for me. I've fought diphtheria. It won't take me."

"You don't *know* that." He is tall, commanding, but exhausted. His hands shake and his eyes are red-rimmed. "Must I quarantine you? Your daughters cannot lose you. This whole fort and I can't lose you."

"This whole fort?" I try to laugh but phlegm chokes me. I sigh too weak to refuse his orders. "I will accept your care once each day if you leave immediately after to gain fresh air."

"Or I may open a door or window." He smiles brightly. He is stubborn and will not budge.

In God's mercy, the long dark days roll on until winter finally becomes spring. Sunlight gradually restores health to many and the terrible sickness wanes and then is gone. By then, I think the good doctor looks twice his age. He is skin and bone but laughs at my concern.

"It is nothing. It's hard to hang enough flesh on my tall frame."

I want to cook good food for him and fatten him up. I tell him so.

He laughs again.

I shake my head. "Doctor McLoughlin, you try my patience."

He surprises me by saying, "We've worked together closely. Please call me John—except in the dispensary when others are present. Then I remain *Doctor McLoughlin.*"

Using his given name is foreign to me at first, but since it seems to please him, I manage the distinction. I sense a deeper friendship growing between us, and I cherish it the way I cherish the lovely necklace of birch links he carved for me.

Thankfully, the doctor enjoys my daughters very much. They greatly benefit from his tutoring and thrive in their studies. He develops a special closeness with my sweet Marie. One ship captain delivering goods hints that a year from now she may receive a marriage offer from Donald Mackenzie, a cousin to Sir Alexander Mackenzie, as is her father, Alex MacKay. Newly knighted Sir Alexander is the exploring cousin my Alex accompanied to the Pacific. We've loved our transition to this fort. I'm not ready to have my girls grow up fast. Surely the ship captain's words are a rumor I don't want to be true.

Weeks and months roll by with little to disturb our routine. By now my girls become experts at knowing what festivities will take place here. Girouard causes excitement by announcing he goes to Toronto soon to marry a lovely young woman willing to join him in this wilderness. After their wedding, they will host a big reception and dance here. My girls are thrilled. I wager his wife will insist on holding more lavish Christmas celebrations in the future.

"When they have their reception, people will come from other places," Nancy says. "You should have told us we'd need fancy dresses here with long skirts for such things."

I roll my eyes. "How can I tell you what I do not know? Things have changed since I visited here long ago. But we have time. We'll buy fabric and you can sew to your heart's content."

One late spring evening, as my girls stroll the fort grounds, the doctor strides to our home. He seems distressed. I offer hot tea as soon as he comes in and takes a seat at the table.

"No, thank you."

"John, I don't know what troubles you, but tea will help you feel better."

"I am not ill."

"But you're clearly not yourself." I pour him a cup anyway. "Are you disappointed that Marie considers Donald? I know you care for her. If you simply tell her you're interested, I'm sure she will change her mind."

Something in my chest catches. I'm happy for Marie—truly. She blooms like a rose, and I pray she has wonderful years ahead. I rejoice to think of my sweet girl receiving the love of a fine man, whether it's Donald or John. Yet I'm also ashamed by the gnawing in my heart that my years for being loved and cherished are over. I did not choose well and suffer the consequences, but at least I have my children.

"John? Will you speak to her?"

"Why should I?" He loosens his collar while his face flames. "I'm hopeless at such things, but it's true I must discuss marriage."

"I knew it. I've seen it coming." I rise to refill his tea cup though he's scarcely taken a sip.

"It's true I love her—as a younger sister." His voice rises. "Marguerite, put down that teapot."

His eyes are wild. Perhaps he is fevered.

"Are you blind, Marguerite? It's you I seek. You are the one I love."

"Me? That cannot be." I splash hot tea on my wrist. "Don't jest."

"It is true." He dabs my hand with his handkerchief and huffs out his words. "I do not jest."

Though his sentiment seems impossible, his desperate gaze shows it is true.

"But, John, I am old compared to you. You are nine years my junior. Plus I am unworthy. You deserve an ideal wife to enhance your career."

"Measured in whose eyes? Happiness matters more than my career." He takes my hand. "Age does not matter. Hardships have matured us, and we've both had more than our share." He stands and pulls me close. His thumb strokes my cheek with great gentleness. "Hear me and hear me well, Marguerite. I have never known any woman like you. You have qualities I long to enjoy for a lifetime. Endless strength and wisdom. Kindness beyond any other woman." His eyes explore my face. "And you are so beautiful."

The shock of his sentiment overwhelms me. "Beautiful? I have lost my youth, and gray streaks my hair." I step away. "You must not think of me like that. You must choose better."

"But I have chosen the best. I think God has chosen. The years have given you much." His voice deepens. "You are everything I desire in a woman. You make me know why God says, 'It is not good for man to be alone.' " He shakes his lion's mane of hair and swallows hard. "As for worth, I am unworthy of you, but will do the best I can."

I raise a hand to silence him. "John, you are an amazing man, but far above me and much younger. I did not dare think you had serious interest in me."

"No?" He takes my hand again. "Surely you knew from my frequent visits. Others could tell. Nor am I the only man to see your worth. I've seen how others look at you. I know you feel legally bound to Alex, although no court would agree, but I'm here to claim your heart."

Despite the winter chill, my skin heats. His

breath stirs my hair, and I find it hard to speak. "I treasured your close friendship but beyond that did not dream. You bless me with your sentiment but must not choose me. As hard as it would be, I will help you find someone suitable."

"Stop. You pain me." He presses his lips to my hair.

I shudder and try to pull away, but he holds me so close, I cannot free myself.

"I long to do more than bless you with sentiment. I desire to make you my cherished wife."

Since he has lost his senses, I must guard mine. The pulsing tic in his firm jaw makes me want to reach out and caress it, yet I must not. We would both be abandoned to a whirlwind of desire, and I will not lose control.

"Marguerite?" He rests steadying hands on my shoulders, his face near mine. "If you cannot answer now, promise you will favorably do so soon."

I draw a ragged breath. "How can I promise what I do not know?" Yet his scent of soap and mint stirs me, making my heart pound so wildly that, despite my resolve, he must see the fabric of my dress rise and fall with each heartbeat. I fight to calm my voice lest it betray me too. "You honor me, John. I have not dreamed of happiness again, nor that anyone could love me again after my years with Alex. I regard you highly, but I am old and worn. You must find the lovely, God-appointed woman you deserve."

His teeth grind. "I have found her and will have no other. God will open a way. When He makes it clear to you, promise you'll accept me."

God in heaven, it is hard to resist this man. "If God makes the impossible possible, and He can keep me from being your detriment . . ."

"You are blind, woman, but I love you anyway." He caresses my cheek again, his fingertips trailing close to my lips. I long for him to trace and then claim them. When I tremble, his smile turns sly. "I think you care for me a little."

"A great deal. Will you wrench my heart right out of my chest?"

"You give me hope. I know you don't yet see our path, but I believe God will make it clear." He pauses. "Yet there is one complication I must confess."

"What is that?"

"When we met, do you recall my crucial need to reach Rainy River? I had been based there before and, after one year, signed a frontier marriage contract with Véronique, a gracious woman of mixed heritage."

I draw back as if struck. Like Alex, John probably found many willing women in places he traveled.

"Wait! It is not what you think." He cups my chin in his hand, and I read the ardor in his eyes. "A year after our marriage, she bore our son prematurely before a terrible storm let me return. Like Peter's Monique, there were complications that the skilled midwife could not assist. She did not survive, though our son lived."

"You have a son? How wonderful." Shock numbs me. "I am happy for any man to have a son."

John watches me. "His name is Joseph."

"Where is he?"

"In Rainy River with Véronique's mother and relatives. He is almost age two. I provide his needs, but if you accept me, I hope one day we can include him in our family." His eyes question but my heart warms.

"If the time comes that I marry you without fear of ruining your life, I would joyfully include a son who is part of you. If he is yours, he is precious."

John sighs as if he is released from prison. "I find him so. He is sturdy and cheerful. But, of course, I am his father. He knows some words in French, English, and Cree."

"Then he's also intelligent like you." I am overwhelmed by the honor this man pays me. "Your child would be a joy, not a burden, plus I love how you cherish my daughters."

"They are a delight to love, but I love you more. Thank you for hearing my heart. It is only you I will marry."

My groan reveals my heart's warfare. "John,

you are a fine man of wisdom and integrity, yet your proposal shocks me."

"Not news of my son, of whom you knew nothing?"

"No, although I share your sorrow in not reaching Véronique in time."

"I'll always carry that regret, though I did everything in my power to reach her. Some say the complications were so extreme that even if the storm had let me arrive, I couldn't have saved them. That might have been even more terrible for me." He rubs the back of his neck fiercely as if he can massage his pain away. "God gives a measure of peace, and now, He gives me the wonderful gift of loving you." He lifts my hand and places it on his chest. I feel his heart beating as wildly as my own. "Feel the ardent beating of my heart and join your life to mine."

God help me, for I am undone. Like a long-frozen river melting in springtime, I might burst open. I lick my dry lips. "How can I resist?"

"Please don't."

"If I become legally free and you still desire me."

"All here believe you are legally free already."

"If my heart feels fully free, although you deserve much better, I would be honored to embrace you and your son." I reach up to caress his cheek, and he clasps his hand over mine. "Our Lord knows you are the only man I truly desire." I turn my head to hide my rush of tears.

"Dearest love, I'm thankful to hear that." He crushes me to him, and I cling as if I might drown the instant he lets go. He kisses my fingertips one by one and sets them on fire. "Always remember it is you I desire. Only you, Marguerite. God will help us build the loving family we desire that will last forever."

How can this fine, strong man speak of need and faithfulness and give glowing promises when I am scarred and broken? "Only God can do that. I cannot."

"But God can. He will unite us in joy, and I believe His purpose in uniting us is larger than ourselves." He blesses my cheeks with kisses.

That night as I pillow my head, all I can think about is this fine man's shocking declaration of love.

Lord, is it possible you will grant me happiness again? At my age? I feel like barren Sarah hoping for a son, although so advanced in years she scarcely dared believe the angel.

Outside, the night is quiet. I hear no divine response except the assurance that God gives good gifts and brings clear answers in His time.

Chapter 10

Fort William on Lake Superior, late 1811

In fading afternoon light, John McLoughlin trudges to our home across Fort William's quadrangle, every part of him looking heavy-hearted. He walks with the deliberate gait of an older man, hardly watching his steps, except his feet know our path so well. As he climbs our porch steps, one mittened hand holds a packet I don't recognize. I open the door before he knocks.

"John, you are burdened."

"Yes." His gray eyes hood. "Your son Tom is safe, but news of Alex is not good."

My hands fly to my face. "Tell me!" My fragrant venison stew bubbling on the wood stove behind me spits, and I smell scorching meat. I rescue the pot by pulling it to the side and wipe my hands on my apron before sinking into a kitchen chair. I signal John to do the same.

"We've heard rumors of trouble on the Pacific Coast, but I didn't tell you until I knew more. Facts have now come." He holds out a muslin-wrapped packet. "This came by the last boat of the season, addressed to Marguerite MacKay,

Sault Sainte Marie, naming your son, Tom, as sender. The sailors on board knew you live here now."

"A ship came this late when we already have ice and snow?"

"Yes. It's miraculous really. The ship found one open channel and rode it in before it froze solid. This message took half a year's time because of the great distance. The sailors whispered that Alex and many met disaster on the far side of the world."

"Please give me the news." My hands twist in my lap.

"Let's read what's inside." He places the packet in my hand as his eyes search my home. "Where are the girls?"

"Marie is helping the head cook plan desserts. Nancy and Catherine are still in school."

"Good." He leans forward and rests his forehead against mine. "Be brave, sweet, if this letter confirms what the sailors say."

"With God's help." I split the packet's red wax seal with a fingernail, and my trembling hands withdraw two stiff papers. My eyes blur. "Please, John. My eyes cannot focus and I don't read well anyway. Will you please read it?"

"Of course." He opens and smooths the folded sheets. " 'Dearest Mother, it is hard to be far away from the ones I love. Please forgive my imperfect penmanship and spelling, but you need to be informed of recent events. Conditions are more primitive here than you can imagine, but we slowly make progress.

" 'Please know that when Father took me to Montréal, I did not know his plans. I think he was unsure himself. He only promised we'd have a grand adventure, which we did. People made much of us for half a year before I knew we would not return home. Despite Father's thirst for wealth and advancement, he liked Montréal less than expected. I would not care to live there myself.' "

I smooth my skirt to quiet my hands. "Thank God for that."

John nods, and then continues. " 'The American millionaire, John Jacob Astor, came to Montréal and promised Father great rewards and a larger place in history than from crossing Canada with Mackenzie if he'd help establish a fur-trade empire in Oregon Territory. I write from there now, and it does show promise, although not all has turned out as we hoped. After we began building Fort Astoria, named for Astor, he assigned Father to lead a fur-gathering expedition in far northern waters where white men had not been before, but left me here for work and school. Sadly, rumors that it could be dangerous proved true. Before I share those events, I'm troubled to have no reply from you to the letters Father and I sent you from Hawaii.' "

John lifts his eyes. “Hawaii? Did you get such letters?”

“No, nothing. But Alex is a restless man. Through the years I’ve learned to expect none.”

John makes a strangled sound and reads on. “ ‘Astor named Father a senior partner and promised me advancement, too, if I’d stay. Our ship’s first port after Cape Horn was Hawaii for fresh foods and water, strong timber, and delicious tropical fruits as you know from what I wrote in my letter. You and the girls would love it because Hawaii is paradise. That’s why I also sent the detailed drawings.’ ”

John searches my face again.

“No, nothing. I’m sad not to have Tom’s letters and drawings, for I would love to.”

“Perhaps they’ll still arrive. It’s sad that so many letters get lost in this wilderness. I’ll continue. ‘Again, it troubles me not to have your reply. I pray you are well. Distances are great and ships slow, but I long to hear from you and my sisters.’ ”

I dab my eyes. “It’s not yet two years, but he sounds full-grown.”

John nods. “I haven’t met him, but hardships mature young men. I like what I hear. Are you ready to hear more?”

“Please.” I wipe my leaking nose with my handkerchief.

“ ‘You taught me not to speak ill of men, yet

Captain Thorn is rightly named. After Father barely suppressed the mutiny Thorn caused near Cape Horn, Father described him as impatient and hard, treating our crew as free men should not be treated. Father calmed the crew with difficulty but promised the first question he'd ask Astor whenever he next saw him would be why he put such a reactionary hothead in charge of our ship and men.' "

John looks up, smiling. "Excellent. I've heard of Thorn, and that is an important question someone needs to ask." He turns the sheet of cramped writing sideways to read words written in the other direction. " 'Once we arrived, we began fort construction. Then Father took the *Tonquin* north on a fur-trading expedition to far-northern waters to natives who had not seen white men. The voyage sought sleek otter and sable furs worth high value. I begged to go for the adventure, but Father wished me safe and left me in the care of my tutor. Alexander Ross works me hard but is fair. I'm learning much.' "

John searches my face. "This is well-written. If Tom tires of building, I'd gladly train him as a clerk."

"I'd love that."

He continues. " 'I am sad to share terrible news. It took six weeks for word to reach us. Five days ago, a Russian ship brought us the sole survivor of the *Tonquin*'s sixty-two-man crew. Sadly, it was not Father. The survivor told us that Thorn so enraged the natives, they rushed and attacked the ship. He said Father acted bravely and as a last resort ignited all the gunpowder on board to destroy the ship but give them all a chance to escape. However, Father and every man except the one survivor was killed. Most were cut down on the ship. The rest perished in the sea, Father among them. I'm thankful one man survived to bring us word, or we would know nothing.' "

My gasp flutters the page.

"All of those men cut down? Alex dead in a cold, open ocean with no one to bury him?" How like the haunting dream I had scarce two years back when Alex returned saying he would leave us forever. My body shudders. "John, I feel as if the *Majimanidoo* monster my mother and her people feared—*he who walks hungry across the land*—has returned and eats all in his path without mercy."

John tenderly strokes my hair. "Such monsters are real, Marguerite. Many remote tribes tell tales of such creatures and are somewhat more in tune with spiritual things than people we typically call civilized. I've felt that monster's breath on my own neck during extreme sickness or danger. Many stories are too strange not to believe."

"You're right." I stare at Tom's pages. "Does he say anything more?"

"Yes." John lifts it near his eyes. " 'Sometimes

Father wept when he spoke of you and the girls. I think he regretted leaving you behind and might have returned—though now, he cannot.' "

I drag my finger along my lip and bite it so I will not cry more. And yet, Alex is a man to be pitied. "It's hard to believe he is gone."

"For over six months already, Marguerite." John pulls my finger free and kisses it. "At the end Tom adds, " 'I'll work hard to make you proud, Mother, and send funds as soon as possible. Please tell Marie and Catherine I miss them—even Nancy. I'd come home now to lead our family but can do better by staying longer to get promoted. I want to provide well for you enough so one day we can be together again.' "

John shows me the page. "And he adds this flowery signature. I also respect what he writes next, Marguerite. 'Mother, I know when your father was killed, it was very hard for you. I will work hard to be promoted so you and the girls can count on my support. It may not be much at first but will increase with time. I will always do my best, I promise. You are beautiful, Mother, and courageous. With all my love, your son, Thomas MacKay, Esquire.' "

I hear a catch in John's voice. "He's not yet fourteen," I whisper. "I'm amazed at his commitment."

"As am I. He's clearly almost a man, and a good one. You've done well by him, Marguerite."

"And God has answered many prayers." I caress the letter written by my son's hands, expressing words from his heart to ours. "It is my fondest wish one day to be together again—perhaps even in Oregon."

"May God fulfill your wish." John observes me folding the pages back into their packet as he speaks. "May I write Astor that you accept your role as Tom's parental guardian, but allow me to be named as a close friend who guarantees the legal issues and finances until he comes of age?"

I look into his serious face. His eyes are so tender, I can scarcely bear his gaze. "If that is what you wish."

"It is, truly. Now, please don't think me unfeeling, Marguerite." John clears his throat, and his Adam's apple bobs. "I speak from having very deep feelings. I'm terribly sorry Alex made the choices he did, for he was a courageous man, and I thank God Tom was spared." He takes my hand. "This tragedy removes the obstacle in your mind to our marriage. This is a sudden and great shock. I know you will need time to consider this, so I will not press you for your answer tonight. Yet in every sense, I hope you realize you are now a legally free widow with the full right to remarry."

"You are right," I whisper.

His finger caresses my cheek. "I understand that you need time to process losing Alex."

"Thank you. It is a shock, although in most ways, he has been dead to me since the night he told me he was leaving." I sink deeper into my chair. "I am grateful to hear he died bravely. May God have mercy on his soul."

John sighs deeply. "I've been present when many men have died, Marguerite, and God *is* merciful. As Alex saw his end coming, I believe he called upon the Lord's mercy." He moves his hands to my shoulders and gazes into my eyes. "We must help your girls face their father's death, but be assured, after a decent period of time, I will come again to claim you as my bride. After his callous treatment of you, everyone here believes you have full legal right to remarry, but surely his passing also ends every remaining question in your heart."

Before I can reply, my girls burst through our door, and the younger ones drop their books in a heap. They are so full of activities at first they don't notice our sober faces. Until Marie senses something amiss. She looks from me to John so Nancy is also now aware.

I step near and put an arm around them both as John pulls Catherine to him. "Be brave, my dears. The boat that docked today so late in the season, brought news from the West Coast."

A line deepens between Marie's eyebrows. "Is there word of Father and Tom?"

John's voice gentles. "Tom is fine but your father—"

"Yes?" Marie whispers while Nancy only stares.

I hold them tighter. "Your father showed courage but met great harm."

"And Tom?" Nancy squeaks and clutches my arm while Marie sinks to the floor from my grasp before I can catch her.

"Not Tom, darlings. He is safe in Oregon. But he wrote of a disaster that struck Father and took the lives of all men with him, save one, on a northern voyage."

"All save one?" Marie clasps her hands. "When they left before the sun rose on that last morning and I couldn't say goodbye, I had a terrible feeling I might never see Father again."

"Not on this earth, darling, but God keeps the hearts of those committed to Him."

"But Tom is well?" Nancy stares like she's trying hard to picture the West Coast scene.

"Yes. He wrote this letter just received." I hold it up.

Her eyes turn to look at the packet. "What does he say?"

John reads Tom's words aloud again and afterward pulls us into his long, strong arms. "I'm so sorry, girls," he murmurs into their hair, "yet it's wonderful that Tom lives. I know nothing can ever replace your loss, but I pledge to help you, and your dear mother and Tom—if you will let me."

"Thank you, Doctor." Nancy says. "You're good to us and we love you for it."

As my girls calm, John and I exchange glances. They have lost their father, but we thank God their brother has been spared.

Brave Alexander MacKay, father of my children, already dead to me before I had this news. He carved a bold path through the wilderness and gained acclaim but is senselessly dead. Despite the heartache he caused me and our children, I hold nothing against him. No matter what he has done, no one deserves to die alone in an unknown, watery grave.

I am awestruck at how closely these events parallel my premonition dream the morning he left. And yet God eases this hard time by the deepening love radiating to each of us from Doctor John McLoughlin.

"Oregon sounds wonderful, though impossibly far," I say, holding Tom's letter again. "I'm glad my girls copied Peter's maps, so we can understand something of the mountains and rivers between us and where he is."

"I'd love to travel there myself," John says, a faraway look in his eyes. "And one day there might be opportunity—perhaps for all of us. Increasingly, the Company says the future lies westward. They foresee a strong trading center being built there."

I take a sharp breath. "Could that actually happen?"

"Based on recent events, it's quite possible. In fact, new developments have already begun, and your son is probably a part of it." He shakes his lion-like head. "We must patiently wait and see."

"Perhaps not patiently," I add.

No matter what comes of my relationship with John McLoughlin, I'm thankful to love and be loved by this man who dares to dream but also faithfully serves and manages to find contentment inside every single day.

Chapter 11

Fort William on Lake Superior,
early Spring, 1812

Six weeks after Tom's letter finds its way to me, John crosses the fort's quadrangle, a less confident smile wreathing his handsome face. As he climbs our porch and shakes snow from his fur-lined coat, I glimpse a rolled-up paper in his pocket. When he steps inside, he takes me in his arms, kisses the top of my head, and from his great height, drops to one knee.

"John, what are you doing?"

"Seeking to win you." His dear dove-gray eyes search mine. "I hope these long weeks have been enough time to consider my proposal, because my heart feels I have waited forever. I cannot endure more days without your answer. Please marry me, Marguerite."

I catch a breath.

His voice strengthens. "I will also keep reaching out to Tom to nurture him in caring friendship."

I study his strong fingers wrapped around mine. "I appreciate that. He has been through so much. I know you would be wonderful with him."

"Thank God." He lifts my hand to his lips. "I

will love your children as my own. Please become my cherished wife. From this day forward, let us forget the sorrows of the past and walk together into a joyful future joined as one."

A knife twists my heart. "Despite my deep feelings for you, my fears give me caution."

"Your fears?" He startles as if slapped. "But I feel your happiness when we are together."

"Yes, that's true, but—"

He rises and lays a gentle finger across my lips. "Before you answer, tell me your fears. With all my heart, I will always cherish you and your children as you deserve, as you have never been honored before."

"It is not you I doubt. I know you love and protect us, but I cannot let you limit your career by marrying me. I did that once. The results were terrible."

"My future? I've told you, I want none apart from you. I will be happiest with my beloved Marguerite at my side."

"John, you don't know all I've suffered from Alex. Do you understand the labels and insults Montréal policymakers give to mixed unions with Métis or Cree? They scarcely consider us human, yet that is who I am, mixed Cree and White. I won't ruin your prospects with the Company."

"Bosh. I hear their foolish comments but disregard them. Besides, any man's worth should stand in his own actions, nothing else. Please hear me. Instead of hampering my future, you make me a better man. True, I don't know all you suffered with Alex, but I am not him." He bends on one knee again. "Honor me with your agreement, Marguerite. I've asked God to help me write a *façon du nord* in my own hand that expresses all in my heart."

Another *façon du nord*? The same document that Alex used to betray me? Yet, that is common policy here. My heart is a frightened bird trying to escape my chest. My eyes can't bear the sight of another stiff paper worthless in eastern Canada. But John is so determined I almost smile. On his knees he is taller than I. His earnest face and voice assure me he means every word he speaks. Despite my love for him, I shiver.

His expression is tender. "Dear heart, talk to me."

I can't control my tears. "I've told you I cannot marry you. You need a worthy, suitable bride."

"Look at me." He cups my face in his hands. "That's impossible when I've already found her."

I cannot meet his gaze.

"Marguerite? What pains you so?"

These cabin walls fade until I see young Alex MacKay binding me to him with his *façon du nord* that proved meaningless and broke my heart. "Forgive me—Alex's contract meant nothing to him. I know you are a different man, but my heart still fears and aches."

When he strokes my cheek, I tremble. His hand stills on my face. "I am not Alex. Please, may I read loving words from my heart?" Though John seldom wears glasses, he plucks a pair from another pocket and perches them on his nose, then unfolds a piece of paper. "I begin by naming all the things I so love about you. 'You are brave and undaunted by hardship. You allow God to transform adversities into strength for you and those you love. You sing your father's songs, keeping beauty and courage alive, and I pledge to do the same.' " He gives a tender look. "I've written too many words. They alone can't express all I feel. May I rise from my knees before I grow stiff?"

His seriousness makes me laugh now. "Of course. Come sit by me." I sit and pat the place next to me on the beautiful birch bench he built for the girls and me when we moved here.

He settles with a sigh, his long legs extending far beyond mine. "Do you remember the Bible story of David before he became king? How he found his Abigail?"

"I'm not sure. I remember stories my father told. The pages of his Bible were tattered. I don't recall that one."

"I will read it to you and the girls tonight. David and Abigail's story parallels ours. She also had a first husband who didn't deserve her."

My mouth drops. “She did? Was his name Alex?”

John laughs heartily. “No, although two Alexanders are named in the Bible. Abigail’s first husband’s name was Nabal which means *Fool*.”

“You’re teasing. The Bible says that?”

“Yes, I guarantee.”

His shoulders shake, and the chiseled dimple in his chin makes me want to kiss it, but instead I narrow my eyes. “Scandalous.”

“I think a better translation for his name in their story might be *Alex*. The Bible teaches all subjects well. I follow it carefully and praise God for leading me to you. Now I’ll read more of my contract.” He unfolds the page again.

I expect to hear the standard arrangements in Indian Country, but he adds more precious words.

“To the usual agreement, I add these vows from my heart and will gladly add all other promises you desire. ‘I, John—Jean-Baptiste—McLoughlin, born in Rivière du Loup, Quebec, serving the North West Company as physician and trader, pledge to wed Marguerite Wadin MacKay, she being born in Indian Country and agreeable to our union, and vow that when it is possible, our marriage will be solemnized by a visiting clergyman or priest.’ ”

When he mentions a priest or clergyman, I gasp. No man in these parts promises divine clergy. Certainly not Alex.

John takes my hand. " 'Our signatures proclaim our marriage sacred until we enter God's eternal kingdom.' " He lowers his paper. "Is it enough, Marguerite? Will you accept my contract and pledge?"

Even now my mind wars. "John, I'm deeply touched. You hold my heart, but will you think me awful if I ask a few more days to pray and consider?"

"More still?" He groans to the depth of his being. "More days seems an eternity. I have expressed my love the best I know how. Forgive me if I fall short."

My hand rests on his arm. Through his coat sleeve, radiating warmth stirs me. "John, the problem is not you. You do not fall short. You could not. I'm sorry for my faintheartedness."

His brow furrows. "No. It is broken-heartedness that alarms you, but I understand."

I marvel that this towering, strong man, who can show temper and sternness during leadership crises is so very gentle with me.

He strokes my cheek again. "I will love you until all fear leaves and there is only joy and peace in your eyes. What do you most long for in marriage?"

I withdraw my hand from his arm, but I still feel his heat. My own responding warmth flushes my face and, though long married, I'm suddenly shy. "If God permits, I wish to birth healthy babies with a loving husband who will cherish his family. One to whom I would freely give and return all the love, passion, and respect you deserve and provide."

"You shall have that and more with great abandon." He kisses the tip of my nose.

I grasp his hand. "My helpmeet will welcome music into our home and laugh with me, sing with me, or grieve and pray through whatever stages touch our lives."

"I willingly promise. I will add dancing to your singing and declare your mourning is ended."

This wonderful, accomplished man asks what *I* desire? Seeing the earnestness in his face and hearing the love in his tone suddenly helps my heart believe that God has brought me John, this warm, loving man for lasting happiness, whether I ever feel worthy of him or not.

He sees a shift in my face, for he leaps to his feet. "Marguerite? Has something changed? Do you now believe?"

I clutch his hands and try to steady my voice. "God has dropped peace in my heart and made me sure. The flames in my heart rise to ignite with yours and burn a loving, warm fire. If you truly understand that taking a mixed-blood wife will injure your career and still want me, I accept all you've written, for you . . ."—I can barely speak—"embody every desire I dared hope for and more."

“Dearest.” He thumbs away the happy tears flooding my cheeks. There’s moisture in his eyes, as well. “Each tear is a precious pearl, for I also know something of pain. Every day I will live the truth of our love before you until your heartache is gone.” He clasps my hands between his strong ones, cradling them against his pounding chest. “Believe the beating of my heart if you ever doubt the sincerity of my words.”

His heartbeats are sure and steady. The adoring gaze in his dove-gray eyes calms me. His breath heats my face, bringing my heart to full surrender. “I believe, John.” And then his lips sweetly claim mine.

“Darling Marguerite, you possess all of me, and my heart does not lie. I will hold nothing back.”

Whatever dam locked my emotions from the time of Alex’s betrayal bursts open now. “Oh, John, I love you so.”

His kiss becomes insistent, passionate. I fling my arms around him with abandon to hold him tight. My lips pursue his, searching, finding. My hunger unleashed after so long a time is not easily satisfied. We become giddy with love, exchanging many deep, lingering kisses. “You could find a worthier woman,” I murmur, “but when you hold me like this, my fear flees.”

He again rests his finger across my lips. “Shhhh. Never speak ill of my chosen bride. You champion others, yet don't adequately regard yourself." He delivers more kisses.

Soon I can think of nothing else. I am gift-wrapped in love. "John," I finally manage, "let me breathe before I faint. When you kiss me, it arouses such longings, I may die and my girls become orphans."

"At least you would enjoy the process, and I am a doctor. I would restore you to life." His eyes gleam as he lifts my heart to heights I have not known during seventeen years of marriage to Alex. "I have medicine to revive you if you faint and will give you new lessons in love every day. And later when we can solemnize our union before clergy, we will."

Any last bit of hesitation is gone. I know of no other man in frontier Canada offering a contract including sanctioned marriage. "I gladly accept." His brow is noble above his dear mouth. I love to trace his lips with my finger. "Your words are perfect because you've poured your passion into them."

He kisses my fingertip and moves to the table. "When a man longs to express all his heart holds, it becomes easy. I also asked the Lord to help me." He sharpens his quill and signs his name at the bottom of the paper with a large flourish, then holds the quill to me.

I write my full name above his in the awkward block letters I've learned.

"I will teach you to value yourself as you deserve, starting now." He kisses me soundly again. I've been starving to death for such love and may never get enough.

After dinner the following Sunday, with the girls and me in our best outfits, Girouard witnesses and signs John's document with my name in agreement. I am now Mrs. John McLoughlin. Certainly, Alex had no desire to legitimize our contract before clergy, though occasionally one did pass through. John is wonderfully different from Alex.

Our friends congratulate me on my choice. Many tell John he has chosen well too. When Peter Arndt hears, he is ecstatic and writes, "When this trouble calms, I will host a reception there none will forget. I am happy your romance began at Sault Sainte Marie."

God has answered deeper prayers than I knew. At age thirty-seven, He has blessed me with marriage to the finest man I've known. Before, when I gazed in my mirror, I saw a work-worn woman aged by hardship. Now I see a cherished, rosy-cheeked wife delighted to tend her home, family, and gardens. When my life seemed dark beyond the dim circle of our family's fireside and threatened by circling wolves outside, the good doctor claimed me as his and also made my girls and Tom his own. He further enriched us with his son, Joseph, who fills my arms as my own child.

Joseph's eyes are blacker than John's and he is darker skinned, but he will be as tall and echoes his father's expressions. We love him.

The day I met John is the happiest in my life. People say young, long-legged Doctor McLoughlin cut distances in half taking stairs two at a time. After our marriage, he laughs more and jumps steps three at a time.

Chapter 12

Fort William on Lake Superior, Summer, 1814

As disturbing reports drift in from the outside world, at first we think we hear of small, unrelated skirmishes between distant forts, but soon realize war is building between the two biggest fur-trade companies. This contest is like two powerful brothers jousting for control in a quarrelsome family, maybe like the Bible story of Jesus's disciples arguing over who will be greatest.

News comes of attacks against our North West Company posts by Hudson's Bay Company employees to the east and south of us. Both accuse the other of over-trapping beaver and challenge land ownership with force. When Americans try to capture Sault Sainte Marie, John and others are ordered to come and relieve that fort. Yet, the next day a runner brings a different message, saying stay home and guard Fort William because greater threats are coming from Grand Portage.

We are glad for each day John remains at home. We have time to explore deeper parts of our love, and I am soon with child by this man I love so much. My daughters are happy we will welcome a child. I've said nothing to Marie that a sea captain may pursue her. That story seems untrue or delayed which brings me great relief, for I love having our family gathered together around our hearth, especially now that we are whole and happy.

"Pray for Uncle Peter's safe arrival," we cheerfully tell the girls each day, although they don't need reminding. In fact, they often remind us first. We can't wait to introduce him to Joseph, who Peter has not seen, and to our soon-coming babe. We are thankful John managed to bring Joseph here after a quick trip to Rainy River. This cheerful, lively toddler does antics for the girls who compete to spoil him. We write Peter funny stories about Joseph and assure Peter that when he arrives, he will also fit perfectly into the hearts of all here.

"No need to worry about him," John assures us. "Peter is wise and his fort is built so solidly even termites have a hard time burrowing through. The Americans would have to tunnel underneath or build another Trojan Horse to get inside." John tells us the story of the Trojan Horse which makes us hoot. "Besides, Peter should be here soon to receive all the love we've stored up for him and to badger me to hold our baby on his knee as soon as it's born."

"And he'll enjoy Joseph." I tousle the boy's dark locks. "I'll cook Peter's favorite dishes and spoil him like he always did us."

“Maybe he’ll come today,” my Catherine says. “I miss him this much.” She spreads her arms wide.

Time flies by, and soon my doctor husband delivers the infant son he places in my arms. Our boy is well-formed and strong, having his father’s dimpled chin and thatch of hair a bit lighter than Joseph’s. We name him David for John’s younger brother. He resembles Joseph but is uniquely himself.

Our baby becomes the other young prince in our home. My nearly-grown girls are delighted with him. We didn’t know our log walls could expand to hold such joy. I care for our family and do daily tasks with a singing heart. The crowning touch will be Peter joining us. We make his room cheery with colorful quilts and bright pillows the girls and I stitch. John builds a comfortable padded chair, and I braid a warm wool rug for the floor.

Ten days after David’s birth, a man who escaped from Sault Sainte Marie reaches us with terrible news. On July 14, 1814, Americans over-powered Peter’s fort by first setting surrounding houses and sheds ablaze. Peter and his men formed a bucket brigade and drenched stockade walls to keep them from igniting, but an attacker sneaked in and torched a barn full of livestock. Faithful Jules saw him. The man reports that Jules bellowed like a bull and laid his nose along his musket barrel to line up his shot. An American sniper saw Jules and shot first. Jules died.

"If Jules hadn't yelled," the messenger said, "he might have gotten his man. When Peter saw Jules drop, he grabbed his same hot musket and fired through a slot in the fort wall, but that lucky sniper saw sunlight flash from the iron barrel and fired the shot that struck and killed Peter."

I collapse into a chair. My girls chorus my shocked thought. "Uncle Peter? Dead?"

"Yes." The exhausted man nodded wearily. "I'm so sorry."

"Impossible!" John smacks a fist hard into his open hand. "He was to arrive here any day. Many of his packed belongings came on this week's boat. Workers just carried them to us."

Indeed, two men had delivered an assortment of boxes. At the top of the first carton we found gifts chosen and labeled for each of us, including for Joseph and our newest baby. We drown in fresh tears, which makes Joseph and our baby howl until John consoles us all.

"You knew him longest and best," John says, encircling me in a sweet embrace, "but in my heart Peter was a father to me too. It is unthinkable he will not walk through our door."

Late that night, in our bed and cradling David in my arms, I tell my husband, "So many fine men are senselessly cut down. First my father. And your father dying young. And now Peter, who was ready to join us in retirement after his long years of faithful service."

"Alex cut down too," John adds quietly as he chucks our cooing infant under his chin.

"I do not forget. He is part of our children's lives, but you have more than replaced him in mine."

"Thank God, for you are my life's treasure." John entwines his fingers around mine and our hands mesh. "We have Peter's letters sharing his joy in coming to keep his memory green."

"Missing him is our greatest loss," I say. "Thank God for our good year at Sault Sainte Marie."

"Yes, where God let me find you," John adds, his dove-gray eyes warming mine as he tucks baby David into his cradle.

We stand, hands joined, and pray blessings over our son.

"I'm glad we named our baby for my brother," John says, "though I'd thought of adding Peter as a second name to surprise him when he came."

"I would love that." My heart catches. "David Peter, it is. We will tell our sons about your brother and Peter so they absorb both men's good qualities."

The next morning, Marie presents a charcoal likeness she has drawn of Peter that looks so real, I expect him to take his pipe from his mouth and tell a droll story after puffing smoke wreaths above his head. I place Peter's portrait on our mantel to stand in honor from that day forward. Messengers coming later from the burned fort tell us that friends laid him to rest near his wife and child. Jules and others lie in a revered place nearby.

"Where will this pointless war lead?" I ask John that evening when our house is quiet and we drink a last cup of tea together. "So many feel despair. When will this craziness end?"

"Only God knows," he says. "Wilderness wars start in the board rooms of financiers and government men in London, Montréal, and Washington. To regain peace, leaders must abandon profit motives and seek more of God's care for the people they lead." He gazes across the room, seeing what, I do not know. "If not, senseless slaughter like Sault Sainte Marie will be repeated across this land but accomplish nothing."

I tremble and grip his arm. "How long will they let you stay here without ordering you into harm's way? After all, you are one of our main leaders. I cannot bear to lose you too."

"For now, I'm assigned here, though there is no guarantee for the future. The next dispatch from Montréal should explain more, but you will not lose me, my love. If I am ever taken before you this side of heaven, our Lord will care for you and our family." He opens his Bible and reads a verse my father especially loved. " 'I will never leave thee, nor forsake thee . . .' There may be times we will be apart—"

"By God's grace, may they be few." I hear alarm rise in my voice.

He places his hand over mine. "Marguerite, we are joined in an unbreakable bond that holds us securely together."

"I believe that, John. Yet having found happiness, I sometimes fear it may be ripped away."

He opens his arms and draws me into his embrace. "Not even the fiercest storm can destroy a home built on God's rock like ours is."

"Still, I would not enjoy that test." I sigh and rest against him. "I will try to trust, but it is hard." We move to our bedroom and I stand on tiptoe to kiss this fine husband the Lord has given. "I thank God for you, John. Even for poor Gaston chopping himself with his axe so you needed help stitching him up."

"Yes. He was our Cupid," my sweet husband says. "I owe the man. But I need your love as fiercely as you do mine." He pulls me close, tucking me into my special place under his chin and kissing the top of my head before claiming my lips in a kiss that sends lightning to the core of my being. After two years of marriage, his love still has even greater power over me than before.

"You own me forever, as each day will prove," I say as I surrender to him kissing me again.

After more long embraces and finding comfort in each other, sleep won't come for me. Eyes open, I lie thinking of families with no husband or father to lead them.

Lord, I'm selfish, but in these tense days of conflict and wars, please safeguard precious John and our family.

I pray for Tom too. I gaze into darkness, safe and content, wondering when the next Company dispatch from Montréal will arrive and what its words from faraway places will mean for our lives.

Chapter 13

Fort William on Lake Superior, late Winter, 1814

Every day I thank God for the man to whom I pledged the remainder of my life. I love the united team God has made us. We see most patients in the dispensary but treat occasional emergencies in our home. We're in tune with each other. I easily know what equipment John needs before he asks. As Company pressures grow, I support him in every way I know how with all the strength and love I can muster.

Unlike Alex, because John is a compassionate doctor as well as a shrewd trading manager, he tries to leave stress behind when he comes home to our family each night. We race to meet him at the door with hugs and slippers, for he is our tall, strong, sheltering tree. Joseph is a strong four-year-old who tackles his daddy's knees. Chortling, David toddles close behind.

"How are Daddy's boys?" John booms. He shrugs out of his great coat and hangs it on a peg by our door, then swings Joseph high before also lifting David to the ceiling. Both boys squeal with delight.

After surviving Joseph's and David's onslaughts, he gives me a sweet kiss. "How's my bride?"

“Fine, now that my groom is here.” I relax in his arms and he kisses me as if we are the only two people in this world. I feel young and swept off my feet again by this handsome man who lavishes more tender love on me in our first few years of marriage than I ever knew with Alex. We release each other to give attention to our family.

“I cooked dinner,” Nancy boasts, crowding close for his praise.

“Catherine made her first dried apple pie for dessert,” I say.

He rewards Catherine with his biggest smile as he carries her pie to the table and pops a buttery crumb of crust in his mouth. “God bless you, girls. No man anywhere has a finer family.” He takes his place at the head of our table and stretches his long legs. After praying and filling our plates, he listens to our reports of the day but finally says, “We received a new Company dispatch today.”

My heart tightens. Something in his tone warns me. I gaze at him through rising tendrils of steam from our serving bowls.

“With what news?” I ask, wishing the outside world would not invade our home.

“Forgive me.” He sighs and lowers his fork. “I should wait until we’ve finished eating, yet I’m burdened. Our continent is a powder keg that may explode with a single match. The trouble is many hands hold matches these days.”

"Did the dispatch give you future instructions?" I hope he will say that everything will calm soon and return to the way it was.

Instead he says, "We're told as tensions rise to consider all Company actions very wisely to weigh repercussions. War could easily break out at several points."

"Oh." I rise to bring tea to the table. Faintness swirls around me and I quickly sit again. Our world has instantly become a more sinister place.

John stares into space, his hands idle.

I touch his arm. "Is there more you can tell us? I also hope you'll finish your meal if you can."

"Thank you, sweet." Yet after his next bite, he pauses again. "Forgive me for bringing trouble home. You've made wonderful food, but I can't do it justice now." He wipes his mouth and lays down his napkin. "Besides strong conflict between the two strong fur-trading companies, the tensions between my two roles as fort manager and doctor divide my heart. In truth, providing healing to my fellowman lies closest to my heart."

"I know, John. That's how I think of you most."

He pushes his straight-backed wooden chair from our table and jostles David on his knee. David rides his daddy's galloping foot and leg. He speaks over our son's giggles. "Divided loyalties between being a good medical man and a wise trading merchant puts me in conflict. It's hard to do one well without neglecting the other, yet I must accomplish both."

"Your trading profits are good, and the Company praises your business sense. You have saved the lives of so many people near here that many mothers name their babies after you." My eyebrows rise. "There are quite a few young Johns in diapers near Fort William these days."

"Johannas too. It's a fine compliment. Perhaps we should add our own John Jr. or Johanna to the group." He catches my eye. "However, it is our children's mother who most captures my heart." He leans past David and gives a tender kiss, unconcerned by the hubbub of our children around us.

Although he is nine years younger than I, the stresses of leadership and daily hardships are aging him. Worry lines intersect the pleasant crinkle lines around his eyes. Before we met, he had completed his first apprenticeship at Rainy Lake west of Fort William. Next, he built and established the post at Sturgeon Lake and wintered in Nipigon, Lake Superior's northernmost, least desirable location. He won the hearts of people everywhere for his medical care while his trading skills boosted profits. My pride in his accomplishments warms me. How is that I deserve such a man as my husband?

He lifts David to the floor, then leans forward and rests his elbows on the table. "This dispatch says little, but it warns us to wait and be prepared. I'd rather have clear declarations of war or peace than to live in prolonged tension between the two."

Even our little boys are quiet when we bow our heads and take more time than usual at family prayers that night.

A week later, another schooner arrives. News often accompanies the vessels, and I am eager to hear any updates from John when he comes home. From the window, I see his approach, and the sight of his stooped shoulders raises my alarm. Yet, he greets us with cheer and carries on cheerful conversation at our dinner table.

When we have finished and enjoyed the fresh shortbread Catherine has mastered, I push my plate away. "Share today's news, John, for you are clearly burdened."

"Thank you." His face is haggard as he lowers his fork. "I'm sorry, love. Yes, the conflict and dangers grow. I did not think things could be worse than the attack on Sault Sainte Marie causing Peter's death and more, but I was wrong. New problems arise on every side. My divided Company roles increasingly contradict each other." He sighs. "And I am only one man."

Marie asks, "Don't they understand that you're meant to save people?"

"Not always." He folds his napkin. "Let me

explain. When Cabot reached Canada by ship from France two centuries ago, he and his men only cared about what they could carry back across the ocean. They took timber, fish, and furs, mostly beaver pelts that sparked a fashion craze that actually hurts more than helps native trappers."

"A fashion craze hurts," young Joseph echoes. He pounds his fist on the table, but a smile softens his angry gesture. His features resemble John but with browner skin. Despite sweet dimples and a winning smile, he is sometimes scorned by whites, who I find best prefer people who are most like themselves.

John kisses Joseph's chubby cheek. "Greed makes men venture farther to trap more pelts for rifles, axes, knives and blankets, mirrors, and trinkets for their ladies."

"We like those," Catherine says.

Sorrow clouds John's face. "Those items are not the issue, but most traders also trade alcohol, and that is a problem. Firewater inflames natives' minds until many lose reason. They fight and kill each other, even members of their own families. Drunkenness is behind too many of the injuries I treat."

"What's the answer?" Marie asks.

"No easy one." The furrows in John's forehead deepen. "The Company desires to prosper, but I believe it also has moral responsibility."

"I'm sorry, John." I rest a hand on his arm.

Nancy taps her chin, thoughtful. "In school they taught about the Jesuits and traders coming to Canada with conflicting goals. The Jesuits named this land the New World. They hoped to create the Bible's new heaven and earth here."

"My mother said early priests treated her people kindly," I say, "but many of the trappers cheated her people."

"I'm afraid that's often true," John says. "Opposing goals often spark war."

I shudder as Joseph chops our table in front of him as if his hand holds an axe. "War," he repeats and frowns.

John wraps Joseph's small hand in his. "War will never be your calling, son. I will train you well, perhaps teach you medicine. The tensions grow worse daily. I fear where they lead."

His words make me tremble. I smooth the locks of his leonine hair before using both hands to knead the knots from his shoulders. "But your life points men in the right direction."

"I hope so. My trading role needs to support our family, plus what I can of brother David's medical school costs. Our family was so broken after Father's death, I still want to help them. I will never let ours endure such hardships."

He swallows hard. "I saw Mother and my brother and sisters suffer terribly. I still wish to assist them while providing the care you and our children deserve. I hope you understand."

"I do." He looks so miserable, my heart aches. "John, look around you. We have plenty of everything. We lack nothing. Besides, I know how to stretch funds or find food almost anywhere if needed."

"I know. You've proven that often, but I don't want you to have to. The Company considers profit king, but I can't live that way. They leave it to our conscience whether we sell liquor or not, but point out how much it increases profits."

"I remember." I swallow hard. "Mother said Father's conflict with Pond was partly based on how they treated native people. Father wanted their good, partly because of Mother's and my heritage. He didn't allow liquor in our fort."

"That's good. I agree." John shakes his head. "We're to be stewards of the people we encounter. Native people must not be taken advantage of."

I take his dear hand. "I love you even more for putting my people's welfare first."

"More?" His eyes light. "How can that be when you already said you love me with all your heart and could not love me more?" He rises from our table and leans against our fireplace.

I follow him. "Because my heart grows bigger and fuller in our happy marriage. It expands so much, my feet float from the ground like this." I lift my hands as if I'm rising.

"Ha-ha. I want to see that. Show me."

I leap up into his arms, which makes our children laugh.

He sets my feet on the floor but keeps his arms looped around me. "The Bible is right when it says he who finds a wife finds a good thing."

He tousles David's hair and thanks our daughters for dinner. The girls clear the table and wash our dishes while the boys plays with sticks and blocks of wood, building a fort. John and I sit near our fire and watch the burning pine logs pop and snap as they settle.

"I'm sorry," he says. "My convictions burden you, but I sense hard times coming—like knowing in late summer it's time to store up for a harsh winter. Warring factions increase. I dread where they'll take us." John draws a weary hand through his thick hair. "I doubt I can be both a good trader and doctor much longer. When I meet my Savior I want him to say, 'Well done, thou good and faithful servant.' Nothing else matters."

"You will, Father," Marie calls from putting plates on the shelf, her solemn expression matching his. I marvel at how she absorbs and reflects his own heart when he is not her natural father. Yet as time passes, the girls all call him Father, which he loves.

"I pray you're right," he answers. "I thank God for each of you." He looks around the room then directly at me. "Especially you, wife of my heart.

You strengthen my life and inspire my every thought." His eyes bathe me in love.

After bedtime prayers, we tuck our youngest ones under warm covers. Once we retire, I hold John close, praying peace over him, until at last he sleeps. But I cannot. I, too, sense a growing storm. My mother's heart wishes to hold every family member close and safe, yet few wives and mothers throughout history have ever had that privilege.

God, give us Your wisdom and mercy for the days ahead. I pray that prayer often.

Chapter 14

Fort William on Lake Superior,
early Autumn, 1815

Beautiful morning sun burning through dark clouds steals my breath. Golden light edges the black with glowing bands of salmon and rose as the colors flash across the horizon. Nature's beauty teaches me that life's storms only last as long as God allows. The Lord limits harm and shelters us. He also blesses John and me with the arrival of another son. We name him after his father, and I pray this fine young one grows to be as wise and compassionate as his namesake. For now, we're to stay at Fort William, but John is told to be ready to move elsewhere at a moment's notice.

The tensions between the warring fur-trade companies shift back and forth like the seesaw John made by balancing a plank across a log for Joseph and David. They love their game and play it every day, taking turns trying to bump one another off of the board. It takes skill to keep it balanced enough to stay on the plank but no skill at all to fall off and suffer bumps and scrapes.

John observes the pair. "My ability to manage medicine and company trade is like that too.

I stand an equal chance of getting bumped and scraped." He laughs while his eyes remain serious.

I am glad he's taken a break from his fort office and the dispensary. He needs time with the ones who love him to ease his worries, and I selfishly revel in my time with him. But that afternoon, when all three boys are sleeping, there is an urgent knock on our door. A man slipped while using a skinning knife and cut his arm badly. Without hesitation, John rolls up his sleeves and washes while I disinfect our table. My skilled husband stitches the man's slashed arm as beautifully as I sew colored beads onto moose hide moccasins.

After the grateful man leaves our home and we're cleaning up the bloody mess, I say, "It takes a special man to fill your shoes. In these tense days, I wonder where your unswerving commitments may take you."

"So do I."

Curiosity seizes me. "When did you first know you wanted to be a doctor?"

"Early," he says, taking the soiled cloth from my hand and wringing it in a basin. "I always hated seeing people maimed or dead when minimal care could save them. I wanted to learn what I could, even if I never made it to medical school."

"But you did."

"Yes. I worked hard, and the Lord graciously opened the door."

"Do you think our sons will follow your footsteps?"

He smiles. "Or our daughters? Perhaps. I wouldn't mind but won't force them. I hope they at least learn enough basics to help during emergencies, so no matter where they are or what they do, they save lives. But I'll also insist they learn your wilderness skills."

"Our daughters already do. Joseph is almost old enough to take along, too, but I keep telling you they are simple woodland remedies."

"Simple, perhaps, but available nearly everywhere if one learns and looks. They are essential for people to know and very effective." He takes a clean cloth and gives the table a final swipe before returning the unused rolled bandages to their shelf. He embraces me. "Thanks for helping. Since the girls aren't home from school yet, I'll set the table for supper. Doctoring whets my appetite for your moose roast and gravy."

"And oven-roasted potatoes?" I tilt my head and see his eyes twinkle. "I can't decide if doctoring makes you hungry or your tall frame needs constant filling."

"Both." His laughter explodes as he gives our table a final rinse with disinfectant and covers it with a cloth. "Mother gave up trying to fill two constantly hungry sons. When we were still young, David and I spent time with Uncle Simon and his fur-trader friends. Hearing their adventures made us want to explore. We soon understood that the lack of medical knowledge had cost lives." His eyes hold mine. "I've wondered if your father might have survived with better care, even if his leg had to be amputated."

His words jar me. "I've thought the same. He would have hated being an invalid, but I think could have managed well and cheerfully with a wooden leg."

John nodded. "Many people do. The way you describe him makes him sound unstoppable—like his daughter."

I drink in the admiration in his eyes. "Thank you, John. You describe him well. In the days he lingered, Mother used every remedy, but nothing could repair the shattered bone or massive blood loss." I shut my eyes. "It hurts to remember."

"I'm sure. I've just heard of a technique for transfusing blood from healthy persons to ill ones. If it works, it is miraculous."

I give a sharp intake of breath. "Can that be true?"

"I'm not sure. It sounds impossible in wilderness conditions, but I'll research the procedure and learn if it can work here or not."

"At least Mother and I shared our love with Father in the three days before he died."

"Not everyone gets that opportunity."

He presses a kiss to my forehead. “When I turned fourteen, Mother sent me to Quebec City to apprentice with Doctor Fisher. He trained me so well, I was accepted to medical school and gained my license within four years. That’s when the Company hired me as a surgeon-physician and trading clerk at low pay but with a promised raise in ten years. Thankfully, that time comes soon.”

“People’s appreciation of your care will guarantee that increase.”

He nods. “Unless I’m penalized for not maximizing Company profits.”

“Surely they respect you as a man of conscience. I’m sure your good reports far outweigh any bad. If Company leaders came here to spend time, they would see the great demands on you.”

“None are likely to do that. It’s too rustic and time-consuming to get here.”

“How soon will you know about the promotion?”

“My tenth work anniversary is in two months. Our income will nearly double once I’m a full partner.”

I kiss his cheek. “Don’t worry, John. We are well and happy. The love you lavish on us is worth more than money. Besides, in our marriage contract, I agreed to cherish you for richer or poorer, in sickness or health. I am happy and intend to keep my word.”

"God bless you, Sweetheart." His eyes still seem to show some anguish, but he looks like a bit of the burden has lifted. "My mother suffered such lack, I vowed my family would never experience those circumstances."

"John, I'm happier than I dreamed possible. We have much more than money. With your father dying young, of course you want to support your family. I love and respect you for it and would have you no different. I would want to do the same for my mother if she lived. We are rich in things that matter most. I desire nothing more."

I smell my biscuits burning and dash to the oven just as I hear John Jr.'s wake-up cries and our girls' feet on the porch. "Goodness. Everything happens at once. But let me serve this meal before our food is ruined and the king of my heart and his children faint from hunger."

"Yes, please." He breathes into my hair. "I pity those on kings' thrones who don't have love, for then they rule in title only."

After we greet the girls and rouse our little boys up from naps, John sits in his chair and spreads a napkin across his knees. No one complains as I bring slightly scorched biscuits to the table. My husband grabs my free hand and kisses it before stealing a biscuit crumb and popping it into his mouth. "Delicious. Is there jam for this heavenly bread?"

"Yes, the children found a late raspberry patch yesterday."

"No bears wrestled them for the fruit?"

I give him my best smile. "I wish one had. Then I might serve fresh bear meat as well. I kept my musket close while I did laundry, but no bear came."

He chuckles. "Pity. But one may have the misfortune to do that another day. You are exceptional, my love. Right now I'd rather hold you than eat." He nuzzles my neck, reaching to loosen the hairpins fastening my hair.

My cheeks burn, and I wave him away with floury hands. I do not wear my hair in long braids like most native women, but in the style Father said his mother in Switzerland wore hers, in a piled crown. John loves to release my hair and run his hands through its length. "Not now. I must feed our family."

"Never mind," he says with a teasing smile. "I'll free your hair later." He sings as my father once did,

"*Marguerite, gentille Marguerite,*
Marguerite, je te plumerai,
Je te plumerai la tête, Je te plumerai la tête, Et la tête, Et la tête,
Marguerite, Marguerite, O-o-o-o."

I dish up roasted potatoes and steaming roast moose and we eat with relish until the food is gone.

Later, in the privacy of our room, John removes the pins in my hair, letting it fall around our faces in a curtain as we hold each other close and are one.

We hear snatches of events in the outside world but nothing sure until young Donald Mackenzie finds us at Lac La Pluie where John tries to block Hudson's Bay men from moving west. Donald does wish to marry Marie. They're little acquainted, but as they visit together, he captures her interest. Once she says yes, she and her sisters giggle like children.

When John and I approve, Donald tells us that Scottish captain, Robert McCargo, who sails a Company schooner on Lake Superior, will soon come seeking Nancy's hand. "In fact," Donald says, "he talks of naming a Company ship for her."

"A ship?" I lift an eyebrow. "For our girl? Can he do that?"

"I believe so." Donald leans back, contented, and spreads his hands across his chest. "Robert is a man of his word, as you will find once you know him."

John's eyes dance. "Such promises are the ways of men in love. I would have named North America for you, Marguerite, if that Italian mapmaker hadn't scrawled his name across it first."

We all laugh, and John lifts and whirls me around. Then little David raises his arms to be picked up and twirled. Mackenzie looks as if he longs to do the same with Marie but watches hungrily without taking such liberty.

How has time flown so fast that our girls approach marriageable age? What Mother told me long ago is true—nothing stays the same for long. Busy building trading in this wilderness where our forests, lakes, and rivers reach American prairies to the south and west, I suddenly notice my girls have matured. As they consider leaving our home to start their own, outside forces stretch our world to the breaking point.

The nation to our south flexes its muscles and makes us wonder where and when the next invasion will occur—for it is inevitable. John and I treat local sicknesses to keep them from becoming epidemics and study nature's signs to learn if the coming months will be mild or fierce. Will next year's furs be luxurious and valuable? Or of poor quality and little value? John constantly studies London prices for ermine, mink, lynx, wolverine, marten, and muskrat skins and advises trappers to trap accordingly. Beaver remains king. Good pelts reaching London earn top price, and John improves ways to ship them.

My father taught me the preferred trade

goods natives desire—blankets, buttons, mirrors, ribbons, gunpowder, knives, flour, bacon, and other foodstuffs. Company policy lets each trader decide his own alcohol policy, but John still won't supply it, despite its high profit margin because so many natives who taste it become enslaved and harm others or are injured themselves.

John is called away for another meeting at Fort William. He is gone nearly a week, and when he returns, we welcome him with hugs and cheer. He pulls off his boots, then slips on the moose hide slippers I've stitched and lovingly beaded for him. While the girls work together to put dinner on the table, John sits next to me beside the fire and cradles John Jr. in his arms. I treasure these tender moments. John refuses to relinquish the baby while we eat. Good food warms us, but we mostly bask in the joy of being together again. When the meal ends, John places John Jr. in his cradle. The girls clear the table, and my husband draws me aside.

"Marguerite, there is news of unbelievably high fur prices in Europe, and of imminent wars as alliances change between nations. The talk of merger between our competing fur-trading companies seems more serious than before, but I don't know when it may reach us."

I rest my head on his shoulder, so happy to have him home again. "I often hope we're so far from the world capitals where those things happen that they can never affect us here."

He kisses my brow. "Oh, my sweet, if only that were true. There is also word from the West Coast, and it is not good. More reports of John Jacob Astor's doings—startling events from that side of the continent. Despite losing the *Tonquin* with all on board except one, he didn't abandon his scheme for a Pacific Coast empire. He's from Germany, neighbor to your father's country. I don't think I've heard of a man more driven."

I purse my lips. "Are most Germans so aggressive and bold? Or is he an exception? Are Swiss people different? Father worked hard but was not unreasonably ambitious."

"Astor wanted great opportunities. After doing business several years in England, he learned of rich fur-trade profits in America so crossed the ocean and began merchandising vigorously." John taps his forehead. "The man does everything vigorously."

I fist my hands. "Yet doesn't take risks himself—only sends others, even boys, to build his kingdom for him."

"That is true."

I bristle. "I don't wish to meet him."

He suppresses a laugh. "He should fear meeting you! Unfortunately, he controls your son's future."

I stiffen. "I don't like him controlling Tom. I pray that can change."

"There are some developments in the works that could alter things. Astor had approval from President Jefferson to build his fort there at the mouth of the Columbia where Lewis and Clark wintered. He boasted he would build a world-famous empire stretching from the Great Lakes to the Pacific and from Canada's border to Mexico with endless resources." He grimaces. "He may yet succeed."

"But he's no king or emperor." I snort.

The girls have finished washing the dishes and put the extra food back in our larder. Joseph has carried in more logs for the fire. The children gather around us. I understand their desire to soak up more good family time with John being home.

"What of Tom's future?" Marie asks. "Is he safe? I heard something about that fort changing hands due to the present conflict between the United States and England."

John's eyebrows lift. "You are a wise young woman. Few stay abreast of such things."

"It affects our brother."

He nods. "Yes. And us and, truthfully, everyone in our North West Company, as well. I promise I'm watching world events and keeping my ears open. Astor has a good business head and avoids most risks. Even when he sent Alex's group to Oregon by ship, he made sure he would succeed by one means or the other so sent out another team overland to see which could arrive first. Both left New York that September." His eyes dance. "Do you know who reached the Columbia first seven months later?"

He enjoys quizzing our girls. The older two lean forward, liking his challenge. Now that his promotion will soon be secure, he offers them education back east if they wish to train as teachers instead of immediately marrying young. I was Marie's age when I married Alex.

"By ship," Marie answers. "It is slow but dependable."

"But bad if you become seasick," John teases. "In most seasons, wild storms batter South America's tip, with many vessels lost."

"By land, then," Nancy says, "though I prefer ships myself." Is she thinking of her smitten captain, McCargo, who is captivated by her pretty face and lively words despite seldom seeing her?

"On land they might encounter Indians," John says, "though there are fewer attacks recently. It's hard to imagine, but another hazard by sea is winds failing and sailing vessels being trapped in doldrums, going nowhere and the crew running out of food and water."

"How hideous. I hate the idea of sitting unmoving on listless seas," Nancy says, "unless you share the time with someone you enjoy." Her eyes become so dreamy, we laugh.

Today John's eyes look bluer than gray. "You both answer well. Astor's overland team reached Oregon two weeks before the others. They began building immediately, and when the others came, they finished the outer structure together and began fur trading. Guess what they named the fort?"

Marie cups her chin. "Pacifica?"

"Columbia," Nancy says, "for the river."

"Good choices, but it's named Fort Astoria to establish Astor's name there."

Nancy frowns. "That's pompous!"

"I think his actions speak for themselves," John says. "As soon as the fort could function, he sent the *Tonquin* north to buy otter and sable. You know the rest."

Marie drops the knitting she's been working on. Her ball of wool rolls across the floor as tears flood her eyes. Without a word, Joseph retrieves it for her. She gives him a tender look and a quick hug around his thin shoulders. She says tartly, "Astor should have gone himself and be punished for making others take risks he won't take. I hope Tom is not impressed."

"He might have been at first since Astor is his powerful employer, but he's probably less enchanted now." John adds another log to our fire. "Many men face hazards for fame and fortune they wouldn't take otherwise. Ambition lures many souls to danger and death."

“But it should be at their own risk.” Marie’s voice is stern.

“We’ll pray Tom realizes that earthly wealth melts this fast”—I snap my fingers—“without guaranteeing happiness. Surely, your father’s death is a lesson he won’t forget.”

My daughters have lost their father, but their brother lives. I’ve lost the husband who fathered our children and then left us behind for broader horizons. Now his abandonment doesn’t seem important. God has brought me to such a better place.

John pulls a paper from his inside vest pocket. “After all this talk, I can’t believe I forgot to tell you. At Fort William, I finally received this written notice that I’m officially Tom’s stepfather. Now I can help direct his future and supply needs beyond his earnings. I am as responsible for him as if he were my own, like each of you.” He looks tenderly around the room.

Tears stream my cheeks as I grasp his hand. “John, each time I think I cannot love you more, you give me greater cause.” I rest my cheek against his. “Thank you with all my heart.”

He pulls me close. “How can I do less? He’s part of you and the girls and our little ones. You’re all forever joined to me and now our larger family. I am thankful to be home!”

My daughters show their love by refilling his tea cup when he’s barely taken a sip.

"You spoil me." He beams. "How I thank God for this family."

"We do more for you," Marie declares, and Nancy and Catherine nod. My girls' eyes brim with moisture.

"Before long it will be Christmas and then the New Year," I say. "I wonder what changes and surprises next year will bring."

"Only good ones," Marie says confidently, her face shining. Whether she thinks of education or marriage, I cannot guess but wish I knew. "How I'd love Tom to be home with us by summer," she says.

"That's unlikely. He'd have to leave now to manage it, and winter is a bad time to travel." I rise and give her a hug. Our fire has died down but our yawns tell us it's almost time to go to bed. I pat Marie's hand. "Tom has signed a work contract, but we'll write another family letter to give him our news."

"A long one," she says.

"I do hope someday we can go to him," John says with a distant look in his eye.

I study his face. "Do you think such a thing is possible?"

"These are changing times. Anything is possible if God makes it happen."

Like a singing bird in springtime, hope builds its nest in my heart.

Later, as my dear husband tucks David and

John Jr. into their beds and our main room empties, Marie puts her hand on my arm, "When I think of marriage, I want someone like John who combines gentleness with strength. I like and respect Donald—what I know of him. But we've had little actual time together. I'm not sure we've built enough love to last a lifetime, and hard times require that. How can I be sure he's the right husband for me?"

I sigh to my toes. "Dear daughter, that's the question every young woman wishes to know. I'm no expert, and young men in love are very persuasive." My thoughts fly from Alex MacKay's urgency to John's gentle patient persistence. Between them is all the difference in the world. I sit again and pull my eldest daughter's head onto my shoulder, running my fingers through her soft brown hair. I am amazed at how quickly she's matured from being my eager child helper to this lovely young woman ready to embark on life.

"It's hard to know, but you and I have prayed much. So has John. I'm fairly sure Donald is praying too. We will trust God to guide the stirrings in both your hearts."

"Thank you. I love you, Mama." She kisses my cheek and blows out the candle on the mantel.

"And I you, dear girl," I whisper after her, "forever and always." I sweep a few escaped embers back into the main fireplace and turn to our bedroom. John now stands in our doorway with his arms open to me. I go eagerly.

He and I pray even more for Donald Mackenzie and Marie in the days following. Despite our prayers, Marie's uncertainty remains. In fact, she seems less sure of their match—or its timing—rather than more. I try to understand. Does she think of going east to gain more education first? Or simply not feel ready to leave home?"

"In such uncertain times," she says one day, "it's important to be exactly where we're meant to be in case calamity comes. I would not want to be away where I could not return quickly to our family. My heart aches for Tom. It must be awful for him to be there alone without family."

"I think it helps that he's a boy," I say. "You know him, always full of pranks and adventures. He's at least seeing amazing new parts of the world."

"Yes, that part's wonderful. Still, it would be less enjoyable without my family around to enjoy it with me."

I don't tell her so, but that's exactly how I feel. I pray for each of my children daily, usually without asking the older ones too many questions. I'm thankful for each added day we enjoy them home with us, for I had left my mother's side years earlier.

Chapter 15

Indian Country, Central Canada,
late Autumn, 1815

The fur-trade wars are fierce reality. We no sooner celebrate John's promotion to full partner than they assign him to a fort far west in charge of Athabasca, where my father was slain. They say John must guard this crucial western outpost from encroachers and competing fur-trade activity. We respectfully decline the post, believing it is not good for our family. Company officials then offer us the most northern and remote Nipigon area. John has served there before and knows its bleak surroundings. Forced to choose one of the two, we finally accept Athabasca, despite my nightmare memories.

The house I shared with Father and Mother still stands but is smaller than I remembered—a doll house partly caved in. I place my hands on my hips and frown. "It's not that bad for all the years that have passed. A few replaced logs will make it usable again."

"Yes, for as long as we'll need it," John admits. "Still, I'm grateful it's this solid."

Although this is the place where Father was shot, the overpowering evil is less than I expected. I think Father's prayers have left a blessing. Even the adjoining trading post has survived fairly well and has sometimes been in use. In fact, entering it again, Nancy finds my initials carved in a log wall with dates marking my growth. She points. "Look, Mama, I'm taller than you were then."

But the shady spot shrouded in trees behind Father's post does hold great darkness. There Pond and his man camped and plotted before entering our home and firing the fatal shot.

"*Majimanidoo*," I whisper. "That sinister thing with no soul that kills and eats but is never full." I clutch my husband's arm.

"I have known it in northern places," he says, "but it also lives and festers here." He kicks a rotted stump, and the crumbling earth reveals fingers of mold that release a gagging stench. We tread it down. He scans the thick stand of trees surrounding us. "Besides priestly exorcism, the best cure will be cutting down those massive giants and let in healing sunlight."

In the two months left before winter sets in, instead of having employees help cut those trees to open the area, he has our family work together. We fell the trees, then chop and split the log pieces to burn in our own fireplace. We uproot nettles, thistles, and wild vines that have flourished and create a sunny, safe, open place for our children to play.

"We build muscles," he says, "plus it warms us during the cutting and chopping. The wood will warm us yet again as it gives heat and light in our home. Besides, there's something healing about cutting and burning things from dark places that weakens their hurtful memories and ability to harm us forever."

I had never thought of it that way, but his words bring peace. Soon, winter snows dress our landscape in virgin white. When the sun shines, this world becomes sparkling diamonds despite the horrors that have happened here. I'm thankful many people come for trade and medical help. Busyness makes time go faster. Once spring comes, we'll only have four or five months left to fulfill our contract.

Despite my best efforts, I'm vulnerable to fears and depression here at times. I fight dark or unreasonable thoughts that try to shroud and suffocate me. I tell myself that I can surely survive a year. When the attacks come, I make strong efforts and pray but feel most safe and whole when John holds me and prays over me.

This is why John looks troubled when he is ordered to go to Fort William for an end-of-year meeting. "I'm sorry, sweet. I was hoping my presence would not be necessary, but they insist."

"I know that's a compliment. I'm glad they value what you contribute to the Company."

He pulls me into a hug. "I'll go and return as

fast as I can. Our Lord and my prayers will cover you."

"I know dearest. I'll be all right." I sag against him, my hands resting on his strong shoulders. "But promise you'll only be gone as short a while as possible."

"I do. See this?" He sticks out one of his long legs. "I'll go and be back again as fast as these long legs can carry me." He looks out the window. "My bones tell me another cold front is coming. Joseph and I have stacked firewood high outside, and you have enough food. But I'm asking you and the children to stay inside while I'm gone, so I won't worry."

My hands fly to my hips. "John, I am capable inside or outside of this home. You shouldn't worry."

"I know, dear. And courageous. But humor me. You find this place where you lost your father unpleasant. You're doing well but are not always yourself here."

That much is true, but we won't have to stay here that many months more. I wonder if he's preparing me for something more than a cold spell. "Do you know what this meeting involves?"

"Not entirely, but there have been growing threats from the south. I promise, after this meeting, no matter what, when our year is up, we will leave and not come back."

"Please hurry home though. I am my best self when we're together."

"That is true for me, too, love." He kisses me soundly and repeats his safety requests and instructions one more time.

I wrap my arms around his neck to linger in his embrace, absorbing strength from this good, sheltering man. "John, I'm a grown, capable woman, but you make me feel like a cherished child."

"You are greatly loved, but no child." He kisses the top of my head again. "You are my lovely wilderness wife who means the world to me."

My heart stutters at his words. His *wilderness wife?* That's what Alex said before abandoning me. That is how my *façon du nord* contract with John is worded, except he added more words, and I trust there is so much more between us. He added phrases promising a church-sanctioned marriage when possible. That has not happened yet. It is hard to arrange such things in this wilderness. Yet every day, John's words and tender expressions show me much more love than Alex gave.

"John," I answer him, "as for staying inside, you know I obey you in almost everything. But if the need arises, please trust I will do what I need to and manage well."

"Yes, I'm sure of it." He bends and kisses me again. "You've rescued me several times and surpass me in many skills. Still, every man likes to know that his family is safe while he's away."

I place his hand over my heart. "Feel my love beating for you here. You must promise to stay safe, too, for these are hazardous days and you are my life. Don't let your meetings keep you past Christmas. Tell them your family needs you. Come home as soon as you can."

"I promise."

The family and I gather around him to strengthen him with prayers and hugs. He tenderly embraces each of us before he belts himself inside his bearskin coat, the fur side inward. Last of all, he ties on the sturdy birch snowshoes I've made him, then he swishes away in long sweeping strides. He disappears in winter's thickening gloom. I make a small calendar on the wall in our room where I can mark the days until his return. I pray they are as few as possible.

People and animals move little during winter days when the sun barely curves above the horizon. Temperatures plummet and frost penetrates our cabin logs until they crack and pop like cannons. The northern lights dance in such vivid colors, sometimes we rise in the middle of the night to see them. Finally, outside temperatures rise enough for sundogs to form a haze around the sun, announcing milder days after constant cold with heavy snow.

"What are you doing, Mama?" Marie asks as I strap on my snowshoes.

"We have plenty of wild rice, dried vegetables, and pemmican," I say, "but I'd rather save those for travel days when we leave here. I've only checked the snares and traps nearest our cabin. Today I wish to go farther before colder temperatures return."

She knows me well and waves me through the door. "Go ahead, Mother. You deserve a chance to clear your lungs."

I push on through sunshine that turns all snowflakes to jewels while my breath rises in plumes. When I find empty traps and no animals along game trails near home, I travel more, my limbs glad for the stretch. But when the sun dips low, I turn for home. And I hear something. A feeble cry.

I stop and listen. What is it? A bleating deer? A young fox? I push my parka hood back to hear better. No animals give birth in winter, except bears in their dens. This cry sounds human. I follow the faint occasional noise, noting its direction, not wanting to journey so far from home I can't return by nightfall. Before long the cry leads me to two snowy mounds below a tall evergreen.

The cry is so muffled, the wind barely carries

it, yet I am sure I hear a living infant. Heart pounding, I remove one snowshoe and scoop the piled snow aside. I uncover a woman with a babe tucked inside her clothing against her breast. I gasp and release a piercing cry that will signal Marie to come. Then I dig in the next mound. I find a man with his arm flung over the woman and child. I surmise they are a family. Frostbite spots whiten the adults' cheeks, but not the babe's. Its cry is feeble. None will survive long without help.

I build a small fire using the flint and dry feather sticks I always carry. Next, I gather bark and nearby fallen branches to feed the flames. Then, I finish brushing the family free of snow and gently move their limbs. Marie arrives with blankets and medicine strapped to a travois.

The husband stirs first. His eyes flicker under frozen lashes. "Where? Who?" He reaches for his wife but falls back.

Marie removes her moose hide mitts and chafes his frozen hands and massages his heart and chest through his pitifully thin coat. She gapes at me. "Mama, how did you find them?"

"It is the Lord's doing, a Christmas miracle." But why do they travel in such conditions? Where do they go with so little preparation? Still, even if they are enemies, we must help them.

Slow to respond, the wife fumbles at her breast and, through half-frozen lips, mumbles, "Ba-by?"

Her wild eyes convey the desperation all mothers understand.

"Your babe is safe," I tell her, showing that I've bundled him papoose style in blankets tucked inside a tanned moose hide. "I'll nurse him myself if you cannot."

She points to her feet. "Can't feel toes."

Even with the items Marie brought, in growing darkness and plunging temperatures, this family needs immediate warmth. I pray aloud, "Dear Lord, send something alive, a deer or moose."

The man's blue lips move. "*Mon Dieu*. Merciful God." His teeth clatter.

A large animal lumbers our way, snapping branches. It halts, walks forward, and breaks more limbs as it crashes toward us. A huge bull moose stands near, unconcerned and curious. Marie hands me my loaded musket in one smooth movement. I steady my shaking hands and pray. When he advances two more steps, I aim and fire. He drops where he stands.

"*Merci*, *Mon Dieu*," I say from a grateful heart, and the man echoes my words. I take the large knife Marie offers and plunge into the animal's belly.

"Quick, *Vite*," I say to the nearly frozen man, in my hurry lapsing into French. I roll him against the moose and push his numb hands into the steaming mass of intestines of this beast God has sent.

"Ahhh," he cries, answering in perfect French. "*Mon Dieu*. I feared we might never be warm again."

"God be praised, *Monsieur*." I place the woman's hands and feet in the animal's cavity. Then Marie and I skin the beast. We drape the family inside the steaming hide, not minding the smell or mess, for it saves their lives today. While they rest, Marie and I cut the meat into quarters.

As we've worked, the temperature has plummeted. We must hurry home. We place the family in the center of the sledge and pile meat around them. Marie and I serve as the pack animals and pull our precious load through the darkness, following the same footprints that brought us here.

Flickering fire and candlelight wink from our cabin windows. And then we are thankfully home. As we enter the warm room, I call, "Nancy, Catherine, heat broth and tea." Both act instantly, experienced in crisis.

Soon man and wife rest on soft hides near our fire, and their hungry infant finds sustenance at his mother's breast. Our guests recover but can't travel in this unrelenting cold. We joyfully redeem the time, our hearts building friendship.

John returns from Fort William seven days after his departure, weary from trudging through log-popping cold. I swing open our door and usher the snow-speckled, bundled giant loaded with packages into the house. Our children whoop and rush to him. He sets the packages aside and bestows hugs, then says, "Step back, please, and let me remove these trappings."

Laughing, the children obey. He unlashes his snowshoes, tugs off his coat, and opens his arms to me. Then he stops, noticing the new happy smiling faces. He blinks rapidly. "What is this?"

"François, his wife, Bodette, and their infant, Claude." I gesture to each as I make the introductions.

"But who are they?" John asks, his brow furrowing in confusion.

"Visitors your wife rescued, *Monsieur*," François says in perfect French. "She saved our lives."

"Why am I not surprised?" John says. His eyes briefly question me, then he moves to the table and sits. I sit near him, and our children gather around him. "From your accent, you are Québécois, like me. These are harsh days for travel. I would rather have not gone all the way to Fort William myself."

"True, *Monsieur*. We were foolish, but God had mercy." His eyes brim. "I am from Quebec, but recently worked at Grand Portage."

John bristles. "That's an Americans' post."

"Which is why I left, *Monsieur*." He lifts his palms. "My brother trades with the Americans, but I will not. I'll stay poor and independent, but not aid the enemy."

My husband's eyes narrow. "Life is complicated in these times. What brings you here? Where were you going, and why?"

François stares into the fire and then points to Bodette. "My wife is fair-skinned although part native. She was not well-accepted. I seek a better life for her and our son. Bodette has family among the Bois Forte people to the west. We thought warm weather was holding, so we risked our late departure. We go there for a fresh start while the border conflict resolves."

"*If* the border resolves." John's eyebrows beetle as his eyes pierce—more like glinting steel now than the comforting dove gray I adore. "You are wise to join her people in these times, but you have entered Canada, man."

"So your wife told us." He studies my husband. "When a mild spell followed severe cold, we called it luck and traveled. I know now I was a fool."

"It was especially unwise with an infant." John glances at the little one, his voice harsh.

"But God was gracious. We had a travois with one sled dog, and a second carried our packs. Magnetic rocks in the Iron Range threw my compass off, calling every direction west and sending us in circles."

John's expression softens. "That happened

to me one summer when I first came. But it mattered less in warm weather."

"I tried many ways to find directions, but the snow fell deep, and we became lost."

"We had many days of heavy snow without a break," I tell John, relieving Bodette of her infant and rock him in my arms. Our little David extends a finger and strokes the baby's cheek.

"I tried to build a snow shelter," François says, "after a timber wolf killed our travois dog. Our pack dog, crazed by fear, broke its traces and vanished."

"Timber wolves are bold this year," Nancy says.

"Yes. When it was bitter cold, too dark to see, I despaired of life. We huddled beneath a tall evergreen for shelter and I struck a fire. As warm smoke rose, it loosened the overhanging snow on branches and dumped piles that extinguished our fire and buried us. Still, people sometimes survive inside snow shelters. We prayed for God's mercy." He fingers the Catholic medal around his neck. "We commended our souls to God, and then your wife came."

François nods my way. "When I saw her, I thought she was an angel come to guide us to heaven. And indeed, she has." His sweeping arm points out the joy of our family and the warmth of our home.

I have heard his story already, but I wonder

anew that this man was foolish and desperate enough to build a fire under snow-laden branches. Or perhaps simply inexperienced. My native friends would use a harsher term. But it's clear God protected them.

John's stern gaze fades as tenderness softens his face. "Marguerite, why were you outside in such conditions?"

"Only briefly, after the storm ended, to check snares and traps near our home." I take his hand. "I only went a short way past the river's edge where, by God's grace, I heard the infant."

The baby gurgles on cue, and when John bends near, little Claude grips his finger. "Incredible," John says.

"Smart baby," I say.

"She saved us," François exclaims. "The fact that we sit here alive is proof that God is merciful and your wife is His angel."

"I know both things well." John smiles and takes baby Claude from me. He can never resist babies and always seems most gentle when cradling an infant. "She is one of God's best."

"Indeed she is," François says. "With the land frozen and the wind howling like a demon as darkness came, your wife asked God for a large animal, and a moose appeared."

"Maybe you saw the scraped moose hide stretched outside to dry," I tell John. "Some of its meat is in that rich stew bubbling on our fire."

Our guest kisses his fingers and waves them to heaven. “Your wife is *magnifique*. She saved our family in a Christmas miracle, and here we are.”

John smiles and returns Claude to me. “Since the first day I met her, I’ve known she is God’s angel. God be praised for your survival.” He stands and exchanges a firm handshake with François. “When this cold spell ends and the earth is less frozen, I will arrange business west and north to help you reach your Bois Forte people. I think we can strike across the border safely and deliver you without meeting hostility. Thank God for your happy ending—these are blessed events to end one year and begin another.”

François holds a hand over his heart. “God bless you and your family one thousand times one thousand forever, Monsieur Doctor.”

“You are a guest in my home. Call me John.”

“One thousand times ten thousand,” Bodette adds. “*Ten* thousand times ten thousand forever. We would not live if it were not for your wife.”

“So much thanks?” John laughs. “In truth, The Lord deserves all the thanks.”

When John and I at last have a private moment, he lowers his head to his favorite place in the curve of my neck and buries his hands in my hair. “Thank God you saved our guests, but in these dangerous times, we must question the loyalty of everyone. We know little of them or their story. And since American territory now adjoins

Company lands—" His eyes turn brooding. "Strangers could try to win our confidence and learn secrets or betray us."

I pull back in shock. "Folks so near death?"

"It is unlikely, but not impossible." He clears his throat. "How did you explain my absence?"

"That duty demanded you make a last trading trip before Christmas."

"That's wise. For their sake, in their remaining days, please teach them survival skills. They need them, and it will help our children to review." He kisses me softly, and then lingeringly. One kiss leads to more urgent, demanding ones, and we forget the Company, our American competitors, and everything else in this hurting world, only taking comfort in each other.

Chapter 16

Indian Country, Central Canada,
early Spring, 1816

During more days of swirling snow, we stay near our cabin and practice following compass directions and telling time from reading tree moss and shadows. I teach François and Bodette how to find food where it appears there is none. We craft snowshoes from pliable birch branches and pile snow into high mounds and then hollow the mounds out with a snowshoe. In emergencies, I tell them, people can survive inside these shelters for days with only body heat.

Crowded around our table, I share a story for their and also my children's benefit. "When I was young and Mother and I traveled through hill country, we were once swept into the edge of an avalanche," I say. "As surging snow captured us, tumbling us like rocks in a stream bed, we couldn't tell up from down. Mother clutched me as the force buried us and at last pushed us against a tree trunk. Despite her terror, she thought to rip off a branch and poke it every direction until she reached the surface. We breathed sweet air again. Rotating the branch, she made a bigger hole, and we crawled out."

François's eyes grow huge. "*Alors*, what a close call."

"Yes, I will never forget the crushing snow that buried us and nearly became our tomb. Our lungs burned, but God helped us breathe again." I draw a deep breath now. "The experience made me eager to learn all I could about God and wilderness survival. I am glad to share this knowledge with you."

"Now I can also help others," François boasts, thumping his chest. "And sing your praises. We can never thank you enough."

"There's no need for thanks. God arranged it. These skills are things Mother and her people taught me." I squeeze Bodette's hand. "You will glean more from your people, and one day your fine boy will become a master hunter and woodsman."

After six days, the weather improves enough for John and a local hunter to take the young family on their way. "God bless you ten thousand times," they call.

"God bless and keep you safe," I shout back. We don't know what the future holds for any of us in the days ahead, but we'd like to stay in touch somehow. Perhaps sometimes we can cross to their location. Maybe they can visit us again, but not near Christmas.

When John safely returns from guiding them, he shares full reports from Fort William he dared not say in front of our visitors. The word is that every outpost should expect attacks. "Here are more amazing facts," he says. "I knew nothing of John Jacob Astor before his venture with Alex, but now hear his name on every side. He suffered crushing setbacks when he lost the *Tonquin*. After the 1812 war, he had to surrender his holdings to the Hudson's Bay Company. Now he is a poorer but strong player seeking wealth in other arenas."

I make a face. "Does history change so fast?"

"Sadly, yes, but the Oregon change should improve things for your son Tom."

"Even if he works for our competitor?"

"Yes. They are a well-run organization. If they didn't illegally insert men into our Red River area, we might partner with them. But America's government is closely scrutinizing Astor. He may face trial for several questionable moneymaking schemes."

"Including Oregon?"

"Especially Oregon." John links his fingers on the edge of the table. "Because from there, his Pacific trading network exceeded England's on the Atlantic. His trade triangle brings slaves from Africa to the Americas, and then sugar, tobacco, and cotton to England, and rum and cloth back to Africa, and—of course—taking slaves from there again. It is a heartless yet profitable plan."

John spreads out a world map that Nancy had copied. "Let me show you Astor's trade triangle.

He has circled the world by bringing goods from New York to the West Coast to trade with natives for fabulous furs. The *Tonquin* was to gather otter and sable to sell in China at high profit. From there, he brought back teas, silks, and luxury goods to New York and London for staggering fortunes."

My stomach burns. "Does he always pursue opportunities that endanger employees? It's a wonder he doesn't pursue political office."

"Please don't say that out loud," John sputters. "He may get the idea. It's unthinkable but not impossible. For now, he's busy pursuing greater wealth."

My heart numbs. "May God judge such crimes."

"He will," Marie declares. My gentle daughter's face flames and her hands fist. "Something must be done, but what?"

"Pitifully little at present," John answers. "Evil thrives, but in England they at least talk now of ending the slave trade. Christian leaders will eventually do what's right."

"I'm thankful my native people seldom took slaves."

"You're right. It's sad when uneducated people show more compassion and wisdom than educated ones. It seems riches and education can harden hearts."

I expressed my viewpoint as if I am European, which I am through Father. Yet when I discuss

European conduct, so different from Father's ways, I prefer native standards. Here, in Indian Country, women of mixed blood married to white traders are treated like whites. Yet beyond our border, I'm told it is not so. What does that mean for our children?

"Increasing profit seems to be Astor's God," John says. "He boasts of church ties, yet his Golden Triangle fills his pockets and injures many. America's government tolerates him because he pays high taxes, but recently it watches him with a closer eye. Now with fresh outcry against the opium trade, he has entered real estate and just become America's first multi-millionaire."

"At the expense of others." I take a sharp intake of breath and shudder. "That is disgusting. I'm sad Tom first had his father's example, and then Astor's. What will become of him?"

John's smile reassures me. "Sweetheart, besides losing his father, Tom has seen many serious life lessons. He is not only his father's son, but yours also. Your example and prayers will prevail."

I bow my head. "I pray constantly for good character to grow in him."

"I pray it, too, and it is happening."

Tom writes more good letters in an improved hand. He makes progress in his clerk apprenticeship under Hudson's Bay management.

In a recent letter, he pens, *Mother, I miss you and my sisters, and especially your cooking. No one here comes close. Thank Doctor McLoughlin for his letter saying he is my guarantor. I hope when Father's estate is settled, there will be some funds available to send my sisters.*

"Is that likely?" I ask John.

"I doubt it. Funds are devoured by attorney fees—especially since Alex was far away from any standard bank. He invested heavily in the *Tonquin* voyage, which failed, yet there may be profits besides. Tom speaks well of his mentor, Alexander Ross, who all say is trustworthy. If anyone can improve Tom's situation, it will be Ross."

Tom also writes about his time with his father in Montréal and describes Astor's coming: *Astor is impressive in every way, a flashy dresser who at times disperses money like scattering leaves in autumn. At other times, he is tight. His promises of fame and fortune captured Father. Me, too, but that spell is broken now. Don't worry, Mother. Astor's influence is like my first taste of liquor. After the first hot rush, I don't like its taste or effects and will not form that habit. Some men swallow liquor once but never touch it again. That's how I feel about Astor. I am now free of his influence.*

"Thank God," I say, holding Tom's letter to my breast.

John embraces me. "He's your son, Marguerite. Are you surprised that God gives him wisdom?"

"No, but I am grateful. However, his apprenticeship is now with our competitor, and I know little of the Hudson's Bay leaders and policies. The North West Company ruled everywhere I've lived."

John huffs out a breath. "You needn't worry. There will be changes, but overall the Hudson's Bay Company runs their business well. They're a century older than us, and were started by royal charter, but once they saw our profits in Canada, came demanding a share. Add the upstart Americans pushing up from the south, and these become dangerous times."

"And leaves us where?"

He huffs out a breath. "If I knew, I could rule all North America. We're told to remain peaceful but be prepared for anything. We hear dire threats rumored. New ones rise like pus-filled boils that could break open and spread disease across the continent." He leans down and rests his forehead against mine. "We live on a powder keg, but it can only ignite if God allows it."

I toss and turn that night. Sleep does not come easily. When it finally does, I dream of noisy clanking metal, crackling flames, and hear the screams of people fighting for their lives. Will what I'm seeing really happen? For my life is also shaped by my mother's other gift of inner seeing and hearing of events before they occur. Mother said God gives this to those of our native people who respect nature and listen to its creator. Did my gift fail me in my dream of seeing Alex perish? Was I meant to warn him? Or did he alone choose his fate?

In tonight's vivid dream I see Tom, tall and more confident than the eleven-year-old boy Alex took from me. He stands in a dim landscape surrounded by fog banks over rolling seas. I have only heard of oceans, not seen them, yet I might have in many dreams and this is one. Gradually, the scene brightens to colors as Tom explores his world. Then, I join him and, when he sees me, he rushes forward like a boy running home after a long time away. He towers above me, and as he lays his cheek against mine, I feel the soft down and first bristles of his forming beard. He laughs and lifts me above the ground.

"Put me down, Tom," I say. "I'm no small woman. What are you doing?"

"Showing you I'm grown." His teeth gleam white. "Say please, and I will."

I look up, smiling. "Please, son."

As I awake, though my son remains on the far side of this continent, I'm at peace that Thomas MacKay is well and shall do well. I tell John my dream.

He gazes at me with loving eyes. "Dear heart,

I hope one day we can bring Tom home or go to him in Oregon."

"Either choice would give me joy. In the meantime, I'm grateful for the Lord giving me peace that Tom does well."

I thank Him again that He comforts and for this husband He has given me.

Lord, all parents want their children safe. I do long to see my oldest son again.

I have the assurance that someday, somehow, it will happen.

Chapter 17

Fort William on Lake Superior,
early Autumn, 1816

We end our year in Athabasca, and I am stronger for it. To our joy, Company directors keep their word and return us to Fort William with John in a higher position still. On this chilly autumn morning, leaves fall from trees, pelted by driving rain. In mid-afternoon, the temperature drops and hail hammers our cabin windows, but the children and I stay safe and busy inside. With the weather nasty, I require our older boys to stay in and play games in a corner. John is reconciling account records in the main fort office all day, but in late afternoon, he climbs our porch steps and knocks mud from his boots.

"Oh ho," he laughs, opening our door and seeing our girls and me surrounded by colorful fabric swatches and bolts of cloth spread around the room. "What a lovely picture. Shall we open a mercantile? Perhaps our sons can be shop-keepers."

"No!" Joseph says fervently, having no interest in his sisters' dress fabrics. "We were made for outdoor tasks. Can we please go outside? We'll even stack firewood." He looks up, eyes hopeful.

I see him already developing skills as a fur-trade bargainer.

"Fine," John says. "The weather's not as bad as it was. Just keep yourselves out of trouble."

"Hooray!" Joseph and David rush outside. Soon I hear pieces of firewood knocking together. I think they say something about building a mud fort, but John has told them to stay out of trouble, so I discount the idea.

Nancy holds a lovely turkey-red floral muslin under her chin and studies her reflection in the mirror. "No. Too busy," she says.

Marie fingers a soft indigo chintz. "I can't decide about dress lengths or when to leave home. Do I marry soon? Or seek more education in Montréal and teach first?"

"That's the same old question," I say.

"Only you can decide," Nancy answers. "I shall do both, marry my boat captain *and* travel." She twirls and her ruffled skirt puffs out in a circle.

"Leaving home early like Tom is not bad," John says, "especially for boys. I did the same. Those experiences brought hard years but also maturity. Still, if you girls are content at home for more years, that gives us joy. Life would be far too quiet and not full of surprises without you." He blinks several times and turns away.

Pain gnaws my heart. I'm not ready for them to leave, either, but I won't tell them so.

Marie lays aside the indigo for a brighter plum.

"Which is worse? For us to take husbands? Or sit home becoming old maids like wrinkled winter apples?"

John guffaws. "Girls as lovely as you? And such good cooks? I'll more likely have to beat off suitors with a club. They must win my approval first you know."

Both girls laugh but seem pleased. Marie arranges the plum into a modest top with puffed sleeves, apparently caught up in dress-making again. But John and I lift our eyebrows. Is she expressing greater hesitation regarding Donald Mackenzie? What do her questions mean?

It's growing dark outside and it has begun to rain. I go to the door, intending to call the boys inside, and they burst in as quickly as black bears dashing for honey. They're slathered head to toe in mud, but their smiles gleam.

"Stop," I say, trying to keep them at the door where they tumble over each other. "Nancy, would you please rinse them in the wash tub while we gather up these fabrics before they get muddy?"

She huffs. "Why me? Remind me not to have sons." But she smiles as she helps them.

When at last John and I retire to our room, I ask, "Do you think Marie is less sure of Donald? What has changed? Nancy seems quite sure of Captain McCargo. I like his perseverance, though it may take her from us sooner than I wish."

John shrugs. "I am not a good predictor of young women's feelings. I'll leave that to your heart and intuition, but Marie and Donald have hardly seen each other. If I were either one of them, that would give me concern."

"Maybe this is how my poor mother felt when I married and left home."

"I'm sure of it," he answers. "But though our children leave, I will stay." He gives me a resounding kiss.

Each year I'm married to this man, I find deeper kindness in him. Except, due to his childhood hardships, he loses his temper when he sees injustice. Days earlier, Marie saw John shake with rage and throw a trader into a muddy ditch for sneaking liquor to the Indians. She described the scene, then asked, "So much anger? He nearly hurt him, although the man did have it coming."

"John possesses a keen sense of justice. He'd like to see conditions fair and just for everyone." While I dusted items on the fireplace mantel, I reminded my girls of his childhood. "After his Irish Catholic father died leaving three young children, they and their mother moved into her parents' unhappy Protestant home. They heard their deceased father constantly blamed for every wrong in the universe. John and his siblings left to be on their own as soon as they could manage."

"That sounds awful," Nancy chimed in. "It's

not bad being poor if you're happy, like we've been."

I kissed her cheek. "We've proven that in hard times, haven't we? John at least had the influence of his uncle, Simon Fraser. He's the trapper-explorer who also followed the wild western river named for him."

"I remember," Nancy said. "We copied it on our maps."

"That's right. He inspired John to study medicine and later join the North West Fur Company for its opportunities."

"I know his early days in distant outposts were hard," Marie said.

"Yes, but also adventures. He's not afraid of hard work, and we met him on his assignment to Sault Sainte Marie." I stepped to the door and shook out my dust rag.

Nancy sighs. "I admire any man who makes his own way. That's a quality I'm looking for."

I'm sure she was thinking of Captain Robert McCargo. Now, I share our conversation with John, and add, "The girls respect your life journey, John. Of course, so do I."

"Thank you, sweet. I thank God it brought me to you."

I curl his sideburns around my finger, glad he keeps his chin clean-shaven for me to enjoy his lips. Most native people can't grow whiskers and so prefer our traders to be clean-shaven. They say seeing a man's open face helps reveal his character.

"As the oldest son," John says, "I worked hard to support Mother and my siblings. I promised myself then that my own family would never suffer like we had. That's why I'm determined to provide well for you and our children so you never lack."

His fist clenches, and I clasp it between my hands. "John, I'm sorry for your hard years, but you succeed well now. Being short of love would be far worse than being short of funds. Besides supporting us, I'm proud of you for assisting your family. You pay much of your brother David's medical school and send funds to your sister in the Quebec convent."

He smiles fondly. "Marie Louise is her own success story, although our Protestant grandfather probably still rolls in his grave. When she desired more education, it was only available in a Catholic school. Grandfather predicted she'd convert. He promised that if she did, he'd disinherit all of us, which is exactly what happened."

I gasp. "He cut off all of you for that?"

"Yes. We didn't see him again until he was in his coffin at his funeral."

I shake my head in disbelief. "That's sad."

"In many ways, he taught me what not to do." John stretches full length across our bed. "If our girls want more education, going to my sister in Quebec is an option. Marie Louise would love hostessing them, and they would love her."

"If she is anything like you, I cherish her already." I study John's face. "I don't see how anyone could feel so strongly about religion they could ever disinherit loved ones for choices."

"It's hard to believe, but you didn't know my grandfather. Do you know distinctions in some religious orders and beliefs are actually shown through the fabrics and colors clergy wear?"

"Seriously? Like our girls choosing dress materials?"

"Yes. Each color means something. Catholic cardinals are robed in scarlet while the pope dresses in white or gold. Lower clergy wear black, gray, or brown."

"But beliefs should be simple." My forehead wrinkles. "Our Lord said we must not allow divisions but should treat others as ourselves."

He shakes his head. "Marguerite, you say you're unschooled because you lack formal education, yet you're wiser than many educated folks who fight wars over religion. I should add you to our Company's advisory group. You make more sense than many there."

"Don't make me laugh. I'd rather stay home. But if warring fur traders and nations followed good sense, most conflicts would end, wouldn't they?"

John nods. "Probably."

"Mother couldn't read Father's Bible, but she lived by its principles. She struggled to forgive Pond, yet in time understood that Jesus forgave even those that took his life."

"That's amazing." John pulls me close. "I wish I had known her, but I'm thankful to have you."

"She would have loved you, John. She didn't have peace when I married Alex, but I was so headstrong. It's best she died before she saw the outcome."

"Any parent hates to see their child suffer."

"I wonder if Pond ever asked the Lord's forgiveness for killing Father and the other trader later on? Yet how can I judge when I also fall short?"

John startles. "You?"

"But I do. You don't see the darkness of my soul." I chew my lip. "My marriage to Alex was ill-advised. Thankfully, I follow our Lord's guidance more closely now."

"Yes, sweetheart. I thank Him for bringing us to each other. You are my life's best gift." He lifts my hand to his lips, kissing each finger before taking me into his arms. He extinguishes the light and we burrow under the covers. He nuzzles my hair. "No matter what happens in this world, we shall always love and encourage each other."

"Always," I answer. And say again, "Always."

• • •

The Company orders John and several other men to go to Fort William for emergency planning. We are thrilled when they return in late September. My husband who tries to leave his worries outside the door cannot hide his distress now. He holds his tongue until the children are in bed, and then, in the privacy of our room, explodes with angry words.

"There will be hell to pay. The conflict between Scottish crofters at Red River against the Métis who have trapped and hunted for us there for a generation has led to massacre. The details are muddy, but despite our men being nowhere near, we're blamed entirely because Lord Selkirk protects his Scots. Rumor says he wants us convicted for the massacre and may bring mercenary soldiers here to make it happen."

"Here to Fort William? I can't imagine that. Will he declare war?"

"I don't think he'll go that far. Some say this can be settled in London and Montréal board rooms through new treaties and money changing hands. We shall see."

Some nights, John is restless in his sleep, groaning unintelligible words. First we hear soldiers will come. Then, that they won't. We grow weary of waiting and imagining, wishing we could resume normal, peaceful lives.

One brisk mid-September morning, John and

I are up early. He sits at our table balancing accounts while I sweeten porridge so its tantalizing smell will rouse our children from their beds. I'm also adding to the grocery list I'll send to McCargo for the next time he sails here. His trips seem more related to seeing Nancy than bringing fur-trade supplies. He is a welcome figure at our table.

The pale yellow sun is beginning to burn away wisps of fog along the lake to warm this day when a guard raises the alarm. He points to the southern edge of our curved shore where brightening sky meets Lake Superior's glacier-blue waters. They're still far away, but a flotilla of canoes brings blue-coated soldiers.

John raises his spy glass to our cabin window. "I believe that's Lord Selkirk in the first boat wearing the tall, plumed hat. Company dispatches describe his sharp profile and jutting chin, which I see is true. Here. Look for yourself." He hands me the glass.

I move aside the curtain. The canoes land, and Selkirk must orders troops to play instruments as they march, for we soon hear martial tunes blast from bugles, pipes, and drums. John's forehead furrows. "Perhaps they hope to terrify us."

The loud noise brings our children clattering downstairs.

"What's happening?" Nancy calls.

"Don't be frightened, but we have visitors."

John says cheerfully. He drinks in the sight of our children as if he's imprinting their faces on his heart.

"Visitors?" Marie asks.

"Yes." He points. "Scottish Lord Selkirk and his troops. They are upset about the rebellion at Red River and probably come to discuss that. We'll know their intentions soon."

"Why do we let them come?" Joseph asks.

"For now, it's the right thing. We're not sure what they want. Remember the Bible says he that rules his spirit is better than he that takes a city. Reacting could throw us in confusion and give them the advantage. I won't do that."

The soldiers march in cadenced steps through our fort's open gate.

"Why are they coming inside? Why didn't we barricade our gate to keep them out?" Nancy asks, as if someone has blundered.

"They would barge in anyway," John answers. "Let's learn their intentions. Even though we're outnumbered, the Lord will help us."

Still, it's a terrible thing for us to see blue-uniformed soldiers march into our fort waving battalion flags and brandishing weapons. When they reach the first barracks, they start calling out names. The first they call is John's visiting uncle.

"Simon Fraser? Surrender to the custody of the crown."

"That's not good." John's body tenses as a door opens and Simon appears. Instead of treating him with respect, one of Selkirk's officers reads charges and snaps him into handcuffs. The same soldier then calls out thirteen others. As the list grows, John's skin purples. "Look at their strategy. They're arresting our key businessmen, not possible agitators."

Months ago, at the first rumors of trouble, he and his uncle had checked the activities of our partners, agents, and employees on the massacre date to see if any might have had part in the Red River events. None did.

"I'm grateful," Simon said, "that I'd already gone far northwest trading furs when the Scots burned Fort Gibraltar. When I returned, I still saw stockade foundations smoldering." He shook his gray head. "Tensions were very high."

John's shoulders had eased. "While it's possible a few Métis who trade with us might have been near the area, I believe they obeyed my orders to avoid all contact. Witnesses say Selkirk's colonists had been rebuilding the stockade but not quite finished when different Métis came, desperate for food.

"As they approached, Governor Semple himself fired the first shot. Within minutes, he and nineteen Scots were dead by return fire while only one Métis trapper was slain."

"That matches my signed eye-witness reports,"

Simon had said, pulling crinkling parchment pages from his large leather pouch.

"Keep those," John told him. "We'll probably need them."

Now with Selkirk and his soldiers here, it seemed our whole fort was put on trial.

"What I resent most," John says, looking out the window, "is Selkirk making no attempt to discover the facts of who was involved. Hudson's Bay officials fully blame us for the massacre, although evidence shows we were nowhere near."

"Won't a court of law discover the truth?" I ask.

John slants a probing look. "Only if it wants to."

We watch the soldiers arrest John's uncle and then handcuff two partner-managers, three agents, four clerks, two lesser clerks, one scribe, and a bookkeeper. Only six are Métis. Fire blazes hot in John's eyes.

"What will you do?" I ask.

"Nothing for now." John grinds his teeth. "It's not cowardice. The Lord is restraining me to watch and be wise before I act. I believe Selkirk knows that those he's arresting had no part in a massacre, but he's making them examples to warn others he thinks might interfere with his settlement plans for a Hudson's Bay's takeover."

It's chilling to see iron cuffs lock men's arms tight behind their backs and hear the rattle of chains as the fourteen men are marched to the brig near our home.

John turns away from the window. "That's about all I can stand. Children, it takes strength to let the false charges proceed before I act, which I believe God is instructing me to do."

We gather around John. I rest my chin against his shoulder, feeling his strong body tense. "We hate this situation but will never think you weak."

Joseph says, "You're no coward, Father. What is your plan?"

"You shall see."

Joseph eyes a musket standing in the corner.

"No, not that," John barks. "We must give them no cause to charge any of us with resisting arrest. Please go to your rooms. Don't come down until Mother calls, no matter what."

Joseph slumps, and his face clouds as if his heart is breaking.

"No matter what?" Marie scowls as she shepherds our little ones upstairs. "May the Lord strike them flat like He did the companies of soldiers sent to arrest Elijah."

I stare. Where has her fierceness come from, yet it burns in my breast too.

John hugs me as the sound of marching boots draws near. "I love you, Marguerite. We will pray for each other constantly."

Men climb our porch and someone pounds the door. John opens it, his mouth in a tight line, shielding me behind him. “May I help you, gentlemen?”

The soldiers fall back, almost like when Jewish guards came to arrest Jesus.

“We seek John McLoughlin,” an officer says. Given John’s tall stature, he surely knows who he is.

“You have found him.”

“I inform you that we have charged fourteen men in your employ with twenty-one counts of murder for their part in the Seven Oaks Massacre.”

“Preposterous. They were not there.” John’s face whitens except for two bright spots blazing on each cheek. He exhales in sharp puffs, but his voice holds steady. “I see you’ve arrested six Métis among the fourteen, yet we have proof none of them were near Seven Oaks on that date. In fact, we possess signed witness accounts confirming that Semple and his men fired the first shot and sparked the entire incident and deadly results.”

The officer scoffs. “Of course, you have signed testimonies stating you were nowhere near. That’s what we expect your witnesses to say. No matter how many men you parade through court, or how many ignorant trappers you have mark their *X* on parchments, these men will be tried and found guilty by King George IV’s court in Montréal.”

A tic pulses in John's jaw. "Gentlemen, in light of your prejudice, our men stand no chance of fair defense. Since you levy false charges against those who were not present at Seven Oaks, take me too. I will volunteer to go along and exert my power to gain a fair trial. I surrender to you as the North West Company director of Fort William to accompany and defend them."

The officer blinks rapidly. "You're mad. Your name is not on our list."

"Then add it." He squares his shoulders. "My place is with my men. Assistants here know my standards and will direct things in my absence."

The soldier still stares. "Actually, Selkirk will appoint someone in charge if you go. But, man, if you're found guilty, you will die by hanging."

John does not flinch. "Or the truth will be known and we'll all return free men."

I shudder. My stomach is sick. For long moments there is no sound, although I'm sure my heartbeats are louder than the rat-a-tat of drums outside. My blood chills. I who have survived prairie blizzards and a snowy avalanche shiver uncontrollably with this greater risk.

John embraces me. "I'm sorry, Marguerite. God assures me that if I stand with our men, we will win and return free."

"I pray you are right. What about Simon

Fraser—he is old but wise. Can he represent the group instead of you?"

"The trip is arduous. I believe the Lord asks this of me." The tilt of John's head allows no disagreement.

I nod dumbly as John strokes my hand. "Among my papers you'll find details for our family's care. I'm confident you will manage well until I disprove these lies and come home."

I tremble, but the love blazing from his eyes strengthens me. My body clings, wanting to remember John's good smell and the feel of him—this husband who completes me as no one else on earth can. This man God has given, who He surely will not take away.

The officer pulls John from my embrace. "Come, man. Since you are determined to suffer, get on with it."

John slides long arms into the sleeves of his frock coat and dons his heavier overcoat. He picks up a small satchel from behind our door that I did not see him pack. Through blurred tears, our daughters' pinched faces gaze from the top of the stairs. Our sons look down through eyes more sorrowful still.

I watch John travel the promenade path he's crossed so many days, but this time in shackles. Autumn's colored leaves flutter to the ground. His feet crush crimson maple and golden birch leaves, releasing their spicy scent on this day of gloom.

He manages one quick glimpse over his shoulder. “Pray, my sweet.”

“Always.” I lift folded hands.

In full regalia, topped by his tall, plumed hat, Selkirk watches John approach, escorted between armed bluecoats, and steps forward. “I know you were involved, McLoughlin, no matter what you say. By desiring to go to trial in Montréal, you admit your guilt.”

“I go to prove the innocence of all.” John’s eyes challenge as if he cannot believe even wilderness law proceeds without proven evidence.

Uncle Simon sees John approach. I cannot hear his words but read his glowering expression.

As John advances, Selkirk loudly says, “Fifteen of you face capital punishment for murdering twenty-one men in the Red River Massacre. The crown orders you transported to Montréal for trial by the crown before Lake Superior is too frozen to travel.”

“That is unwise,” John’s voice thunders. “It is already too late in the season. To make men travel now is almost a death sentence. Be warned that the God of heaven judges the actions and hearts of men.”

“We have lawful right,” Selkirk answers haughtily.

My lungs seem incapable of drawing breath. How can I live if I cannot breathe? I can stand no more. I rush upstairs to join our children, and we all fall on our knees. "Lord Jesus. Have mercy! You alone can save John and our men. Please intercede. Stop this terrible evil."

Chapter 18

Following our men's arrest, the day drags like eternity. We do small tasks but constantly glance across our leaf strewn promenade toward the brig. How are our men faring? How is John?

After dark, a furtive sound scrapes at our back door—more of a scratch than a knock. I wave our girls, Joseph, and our littlest ones upstairs to safety while I open the door a crack. I see one sad glimmering eye, and then the face of Aubergine, one of John's most trusted assistants. His family name is unpronounceable but is spelled similarly to eggplant, the purple vegetable, in French, so *eggplant* he is called. In truth, it fits him, for he is jolly and ruddy, especially when he drinks, which is often.

"Madame McLoughlin?" His tone carries sorrow. "Many good men wait in your backyard to stage an uprising to free John and the others from prison. Our plan is well-made. Simply say the word and we begin."

"You want me to approve an uprising?" Picturing John and the others back home in the arms of loved ones makes my eyes sting. Those sweet thoughts are followed by images of our fort in flames, our homes lost, our women and children slain or abandoned in coming harsh winter if we resist these armed men.

"Step inside, Aubergine. Explain." I motion our children to stay upstairs, even our older girls, so they cannot be blamed for overhearing any news of mutiny.

"Anything less than their full release is unforgivable," our friend blusters, his suffering face showing the revenge and murder that fills his heart. "That pompous Selkirk attacks honest men without respecting the years of work we've invested here to make this wilderness our home. I don't begrudge the suffering Scots a place to live, but in this vast wilderness, why must they steal ours?" He flexes his massive right arm, and muscles ripple down his leather coat sleeve. "I long to lift Selkirk by his neck and fancy hat and toss him into the lake for the fish to eat."

"Aubergine," I say, "would you be so unkind to fish?"

He quietly chuckles, showing one broken tooth in need of a dentist. "Humor is good medicine," he says.

When I lay a calming hand on his arm, it jostles his coat and reveals a long pistol tucked in his belt. "What is this? You are usually a peaceful man, not violent."

"There are times, Madame." His jaw is granite. "Every man has limits. These arrests break our hearts. They falsely accuse our leader and friends of crimes they had no part in." He bends close. "It will be easy—tonight we shall seize

Selkirk and his aides while they sleep and hold them hostage. The price for safe passage to their canoes will be to free our men and leave our fort while leaving a number of their men behind to guarantee they keep their word. We'll see how they like that turn-around. And we have plans for their vessels." He utters a fiendish laugh and rubs his hands together.

"What plans?"

"They will enter their canoes but find them less dependable than before."

"What do you mean?"

"Weakened spruce-ribbed joints make tarred seams come apart in the water so they can't travel far. If they are lucky, they'll be near enough shore to live. If not, God has decided their fate."

"You are serious? And if you fail?"

"We will not." His throat rumbles like a bull moose, and he thrusts his bearded face near mine. "Don't speak of failure. We will risk everything to end this injustice."

A shiver chills me. "Dear Aubergine, thank you for your loyalty. The accusations are unjust, but John does not want violence. He believes God has given him this assignment to win justice and that the court will see the truth."

"A British court when Métis are involved. How can that be?" Our friend rocks back on his heels. "God Himself stands little chance in Montréal's courts, Madame. Pardon me, but we believe it is a fool's errand, like Jesus Himself standing before His accusers but being crucified when He was innocent. How can we hope for fairness when the court authorities are so far away and care little for our case in this distant wilderness? Besides, they will likely side with the Scots and the Hudson's Bay's claims instead of our people of mixed blood." His chest heaves as if his heart will crack.

"In honor of John and what he believes he has heard, we must have faith," I say.

"In honor of John and all that is good, we must try to free them," he says. "If these men go unchallenged, their success will drive us and all we have established here from this land."

"But you know if you win by violence, feuds and revenge will grow."

"We must take that risk." His eyes hood. "Please understand, we must end this travesty. The courts in Montréal will not give justice."

His words strike hard. "I do understand—like they failed to judge my father's killers."

"Exactly, Madame. You will join our cause?" He scowls the question so fiercely, his brows meet in the middle. "There are constant legal failures concerning us. Our wilderness is far beyond their attention or care, yet they bleed us dry for profits."

"You are persuasive."

"You know I am right."

I scrub my face with both hands and draw a ragged breath. "Of course I also long for our men to be free, but not at such cost. John says that through history, nations fighting civil wars only destroy each other. A victory won tonight would not end this conflict or bring lasting peace. It would only increase our problem."

Behind me I hear a whisper of sound and whirl to find Nancy, although at first she is so changed, I hardly recognize her. She has smeared her face dark with some substance and wears men's pants. She wears one of John's shirt tucked into a thick, leather belt with dueling pistols stuck in on either side.

"Darling, what are you doing?"

"What you should be doing. Fighting for freedom. Behind our home I see men hiding in shadows and Aubergine here armed and excited. I can guess their intention." She winks.

Aubergine's eyes flash approval. "*Sacré bleu.* You are bold."

"Like my mother."

My heart chills. "Nancy, not like your mother tonight. Please stop and think. Sometimes you are too bold." At first, I didn't recognize the woolen trousers she wears as those I used to ride my horse astride next to John, not sidesaddle as he says city ladies somehow ride. When any folk here look at me strangely, he guffaws and boasts, "You should see how she stays with me on woodland trails and even gallops ahead. No woman rides better."

Nancy holds another pair of trousers toward me. "I brought you some, too, if you'll join us. I know you love Father. We'll smear our faces and screech so they think fierce Indians want their scalps and the shiny buttons from their uniforms." She dangles the trousers, tempting me.

"Oh, daughter . . ." I groan and nearly bend double, clutching my middle with the anguish of this situation. "I truly love him and see your cause, but John wishes to fight with prayer, not force. This test is horribly hard. My mind tells me his chances are poor."

"Worse than poor. He has none." Our friend swipes both ends of his mustache into points and shifts his large feet. "What shall I tell the waiting men? They await your word, Madame?"

"Tell them . . . Tell . . ."

I can't think. My heart forgets to beat. And then I say in a rush, "Please thank them for their courage and devotion. As much as I long to crush these invaders, for the love of my husband, I must obey his wishes and support his choice."

"And do nothing?" He gasps loudly, incredulous, while Nancy adds her own rude sounds.

"Do pray for him though and the others," I plea. "The risk is terrible, but he believes it is the only path."

"Pahhhh, rubbish. I love and respect your husband, but this time he is wrong." Shaking his head, Aubergine melts into the darkness. The men awaiting him fade deeper into tree shadows too. Nancy huffs her way upstairs. She doesn't need to speak to express her disappointment.

As much as I loved this morning's brilliant sunrise, I remember nothing of tonight's sunset, although surely God provided one. Whether it shone with fair colors, promising sun tomorrow, or signs of a building storm, I cannot say. With John arrested, the world dims to black and white. It is hard to believe we will ever enjoy clear sunlight here again. Yet, I do recall the bright yellow disk that rose and burned through fog this morning on this day that so greatly disturbed our lives.

Dear Lord, send enough warmth and light to end this suffocating darkness so we do not die. Return our world to light and sanity again.

Much later, I climb into bed sick with worry. I shift the covers and move to John's side of our feather tick, inhaling his smell, fitting into the hollows his body made just this morning when we had fewer cares than face us now. To think of him, and send my love, I will sleep on his side of our bed every night until he returns safely again.

Chapter 19

Appropriately, the sun barely shines the day following John and the men's arrest. Thick fog spreads like a living thing and swallows distant buildings until it's hard to see far at all. We prepare food, and John's aides carry it to the brig for our men, then Aubergine brings back empty bowls and news.

"Selkirk started interrogations last night," he says, his dark eyes snapping. "Our fifteen confess only their innocence, no guilt at all, so he says he will send all to Montréal for trial."

That far? For the Red River Métis, even Fort William is farther than most have traveled from their homes since birth. "Winter storms come soon," I say. "Doesn't Selkirk consider our weather conditions? He may be sending our men to their death."

"He knows little of our weather," Aubergine says with contempt, "and does not seem to hear reason or care." He slants an approving glance at Nancy as she slips closer to hear. Captain McCargo would be wise to claim her soon before our friend here offers her a marriage contract of his own.

The man nibbles his mustache and asks if I've changed my mind about an uprising since I've had a whole night to consider. "If we don't act soon, those arrested must rely on God alone, for Selkirk can't guarantee delivering them safely anywhere." His eyes plead. "There's still time, Madame. Our men remain ready and willing. Nancy can help, too, even if you feel you must stay back to protect your children."

His eyes measure me as if he is assessing my courage. He cannot see the high cost I pay to support John's decision to accompany the prisoners to seek a fair trial. Before the law, John is now equally charged and also fighting for his life.

"I cannot disobey John's wishes."

"Cannot? Or will not?" Aubergine's face darkens, as if he considers God's defense to be little help.

"The truth is, I cannot."

"I feared that would be your answer. That's what John said you would say."

"What?" I intake a sharp breath. "You saw him? Talked with him? How is he?" A thousand questions fly to my lips.

He relaxes his stance and gazes toward the brig. "I shuffled past guards earlier to collect his tin cup and bowl and spoke in French only, which few German-Swiss bluecoats know."

"Thank God. You told him your idea of hostages and boats?"

"Enough that he understood our willingness."

“And he said?”

“The same as you.” Aubergine sighs and studies his moccasins. “He depends on God’s deliverance. Like Moses leading his people from Egypt, he believes the sea will open for him and his men but swallow Pharaoh and his chariots.”

“May that be true again.” I cannot speak, only grasp Aubergine’s hand.

He swallows hard and looks forlorn. “We have no choice then, but only to wait and see what God will do.”

“Yes, dear friend. We will wait and pray. But don’t look like it is so hopeless.”

The next fourteen days crawl by. Iroquois paddlers from far eastern Ontario arrive in three large freight canoes to carry our men to trial. Selkirk assigns bluecoats to go with them since he also needs good soldiers here to maintain strong defense to hold control. While he insists that the Montréal trial will judge the Hudson’s Bay claims to be true, his defensive tone indicates a need to convince himself.

Outwardly, most fort residents appear calm, like the deceptive smooth skin that forms on the surface of a good thick pudding as it cools, making it look ready to eat, while scalding heat bubbles beneath. It smells and looks enticing, but the eater may get badly burned if he spoons the food in his mouth too soon. Lord help me, I would like to see Selkirk badly burned.

Silver frost patterns the trees in early mornings but melts by noon. Each day a thicker skim of ice builds up along the lake's edge and spreads as frigid waves lap against rocks and ferns. Daily, the ice extends farther out and stays longer, except where bright patches of sunlight melt its progress. Fierce winds strip autumn's last leaves which crunch underfoot, making pungent leaf mold scent the air, reminding me of death and decay.

I worry about how few clothes John and the others have. As wife of the man in charge, I request an audience with Selkirk, who has usurped John's position. He sits behind John's desk and does not rise when I enter.

"What do you want?" he asks abruptly, obviously resenting a request from a woman, and perhaps a native woman, at that.

"I'm concerned about the needs of my husband and our innocent men."

"Innocent? Pah," he barks in a monotone without looking up.

"The court will decide." My voice sounds strangled. "Instead of transporting so many men, why not hold the trial here next spring and bring a judge from Montréal?"

He looks up again now, his eyes angry. "You dare tell me how to do my job? Crown magistrates in Montréal should not be inconvenienced by distant troublemakers. We will make such an example of these men, it will discourage other uprisings before they happen." He drops his gaze and shuffles papers, a sign that our interview is over.

I do not budge. "May the families bring our accused men more clothing and food before their long journey?"

"No." His nose is as pointy as John describes—like a mole or fox. He doesn't wear his plumed hat now. His mouse brown hair hangs lank on both sides because he is bald on top. No wonder he wears his impressive hat so constantly—even at the table. I will tell John when next I see him and we will laugh together. "The fifteen prisoners are the guests of the crown. Their welfare is our concern."

I am a child again seeing Pond *accidentally* shoot musket balls into Father's thigh. Maybe Aubergine and the others are right. It would be satisfying to restrain and pummel this narrow-eyed fox and teach him the price of injustice. But then when I least want to listen, inside my head I hear John's voice reciting a reminder from God's Holy Book, "Ye have heard that it hath been said, An eye for an eye, and a tooth for a tooth: But I say unto you, That ye resist not evil"—

Lord, this is so hard.

My hands twist. "Please reconsider," I tell this vexing man.

"The matter is closed. Leave so I may work."

"May you fulfill your duty as God wishes you to." My long skirt flounces as I go.

Despite Selkirk's effort to keep our men's departure secret, one of Aubergine's friends overhears the plan. At daybreak two mornings after my meeting with him, our men are led to canoes at the cold lake's edge. The men's families line the way. We softly call our loved ones' names with our hands outstretched, yet we may not touch. We also speak encouragement to the six Métis here without loved ones. Bluecoats stand in place at intervals to keep us distant, their flintlocks or muskets ready, as rattling drumbeats set a quick pace for our men's march to the canoes. They are not handcuffed now, but a stout cord wraps around their waists and links them together—a leather cord I am angry enough to bite in two with one snap of my jaws, like I once saw a wolf do to win freedom from a snare.

And then John is abreast. Our eyes meet in embrace. His lips curve upward and his face is confident, a man at peace. But I also see exhaustion. My breast aches to hold him close, even now to cry out for uprising so those here whisk our prisoners away. But I am John's wife and will do him honor. I uphold his decision to trust the Lord, although fear strangles my heart.

Please, Lord. Give us mercy.

John mouths, "I love you," which I return.

After one fleeting smile, I watch as he and the others trudge past to the shore of this vast lake that stretches beyond the horizon to a world in eastern Canada I cannot imagine. Three canoes await. Two carry various fur bales and trade bundles and several soldiers. Our prisoners and two soldiers are ordered into the third canoe. It is so overloaded it already begins taking on water as they shift. Selkirk is inhumane to subject our men to travel in such hazardous conditions.

Alex MacKay went far west to build a fortune and rode a ship destroyed by men, not water. May God protect John and his men on this poorly equipped journey. My heart thinks of Jesus asleep on another storm-tossed lake, the boat filling with water. Of that Galilee storm, my John often says, "What God did then, He can do any time." The thought brings comfort.

Paddles enter the water as rowers call out cadence, and the skirl of bagpipes on shore mark their departure. Selkirk instructs the pipers to play, "God Save the King," which they do once, but quickly turn to "Amazing Grace." My heart soars as that hymn's message joins our prayers in committing loved ones to God. Selkirk stands in full regalia, his hat plume waving and his dress sword shiny. When we sing "Amazing Grace," he frowns but stays silent.

We watch until canoes and men become small specks near the horizon. This morning's sky is gauzy blue, though dark clouds rim its northern edge. After the canoes depart, I despair that we can have no news of our men until spring comes and ice melts. My heart reels at how long it will be until I see John again. Or if I will see him again in this life.

Dear Lord, have mercy on me and my children!

Chapter 20

Thrashing and wrestling through this terrible night, I don't expect to sleep at all with John gone, but in that blackest period before dawn, I sink into exhaustion. Tangled in our sheets, arms embracing his pillow, barely an hour later I squint my eyes open, unsure at first where I am or what has happened. But my clenched stomach tells me Selkirk's canoes have carried my husband and the others far away, much too late in this dangerous season.

As we gather downstairs, the children willingly sing and pray, looking at me for assurance. I'm comforted by them. "Selkirk should have accompanied them. Then he would respect our land and weather," I mutter, aware I'm not being the example I want to be.

"He'll be fine, Mama," Joseph tells me. "He's doing God's will." Joseph's face shines with all the confidence in the world.

Our Savior said a little child shall lead them, and I'm seeing the truth of those words. I breathe deep. "Yes, of course. What shall we eat for breakfast?" They're full of suggestions, so we splurge and fix pancakes plus potato patties and bacon strips. Things feel more cheerful with our bellies full.

Our day staggers on. I keep John with us by talking of him constantly. Some memories bring laughter, such as the evening when he explained how American colonists criticized England's king by tucking insults inside nursery rhymes. "Humpty Dumpty" describes the king's brain getting so scrambled by a blood disease he couldn't rule or answer letters. That illness contributed to the war.

I share another rhyme which teases about the ragtag Colonial army opposing George III but winning. The children recite it with me.

> Georgie Porgie, pudding and pie,
> Kissed the girls and made them cry.
> When the boys came out to play,
> Georgie Porgie ran away.

I think but do not say that I might run away too. Or maybe I will fashion a rhyme about pompous Selkirk and his tall hat to make John laugh when he returns. I plot a rhyme while also beginning the task I'd postponed for too long—first dusting the logs in this main room and then rubbing rendered bear tallow into them until they gleam and shine. The girls and I roll up our sleeves and each attack a wall.

With a glint in her eye, my Nancy says, "Do you know Lord Selkirk's full name is Thomas Douglas, Fifth Earl of Selkirk?"

"I do," I reply. What a mouthful. "He'd hoped to help penniless Scots who'd lost farms in their country by getting them land here, except they didn't know our climate and nearly froze to death. The trouble is, he hadn't researched to see whose land it was or who was using it. He had no right to give it to anyone."

Marie props her chin in her hand, smearing a little bear fat on her face. "Let Aubergine and the others send him to lands far west where he can be king and leave us alone. But where?"

"Perhaps along the river that Father said flows north to the Arctic," Nancy answers. "That could be a good experience. And in canoes as unreliable as those he gave our men."

No wonder John says Nancy could fight in an empty room. I can't avoid smiling. "That sounds fair."

We laugh and rub harder.

I send Nancy a questioning look. "Where do you get your liveliness, girl? Not from me. Your tongue is sharper than mine."

She drops one hand to her hip and raises an eyebrow. "Don't be sure, Mother. It's not from Alex MacKay, because he's been gone so long." Now her dimples flash. "You've shaped me most."

"I'm bewildered." My cheeks burn. "Your fire is from me?"

"You doubt it? Although John gentles you now."

I shake my head. "Thank God for that. What will Captain McCargo do if you two ever disagree on board his ship?"

She stops rubbing again and turns. Her smile could melt stone. "Why, I will be so sweet that we always agree. He's ten years older and says he's waited forever to find someone as lovely and lively as me." She twirls then, cloth in hand, like the belle of a ball. "But I suppose, if I give him too much trouble, he can tow me in a dinghy behind."

"I can picture that. I've heard of such things."

Joseph comes in from stacking firewood and hears the exchange. He points fingers at Nancy and guffaws.

"You'd best not laugh too hard," she warns, "or I may cut too close the next time I cut your hair and nip your ears." That's no idle threat. She's done it by accident before.

I giggle. "A lovely, lively bride. Towing you behind might be fitting. I agree he could not find your equal anywhere in Canada."

"Or beyond. He says he has crossed oceans and found no one as sweet and fascinating as me." She flutters her eyelashes.

I shake my head. "May the Lord have mercy. Is he impressed with your humility too? Have you put a spell on the man? I hope he knows what he's getting in a bride. You'll likely lead him a merry chase."

I turn to my sons. "Be wise when you marry, boys. Get a gentle, kind, hardworking woman."

"Nancy's so pretty, that's part of her charm," Joseph says. "But if we ever leave you, Mother, our wives will have to be as pretty as you and as good a cook."

Joseph hardly knows what he's said that strikes us funny, but we laugh so hard, he and his brothers look at us like we're soft-headed.

The log walls now shine. Even the few sunshine rays that enter our living room this increasingly cloudy day are multiplied and add brightness. I step back to admire our results.

"I will lead my captain a merry chase," Nancy declares, "but a happy one so he never looks elsewhere." She steps to the door. "The weather is worsening. It's more dreary than nice with a cold wind. Would this be a good afternoon to remain inside and sew dresses for my wedding trousseau? I want everything ready when Robert drops anchor next spring."

"Yes, it's a perfect day for that." My heart cheers. "By some miracle, when your beloved arrives, I pray that John and every man arrested is on the vessel with him."

Nancy's sudden hug conveys sweetness and spice. She is a fresh-baked tart stuffed with sweet and sour red cherries at the same time. "We agree, Mother."

• • •

Already twelve days have passed. No additional soldiers have crossed the lake. We doubt Selkirk has received word from outside sources. It's terrible not having news of John or giving him ours. I see no way to write until an Indian hunter traveling from the west enters the fort. He says he will deliver a message for me, so I sit down and write.

> Dearest Love,
> It has been twelve days since your departure, and never has time passed more slowly. Heaven's clock has stopped or drastically paused. The same sun, moon, and stars shine over us both, yet we can't see you. We constantly commit you and the others to God's care and pray for you. It's hard knowing we may have no news of you before spring.

Seeing me struggle with this quill to print my best words, Marie writes my words in her beautiful script except for the personal intimate words I add at the end.

> We're doing well despite this strange world ruled by Selkirk. Working hard keeps us sane. Come home quickly. I plan to make our home spotlessly clean and

shining. Our David is thrilled to see three pumpkins turning orange in our yard. I still wish we could raise baby goats. Please consider that after you're home. When that day comes, we'll find a way to keep them out of our vegetables and help them avoid the soup pot.

Nancy works on her trousseau and moons over McCargo. Marie does wonderful work in the dispensary and delights me by compounding new medicines from fresh plants and herbs more creatively than I. She has a gift and illustrates descriptions of medical herbs as well.

I ask God to help the court hear your true account to save you and our men. We uphold you all at each meal and always before bed. Truly, I pen these misshapen closing words in my own hand. My love embraces you. I hold you close to this heart that beats in unison with yours. Thank you for loving me as I do you with all my heart.

Your loving, longing, faithful Marguerite.

I roll my letter in a thin piece of deerskin with John's name outside. Running Wolf is a lean leathery man who thinks he will overtake John and the others. I have more faith in him finding John than in mail passing through Company channel.

He tucks my thin roll inside his fringed buckskin shirt under a thicker hide. "My feet search the wind," he says, lifting a hand in farewell.

Running Wolf is well-named. When he leaves, his moccasin protected feet skim the snow and dart between shadows until there's hardly a sign he's been with us.

Our dreary days are unremarkable. To pass them well, beyond ordinary tasks, we start special projects to fill the time. After rendering excellent bear fat for baking, I have enough extra tallow for candles and decide to teach Catherine to make them. She's happy to be my main big-girl helper for this task and does a fine job.

God or the devil makes Selkirk a little more tolerable, for he develops painful boils and comes to me for treatment. I'm sure he regrets sending John away now that he needs a trained doctor. The boils on his posterior make it hard for him to sit. Marie helps me drape him professionally for privacy, but he is mortified. He doesn't know how he got his affliction. I've heard John mention infected blood. Aubergine calls it God's judgment.

Nancy does her part amazingly well, tongue

tight in her cheek to keep from blurting angry words. She wields a sterilized knife to lance and bandage the lesions without the blade stabbing deeper than it should—though I am sure she is tempted. After, she asks about his pain, she gives St. John's Wort and Valerian root to calm anxiety and bring sleep. I hope they will improve his temperament.

Gentle Marie hates to see anyone suffer, so she makes poultices for him. If she doesn't accept Donald's marriage offer, I picture her becoming a kind teacher, or perhaps a nun because only their schools provide advanced education.

When we finish, Selkirk seems docile and mumbles thanks. Later, his aide brings a quarter of fresh venison plus a basket of salted fish, which made us think kindlier of him.

Despite his harshness toward people, once the girls and I treat his tormenting boils, he sends more patients our way. I believe he begins to regret his actions. He mentions that his acts were simply to support Hudson's Bay's claims for disputed areas. He always includes food or household items as gifts and usually asks about John. Does he not know that we can't receive news of John without it passing through Selkirk first?

A Monday in early November promises more sun and warmth than usual, so I'm inspired to give our quilts and bedding their last wash before winter sets in. Marie supervises Catherine making more candles while Joseph watches the younger boys in our yard. Nancy and I haul our large copper kettle to the front porch, and we are heating water when Selkirk's aide approaches. He carries what we think is a haunch of meat or bundled furs. Then it stirs, and he puts it down in a hurry.

"*Gott in Himmel*!" he blurts in German-Swiss and steps back. "Lord Selkirk said to bring you this. If it lives, he will pay for its care."

That piques our interest. The bundle moves again and rolls a ways along our porch. As Nancy and I stare, the aide tips his hat and scurries away. When I gently poke the bundle with my wooden laundry spoon, the fur pooches out in that spot, as if something inside responds.

"How strange." We bend down for a closer look.

By now, Joseph is interested. He always carries the fine folding knife John gave him. He cuts the cords, and the bindings fall away. The fur coverings separate, and a filthy form springs free and uncurls itself.

"*Splait*?" An unearthly screech and hideous smell push us back. I would have been less surprised if a demon from hell had sprung among us.

Joseph closes his knife and gags. Nancy lifts a cloth to her nose and asks, "What is it?"

"I can't tell yet."

"*Splait*?" the thing croaks again as if asking a question. I advance and peer to see if it is a shaggy dog or bear cub, but then recognize a human child of perhaps four or five years unwinding its limbs to stand teetering before us. Black eyes peer through matted dark hair. The buckskin rag covering its bony body has tears revealing skin the same dark color as the buckskin. I start to count ribs, but the overpowering stench forces me back.

When I make myself step close again, the child dodges and grips its soiled fur tighter around itself. I look for welts or infection but only see caked excrement. Whether the child is a boy or girl, I cannot tell. Its fingers and toes resemble curved claws with broken nails. It rocks on all fours, and again says, "*Splait*?"

Suddenly Joseph gasps. "I remember. That's how they talk where I used to live." His eyes water as he steps near. He resembles John most when his noble brow frowns to understand something. How I love this bonus son. "*Splait*?" Joseph repeats.

The thing's mouth spills garbled sounds.

"It's mongrel Métis French, Mama," Joseph explains, "with Indian words mixed in. I think it's saying *s'il vous plaît* and *eau* and *pain—please, water,* and *bread*. May we give it some?"

"Of course." I signal Nancy, and she dashes off. I offer the child a cup of water from our barrel.

The poor thing guzzles instantly. Drips streak clean paths through the dirt and grime coating its cheeks and chin. It noisily drains a second cup, and then a third.

Nancy brings a basin of water and towels with the bread. We let the child eat, then I gingerly draw the child into the water and splash its limbs in a game. The child gurgles and finally laughs.

I brush its filthy hair aside and rinse crust from its eyes. The child calms enough for me to peel away the buckskin rag and cleanse its body. She is a girl. After changing the water several times, I gently wrap the tiny thing in a towel. By now Marie and Catherine have joined us. Catherine brings more bread, which the girl snatches and devours like a dog tearing meat.

I send Joseph to ask Lord Selkirk's aide to return. He crosses our rectangle asking, "Have you called me to claim a corpse?"

"Not at all," I say a bit too loudly, not understanding how anyone can give up so quickly on a living being. When I partially lift the towels draping the girl, he seems startled to see a human child eating bread.

"*Gott in Himmel*," he says, "it lives. How is this possible? You have done wonders."

"It's a beginning." I tuck the towel around the child's shoulders. "What does Lord Selkirk want done with her?"

"I don't know. I doubt he expected it to live."

On examining the little one more closely, instead of curved claws, I find short, discolored fingers and toes, actually stunted, making it difficult and probably painful for her to use them. My heart aches to know what John would advise. I'd never seen such an extreme condition when he and I treated patients together.

When Joseph rattles off more mongrel French, the child waves seven fingers. "She thinks she is age seven," he says.

"Impossible," I say quietly, since she is so small. I turn to Selkirk's aide. "Where did you find her?"

He shrugs. "Somewhere far away. We're not exactly sure."

"Share what you know." I give the girl a cup of milk, and she gulps it too.

He peers across the open quadrangle as if he wishes to escape. "Her father may be a trapper gone for long periods." He points west. "Others say he may be among those arrested and sent east to trial—we're not sure."

"What? How can you not know?" If I were a man, I would have struck him. Instead, I glare so fiercely, he steps back.

"She came from a cabin on land belonging to Pierre Pelletier, which means *pelter* or *trapper*. But there are many with that same name. There is a Pierre Pelletier among those arrested and transported to Montréal, so that connection is possible. The wilderness cabin is remote. Someone passing by discovered the child by accident. If they had not found her, well, she wouldn't be alive."

"Why wasn't more done the instant she was found?"

"The man finding her was busy gathering gold dust and furs. When he found a stinking human mess, he wrapped it in pelts and figured God would decide if it lived or died. He brought it to us along with his furs, but left quickly, saying nothing. Our workers failed to notice that one bundle held more than pelts. At first they believed the life inside beyond help. Selkirk said bring it to you."

"Surely, more is known."

He spreads his hands open. "Very little. This part may not be dependable. Rumor says the child's mother died years ago from a pox, so the grandmother cared for the child but died recently."

Whether the child before us understands us or not, our tones must convey meaning, because tears course down her cheeks. She and Joseph exchange more garbled sounds. When she lifts her hands like two birds in flight, I see her stunted, terribly deformed fingers more clearly. Something dreadful has happened to this child.

"*Frostbeule*, frostbite," the aide confirms, indicating her mottled skin and stubbed deformities.

"If the rumor is true, when the grandmother died, the cabin fire went out. Since the father was away, this helpless thing—"

"This child!" I correct.

"This child probably entered the woods to gather firewood, except a blizzard overtook her and froze her hands and feet. It's a wonder she lives." He removes his cap and wipes his brow. "The rest is so fantastic, you'll think me mad."

"Let me decide."

"The man says he found her in a cave or den guarded by, how do you call it, *a lion of the mountains?*"

"A mountain lion," Nancy answers, eyes bright. "They're also called cougars—big cats."

"*Chat*," the child echoes with liveliness. "*Le gros chat*!"

When Joseph speaks more guttural words, the girl curls into a ball with her head tucked in tight.

"What does she say now?" I ask.

"It's sad." Joseph keeps his eyes on her. "During a storm, after frost had damaged her hands and feet, she entered a den and slept. A big cat came in from outside."

"*Le gros chat*," she repeats, her eyes happier now.

"At first, she thought the cat would eat her, but instead it fed her scraps of meat and warmed her. It guarded her many days until a man arrived. He saw the cat near the den and killed it for its fur, not knowing it guarded a life."

The aide interrupts. "When we told Lord Selkirk the bundle held something alive, he said bring it to you, that you would know what could be done. He will pay the costs."

I stare at him in surprise. "Costs? This is a child's life."

"We didn't know it was even human, Madame," the aide insists.

I give a withering look. "Anything alive needs care." I cross my arms and look at him with disdain, and he hurries away. I turn and gather the child into my arms.

My heart aches as I imagine living alone in the wilderness, mothered by a wild cat. Almost like Daniel in the lions' den. The wild animals couldn't eat him but consumed the bad men who put him there. I'm having a hard time not wishing that animals in our forests would come do the same to whoever found this child but neglected her. She's clearly a miracle. She deserves a special name to match and it can't wait for John's return.

The name Evangeline springs to my heart. That's what I will call her, Evangeline. My girls approve. I tap the girl's chest and repeat, "Evangeline." Then I turn and point to each of my children and speak their names. She says them a little more clearly each time and, finally, when I tap her chest again, she smiles and says what we can tell is her name. Then she points to me with a quizzical look.

"Me? Mama," I say thumping my chest above my heart. "Mama," I repeat.

She rests her head on my chest and murmurs something close to *Mama*.

I hold her tight and burst into tears.

Chapter 21

Fort William on Lake Superior, late November, 1816

Our instincts warn us to stay distant from Selkirk's mercenaries, but during the times we must interact they become fellow human beings far from home also sharing the hardships of our situation. When they chatter German phrases back and forth, my face must show a flicker of recognition for one of them suddenly sees I understand.

"*Sprechen sie Deutsch*?" Selkirk's top aide asks after conversing with his partner, already sure of my answer.

I confess that I speak and understand my Swiss father's tongue. "*Ja*, *Schwiiz*," one says, giving their name for the country. Afterward, the troops show greater kindness to the children and me, even more when I bake and serve a rich apple strudel made from dried fruit they provide, like the kind they love back home. They are homesick.

Despite long periods of cold, with our loved ones gone, even commanded by a hostile officer and foreign troops, we still find mercies. One is that because Selkirk is Scottish and does not speak German-Swiss, his troops update me with news of John and the others before Selkirk hears. But we do not get word often. The mercenaries are as restless as us for word of the prisoner brigade that left here so late in the season. Their faces scan the weather and frown.

Another mercy that cheers us all is that, although Evangeline is so undersized, she responds to care like a tender flower bursting open in springtime. Sometimes, in her sleep, she shrieks cat-like, frightening us to death. But when she awakes, she is again gentle and places her soft cheek against Joseph's or mine or rests her ear against our hearts to hear each thump.

When she first came, she knew few English words, but she now mimics our speech and learns quickly. She beams when we understand her, and her joy brightens our days. All in the fort are charmed by her progress and say they wish she belonged to them, despite the care required, but she is ours!

Marie records the story of Evangeline's coming in our family journal, and we share it with newcomers to the fort. Today that includes one of Selkirk's soldiers. This child's arrival is as much a miracle as the Bible's story of the slave girl who pointed her Syrian commander captor to Israel's God for healing from leprosy. Everyone who sees this girl wants to help.

"How can we help her suffering hands

and feet?" Marie asks this afternoon while Evangeline rests. We search John's clinic shelves for frostbite cures, but we find nothing helpful. I focus to recall the natural remedies Mother made to soothe skin rashes, burns, or frostbite, and ask God to help me find the ingredients. "One is mullein," I tell Marie, "the plant with soft, velvety, gray-green leaves and spikes of yellow flowers."

"I know where that grows and think we have some dried." She finds a supply among stored leaves in the attic above John's dispensary. "How do we prepare it? Soak the leaves and make a poultice for Evangeline's injured toes and fingers?"

"Let me think. Mother made a salve to coat the skin." I wrinkle my forehead, reaching back in time to picture her doing it. Using John's stone mortar and pestle, I crush the dry leaves into powder and add sunflower oil until it is a paste. We spread it on Evangeline's damaged skin.

"This is like what Mother used in Athabasca when I needed care," I tell Marie, my memory recalling the day I foolishly froze my fingertips by taking off my mittens in bitter weather to fashion a doll from twigs while playing outside.

On John's shelves, I find medical notes written in his beautiful hand. After years of marriage, I can read most things he writes. I show the pages to Marie. "Look. He describes another treatment.

The horsetail rushes we eat when young and tender in spring are rich in a compound that renews skin. Do you think we have any rushes left?"

Her face glows. "That's what we use when they are coarse and mature to scour copper pots to a high shine. I'm sure there are some in the attic." She finds and brings them.

We create ointments of both remedies and apply them liberally. We are not scientific enough to evaluate them over time to compare the results. Instead, we eagerly slather on both treatments. They smell so wonderful, Evangeline licks the ointments until we distract her by giving her instead the boiled peppermint lozenges we made last summer for sore throats. Her eyes widen with delight as she greedily sucks their strong flavor.

Marie and I spread more ointment on her hands and feet and tell her it must stay on. We fashion small mitts and booties from boiled wool to cover her skin while the ointments work. Miraculously, Evangeline cooperates—I think because she sees how much love we add to the process.

Despite our limited knowledge, the skin on her fingers and toes improves. They remain stubbed and discolored, but when she removes her mitts and booties to eat or play, the skin is smoother with greater flexibility. She smiles like a happy chipmunk.

The German-Swiss soldiers notice, too, and ask if they may try my ointments, for they also suffer frostbite and chilblains in this region harsher than their homeland. They prefer the horsetail ointment to the mullein, which is good, because we have much more of it. Even so, we dole out small amounts to make it last until spring. If the soldiers are still here then, they promise to gather armfuls of what we need, but they hope not to be. We agree.

When temperatures drop and food is scarce because animals hide or hibernate, these soldiers bring treats to our door. They make and deliver toys for the children. Their morale is low, knowing they will celebrate Christmas far from home. Some evenings, when our family sings hymns or carols, a few men join us. We sing in English and they in German-Swiss, but together our songs are beautiful.

One morning, Selkirk arrives at our door, wearing ill-humor like a cloak. He always greets Evangeline first and then proceeds with business. "During Christmas season, we must fight discouragement and find ways to raise our spirits. I'm suggesting we participate in activities I've seen celebrated other places, but I ask you to think of more."

He mentions the *L'Ordre de Bon Temps*, Order of Good Cheer, which he says the great explorer Champlain started his first winter in New France to cheer newcomers overwhelmed by Canada's cold.

"My thoughts are similar to Champlain's," he says. "Besides good food and music, we need games and gifts for the children. Will you help?" He squints through red-rimmed eyes.

How can I not? It will be an event for everyone at the fort and beyond. He's set aside special foods for the occasion, and will provide licorice and peppermint sticks from an unknown source, plus ribbons and small mirrors for women and children. He intends to send out his best hunters for game.

I think of times when God sent moose to meet our needs. First at Sault Sainte Marie when we wintered with Peter, and again the Christmas we saved the lost family buried in snow who needed warmth to survive. "I've seen God provide," I tell Selkirk, and share both stories. "Perhaps I'll go hunting."

He laughs. "Please don't. You must stay safe, Madame. People will mutiny if anything happens to you."

I'm not sure that's true, but if he believes it, all the better.

Marie and I do not ask the state of his boils, but although he requests more of the compound we mixed for him, he seems to sit less gingerly than before.

He rises from the chair and turns toward the

door. But then he looks at Evangeline again. "You've done wonders with that child," he says. He instructs me to go to the store and choose lengths of cloth to make something special for her, plus dresses for myself and the girls and shirts for our boys. He wrinkles his forehead. "There is much wrong in this world, Madame. Perhaps we can set a few things right."

I consider if there is a blessing or provision I might ask for Evangeline, since he would surely give it, but I won't speak without a clear word.

He shifts from foot to foot. "We will make Christmas nice, something special to brighten these dark, dreary days."

"Thank you, that is kind, but even nice gifts can't erase heartache. We must pray for each other since so many families suffer this season. We must ask the Christ child, the best gift, to change hearts." I don't know if he is a man of faith or not, but he reddens and turns away when I mention prayer.

As he secures his cloak tighter, I study his thin neck with rather unchristian thoughts. It is good my years have mellowed me so I am not a woman of violence. I confess my heart heats and then turns to ice at his words. Does he not realize the great pain he caused so many when he sent our men away? Yet he looks so downcast, the Lord makes me merciful.

I say, "Lord Selkirk, God alone can provide the strength to survive these days."

Three nights later, two soldiers come to our door and tell us that two new witnesses of the Red River Massacre have come forward after hearing that John volunteered to stand trial with the accused. John's sacrifice made them bold to speak the truth, although they expect to be punished. "If the men are found guilty, they and the good doctor will hang," one says. "These witnesses do not want the death of fifteen innocent men on their conscience, so have come forward to declare the truth."

The other man speaks up. "One signed a paper and the other marked his *X*. Their reports confirm that Semple was so badly frightened, he started the unprovoked attack, firing the first shot that caused the massacre." Their information confirms that none of our men, Métis or otherwise, were near the battle area or involved in any way.

I grasp one soldier's hands. "God be praised," I say in German. "This is proof Montréal can't ignore if word can reach there in time."

"We will see to it, Madame. The signed testimonies have been sent by a fast courier."

"Even so, everything takes time, so we will pray for God's aid."

My heart races until I can scarcely breathe. Do John and the others still travel the lake? Or do they now advance on snowshoes through frightful drifts? I pray God's protective hand on them.

After these new testimonies come to light, Selkirk's head drops low. However, having initiated such serious events by charging John and our employees with intentional massacre worthy of death, I doubt he sees any way to reverse it. He comes to our house the day after the soldier's visit, requesting cough syrup for his suffering throat and wracking cough. "Fresh testimony has been given and sent," he tells me, apparently unaware that I already know. "Of course, it is false," he adds. "We must await the court verdict and due process." His cough is deep and frequent. His chest rattles.

Although Selkirk has been our strong enemy, I feel pity and give him the treatments he seeks. As he lives, I say a prayer for him. God must help him or he may not survive the winter. John would be proud of me. He never refuses anyone, even when they seem almost beyond the help of medicine or undeserving. "No mortal should make such decisions," John says.

I keenly feel my husband's absence and often hear his voice instructing me in medical care and guidance for our children. Sometimes, it seems I can reach out and touch him. At others, I despair when I can't sense him near. Then some inner eye lets me see him and the others in overloaded canoes battered by storms. I hear John warn the guards as clearly as if we speak in the privacy of our bedroom, his dear voice heavy with exhaustion. I try to draw nearer to hear more clearly, to touch and hold John, but a thick cold wall separates us. I shake off thoughts of more sleep but can't stop trembling.

Lord, I'm so afraid. Let me hear something, anything, from John.

God hears my prayer. At dusk the night after my prayer, there's a commotion when an independent hunter famous for tracking and harvesting bears shambles into our fort. This champion thrives indoors or out in summer or winter. He's grappled with so many bears, he resembles them, and people now call him *Bear*. After reaching our fort's quadrangle and greeting the men standing near the fire, the men point my way. He ambles toward us, shaggy head and arms swinging.

"Mrs. McLoughlin?"

"Yes. May I help you?"

He smiles. "No, I help you. I come from far side of giant lake. Prisoners left here too late in season."

My throat clogs. "They had no choice. Have you seen them?"

"Yes." He rests a bear-furred boot on our bottom step. "They had trouble, but your husband lives."

“Thank God.” I clasp my hands in thankful prayer.

He pulls a small, stained packet from a hidden pocket in his clothes. “From your husband. I’ve kept this safe. No official report.”

I snatch it, my fingers like claws. I dismiss our children, displeasing them. I fumble at an inner fish skin waterproof wrapping, and loose scales coat my fingers, releasing the tang of trout. A thin, rolled birch bark has John’s words written in berry juice. My shaking hands stare at his dancing words until my eyes focus. Bear waits as I read.

> Our love unites us. How hard to be led away in chains. I left my heart with you on shore. We’ve had hardship. I owe my life to Hans-Joseph, an enemy soldier who I can never call an enemy again. Pray we reach Montréal safely and win trial. Please keep this in confidence. I longed to greet you. My words embrace you and our children. Reward Bear.
>
> All my love, John

Blinking back tears, I stroke the bark’s surface. My fingers trace John’s berry juice letters, inhale the earthiness of this thin surface his hands have held. And then I roll the bark back into a thin scroll and lower it down the neck of my dress to hang between my breasts. His message is short and says little, but anything from him is precious.

I rest my hand on Bear's burly arm. It is twice the size of mine. "Thank you."

He inclines his shaggy head and thick neck. "Your husband—good man. I nearly died when a big bear tore me open. Your husband had my guts on a platter and put them back inside fine. I'm strong again." He flexes one arm, inclines his massive head again, and turns to leave.

"Wait. I'll give you food for your journey."

"No. I find or hibernate." In his shuffling gait, he crosses the quadrangle, quickly reaches the fort's far side, and disappears into the night.

My heart pounds. "Lord, what just happened? I needed word, and You brought it. There's been trouble, but John lives." I lower my face into my hands and weep.

Chapter 22

When I enter the cabin, my older children pressure me to know what Bear told me. Nancy says, "We know it regards Father from the look on your face."

I say nothing except it describes hardships but John lives. "I'm sorry I can't share more until Selkirk has an official report, but Father mostly sends his love. Our prayers are being answered. We must continue. Especially pray the eye-witness accounts arrive in time."

Nancy is more subdued than usual. "Yes, Mother. We'll pray until they're home."

I commit John to God's care every waking moment and wish for more of Mother's gift of seeing and hearing more than is easily known. Like her, I sometimes hear distant conversations as if I am present when I am not. I long for greater ability to support John in all ways through this agony.

Yet despite the message's encouragement, that night, I suffer nightmares beyond any I've known. I pray for strength and encouragement. And in the morning, Joseph, eyes shining, comes to me with eyes shining.

"Mother, a white-headed eagle is nesting in the tallest tree past the upstairs window. The other birds have migrated, but this king came now and built a nest." Joseph juts his chin the eagle's direction. "What does it mean?"

"Show me," I say.

He leads me outside to the tree, and the others follow. Even crippled Evangeline half scoots and half flies alongside us.

Joseph is right. Though late in the season with all other birds gone, this eagle builds its nest now. In our presence, it dives, snatches, and carries a large fish from the lake to its nest as we watch. Evangeline lies on the ground below, staring up at the nest. Her face shines with energy and light as if she too might rise and soar. She makes soft croonings in her throat, and the eagle regards her without blinking.

Goosebumps pebble my skin. *Dear Lord, what gifts have you given this child? Is she an angel from you?* John will love her.

The next day, a late storm washes dead fish ashore. We stand on our porch and observe our eagle coming to feast. Then ravens swoop in, diving to peck his head and eyes.

"Mother, help!" Joseph shouts.

The children and I rush closer, whooping, and we pelt the attackers with stones. Our eagle utters shrill cries and spreads his wings, diving at the ravens himself until he drives them far away over the lake. We stand in awe. He didn't need our help at all.

When he alone enjoys the fish again, Evangeline throws back her head and releases the triumphant howl of a wolf pack leader, making all other sounds cease. Will I ever know all that she has suffered during her life in the woods?

My heart believes that somehow this eagle parallels John's struggle. If I compare my husband with any winged creature, it is with this noblest of birds. "You are like him," I tell the majestic creature. Then it preens, opens its wings, and soars high until it is a mere dot in the sky.

"May you and John fly high and live long," I say, wiping my cheeks as chills prickle my skin. Eagles matter to Mother's people, too, so this unexpected presence cheers me. I pray my recent dreams of more monstrous storms and lives lost are untrue. Are my fears from Alex's days? Or do new dangers surround John?

The days are colder, and we busy ourselves preparing for Christmas. We make spiced cider with cinnamon sticks, ration the rum which warms the soldiers as they stomp their rounds, and brew Rosehip and spruce needle teas to defeat scurvy. I visit Selkirk's office and ask, "Who will be Santa?" I cannot picture him performing that role.

"I am too thin." He points to the fine military clothes hanging from his frame. "Aubergine has agreed to preside."

"A very suitable choice." Yet I wonder if that

renegade can bring Christmas cheer without starting a revolution.

"Don't worry," Aubergine says later when I ask about it. "As much as I'd love to create trouble, I'll honor the season. Selkirk has a sack of gifts I'm to distribute, but I shall choose his." His smile is wolfish.

"Will it be coal in his stocking? A switch in his shoe? Or a whip for his backside?" I ask.

"Ha-ha. I'll think of something worse."

"You wouldn't dare."

"Do you doubt?" But his happy smile somewhat assures me. "This time, I'll be a cooperative Christian harboring pagan thoughts," he says. "All the same, they say a priest will come this way to take confessions, so I'll behave. If anything happens to me, I want to be buried in sanctioned ground inside the stockade—not outside with the heathen. Remember that, Marguerite." He makes the sign of the cross as he speaks of sanctioned ground.

"You're not leaving this world anytime soon, Aubergine, but you say a priest is coming?"

Monsieur Eggplant nods. "Yes. He accompanies his brother, a Company surveyor. They suggest possible new Company sites and future mission stations."

"Tremendous. Is Selkirk Catholic?"

"No." He shakes his head. "Scots Presbyterian. But after the Red River Massacre, welcoming any churchman may be an olive branch to calm uneasy souls."

I study his jolly face. "Do you think Selkirk's soul can settle?"

His eyes sparkle. "That's unclear. My men and I are divided but taking bets."

"If Selkirk has requested this Christmas celebration," I say, "he may show some ability to govern after all. But turn around, Aubergine. There's a tear in your jacket that needs mending. Leave it here. I'll fix it by morning."

"I will not." He sputters and turns eggplant purple, hugging his coat tight to him. "I'm usually tattered. What will people think if I appear neat and tidy?"

"They'll think what they want, mostly that people help each other in this hard land."

"Well, if you insist." He shrugs out of his coat.

My thoughts fly. "Do you think the priest will perform weddings when he's here?"

"With a priest available, some couples will probably drop wilderness contracts to have church-blessed marriages."

"I don't blame them." My sigh reaches my toes. "If only John were here." My heart longs for our vows to be blessed by a clergyman of any faith. I'm happy Marie and Nancy's suitors haven't claimed them yet, for with John away, I'd like to have my daughters home with me a while longer. When their wedding times come, I wish them both to be church blessed. I believe sanctioned beginnings make strong marriage unions, no matter what events come to this wild region.

Instead of brooding after Aubergine scurries away, I think more about Selkirk wanting these to be days of cheer and cheerful distractions. I think of Peter Arndt's delicious, flamed puddings, and I request ingredients. Selkirk offers me dried apples and raisins, and when a bear unwisely strays from its den, I drop him with one shot. I turn him into a fur rug as well as roasts, rendered lard for pies and cakes, delicious mincemeat, and tallow for soap and candles.

The next time I see Aubergine, he looks more like a northern Eskimo than any Santa. He wears rich furs with the fur turned inward and stitched into a handsome parka. His bushy beard and eyebrows are frosted white like Father Christmas, and a team of yapping husky dogs pulls his large, decorated sled that races through our gate into the fort's quadrangle. Half of the fort's inhabitants come out to witness this exciting arrival.

He sees me and waves, scattering snow as he swishes to a stop. "I bring you a brother and his brother."

"What do you mean?"

His grin is pure mischief. "I bring you a priest and his brother. Will that satisfy you?"

Two well-bundled lumps on the sled throw aside blankets and escape imprisonment. "*Merci*,

Mon Dieu," the black robed one cries. Both men beat their hands for warmth and stomp their feet to restore circulation.

Aubergine introduces our guests. "*Mesdames et Monsieurs*, meet Father Mathieu and his brother, Claude Gauthier, a fellow North West employee." Aubergine waves me forward. "Gauthier, Father Mathieu? This is Doctor John McLoughlin's wife, Marguerite."

"A pleasure, Madame." Gauthier has the weathered look of an experienced Company man. He will know Father's voyageur songs and Alex's woodland skills. He bows from the waist.

His brother, the priest, closes the distance and takes my hand, bending over it as if in prayer. "*Enchantée*, Madame. My prayers have remained with you since I heard of the travesty against your husband and the other men. It is God's marvel so many survived after the cruel accident and drownings on their journey. May God help them complete their mission and return."

"Drownings?" I've had the short birch bark note from John but had no idea it was that serious. I thought perhaps John suffered from cold and a soldier helped him. Those around me are struck dumb.

"Accident?" one wife says. "Explain. You took twenty men east and we've had no report. How are they? Is their number less?"

Thankful at least to know John lives, the earth

still shifts beneath my feet. When I wobble, Gauthier grasps my arm to steady me.

"Madame, though your husband is terribly wounded, he lives." He says more, but an inner noisy clacking horde of ravens rises from some hidden dark place to dive bomb my head and pierce my breast. Evil conspires to destroy me and our other families here. I would fall except Aubergine also darts in and supports me.

"Speak, man." Aubergine's eyes glitter, and he leans forward with his other hand clenched as if he might strike the priest. "In God's name, what do you know? If there has been tragedy, tell everything before we go mad."

His shouts and threatening gesture revives my senses and drives the ravens away. "You must not, Aubergine. God alone will help us survive what we must and avenge our men." But I still clutch his arm.

The black robed man crosses himself. In the next moments, he and his brother share the awful truth of the terrible late autumn storm on Lake Superior that swamped all three canoes and drowned Métis, whites, and several Iroquois paddlers on the ill-fated trip to Montréal. At first, the priest and his brother can't agree on the names of the dead, living, or injured. They are mixed up. Some men's names appear on both lists. Neither do the Gauthiers know how seriously hurt the injured are.

"Think, men," Aubergine shouts, his face darkening like someone suffering apoplexy. I restrain him lest he strikes the churchman.

The two brothers confer in quiet tones. Finally, they agree on most names of the lost but not all. There were eight lost. Moans and wails rise from the crowd.

"McLoughlin lives but is greatly changed," Gauthier insists.

"In what way?" My voice breaks. "Have you seen him? Were you there?"

"No. But I survey Company sites and met soldier guards who helped recover the dead. They came seeking replacement canoes and told the tragedy. They described your husband."

"And said what?"

"His icy ordeal so shocked his body, his hair instantly turned snowy white like an eagle's. Men now call him the *white-headed eagle*."

"The white-headed . . . ?" My voice breaks.

My children have gathered around us in a tight knot. Eyes wide, even Evangeline seems to understand something is terribly wrong. Sucking her damaged fingers, she makes soft crooning noises in the back of her throat and rocks back and forth.

Joseph's gaze meets mine. "Our bird, Mama."

Selkirk rushes forward so fast he stumbles. The men repeat their report, and Selkirk stands at grim attention, as if hearing the shocking details of these deaths grieves him personally. I have no wish to defend him. My heart is stone. I reach my arms around my children to pull them close, though in truth, their young strong bodies hold me up.

"How many again?" Selkirk demands.

Father Mathieu says, "May God be praised, it was not more than eight, although losing any is heartbreak."

"Although many are weak and ill, they may have reached Montréal by now," Gauthier says. "We pray the trial begins soon and reaches a clear court verdict."

Lord Selkirk frowns. "There is only one right way for things to end. When the men are judged guilty and hung, drowning may seem more merciful."

Those standing near give sharp gasps. Fists clench. Several strong men advance on Selkirk, who moves away from the crowd and closer to his bodyguards. He buttons his uniform jacket more snugly around his neck and rests a trembling hand on the hilt of his dress sword. "Surely you understand what I mean."

"We understand you, all right," says one accused man's son, snarling. Dark looks and growling murmurs seem to impact Selkirk as much as if he is pelted with stones. His lips tighten, but now he keeps them closed.

"Merciful God." I can find no other words.

Gauthier and his brother look at Selkirk as if they have reported well and expect reward. He ignores them and points to the fort buildings. "Aubergine? Find them lodging."

"Oui, Monsieur."

"I'm a Scot. Speak English to me." His frowning gaze moves to the dogs. "Why, those animals are superb. Give them shelter and food. I have use for them." As the sled pulls forward, Selkirk slumps and says to no one in particular, "When will this cursed trial end? When will life be good again?"

When no one answers, he turns to me. "I am sorry John suffers, Marguerite, but thankful he lives." He searches the leaden sky as if it holds a scroll containing answers and then again scans my face. "You will still help make us a special *joyeux Noël*—won't you?"

"I—I'll do my best." I give a feeble curtsy.

"Your best will be more than enough."

One of his shiny boots kicks a frozen dirt clod far as he still holds his brooding eyes on mine. "I did not wish to cause harm—only to discharge my duties as I understood them. Please don't be formal with me when we speak privately. I count you a friend to whom I'm indebted."

"Of course, sir."

"Thomas. My Christian name is Thomas." He

pushes his tall heavy hat more firmly in place and retreats to his residence.

So is my son's in Oregon I say to myself as Selkirk strides away.

Chapter 23

Winter solidifies our world to iron while Fort William and our whole region quakes with the unthinkable news of eight lives lost. We discuss the names of those believed lost and guess who remains, glancing at each other hopefully. We pray our remaining men have now reached Montréal, but we have no word. Perhaps they've already been tried and set free to return home.

Meanwhile, our family checks the white-headed eagle's nest daily. Will he stay or leave for a very late migration like all other birds have? I don't tell the children I think John's life parallels our eagle. However, when they hear that John's hair is now pure white and that he's called by that name, they make the connection.

We ask old-time voyageurs the ways of eagles. Finally, old wise Jean, with one eye destroyed by a wolf that survived its snare and sank its teeth in him, touches his red cap. "I've long studied the ways of God's creatures. All eagles migrate, but sometimes one stays behind for a special purpose. Mature eagles fly faster than our best racing canoes can traverse rivers. They soar to dizzy heights and glide great distances. Their piercing cries are heard farther than any other bird you'll ever see."

Evangeline's dark eyes flash, and she makes plaintive sounds that pierce our souls. Her crippled hands mimic winged flight as she repeats her sharp cries again. Somewhere, somehow, this child has known eagles well.

"She is a very special child. She is what we call an old wise one." Jean taps a spot above his good eye. "Most eagles fly south to lakes and streams that stay open. I have not seen one stay behind this long, but the old natives speak of it."

Our eagle lingers until Lake Superior freezes solid with few open patches left. And then one morning he is gone, nest empty, leaving our hearts empty too. My heart pleads. Lord, *I understand many ways of nature, but not this. Don't let our eagle leaving mean bad things concerning John.*

The nest is empty for days. And then a week. Then it is almost two weeks, with fresh snow falling, when Joseph comes running home.

"Mother, our eagle is back!"

"Are you sure?"

"Yes. Come see!"

We race to the tree, rejoicing. It may be our imagination, but the mature eagle is back in the nest, looking larger and more powerful, his head whiter. He preens and calls, his noble head fixing his dark, keen eyes upon us.

"What does it mean?" Marie asks. "So majestic—help me understand."

I see this daughter is also gifted with insights

through our Indian heritage. “I’m not sure all that it means but believe having him return is encouraging.”

Joseph says, “I think I know. Minutes ago, I saw him dive three times to the same place near shore. I searched and saw a stream bubbling up in a spot that doesn’t freeze, allowing the eagle to fish.” He salutes the bird. “Besides, he knows we like him.”

“Yes, we do. Very much.” Laughter fills my heart. “Thank you, Lord, for this blessing.”

We are comforted seeing our splendid bird return. He also responds to Evangeline’s plaintive chirps.

When you come home, John, you will find more treasure waiting here for you than when you left.

There is little travel across Canada’s frozen heartland in winter. Two weeks before Christmas, one exception is a platoon of twenty German-Swiss soldiers and their lieutenant come to replace the soldiers Selkirk sent east with our prisoners. Both groups bypassed Fort York held by the British. They skirted Kingston for the same reason but crossed paths with our men near there and gained word of their journey. One replacement named Ernst-Werner is related to Hans-Joseph, the soldier who saved John. When one of the few German-Swiss here from before learns of the connection, he brings Ernst-Werner to me.

"Hans-Joseph and your husband are great friends," the tall lieutenant says. "All things considered, be assured your husband and the others are doing well."

I stare as if my look can dredge added information. "Surely you can say more."

"Your husband again proved himself a hero. They slept in a roadside inn when the chimney caught fire and ignited the roof. Your husband heard the sounds or smelled the smoke and roused warning in time to save the inn owner, his residents, and nearby homes. The only loss was twelve chickens roasted before their pen could be opened. The inn was greatly damaged, but nearby residents were so grateful, they opened their homes to the men."

"How kind." I warm with pleasure.

"In fact, my cousin's superiors are so pleased, they will commend your husband as a model prisoner in Montréal, which helps his cause."

"Thank you. Do you know how he fares physically?"

"We had little time. He has a cough and hoarse voice which could be from smoke. He wears a rag tied around his neck that smells of camphor or something."

"Poplar buds." I nod. "He remembers the remedies I taught him."

"He's an impressive leader. Don't tell Lord Selkirk, but we all hope your husband is vindicated in court."

"Thank you for that."

He steps closer and hems and haws as another soldier arrives with a basket of dried apples. "We wonder . . . That is, we hear sometimes you turn these into strudel?" His eyes shine with longing. "We would chop logs, stack firewood—anything." He turns his head as if ascertaining we are unobserved. Selkirk must not know.

I accept the basket. "Come to our back door after dark tonight."

The girls and I add extra green bark and spruce needles in the stove fire box as the treat bakes golden brown, so the air around our home smells more of firewood smoke than tantalizing apple dessert. The men say thanks in German-Swiss and English, big smiles on their faces.

The children and I thank the Lord for sending us more encouragement. Selkirk does not know of the two military groups meeting or that his replacement mercenaries bring us word. God has arranged that.

As thankful as I am for news of John, I ache from missing him more than words can say. Each night, I lie on his side of the bed, absorbing his strength and thinking I catch a bit of the smell of him. Even after encouraging news, I toss and turn fearing some new danger. I clutch his pillow and pray against thoughts that swarm. Is it more harm from Selkirk? I pray not, for he seems to soften more each day and show some regret for his treatment of John and the others.

In fact, after hearing of the deaths he's caused, Selkirk looks more sickly and pitiful each day. With two new eyewitnesses coming forward, he must realize his charges may collapse. Are high officials accountable if they arrest hastily with wrong information? Or does government privilege protect them? Surely laws govern even those circumstances.

I trust John and those with him will understand that I now even include Selkirk in my prayers.

I doubt John knows that Father Mathieu and his brother, Claude Gauthier, have come and shared details of the tragic drownings. My heart twists.

Please, Lord, I cannot lose this wonderful husband you've given. He is life itself.

I care for our children and try to stay strong but feel hollow. I pray for our Lord to bless John and help him fight and win so he may return to us.

Fort William, Christmas, 1816

For Christmas at Fort William, we put anger and heartache aside to celebrate our Savior's birth. Selkirk amazes us by providing candies and jars of pickled vegetables and preserved figs and marmalades, things some have never tasted. At times, he seems almost cheerful.

On a secret signal when Santa approaches the fort, a bugler blasts, and Selkirk has the gate swung open. He orders our fort bells to ring and shouts, "Come quickly, everyone. Father Christmas has come. Bid him welcome." For that's what folks in Scotland call this jolly, red-coated man.

Father Christmas sweeps in on the large sleigh that is Aubergine's much decorated sled with his dogs unrecognizable they are so draped in splendid ribbons, garlands, and tinkling bells. The children stare without guessing his identity, except perhaps for Evangeline.

"Ho, ho, ho," Aubergine laughs, his belly stuffed rounder with pillows. His scarlet suit looks like a very large British red-coat uniform. His red velvet hat is trimmed with white and the black-tipped ermine fur that decorates the robes of royalty.

The sleigh swishes to a stop scattering snow as Father Christmas emerges, bows, and adjusts the immense bulging brown sack he carries on his back. "If there are good children and grown-ups here to receive gifts, I have many I've brought a very long way."

"There are," Selkirk answers, sweeping his arms wide. "Come in, come in. We've prepared a feast in your honor."

"*Sacré bleu*," he says. "Then I have found the right place." More laughter gusts through the elaborate beard hanging past his waist. Once inside, he says "All please sit while I read the names on these packages."

He squints at the labels and wipes a white gloved hand across his eyes, adjusting large wire spectacles perched on his nose. "Terrible," he laments. "Cold weather affects my eyes. Who will read for me? You there—" He points to me. "Please come help an old man."

I don't want to admit I read poorly, so say, "With so many labels to read, may my children help me?"

"Of course. The more the better."

I call Marie, Nancy, Catherine, and Joseph forward. Though she cannot read, Evangeline also scuttles near. A cheerful cook corrals David and John Jr. for me and gives them things to nibble.

Oohs and aahs rise as every child receives gifts. Faces shine because Selkirk has put thought into each gift given. Despite his harsh exterior, a heart of considerable size must beat inside.

Father Christmas saves the last gift for Lord Selkirk.

"For me?" our captor asks.

"Yes." The jolly figure nods.

I hold my breath. *Lord, don't let it be a switch*

or coal. Let it be something good and thoughtful. Nothing must ruin this day.

The package rattles as Catherine delivers it and stands near as Selkirk opens it. He lifts out a leather vest wonderfully embroidered and beaded with vines, leaves, birds, and flowers. When Selkirk tries it on, it fits perfectly. His eyes film. "Wonderful. This will warm me in this frigid place."

Father Christmas glances my way, but I'm not the only one sighing relief. Next, we sit around the long tables and stuff ourselves with a sumptuous meal. After an hour of delightful songs and skits, we feast again on desserts, not caring that December's short days are already making it dark.

Father Christmas drains his cup a final time and rises unsteadily to his feet. "*Mon Dieu*, you are marvelous people here." He lapses into Québécois French that sounds suspiciously like Aubergine. "*Certainement*, if I stay longer, families farther west will not receive gifts. I must go, but promise to keep being good boys, girls, and adults all year, and I shall return next December 25th."

"We will!" everyone shouts.

He pulls his red coat down over his bulging belly, slips his fur-trimmed white gloves back on, and waves as he exits. He reaches his sleigh and his eager dogs quickly pull him west out of sight.

Soon, we can't even hear his jingling sleigh bells.

Back home, we play games and talk. We are not ready for this night to end but eventually climb into our beds. My heart feels lighter as I hug my husband's pillow. *May you be blessed, too, John, on this night of our Savior's birth*. My thoughts become a prayer.

Dear Lord, please bring my husband home. Help him know how much our children and I long for him. Free him and the others. Bring them safely to us soon. Thank You for this special day and please bless this coming year.

Chapter 24

"Aubergine, you should have been here," Joseph shouts when he opens our door and admits our rotund friend the next morning. "Father Christmas came and you missed him!"

"Missed him! *Quelle douleur*, what pain. What bad timing for my dogs to slip their harnesses and run to the far horizon. I had to chase them halfway around Lake Superior to catch them again."

"So far?" Joseph tilts back his head and stares, being a very literal boy. "That's impossible."

Evangeline hides a smile.

"But he left your gift," I say, bringing a nicely wrapped one from the closet.

"Ummm, this smells like my favorite rum cake. Shall I eat it all by myself?" He lifts the package to his mouth like he will bite it now.

"You may eat it all if you like," Joseph says. "We had lots yesterday."

"You didn't see Santa as you traveled?" Catherine asks.

"No, but you know my eyes are bad. Or perhaps he went the other way. Or flew high above me across the sky."

"He did, he did," Catherine insists. "That's how he travels so far and fast." She licks her lips as she watches him unwrap his cake. "That's my favorite too. I'll share my candy with you for a slice of your cake."

"My delicious cake?" He bends down near her. "I'm not sure."

But when she offers him sticky pieces of her red and white striped peppermint, Aubergine is overcome by a sneezing fit, and I see a grown man ready to cry. "In that case, who can resist?" he says as he cuts his cake into thick slabs for each of us.

Later, he waves me into the pantry in the back of our home, his brows knit in a solid line. "Marguerite, I must tell you something you can't share with anyone."

I tilt my head to look in his eyes. "All right. I've never seen you so serious before. What is it?"

"One of our German-Swiss traveled to the next fort west, giving evidence for a court martial after one man went mad and fled. He became lost and nearly starved, so is grateful to be in the brig instead of dead."

"It's still sad."

"Yes, but his ruling judge came from the east and had a role in John's trial. He brought news."

I clutch his arm with both hands, my nails nearly cutting his coat sleeve. "Tell me!"

"The eye-witness accounts from Red River events came in time. The magistrate accepted them as strong contradictory evidence."

"Thank God." I breathe again.

"He was furious eight died during travel and shocked to hear Selkirk had ordered the arrests and late departure. He said it sounded like the worst case of company rivalry rather than sound government or justice."

"That's true. He is a wise man."

"Our men are pardoned and released—"

I clasp my hands. "Thank God, then John—"

He shakes his head. "No, not John. The magistrate says someone must pay for the travesty of justice. He's ordered Selkirk to defend his actions with John present. John can come home after Selkirk is ruined or imprisoned."

"That's a relief, but another delay?"

"Yes. We have victory but must be patient."

I can't resist saying. "It's good, then, you and your men didn't free John and the others by force."

Aubergine exhales mightily. "Time has passed and lives have been lost, but it is comforting that law still rules in Canada." He brings a finger to his lips. "Remember, this is cause for joy, but you can't let a word slip."

"Understood." I smile widely. "Yet I can hardly keep from singing and dancing."

"That I want to watch."

I slap his wrist. "It will be devilishly hard, but I'll keep quiet."

"Yes. And we must wait."

Christmas celebrations have lifted our spirits during the short, dark, cold winter days while we await news of our men and their return, but no word comes. I begin to doubt Aubergine's report.

Our silent world is hemmed in by falling snow except for the crunch of our boots as we walk paths doing chores. One major change is that with John away, Company headquarters sees the need for a medical man here to fill John's role, so they send a junior replacement. Jacob McIsaac is brought to Fort William by a guide who travels to check conditions at Red River since the massacre. I wish him well, but it will be hard for anyone to fill John's shoes.

The young doctor delays his last year of medical school to gain paid experience. Aubergine brings him to our door and says Selkirk wishes me to introduce the young man to our dispensary and methods.

I'm taller than gangly McIsaac. He'll probably add height and weight in the future.

He covers a yawn. "Yes, show me your facility, but don't explain procedures. My education gives me sound foundations." He, Aubergine, and I stroll from our home across the yard to enter our dispensary. "You're Doctor McLoughlin's married wife?" He examines me carefully as if surprised I'm married to John.

"Yes. Marguerite. I work with him and—"

He waves a dismissive hand. "I expected—Never mind."

"She and John are a strong team here who work wonders," Aubergine says.

"No doubt."

I point to our supply shelves. "I'll show you my husband's medicine compounds and the distillations and extracts we prepare from nature."

"No need!" His nose is not over-sized, yet he looks down it, which brings his watery blue eyes strangely close together. He also frowns and hunches his shoulders, reminding me of some new bug that has hopped into our facility.

"I won't use woodland quackery," he explains, "even if your husband tolerates it." When his shoulders hunch tighter still, I smell something unpleasant. It may simply be unwashed body odor but is more like something dying, like when John and I cut off gangrenous body parts that must be burned. I push that unpleasant thought away but pinch my nose to breathe through my mouth. I also step away.

"What primary ailments do you treat here?" he asks.

I name the main ones, including telling of the Indian youth's severe burns and remarkable treatment and recovery.

McIsaac sniffs. "But they live outside of the fort. I can't be expected to help everyone. I'm to aid North West Company employees and their families, not use energy and costly supplies on forest creatures who do not bring us profit."

Aubergine and I both gasp. McIsaac fails to impress me. I try to be charitable by reminding myself he's only just arrived and probably suffers exhaustion.

I lead him to the back room. "Forgive my thoughtlessness. These are your quarters. I can answer more questions later, but you must rest now. I'll care for the next patients today to give you time—"

"I don't need time, and I insist on only using modern procedures. I've brought the most up-to-date medical manual and pharmacopeia." He draws a thick, heavy book from his leather bag and slaps its cover. "Heaven knows it must be hard to get reliable supplies and medicines in this distant place."

"Yes, often. That's why—"

Aubergine jerks free of the wall he's been leaning on. "Excuse me. There is someone I must see."

I continue giving McIsaac information while organizing his towels and blankets. As he prattles about the wonders of his medical school, my thoughts wander. Is he exhausted? Afraid? Or simply rude? Before I decide, Aubergine returns with Lord Selkirk, who pleasantly requests a refill of the salve Marie and I compounded to soothe his boils. The instant McIsaac realizes who Selkirk is, he stands at attention as if trying to add height and importance.

"I do need more of your amazing compound, Marguerite," Selkirk repeats. "It works magic. I'm grateful to you and Marie." He turns to our new arrival. "McIsaac, is it?"

"Yes. Jacob McIsaac." He extends a hand, which Selkirk ignores. Instead, he cocks his head and studies the young man.

"It's good you've come to help. Marguerite is quite overworked and needs your help. You're fortunate to be assigned here. You will learn much from working with her. I'm sure there's little of her wisdom in your medical school."

"I'm sure that's true." The small man's lips curl slightly. "You want me to work *with* her and learn?"

Aubergine glowers until his eyebrows meet. I almost expect steam to rise.

"Yes." Selkirk's head jerks. "Is that a problem?"

"I thought—That is . . . You intend me to collaborate with a native woman? If she cleans and organizes the place, that's fine, but I don't see her assisting me."

Selkirk stares. "I see. I thought that's what you were saying. How unfortunate. What you mean is you will not be assisting her." He turns to me. "I'm having second thoughts, Marguerite. I know you and Marie are overworked. If I find you someone to fetch, carry, and clean, can you both continue providing excellent medical care here?" There's an odd gleam in his eyes. Almost dangerous. I would not want to challenge him.

"I believe so. We will do our best."

"Your best is excellent." He turns to McIsaac. "On second thought, Company headquarters has made a mistake. A man of your skills and education would be wasted here. There are pioneer situations farther west with folks desperate for the care a good medical man can provide, places who've seldom had that opportunity." He taps Aubergine's shoulder. "I'm sure you know outposts far west that would benefit from this man's services, don't you?"

"I do." Aubergine's smile engulfs his face. "Do you wish to suggest some? Or do you leave me the choice?"

"You may choose. Give him a night's rest, and then take McIsaac west. Even if it takes several days, just inform me later where he is."

"Of course, sir." Aubergine's hands flex as if he might rub them together with glee. He cannot keep the sparkle from his eye. I shudder to think what wilderness realities Aubergine will arrange for this young man.

McIsaac reddens as if his collar is too tight. He seems to sense his future just got away from him. "You're sure, Lord Selkirk? That is—My superiors say this is a good post and sent me with the highest recommendations. I haven't had opportunity to show you—Within days, you would see—" He looks like a whipped dog.

"That's fine, McIsaac. I've seen enough." Selkirk's mustache twitches in his narrow face. "Your skills fit better in a distant place where you can establish a pioneer work of your own. Your training will let you do your educators proud."

I risk a glance at Aubergine, who tries to swallow another grin, and I have to turn away. Selkirk is having fun. Actually enjoying himself. McIsaac shrinks like a squashed bug.

Now Selkirk graces me with a smile. "I must have more of your compound, Marguerite. You have my thanks for treatment more effective than I've found even in national capitals, and I will tell anyone so."

"I'm thankful, sir, and have some here you may have. Always let me know when you need more."

"With pleasure." His hand skims my arm as he accepts the ointment from me. I almost feel affection in his touch.

The next day, Aubergine wakes McIsaac early and tells him to dress for a long cold day or several on a dog sled. McIsaac shivers.

"Where will you take him?" I ask while the doctor hurries to beg a fort cook for food to take with him.

"I may tell you someday, but don't ask." Aubergine's voice bubbles with laughter and something deeper that makes me shiver. "It is a place that will make a man of him. Where he'll treat native patients well or starve. If he learns, he'll survive. If not, he may become another wilderness statistic."

"Are you that heartless?"

"No, Marguerite." He smiles wolfishly. "I'm that wise."

"Does Selkirk know?"

"Yes. And agrees." Within minutes, Aubergine harnesses his dog team, and his sled races westward through frozen mists.

In coming days, although Marie and I stay very busy, I think often of that young man. And sometimes pray for him.

Days later, the whole fort gathers to observe New Year's Eve—passing to a brand new year that we sincerely hope is better than the last. Instead of rowdy celebration, we all discuss our men's chances for freedom and the date of their return. We need this year to bring more peace. Because our fort has consumed so many supplies in recent days, tonight's dessert is fresh snow sweetened with maple or fruit syrups.

At Selkirk's invitation, Father Mathieu says a prayer at midnight. "Lord, we need grace and wisdom this coming year. Savior, You alone hold the hearts of kings and magistrates. Rule our land and heal the souls of men. Help us. Lead us each day." He makes the sign of the cross and says,

"In the name of the Father, and of the Son, and of the Holy Spirit."

"Amen," we say.

"Amen," he answers.

Next, he leads in reciting the rosary. We're not all Catholics but most of us know enough words to follow along in unity. Finally, as candles burn low, we exchange sleepy but sincere New Year's wishes and trudge home in darkness.

The next morning, Father Mathieu and his brother bundle in the dog sled for their journey west. They will investigate new territory before sweeping north and east to survey more potential fur post sites.

Aubergine tells them, "You may meet an apprentice doctor that we've handed off to western tribes. If you come across him, extend kindness. He may desire to return to more civilized areas, but not this one."

"Ah!" Gauthier says with interest. "There's a story behind that."

"Indeed." Our friend repeats his wolfish smile. "I hope the young man learns it well enough to understand and value it."

Selkirk's eyes glimmer. I definitely see his mustache twitch.

Ten frosty mornings later, between the freezing blasts of the next rising storm, men on snowshoes emerge from the trail along the southern edge of our vast lake. They are British red-coats accompanied by two more officers in royal blue. Eager for word of John and our men, I run forward through heavy snow and reach them first.

They want someone in charge. They don't wish to stop and talk with a woman. "Please take us to Lord Selkirk," demands the red-coat with the most gold braid on his coat and empty facial expression. "We come on official business."

Perhaps Selkirk sees through his window, for his front door swings open as we climb the steps to the house he occupies.

"Lord Selkirk," says the leader, "we come in the name of the crown and seek a private audience."

"With me?" Drawing himself to full height, Selkirk scrutinizes the soldiers. "Very well. Come in."

Once they enter his quarters, the door shuts, and half an hour passes. And then longer time. Finally, the officer in charge returns to the front porch.

"Have someone ring the fort bell and call everyone to a meeting in the main hall."

One of John's aides pulls the rope hard and long until the big brass bell clangs out its somber tones. As our people gather in the timbered meeting room, Selkirk stands erect in his dress uniform. Donaldson, Selkirk's top aide, stands at his side, face flushed, as if he swallowed something that demands to come back up.

The second highest-ranking British soldier hands Selkirk a scroll. That soldier then unrolls a matching one and reads in a loud voice, " 'In the matter of the fourteen North West Company employees charged for the Red River Massacre, the crown has found insufficient evidence for conviction. In addition, because Fort William was unlawfully occupied by Lord Selkirk who took matters into his own hands, we order him to restore control of Fort William and surrounding areas to North West Company officials and appear in Montréal immediately to satisfy the demands of this court.' "

Selkirk staggers, his face livid except for several white splotches on his forehead and cheeks. His skin has the ashen look John's medical book describes as leprosy, except we've never heard of the disease being in this place.

Lord Selkirk wheezes but lifts his hand. "You said I could address the people. I wish to do so."

The officer in charge inclines his head. "Proceed."

"Fort William residents, thank you f-for gathering," he stammers. "I am sorry to say recent fresh testimony sheds new l-light on the Red River massacre. The events are not exactly as I first understood. Concerning the hearing in Montréal, my presence is required together with Doctor McLoughlin to resolve final matters for the public record." He waves Aubergine forward.

"Until the return of McLoughlin and the other men, the staff he appointed will oversee daily operations."

Selkirk's voice quavers. "Let me add, it deeply grieves me that the disaster experienced traveling to trial took the lives of eight men. Four were from here. We commit their souls to our faithful Creator." He raises his eyes to the ceiling as if beseeching the Almighty before addressing the crowd again. "Despite initial information to the contrary, I'm told further detailed eye-witness accounts do clear your men of blame. All charges are dismissed."

A collective sigh billows through our group that makes burning candles flicker and brighten. Happy murmurs rise, heads turning to glance at each other, desperate to know more.

"All men have full pardons and all save Doctor John McLoughlin will return as soon as the weather permits safe travel."

All except John. My heart sinks. Aubergine was right. I strain to hear every word.

Selkirk's Adam's apple bobs. "As you've been told, Doctor McLoughlin and I must meet in person before the crown to conclude this sad business. Hopefully all true massacre wrong-doers will be identified and convicted." His eyes survey the entire room. "Th-thank you for your cooperation during my time here. I transfer power now and leave tomorrow to travel east.

My orderly will pack my office and things. May God bless you all." He blinks rapidly and, with shoulders erect, walks stiffly toward the big front door.

Joy? Pity? Anger? Relief? I feel all of those strong emotions at once boiling in my heart. As Selkirk leaves, men pound each other's backs. The wives and children of absent men form small clusters, hugging and weeping.

Face resolute, jaw frozen, Selkirk has almost reached the door when I rouse myself and follow. I detain him with a hand on his arm. "Wait."

As he stops and trembles beneath my hand, my anger turns to pity. I hear myself say, "During these months, I've seen you become wiser and kinder. You've made steps toward amends. May this long ordeal bring you some measure of redemption."

His hooded eyes dampen as he barely whispers. "Thank you, Marguerite. You are gracious. That is my prayer too. Try to think of me kindly. I will always remember you and your family."

"Please greet my husband. Tell him we eagerly await his return. You will stay in our prayers."

His shoulders slump. "I shall. God bless you for your kindness." And then Selkirk, with a red-coat guard following him, passes through the big front door, descends the massive steps, and fades into darkness.

More days pass without news of our men's

return. Never have I known time to pass so slowly. No one seems aware of when their homecoming might be or what causes the delay. It will help if Selkirk reaches Montréal quickly, even though late winter overland travel remains treacherous. Seeing him removed from power and taken east in custody to face serious court charges reminds me of John relating the Bible story of wicked Haman whose fortunes reversed on himself when he tried to destroy God's people.

Now John triumphs, but I grieve all he has endured. His life and body are forever changed. Even if he can't regain his former physical strength, of course we want him home. The loving care of a man's wife and family can do much to restore his health and well-being. Therefore, when a sudden new prayer burden grips me, I wonder if it means John faces some dreadful new test. I beg the Lord for understanding, but it does not come.

As winter finally inches toward spring, the first ship to cut through lake ice and reach our harbor is Captain Robert McCargo, come to claim my Nancy.

I lift my skirts and run like the wind, as fast as in my youth, but Nancy surges past me.

"You're here! Robert, you've come!"

His anchor chain clanks and rattles as it spools out and his ship is securely anchored. As soon as it hits bottom, her smiling beloved leaps from the ship to land and swings her in a circle, rubbing his fiery red beard against her cheek with her arms tight around his neck. "Of course. I promised and have marked off every long day."

After a long moment, he puts her down. Then he embraces and swings me. I feel his total joy.

"Mother McLoughlin, I am so glad at last to be here and greet you."

I smile and as he lowers me back to the wooden pier, lean back my head and blurt, "Welcome, Robert. What about John? Is he here with you?"

His face falls. "I thought you knew he was delayed. He and Selkirk must finalize court matters before the judge. I sailed before that could happen. Rumors report Lord Selkirk must pay steep penalties including all court costs and funds to families who've lost loved ones or suffered harm."

I gasp. "That will bankrupt him."

"But he deserves it."

"It is hard even to see even a guilty man receive judgment, because he showed kindness at times too."

Nancy grips Robert's arm again. "I'm sorry, Mother. I've shared him enough. Robert, please complete your remaining ship duties so we can enjoy time onshore together."

"Yes, sweet." He raises his reddish brows above twinkling blue eyes. "I am sorry John is not with us, but I have eleven men below decks found innocent who are glad to return home and greet loved ones." His wide grin makes his dimples flash. "Climb the deck, gentlemen, and show yourselves."

They've stayed hidden to surprise us. As they surge forward now, they blink in unaccustomed light, and when they see their families on shore after their long time away, pandemonium breaks out. Their loved ones swarm the pier, so crazed with eagerness I fear the wharf will collapse and the ship itself be in danger.

"Restrain yourselves," McCargo yells. "Line up in turn to come to shore one man at a time." They scurry into line, rising on tiptoes and waving and shouting as they glimpse loved ones.

"Thank God for these eleven," I say, "but why not twelve? John should be here." Despite McCargo's words, my eyes strain to see if there is a chance John is among them, hiding. But as the happy, chattering men clear the ship, John is not here.

"Mother McLoughlin?" Robert addresses me again as if the wedding is accomplished and he's already my son. "I am sad I couldn't bring John. Plus, there is one more development."

"What?" I narrow my eyes because his tone carries concern.

"Our Company is so pleased with his victory, he's promoted to lead all merger expansion meetings. While awaiting Selkirk's arrival for the final court appearance, the Company sent him on a quick trip to England to conduct the merger."

I stagger until Robert steadies me.

"A quick trip to England? Is there any such thing when so much needs to be accomplished?" I speak as if McCargo does not know geography, when in reality he has crossed the vast ocean at least twice and I have not even seen it.

McCargo's knit brow begs me to understand. "The judge's favorable ruling gives our Company strong leverage for our merger negotiation. Whatever happens from now on in, John will always be near the center of it. You can be extremely proud. Surely the meetings will conclude soon and he can return home."

"Oh, I hope so, but proud?" My stomach curdles. "I'm always proud of John," I say, and make my face look cheery while terror chills my bones. "His absence is terribly hard, that's all. I so much want to see him."

"He says the same of you."

"You saw him?" I ask with rising hope. "Did he send a message?"

"Let me see." McCargo plunges his hands into his coat pockets, but both return empty. "He intended to write, but the Company constantly called him into meetings. He is talked about everywhere, and the Company swallows all his time. Plus, we sailed sooner than expected because of a gathering storm. I should have sent a runner to him, but there were so many last minute details. We left harbor before dawn, which he had no way of knowing. Perhaps one of my crewmen has something."

But as each man greets me, none do.

"We had to sail so early," Robert repeats, looking as if he fears his future mother-in-law's anger. "And I confess I tired of delays in reaching Nancy." He glances her way and rubs his jaw again, his cheeks tinged red. "We worked like dogs all night loading to depart at first light. Now I wish for your sake I'd gone to John myself." He gives me a concerned glance before his eyes return to Nancy again.

"I understand, Robert. I'm pleased at how totally you love my girl."

He blushes again. "That is easy to do. Surely John will be on board my next trip. Or God grant he arrives sooner on an earlier vessel."

"After first taking a trip to England?" I ask. "Surely, that will take considerable time."

He frowns. "The Company promised him a fast trip."

"Pah." I shake my head. "I don't believe there is such a thing. It is impossible to make such promises. You're a sea captain. You know more about ships and ocean currents than I ever will, but those seem like very empty words."

He hangs his head.

All around is me is celebration. Hugging,

slapping backs and shaking hands like pump handles. Happy chatter fills the air, yet bitterness gnaws my breast. I smile outwardly as if I'm well, but I am not. I will not show weakness before my children or these good people who love John and with whom our lives are intertwined. He is their brave hero, and he is mine.

The evil ravens that dive bombed me at the time of Alex's betrayal attack again now until I can scarcely breathe. Of course, I celebrate the glad return of these eleven men, though my throbbing head and aching heart push me to frenzy. After experiencing Montréal society, will my second husband abandon me now? Until today, I've been so sure of John's love, yet he fully deserves high promotion that takes him to England beyond my reach.

In marrying him, I have been unwise again. I am a simple woman. How could I believe my love could hold any man when I am not his equal? How did I believe a lasting marriage was possible? I was twice a fool to marry above myself again. I force myself to appear calm to meet our children's needs, but anguish cripples my being.

Merciful Lord, besides my older children, I now have two fine young sons I will not let be taken from me, nor this sweet, wild young Evangeline. You see our needs. You know my pain. You may think I'm strong. You know how much I can stand, but I can't survive being abandoned again. After heartache from Alex, and this crushing blow, help me want to live and go forward. To know that even if I am cast off by earthly men, You alone will never forsake.

In the privacy of our bedroom, I tear my hair and beat my breast, throwing myself across our bed where John's pillow now smothers my sobs and absorbs my tears.

In coming days, I stay busy meeting our children's needs, though I fail my own. In our whirlwind of completing plans for Nancy's celebration, she is too busy to notice. But Marie sees.

Hands on her slim hips, she blocks my path as I cross to place our washed plates on the shelf. "Mother, you cook and feed the younger boys and Evangeline, but you don't eat. Your eyes are dull, and your cheeks are hollow."

"You exaggerate." I reach up and pinch my cheeks to make them rosy. "I must have eaten. You just haven't noticed. You've never seen me cook and not eat, have you?"

"Not usually, but I've seen no spoon touch your lips these last days, and I've been watching."

"You must have missed the moments I did." I don't confess that I'm so numb and unfeeling, I can't eat. It has been three full days since I've tasted food or desired any. "In these busy days, I pop bites in my mouth while I work instead of stopping to eat."

"You're sure?"

"Of course." Maybe I'm not lying. I must have eaten—haven't I?

"See that you do," she says. "Better yet, sit down now and let me fix you something special. What would you like? Custard? French crêpes?"

"Nothing now, dear one. I'll eat later. With Nancy and Robert's reception tonight and them sailing tomorrow, I have to take care of so many last-minute details."

"But you must also look after yourself."

"I will. After tomorrow, things will be different." I give a quick hug. Can she feel my thudding heart? Or sense the pain behind my mask? "I must frost Nancy's cake. Why don't you help make sure her dress still fits after these days of feasting?"

"That's a good idea." She steps aside and lets me pass.

I bury my hurt in the busyness of honoring my adventurous daughter who is about to wed her handsome captain. *I'm sorry you're not here, John. Nancy adores you. We all miss you. I know you have to obey strong Company demands, yet surely you could insist on being here now.*

Later, when Nancy's Robert comes by, he takes me aside. "We'll do our best," McCargo promises, "to see John in Montréal when he returns and give your letters to him. You can count on him coming soon. Maybe we can bring him."

"Thank you. I'd love that!"

What is wrong with me? I see strain on Robert's face and am almost glad for it. Do I begrudge John's promotion when the recent alternative was nearly his death? *Lord, help me desire what is truly best for John.* I lift him in prayer constantly although my soul complains like a bleating goat.

Father Mathieu and his brother, Claude, return from western lands in time for Robert and Nancy's wedding. Aubergine cobbles together vows that are better than the standard *façon du nord* and I thank God. Their union is not the full church wedding I wish. That is not available here, but at their reception, Father Mathieu speaks an additional blessing over them.

I deeply desire lasting unions for my children and hope one day to share church vows with John. This wedding, combined with our men's return, brings joy, and our people celebrate by feasting, dancing, and sharing more tales of John's courage. Yet, later, alone in my room, my anguished heart still bitterly complains.

Thank You for blessing my daughter and her captain. My heart overflows. Yet why did You pardon John if success takes him away from us? The best of husbands can be swayed by social acclaim and promotion. I learned that with Alex. Is John forever lost to us?

I hear no answers but determine to trust.

Now the Gauthier brothers arrange to sail east with Robert and Nancy. After their recent journeys west, they are prepared to recommend additional fort sites for Company building to prevent Hudson's Bay intrusion, and Father Mathieu desires to establish more mission stations to the east and north. Both men have been a blessing on their occasions here. They will always be welcome. As they prepare to board the ship, I remember to ask if they met the junior doctor, McIsaac, on their journeys out west.

Gauthier smiles strangely. "He had been there. I'm not sure we heard the full story. He performed basic duties well enough, but his body had difficulty adjusting to the food and harsh surroundings. He might have adapted in time, but instead he joined himself to a small military band completing geographical surveys and returning east. Did you not see them?"

Aubergine and I shake our heads. "No," I say. "No group like that passed through here."

Gauthier smiles at Aubergine and shrugs. "Ah, well. Canada is a big country full of countless trails and rivers to follow. We're eager to explore many more of them ourselves."

Many of the fort's residents gather to watch the newlyweds depart. The wind is fierce but favorable. Theirs must be a short honeymoon, but if shining faces show anything, they are already finding happiness. We stand on shore waving until their ship and passengers pass from our sight.

Once they are gone, Marie amazes me by saying she sent a letter with him for Donald Mackenzie, declining his proposal—or postponing her acceptance. When I ask why, she says, "This is an important time for our family. I choose not to be away."

My mother's heart twists. "But I want you to have your own happiness, not give up yours for mine."

"It's more than that, Mother," but she doesn't explain. Perhaps I have not hidden my pain at all.

Day after day, once Nancy and Robert have sailed away, a long, lonely year creeps by without incident. Life falls into an unchanging pattern of caring for my children on my own, but realizing I perhaps lean too heavily on Marie. I feel guilty. Nothing in me wants to prevent my daughter from finding her own happiness and forming her own family.

"It's not that, Mother," Marie answers again when I question her. "Life will still hold enough opportunities for me. Let me stay home with you a little longer. The years pass fast enough."

Her smile is genuine. She sheds no tears. I turn away so she doesn't glimpse mine.

Lord, thank you for Your beauty in this oldest

daughter of mine. Prosper her with happiness and every blessing all of her days.

As always, I pray You keep John safe through these terrible times, though I must mark off the calendar with no assurance of how many days are left or when he might come. I hate his absence. It's as bitter as gall. I'm tired of letting Company policy rule every part of our personal lives, no matter how much they pay John and although his efforts bring good to so many employees.

Forgive me! Help me be a brave Christian woman willing and able to do what is right . . .

The Lord remains silent. I don't think He is surprised that I find frailty and selfishness underneath my true feelings. It seems surer that I am surprised and not pleased with what I discover.

Chapter 25

Fort William on Lake Superior, late March, 1817

After Robert and Nancy's ship departs, a long cold snap freezes our harbor solid again. Aubergine receives two brief messages from headquarters brought by messengers on snow-shoes. They agree that only a full merger between the two major companies is the only sane way forward. I don't know which side of the Atlantic John is on, but he's somewhere in the center of negotiations.

It's another month before the sun curves above our horizon. Then slowly warming temperatures bring groans and widening cracks in the lake ice that open narrow water channels.

One morning, Joseph looks out the window and shouts gleefully that a ship is pushing and squeezing through an open channel to our port. He races out, leaving our front door wide open. "I can't read the ship's name," he shouts over his shoulder as he runs. "Perhaps it's Father!"

We all run after him, but Joseph reaches the wharf first. He calls, "Is John McLoughlin on board? Is Father here?"

None of the bundled seamen I see on deck resemble John unless hardship has changed him so greatly I can't recognize him.

A captain I don't know steps to the rail. "Who do you seek, lad?"

"My father. Doctor John McLoughlin."

"He's not here," the captain answers, "although, I'm sure he wishes he were. You must be his kin since you're growing tall like him." He drops anchor and extends the gangplank.

The captain turns to me and my brood. He tips his cap, and I see that his face is crisscrossed with lines from sun and wind, but younger than I first thought. "I'm Captain Manahan," he says in what sounds like an Irish brogue. "You must be Nancy McCargo's mother. She's pretty like you."

My face warms. "Thank you."

"We love having your girl in our schooner family, although she leads her captain a merry chase."

"Already? I thought she might." I return a smile, though my heart breaks that John isn't with them.

"Robert wouldn't have it any other way," he chuckles. "He says he's the happiest man anywhere. She's proving herself a good seaman, riding out storms without getting sick—unless that changes with pregnancies." Another hearty laugh booms from his chest.

Pregnancy? Surely not yet. The wind is so boisterous, I grasp a pole at the end of the wharf tight. "She's plucky. Her hardiness will help her then too."

Marie's face lights with understanding for lately she helps me deliver babies too.

"Do you have word from my husband? Any message?" I cup my ear hoping something.

But he shakes his head. "I'm sorry. I wish I did, but I heard he's in London." The captain tosses a hawser rope over an upright post next to me and snugs up his ship to shore. "With the massacre charges dropped except finalizing matters with Selkirk, you probably know the Company made him cross the ocean on merger business."

"I'd heard they intended to but hoped it proved unnecessary."

"I'm afraid he's in the thick of negotiations with top leaders and winning points for us. His trial win gives our side great advantage, though Hudson's Bay men are stalling for more favorable terms. The merger should end military hostilities. We all agree continued conflict would destroy us all."

"Thank God."

He shrugs. "Sadly, some people have short memories regarding war. Their opinions are as changeable as this fierce wind." He tightens the cap on his head. "Your husband is very courageous in facing danger."

"He's courageous in facing everything. I'd heard he'd been asked to sail the Atlantic, but when no further word came, I thought . . . I hoped . . ." I drop my voice. "Do you know how long his commitment keeps him away?"

"I don't. I doubt even Company leaders know. He made it clear he needed to return to Montréal by the time Selkirk arrives, which should be soon. Since he's now our top Company expert in international business, he's much in demand." He fishes a stiff envelope from his jacket. "I have an official report of court proceedings, although his final hearing with Selkirk remains. Who is in charge here now? Who should receive this?"

Aubergine rushes forward on short legs, out of breath and still buttoning the coat I mended for him. "Welcome. I oversee matters until the good doctor returns. Do you bring word?"

"Little beside this court record." The captain hands Aubergine the envelope. "I also have a newspaper account about the trial. Let me instruct my crew on unloading key items, and I'll join you in the fort."

When done, the captain steps forward and shakes my hand and Joseph's before ruffling the hair of our two youngest boys. We guide him and part of his crew to the fort's dining room, where they enjoy a hot meal while local people pester them for news. The captain mops up the last of his moose stew with fresh bread before smacking his lips and pushing his plate away.

"I have the newspaper report in this pocket." He fumbles and extracts it. "As you know, the court findings went against Selkirk."

“Hurray!” a local man shouts.

He unfolds the first published newspaper most folks have seen. “The Gazette from Saint Catherine Street in Montréal printed this in French, but surely someone here speaks that.”

“*Mais Oui*. Let me translate,” I say.

As the captain spreads the paper, I have no trouble reading the headline. *October 30, 1818—High Court Overturns Red River Findings: Lord Selkirk Found in Contempt of Court. Must Pay Stiff Fines for False Charges.*

I translate the article aloud. “ ‘In court proceedings shocking most Canadians, all Red River Massacre murder charges were overturned when Scotland’s Lord Thomas Douglas, 5th Earl of Selkirk, was judged to have acted prematurely in arresting North West Company employees for last June’s crime at Seven Oaks and usurping Company headquarters at Fort William.

“ ‘Selkirk’s arrest and transport of Métis and non-Métis employees, including the fort’s Factor, Doctor John McLoughlin, is blamed for the drowning deaths of eight travelers due to leaving too late in the season in overloaded canoes.

“ ‘Readers recall that the Red River Colony, also called Selkirk’s Concession, was initiated by the Scottish noble on 300,000 kilometers of land given by Hudson’s Bay Company charter. Unfortunately, the land he awarded to displaced, Scottish farmers had long been used by the

Métis serving our Company. However, they had lived and operated there at the junction of the Red and Assiniboine Rivers for a generation, using waterways for trapping and travel and lands for crops. The Scottish arrivals built Fort Douglas which mysteriously burned last year. It was rebuilt when Governor Semple arrived with eighty-four men. Minor irritations produced conflagration and the deadly Seven Oaks Massacre.

" 'Before that, alarmed by increasing hostility between the two fur-trading companies, Doctor McLoughlin and staff planned to visit Red River to pursue resolution, but testimony confirms that the fatal attack occurred before McLoughlin and his men had begun travel to the site. The Métis accused played no part in the massacre.

" 'Instead witnesses state that in the confusion, Governor Semple ordered the first shots fired, which brought returning fire that killed him and the others. Fearful that the accused Métis could not expect a fair hearing, McLoughlin volunteered to go with them to face trial. If found guilty by the crown, all would have met death by hanging. However, all charges against the original fifteen accused have been dropped.

" 'With full exoneration, Doctor McLoughlin emerges as a respected hero while Lord Selkirk must face court judgment for fines and censure. Regrettably, even generous payment cannot replace the lives lost. The crown's verdict confirms that truth and justice still triumph in our court system. While Lord Selkirk's prospects dim, McLoughlin's rise in brightness. The North West Company now sends him to London to lead talks between the two major fur-trading companies for merger benefitting our peoples and nation. Respectfully reported, Alfred Devine, Editor.' "

Although I am wilderness born, John's prolonged absence chills my heart more than the worst winter. Despite our calendars declaring it is spring, late-falling snow absorbs all sound and creates a magnificent but silent landscape. Minimal hunting takes place, but most life stands still. We have no more visitors and no word from back east.

Our white-headed eagle sits majestic in his tree and, against nature's pattern, appears to stay. His presence comforts. From the time of his return, my heart feels more peace as if he tells us that John prospers too.

It is hard having John so distant and sought after that his wife cannot even know or imagine his location and circumstances. Across the sea? That far away? Unavailable to discuss family needs, even by letter? Or is he receiving my letters but not answering? Our children's faces grow sad as time passes but no word comes. I invent excuses.

"Ship captains sometimes forget," I say. "Letters might get lost on overland journeys. Travelers must cross dangerous rivers. Sometimes there are skirmishes . . ." Soon, my explanations sound unconvincing even to me. Twice I dream John is home but so changed in looks and manner we hardly know him.

Reluctant at first to describe their ordeal, our returned men gradually share details ghastlier than any of us wish to hear. Mind you, we can read their stories in their changed bodies and ravaged emotions.

John's uncle Simon is the oldest of the group. We bring him into our home. He suffers aches and pains, but discusses more incidents as he recovers. On one of his better days, we ask him to recreate the trial scene. He acts out testimonies and rebuttals, moving back and forth across our living room and making it appear as if we are present with him in court.

"When the black-robed, wigged judge pounded his gavel, I took notes. I couldn't capture everything, but jotted down what I could of the verdict."

He waves his hands in the most animated gestures we've seen since his return. "I've memorized some key things since. After hearing witnesses and considering all reports, the judge declared the crown presented insufficient proof for conviction and in fact supported the innocence of all accused." You can imagine the jubilation."

"Yes!" Joseph pumps a fist in the air. "What did Father do?"

"Weep and shout in triumph at the same time. The men shot from their seats and pounded his back, shouting he was their Savior, their hero. The judge let the pandemonium roll for some time as we all absorbed the wonder of our freedom. The court clerks and warders who would have led us to death's row instead stood and rejoiced with us."

"I wish I could have seen that," Joseph says.

Simon frowns. "Your father's glad you did not. There were so many deep emotions. The judge pounded his gavel and declared that in the matter of Lord Selkirk versus the North West Company and the Red River Seven Oaks Massacre, the crown found the defendants free on all charges and in fact he would be determining the penalties and resolutions Lord Selkirk must pay."

"I'm sure he's shivering in his boots," my Nancy says.

Simon nods. "I would be. The only problem now is the necessary delay while Selkirk reaches the court for final inquiry resolution with John present. Of course, John didn't wish to remain, but all agree the cause is worth it and hopefully it won't be so very long."

"Frankly, any added time is too long," I fuss. "This case has already dragged beyond two full years—isn't that long enough?" My voice wobbles.

"I know, Marguerite. I agree. None of us will likely recover enough to be fully ourselves again." Deep lines surround his tired eyes. His cheeks are sunken pits. He wheezes when he walks and sinks into a chair when only halfway across the room. The children and I rush to bring a warm quilt to cover his arthritic knees and treats to tempt his feeble appetite.

"We are thankful you're here, Uncle Simon," Marie says.

He clasps her hand and brings it to his lips. "So am I, dear one. We saw God Himself move on our behalf."

"But will it truly end when Selkirk appears?" I ask. "Some say his lawyers seek retrial. Will there not be some technicality they want to unravel to spin out arguments forever?"

He clicks his tongue. "I understand your concern, but I think we're safe. No magistrate will keep retrying the same case forever. John must testify about the canoe trip resulting in the drownings from Selkirk's rash orders."

I shudder. "If that's the final inquiry and John returns from England soon, I'll try to bear it. Perhaps we dare begin to hope our long separation will end." I manage a half smile.

“I think we may safely begin to hope. I could not be prouder of John’s conduct.”

“Thank you. Will you please share more of the journey? Especially the capsizing and John nearly being lost. How he was saved.”

Pain clouds his face. “I cannot. Reliving even part of it costs me too great a price. It’s enough to know that eight men drowned and we nearly lost John. His survival is a miracle. I will always regret I could not do more to help him or the others. It puts me in agony to recall our struggle. I still don’t know how I escaped the icy waters myself. It’s not through any strength or skill of mine. God intervened.” He speaks slowly and haltingly, his eyes studying the floor.

“Forgive me my thoughtlessness.” My arm curves around his shoulder. “I would not cause you more pain for the world!”

“You wished to be there but could not be. You simply wish to understand.” But then he does slowly continue speaking. “We looked death in the face as it stole eight noble souls and tried to take us all. No wonder your native people speak of *Majimanidoo* and *Wendigo*. We saw his ugliness and smelled the stench of death. We felt his breath that raised the hair on our necks.”

Our children shiver and their eyes widen hearing more details of John’s suffering.

I shiver with them. “How terrible, I can’t imagine anything more terrible except our worst plague in Mother's village. John's hair is completely white now?"

He sighs. "Yes. Totally. That happens sometimes when people suffer a great shock. His grandfather's hair went white when he was young. Perhaps it's a family trait, but I blame John's sudden trauma, for he changed instantly."

"Is that the grandfather who sheltered John's family?"

"Yes. He met outward needs but didn't know how to give more. I'm proud that my nephew provides ungrudgingly for those in his care. Now, please excuse me. My aching bones demand rest." He pushes himself up from his chair and limps to his room. "Try to think of John as he was when young and strong," Simon calls over his shoulder. "That is best for you both. Ask God for grace to accept John's changes. He will need your love and support to heal."

After Uncle Simon leaves, Marie asks, "How much is Uncle Simon not telling us?"

"Much, I think. Frankly, I do better knowing the true details than having my mind imagine things."

"Me too," she says. "I will try to hear more facts from other survivors."

After further conversations, Marie sometimes looks at me sadly but stays silent, as if the reality of what John and the others suffered is more than she can bear or wants me to hear. But I am made of strong stuff. After all, at age seven I saw my father murdered. When still a child, I helped Mother fight the epidemics ravaging our villages and bury the dead. I will not name further evils, for although parents do their best to shelter their children, few escape all harm. It is hard to think of John not being physically strong. We want him home in any form and will find a way to bear it.

Lord, strengthen him. And strengthen us for his return. Give us endless love and patience as he heals. Also help us adjust to his new-found fame without missing a step, for I confess I am very afraid.

Chapter 26

Fort William on Lake Superior, Summer, 1819

With John away so many months now, our family routine changes little. The released men not from Fort William return to their home areas and do their best to resume normal life, now that the invading Scots are leaving. Two of our men have found brides and will marry soon. Another's wife has a baby son they name John.

Because of hearing almost nothing from my John, the children and I are unsure what to do. It seems strange to remain at Fort William with him not here in charge. This is Central Canada's command post. This is where he left us and probably expects to find us. And yet, so much has changed.

Now, I sometimes sadly say *if* he returns, for I grow sick of waiting. If he doesn't return soon, my mind pictures going after him with our brood, using my wilderness skills to track him. Or sailing to an Atlantic ship on McCargo's ship to find John, and if he is not there, crossing the ocean.

"We could swim, Mother." Joseph says and makes me laugh. Our youngest boys don't understand the ocean's size, yet swim like fish. Even in winter snow, they make a sport of diving into drifts and propelling themselves forward with strong arm strokes and powerful kicks as if they are swimming.

"*Quelle force*!" Aubergine says when he watches them. "They are like strong young bulls!"

My medical schedule remains the same. Most days I distribute medicines and treat patients in the dispensary, helped by Marie and sometimes Catherine. Little Evangeline is also willing, often scampering through the woods on imperfect limbs like a lively squirrel, bringing me gifts from nature for cures or tonics new to me. Did her grandmother teach her? As she learns more of our language, we share and understand other bits of her story.

Occasional but rare visiting officials or trappers bring news from the east. John's merger talks in London move forward but more slowly than expected. Because his frontier experience is crucial to the merger union, no one else can take his place. Management orders him to stay weeks longer until the critical parts of the talks are complete. That may mean Selkirk must wait in Montréal.

They say he's written out merger guidelines and insists they let him keep his word to return to court in Montréal and to his loving family. They warn me that expanding Company business means he will need to regularly travel between Canada and Europe, putting personal concerns aside. After all, Company growth and welfare are more important than individuals, aren't they? He will be well rewarded.

The promise of financial reward may tempt John. He's known such great poverty and wishes to help his family and ours. That may be a bigger monster for him to fight than cholera or near-drowning or court trials. As more weeks pass without him appearing, doubt strangles my heart.

At spring break-up, when the first Montréal ship enters our harbor bringing food and dry goods in exchange for our furs, their supply officer draws Aubergine and me aside. He says all North West managers agree that John's merger solutions are perfect. They won't be represented by anyone else as their spokesman in London or anywhere.

For over two years, my husband has crossed to distant places I can't even imagine. When rival Hudson's Bay Company leaders in London met him, they instantly recognized his genius and offered him top positions in the merged Company. He will be one of few holding the reins of a vast empire in his hands.

That much success can ruin any man. How can he live content in this wilderness place again? After years as a Nor'Wester employee, he will now be a top level Hudson's Bay Company official. The wheels of change may turn slowly, but they grind into powder.

"What does this mean for our family?" I fuss to Aubergine once the supply officer leaves. "John now works for our competitor, but the transfer isn't yet complete here in Central Canada. You're still under North West Company direction. If our officials consider John a turncoat, must you force us out?" I look at him shyly. "We will do whatever you say."

"What?" the good man roars. "Marguerite, have you lost your senses? After years of friendship, we in this fort are one family. No management on either side of the ocean, not even the Prime Minister of Canada or the King of England, can tear you from us. John is building a strong, wise road forward. He'll complete the merger, end things with miserable Selkirk, and come home as fast as he can. Have faith."

Those last words bring tears as I gape at this fierce friend who instructs me with more wisdom than usual. "Sometimes I have faith. At others? Well, it is hard."

"I know." His look becomes tender. He takes my hand. "Marguerite? Don't think me uncaring. I do understand."

"You are right, Aubergine. And I must trust. It's just that John's been away so long that my heart fails."

He rears back. "You don't show it. You've been

a tower of strength to all of us." His eyes are unfathomable pools. "Have you never wondered why I've not married all these long years?"

"Of course, I have. John gives vague answers that you travel often and love adventure." I think of Alex fathering a child elsewhere and lift my eyebrows. "Perhaps you have love interests elsewhere we don't know about."

"No!" He turns crimson. "Don't think such a thing." He looks deeply into my eyes. "It's because I have never found someone as wise, strong, kind, and beautiful as you."

I withdraw my hand. "Be serious, Aubergine."

"You don't believe me? I am serious." His face pales. "I assure you, John knows it's true. Because of my deep regard for him, I will not overstep my bounds. Long ago, he promised to help me find someone like you, but we both know that's impossible. No one else like you exists on this earth."

"Dear friend, am I to believe you? I—I don't know what to say."

"Then say nothing, but believe me. Such things are best left with God. Rest assured, while blood pumps in these veins, I will do everything to keep you and your family safe and comfortable here until John's return. Yet if for some reason he cannot or does not return . . . then we will see what happens next."

"God bless you, dear friend." His warm hand

clasps mine again before I gently withdraw mine to turn away.

For a long while that night, after my older girls and younger children settle, sleep will not come. Where is John? Does he enjoy his new life? Has his heart changed regarding us? Does he miss me as much as I miss him? Or do his new challenges fulfill him so, he seldom thinks of us?

He is resourceful, a gifted merchant-trader and outstanding doctor. Do dazzling sights and opportunities tighten their hold until international cities become home to him instead of our wilderness places? Why has he not written us when I have written so often?

My heart pains. Stars wink overhead. Through the long night, constellations wheel their patterns across the sky. Does John see these same stars? Or are the patterns over his head constellations we don't see here? Do they remind him of us? Will we see him again? I pray. And eventually cry myself to sleep.

Fort William on Lake Superior,
Midsummer, 1819

Nancy sends word that she is with child and thriving. She didn't announce it earlier until she was sure. Her handsome captain proves to be the most adoring and attentive of husbands. If he has tamed her, that is more impressive than if he has sailed all seven seas. Their baby is due this fall, and McCargo agrees that Nancy should come here so I can help with its birth. That prospect adds joy to my step.

So in mid-June, on the longest day of the year, when their ship sails into harbor, pennants flying, I am amazed. As Nancy and her husband hurry down the gangplank, my heart leaps. Yet as I rush forward, the strain on their faces stops me short. They do not bring good news.

"What is it?" I call before they're near enough to hug. Nancy's rounded form looks fine, but she's still months from the delivery. "Is it the baby?"

"No," she calls. "It's too soon for that."

Robert reaches me first, with Nancy right behind him. We all embrace, but when Nancy throws her arms around me, she bursts into sobs that shake us both.

"Darling, is it John?"

"Y-yes!" Her sobs grow wild and Robert pats my back. Marie, Catherine, Joseph, Evangeline, and our younger boys join us, and we're all crying without knowing why.

As soon as Nancy releases me, McCargo takes me in his arms again, his face filled with anguish. "Don't cry, Mother," he says, though he has tears himself. "How I wished to bring John or good news, yet this may still turn out all right. When he rushed to London to produce the merger, he wore himself out."

"That's no surprise," I murmur.

Nancy grabs my hand. "Yet a blessing is that his brother, David, has studied pulmonary disorders and was in London. Someone invented a medical gadget called a stethoscope that amplifies heartbeats and lung sounds. David listened to Father's lungs. It helped him choose treatments for pneumonia. But then his long return voyage across the Atlantic during storms caused a relapse. The court deposition with Selkirk went perfectly, but so many demands have drained Father's body."

"How badly?" I crush her hand. "He's alive, isn't he?"

"Yes, when we left, but he had to travel again to live."

"Travel again? What do you mean?"

"He was alive but very ill when we last saw him in Montréal. He had to leave Canada immediately to get treatment. When he returns, he hopes to be fully well."

"But every trip presents hazards." I grip my face with my hands. "He left Canada again? I don't understand." I'd like to shake the news out of Nancy, except she's with child. "Where is he?"

She dabs her eyes. "When Robert and I were still two days from Montréal, we got word that

Father had arrived and completed the inquiry with Selkirk. It went well."

"I knew it would."

"When the judge heard both sides, he decreed Selkirk must pay every penalty. We rushed and met Father after in a small inn and found him eager to come to you but delirious with fever and a terrible cough."

Robert interrupts. "When we insisted he get medical care, he roared, 'I'm a doctor and wish to go home!' "

I smile despite this terrible news. "That sounds like him."

"He only agreed to see a specialist at Montréal's new General Hospital because he was too weak to resist," Robert adds. "He could scarcely stand when I helped him into a carriage."

Marie gasps. "Father's in Montréal? But I thought you said—"

"That he had to leave. Yes, he did." Nancy finds her handkerchief to blow her nose.

Marie's voice sounds incredulous. "Then where did he go? South to the United States?"

"No." Nancy and Robert share sad faces. "Doctor Andrew Holmes, the only physician with methods Father trusts was away, so his assistant came. By then, Father was unconscious. On hearing his tortured lungs and awful cough, the doctor prescribed standard medical treatment."

"Standard! You don't mean?" I hide my eyes.

"Not leeches. You know Father hates those."

"I do now," Nancy says. "The doctor said they would cure Father, and we saw many patients treated that way. But when he roused and saw living leeches attached to his arms and chest, gorging on his blood, he went wild."

"I'm sure." I press my hands tight, my nails cutting my palms. "He calls leeches barbaric, claiming they killed President George Washington. It's a wonder Father didn't kill someone."

Robert nods. "He shouted and kicked off the sheets then pulled off the swelling leeches. Before we could stop him, he ran outside to a carriage, bloody and still adjusting his clothing, commanding to be taken to the docks. By the time we caught up, he'd paid to board the same ship that had just brought him home from England, now reloaded and ready to sail."

"But you stopped him?"

"We could not." Nancy pales. "He was so distraught, we couldn't reason with him. He looked near death's door." She wrings her hands. "When he finally explained, it made sense. He said, 'Tell your mother I'll die if I stay here. I'm returning to England for more of David's treatments, or I may never see any of you again. I won't let bloodsuckers kill me!' "

I feel faint. "He was that ill but sailed to England? Can he survive that journey?"

“We hope so,” Nancy says. “He promised to send word as soon as he arrives.”

“Pah.” I make an unladylike sound. “I’ve heard those promises but seen almost nothing. By all that is holy, I can’t stand anymore.” Suddenly our wharf and the faces of loved ones swirl in dizzying circles. I stumble against Nancy, hear concerned sounds, but fall. For a long while, I know nothing.

Chapter 27

Fort William on Lake Superior,
Summer, 1819–early Spring, 1820

Long mid-summer days are cloudy with light rain or heavy haze that the sun can scarcely burn through. Forest fires add more smoke and dust, dulling our world to burnished pewter. Occasional thunderclaps bring pounding rain that hits the earth so hard the raindrops bounce up again. My burdened heart also feels pounded and spattered.

One morning when the skies do clear here, my daughters and I pray that John has sunshine in England and is receiving all he needs to become completely well. He will also need healing in mind and soul after all he has suffered. And when sunshine and his brother's treatments heal him in England, I hope sunlight travels here to renew my hope, because I feel drained, cold, and hopeless, perhaps unable to ever feel the warmth of human love again.

Lord, You hold the sun and heavens in Your hands. I entrust our loved ones to You—John in England or wherever he is, Tom in Oregon, Nancy and Robert on their ship carrying my precious unborn grandbaby. I commit every outcome to You.

Even after praying, I thrash and wrestle through the night. I'm not sure I've slept at all by the time the morning's pale sun tries to push heavy clouds aside. Despite its efforts, it looks more like a dim sliver of moon on a black night than the bright sunlight our Lord intends.

Great darkness shrouds my emotions. I realize now what I should have known long ago. John is a wonderful man with skills and gifts too large for the frontier role he plays here. They are also too immense and in demand for our wilderness marriage to hold him to me. With my heart cold as death, my trembling hand picks up a pen to clumsily print out the words I should have written long ago. I will not have Marie rewrite this one. Aubergine and the Company will find a way to deliver this message to John. It is time.

Summer 1819
Dear John,

I pray that your brother's treatment has again worked miracles for your lungs. We constantly hear of your fame across the seas, especially of your success in guiding two rival fur companies into merger forging a far more promising future for one. Robert says Hudson's Bay officials offer you any post at any location in England or across Canada. Of course, you must choose the best. Some call you a new Solomon. We are very proud.

At the same time, you've been away over two years. That is a life-altering period. I lived through similar changes with Alex. It is an embarrassment to any man of prominence to be joined (I do not say married to) an uncultured woman of mixed blood. While I have applied myself to read and can now print a measure, I am unskilled. I regret that my written words are clumsy, awkward things that look like a child scrawled them.

John, it is time to dissolve our contract, as you must be ready to request yourself. I release you from your commitment to me so you can be joined to someone suitable.

You are a good and loving father. I know you will provide for our children and not leave me destitute. I ask that you let me raise our youngest sons while they need a mother's nurturing. Later you can guide their education and careers. I know we will always share close ties between us.

During our years together, you've made me the happiest of women. You have my lasting respect and wishes for your good health and long successful career. I will always love you but am not your equal in any way. Your growing prominence pulls us apart. Do not worry—I understand and have no regrets.

I will tell Aubergine this document is important and he must send it by the surest way. He will apply the NWC red wax seal to mark it rush and private so that you alone read its contents. I expect no reply—I know you are a very busy man with constant demands. My heart hoped to hear from you more during your long absence, but it seemed heaven itself opposed us. You showed me where the Bible says a man's thoughts turn where his heart dwells, and life events tie you to business. No one blames you. You are highly gifted.

I ask God to always bless you and keep you safe. Be assured, I will only speak highly of you and take excellent care of our children so they represent you well in all areas.

Your caring, admiring friend
and life-long well-wisher,
Marguerite Wadin MacKay McLoughlin

Fort William on Lake Superior,
early Spring, 1820

On a blessedly warm spring day when the children and I work in our garden, a stranger approaches our cabin. He is tall and walks slowly, his shoulders stooped, his thick mane of white hair glistening in the sun.

Suddenly my children gasp and run to him like young deer. They shout and throw themselves upon him. Evangeline also leaps into the pack. Only then do I realize this stranger is my husband. I am rooted in place as he greets the children, even Evangeline. Then he separates himself from them and approaches me. As he comes closer, I see exhaustion and joy mingled on his face.

My heart catches. It has been nearly three long years since Selkirk's soldiers led him and the others away. Although John is only thirty-four, his leonine hair is totally white. Yet somehow that change makes him look even more distinguished, more noble. The top of my wax-sealed envelope rises from his breast pocket. I stand waiting with a fixed smile, my arms crisscrossing my chest until we're close enough to speak.

"Welcome home, John. It has been terribly long."

"To my sorrow. An unthinkable lifetime." He reaches for me but stops, his gaze dropping to my closed arms. His face is haggard, his eyes hollow. "When we left, I never dreamed of being away so long."

My heart pities this immensely successful man. "I'm sorry for all you've suffered—"

He opens his hands in surrender. "And I for you. And to think, most of our letters have missed each other."

"I don't know how many you sent. I only know I received few. Robert brought news of your tasks in London. Your life circumstances now consist of high-level Company mergers. You are accomplishing important things. It can't be helped, but I'm left behind. That's simply the truth."

His face twists. "That is not true at all. I am capable and able to bring change because of God's love and your love and prayers. Forgive me for failing to have more letters reach you, yet I'm not sure what more I could have done to help them succeed. I wrote you often but only received one before this." He taps mine with its broken red wax seal.

"That is the most important one."

"Don't say that. I disagree with its contents and would like to tear it to shreds. I don't know if my letters were held back by the court or failed to catch up to me as I traveled, or what. Surely, there is an explanation. I hope one day all missing letters will be found and you shall be deluged to see my love and devotion."

"They may be at the bottom of the ocean, but it doesn't matter now. I've come to reality."

"It does matter." His eyes search mine again. "May I come in?"

"Of course." I step back. "This is your home. I'll take my things upstairs and stay in the girls' room so you may rest as a man of your stature deserves."

"Don't stand on formality. You're breaking my heart." He waves our children to stay on the porch while he escorts me inside. "What are you saying, Marguerite? Good Lord, I have no stature apart from my union with you, and I want none. What is this monstrous distance between us when all I longed for was to fly to your arms?" His tired eyes blaze. "Nothing in life has meaning apart from you and our children."

My heart turns liquid under his gaze. "That's not what I've understood from all the glowing reports of your success. Many princely distinctions and opportunities are yours. You deserve them all. I will not stand in your way."

His brow darkens. “I want you standing at my side.”

I heave a sigh. “That’s impossible. Please face reality. It is your future I consider. I’m giving you the gift of freedom.”

“Freedom?” He chokes on the word. “That’s no gift I want. Your letter nearly killed me more than my sodden lungs.” He extends his beautiful hands, but when I stand aloof and guarded, he drops them again. His voice breaks. “We will find God’s path through this. I pushed hard to rush home as soon as we returned to Montréal. I bought this for you in London to honor and seal our marriage, for you are constantly in my thoughts.”

He reaches in his other shirt pocket and pulls out a black velvet bag. From inside he draws out a ring of gleaming gold with the largest, most lustrous pearl I have ever seen. He offers it to me with a trembling hand. “Marguerite? This is not wonderful enough, but it is the best I could find to symbolize all you mean to me.”

My heart constricts. I barely whisper, “John. I can’t be that to you.” I close his fingers around the ring and push his hand back to his chest. “I am honored but cannot be partner to a man as highly accomplished as you.”

“Nonsense!” He staggers to a nearby chair and holds the ring in his fingertips as if it is on fire. “Marguerite, I had so planned and hoped—”

"Your journey has drained you. You need food and care."

"Heartbreak drains me if I survive every crisis but lose you." His eyes probe. "Our hardships have also affected you deeply. I'm sorry for that terrible price."

I shrug. "It couldn't be helped. Your absence takes its toll, but I am strong and know how to bear hard loads."

"No one is meant for that. It's been an impossible weight. Some of us are strong during crisis but suffer weakness after." He eyes bathe me in such tenderness, I look away. I fight every impulse to embrace and comfort my suffering husband, but I will make a clean break for his sake. "You are exhausted, John, and must rest. Where is your luggage?"

"I only brought my medical bag. I left everything else on the ship to hurry here. When it docked at our last port and announced a four day delay for repairs, I departed and came here on foot. I would not wait four more days." He releases a shuddering, raspy breath. "I hoped for a very different homecoming."

Are his lungs ruined? "I'm so sorry, John. We're both different people now." I must turn his thoughts. "What do you think of our children? Our young giants?"

"They are handsome and wonderful. You've done well. I'm proud." Yet his smile holds sorrow.

"They are much like you," I say.

"I'm also thankful to also see much of you in them." Now his breath is raspier. "And we have another child too? A little girl?"

I briefly explain how Evangeline came to be with us. My heart clutches as I recall how certain I was that John would love her. I end my explanation with, "She is a special child."

He nods. "That is evident." Then he sighs. "Marguerite, we can renew our love, for mine has not failed."

"It's sad, but too much time has passed. Our paths have grown apart. We are both greatly changed." I turn and add wood to our fire. "I'll start dinner. Do you prefer moose or grouse?" I melt lard in my iron skillet.

"I prefer holding my wife."

"Be sensible. I will always love you, but marriage is impossible now."

"Nothing is impossible." As he reaches for me, I step away and dust flour into a bowl to coat the legs and wings of four grouse. "Joseph is an excellent shot besides being skilled with snares. He brought these four birds home."

"Wonderful." He glances outside at our children and then back at me. "Joseph is a fine young man. You've formed him well." He sinks back into his chair, near collapse, and drops his furrowed face into his hands. Years of crisis and harsh travels have ravaged him. He looks much older.

"Two and a half years, Marguerite. Who could have imagined? I only knew I must help our innocent men win their court battle so they were not hung, and so I did. But Company demands increased."

"And brought you wonderful future opportunities."

"For *our* future. I admit, I welcomed the prosperity and security this could provide for our family, but not at the price of our life together. Nothing equals that."

Evangeline sneaks into the house and creeps near. She looks questioningly at me and then wraps her arms around one of John's legs, pressing her face against his knee. She purrs like a kitten as he strokes her hair, which is as black and straight as a crow's wing. Seeing their achingly beautiful bonding makes it harder for me to stay distant, for I've never stopped loving this man.

Our yard fills with neighbors who hear that John is home. When she entered, Evangeline left our front door open, which now lets others push inside. They shake John's hand or pound his back. Next, Aubergine arrives. Perhaps due to recognizing the tension on our faces, he leads Evangeline outside to our older children. He asks others to wait outside, too, and then reenters.

"Welcome, John. Our hero is home at last." His voice booms as he scoops John into a bear hug. "*Mon frère*, how we've missed you—haven't we, Marguerite?"

"Every moment."

Although John is a big man, he's thinner now. Aubergine lifts and spins him, whooping like a wild man. "You beat Selkirk, you did—beat and ruined him!" He lowers John again and waves a fist, stomping in victory.

"Yes, I won with God's help, but find little pleasure in ruining him. He is broken and may never recover."

"Ruined? Broken? But you pity him?" Aubergine snarls, his voice a weapon. "What about our dead men? What about yourself, nearly drowned?" His eyes shrink to slits. I do not see kindness in them. "It's not time to discuss or debate. Tonight, we celebrate. Come outside now, John. The whole fort is here. Greet this eager crowd. How did you sneak home with none of us knowing?" He leads John forward with an arm around his shoulder, then glances back at me. "Marguerite, this is no time to cook. I'll have our chefs prepare a feast. Don't work. It's time for jubilation!"

Before I can protest, Aubergine lets go of John and lifts and whirls me, too, while I hold an iron skillet in one hand and a wooden spoon in the other. I feel joy and strength in his arms. John watches, his expression pained.

John's celebration dinner is a blur. He wears a weary smile as people crowd around to congratulate him. They don't mention his changed physical appearance but their eyes show concern. "You must rest," many say. "There is no need to resume fort duties yet." Those who stood trial with him thank him again for his leadership and heroism.

John clears his throat. "I must tell you an amazing story you do not know." He waits until everyone quiets and gives attention. "I have just returned from sharing an ocean voyage with Lord Selkirk and know how deeply these events have afflicted him. He needed my urgent medical care."

"*Quel douleur*," Aubergine says. "What a pity."

"He was horribly ill—at death's door."

"Good." A hunter shakes a fist.

"Serves him right!" says another. "I'd help arrange his funeral."

More heads nod.

"As I rushed back to England, seeking more medical treatment to live, imagine my surprise at what God arranged."

"What?" Joseph asks.

"Tell us," a cook says.

"If it involved Selkirk, are you sure God arranged it?" a widow asks bitterly.

"Listen and judge. I reboarded the same ship in

late afternoon before its evening departure. I was so ill, I went immediately below to my cabin to lie down. Although exhausted, I could not quiet my mind from dizzying trial and merger facts. And then, through the cabin wall, I heard the noise of someone occupying the next stateroom. I thought little of it in my exhausted state, but through the night heard strangled coughs and the groanings of someone in great distress."

"How unpleasant," I say.

"To a doctor, it was. The next morning, Wilhelm DeVries, our Dutch captain, assigned me to take all meals at his table. We exchanged pleasantries and he said the traveler in my adjoining stateroom, a Scottish official, would also join our table when he felt up to it. When that man failed to appear at the evening meal, the captain sent his steward to check on him.

"Though well-traveled, that captain knows little of Canada's fur-trade conflicts. When the steward returned saying the traveler still did not feel well, the captain asked me to pay a courtesy physician's visit. Imagine my shock when the steward took me to the adjoining stateroom and I saw the passenger was Lord Selkirk."

I hear several rough intakes of breath.

"Only our Savior knows who was more surprised, Selkirk or me. I assured the steward that the patient and I were acquainted, so he could leave us alone. When Selkirk raised his streaming eyes, he said, 'What? My enemy sails on this same ship?' "

"I'm not your enemy," I told him, "although it is bizarre we are ship companions. The new Red River eye-witness accounts simply do not match your early conclusions regarding the facts."

" 'It's a cursed mess,' he said, and pressed his swollen face into his pillow. He ordered me to leave. I replied that I wouldn't, that the ship's captain had sent me, and as a medical man I was duty sworn to help all in need. I warned him he was seriously unwell, but he refused my help."

"Good." Aubergine glowers.

"Just then, a strong ocean wave dropped our ship into a rolling trough, making the furniture shift. Selkirk retched until he had nothing left. I loosened his cravat and told him I was sorry for his distress, that I would help whether he liked it or not."

I survey the room. John's hearers show little sympathy. Several fist and wave their hands.

John continues. "He said the court verdict ends his life while it advances mine, that the Almighty is against him although he only meant to help distressed Scottish farmers and hoped Canada had space for us all. I explained his desired lands were those already occupied by our people for a generation, but that perhaps solutions could still be worked out."

"Nah. It's too late for that." Another of John's hearers hisses.

"Don't worry, Selkirk also said it was too late, that he must sell all of his assets to pay court penalties and then be bankrupt. His brow was on fire. Blood marked the handkerchief he held to his mouth. I asked if he had consumption. He laughed and said even if he did, it wouldn't matter. When I said he could still have a good life, he accused me of mocking him. When I bowed my head to pray for him, he drew back and said, 'You ask God to help me? You're as strange as your wife. After my harsh conduct, she's added me to her prayer list.' "

John's eyes moisten. "Marguerite, I was never so proud. Joy exploded in my chest. I knew you would do no less."

"Thank you." I avoid his loving gaze.

"In fact, Selkirk thinks your prayers put us on the same ship."

"That was not my request. I only wanted you safely home, but who knows the mysteries of the Lord."

"Selkirk confided one thing more when he was forced to accept my help. 'We crossed one narrow stretch of lake,' he said, 'where every shrieking banshee wind from hell found us. I believe we fought forces from another world. We were not overloaded but that storm sucked the tight chinking from our boat and opened holes until water poured in like hungry snakes come to devour us. Our canoe was awash, filling with icy water. Somehow we reached land.'

"He rested a trembling hand on my arm and said, 'I thought of you then and what you suffered. I didn't mean to kill you or put all of you through terrible harm.' The fact that we reached shore without sinking was God's mercy. I wouldna send anyone in such conditions again."

John looked around the room. "I believe him."

"Fool to believe an enemy," another Red River man speaks harshly.

"Would you have feuds and wars continue forever?" John asks. And waits.

No one answers.

"That's what I thought," John says. Then he holds me in his gaze and will not lower his eyes. "I asked Selkirk how my family was when he last saw them. He said they are treasures to be proud of as I truly am. He mentioned our new daughter, Evangeline, who is already a precious gift and joy to me."

She scoots near to slip a clawed arm around his waist. John tucks her hand into his.

"He spoke of his family in Scotland, how he cannot provide for them once he's penniless although he knows the penalties are just."

Murmurs rumble. Someone says, "He should have thought of that before. You want us to pity him? He had no pity for us, so we don't."

John lifts a hand. "I only want you to know he understands now what he put us through and is heartily sorry. Though this unscheduled, unwanted voyage across the ocean took me and him away from our families, I believe our Lord gave him and me quality time together. We confided our hopes and fears and prayed together. Heaven gained. We lost nothing. When we reached London, my brother immediately rushed on board to thump my chest. I had him treat Selkirk as well. We all parted changed men, which I hope God grants you may actually see one day."

Aubergine makes a rude sound like a blowing fish. "You're telling us this murderous viper so cruel to our men is changed? That we must forgive our enemy?"

John's voice softens. "I'm saying he is no longer God's enemy and regrets having been ours. If our Lord forgives Selkirk, can we do less?"

"Pah!" Aubergine tightens his lips but then stays silent.

"It's hard to think kindly of him," says a returned Métis who suffers a permanent limp.

"I can't make anyone forgive," John says. "I had to fight my own desire for revenge. I only know Selkirk obtained God's pardon and requested mine."

"*Mon Dieu*. Does God forgive so easily?" asks

a sorrowing widow. "Our lives will never be the same. Our children have lost their father forever."

"Truth." Aubergine sweeps the tips of his mustache upward. "John, you have been horribly mistreated too. Almost to the point of death. Your charitable thoughts are beyond me. Only a giant of a man can forgive so much."

"No. Just someone willing to let Jesus work in his life." John gazes at Aubergine kindly. "In spite of your fierceness, I know the tender heart that lives in your breast. If you ask our Lord's help, He'll give it."

"If I decide to ask." Aubergine does not meet John's eyes. "It's getting late," he says at last. "We are thankful you are home, John. You are exhausted and must rest. We need our rest too."

People drift home from the fort's main meeting hall. After we reach ours, I gather essentials from our bedroom to carry upstairs to the room I'll share with my two older girls and Evangeline. As I leave, John takes my arm.

"Marguerite, please. To be here with you again after years of absence—to see you but find your heart closed is torture beyond anything I've endured. Worse than nearly drowning and losing my companions." His eyes are wells of aching sorrow.

I pull away lest I surrender, for I have missed his touch. "John, years ago you added a tender promise to our *façon du nord*, but until now it only remains a frontier contract—not a true marriage. The contract is easily dissolved so you can enjoy a better life ahead."

He stares. "What? Is that the problem? It is only a frontier contract because it is not yet solemnized by a church wedding or clergyman or priest. Those are not easily available. We said our vows before God." He drops onto our bed as if struck by a poker. "You're so much more to me than the *wilderness wife* named in such contracts. I meant my vows and believed you did. You are my true wife."

His agony burns my soul. I lean against our bedroom wall lest I fall.

He rests his hand where my form has pressed into his side of the bed every night he's been away. "It looks like you reached out for me here. How I ache to hold you. I have remained faithful and chaste all this time."

"So have I." I swallow hard. Only men of high character can say such a thing. Alex MacKay could not. Yet for John's sake, I hold back. "I've come to reality, John. After these years apart, separation suits your new opportunities. We will remain friends. Our children will not suffer."

"Marguerite, if you persist, we will all suffer forever."

After a sleepless night, I hear John stir before dawn. I sneak downstairs. His eyes are burning holes. Did he sleep at all? He groans as I step past him, stiff and resolute.

"I prayed you could open your heart, but I see it is not changed." His voice is ragged.

Dear God, I hate hurting this man but it is for his own sake. Does he not know what it costs me to stay distant?

I sigh. "John, it's impossible. We cannot turn back the clock. Our future is clear."

His lips press into a thin line. "If you can't hear or believe me now, I will make one more journey—the most important of my life." What is he thinking? He is beyond exhausted. His cheeks are gaunt, his voice broken, but his gaze does not let me go. "Promise for the sake of the love we've shared and the vows we've made, that one more time you will wait for my return. I will try to complete my task and come home to you as quickly as I can so you can see the depths of my love and the sincerity in my heart."

"John, there's no need. Nothing will change my answer. I've agonized and prayed during these years. It pains me terribly, but this is the right answer."

"You've prayed about this?" His eyes pierce.

"Yes. Long and hard."

He releases a sigh from the depths of his soul and pulls on his travel-worn boots. They still wear the dust of his recent journey.

"John, stop. It's too soon for you to leave again.

Please listen. You are not well enough or strong enough. You will do yourself harm."

"No. I will go. This matters—you matter—so much."

His appearance frightens me. "Let me pack food and supplies."

"I need nothing. It would be weight I'd have to carry."

"How far will you go? How many days' journey? Let me send someone with you."

He shakes his head. "They would slow me down. Joseph is old enough to come along, but this is not his time. While I'm gone, may he stay with you?" His eyes flicker. "Perhaps I've been unfair leaving him in your charge when he is not yours by birth."

His words make me stagger. "What are you saying? He's mine by love, which counts most. Of course, he must stay. We are family. This is his home." I'm thankful our children are not awake to hear what we say. "He is *our* beloved son, John."

His shoulders ease. "That is as I hoped, but I had to ask since other changes shock me." He rakes a hand through his white hair. "I am resigned that prolonged grief and hardship have overwhelmed you, as they would anyone."

"Not grief and hardship alone, although we've had terrible amounts of both. The truth is, I've come to my senses."

"I don't accept that." His lips tremble. "Merciful God who saved my life, preserve my wife and family now!"

I swallow tears. "Don't you see? Your success separates us. I understand now what I should have years ago and not married above myself again. Montréal is a demanding lover that promises men fame and fortune but steals them from those they leave behind. You are higher above my station than Alex was. I should have known, but I followed my heart."

"Thank God you did." He snorts. "But don't compare me to Alex when I am not him! As God is my witness, although I had to spend time away, my heart has remained yours. While I have breath, I will fight anything that separates us. You and I are joined heart and soul."

His raspy chest alarms me. His blue-tinged skin looks more serious than travel weariness alone. I see his pain yet force myself to remain cold. My crossed arms imprison my heart lest it leaps out in response. "We were joined, John, but I have set you free. God bless you always as you pursue the better life you deserve."

"Please understand, dear one." His chest heaves his words. "Separation is no gift. I do not wish to be free. I am your willing captive, as I believed you were mine."

"Reality requires hard choices." My voice is a monotone. "You may not take our young sons for your life in Montréal, as I am sure you would like. You may guide and influence them later."

"What? Take our boys? Do you think—" His hands ball into fists while I stand unmoving. "I'll prove my love by my actions, as you shall see if God preserves me, Marguerite, my heart." He presses one austere kiss to my forehead but makes no attempt to embrace me.

He expels another long breath that sounds like the beginning of a death rattle as he shrugs into his jacket. "I pray God gives me success quickly. I want no life apart from marriage with you." He searches my eyes. "Wait here for me. You have endured nightmarish loneliness in my absences while sustaining me with love and prayers. Please grant me once more the grace we've known in our marriage."

"You mean in our contract agreement." I am surprised at my sharp tone. The raucous blackbirds that attacked me during other hard times in my life sweep in from nowhere to dive-bomb my mind and drive me mad. "I will wait for a season," I say without emotion, "but after a reasonable time, if you do not return, I will ask God where we should go."

"Merciful God." He groans, looking ill. "I long for our marriage to live." And then he passes through our door.

I stand in our open doorway watching his tall, stooped form walk away with long strides.

I'm puzzled that he heads away from our harbor where he could wait for a Lake Superior schooner. Instead, he takes the wilderness trail heading south along the lakes, carrying only the small leather grip that is his medical bag. He does not look back. Soon, distance swallows him.

What have I done? Yet dissolving our contract is the only sensible thing.

Lord, wherever John goes, don't let him suffer more. We have both walked hard roads. Like Alex, his amazing gifts bring him opportunities that cannot include me.

I drop my head until my breathing returns to normal. I have won this contest and am victor, yet my victory feels hollow. My throat clogs. My breast wants to wail its pain like a widow newly made. At least I have not let John rob me of my sons, like Alex stole Tom. I will guard my flesh and blood like a fierce mother bear and slash the heart of any man or beast who tries to take my young from me.

My lips repeat the scripture prayer they have spoken countless times, "God bless and keep you, John McLoughlin. The Lord make His face to shine upon you and give you peace. You will always be the love of my life."

Chapter 28

I stumble numb through this morning's chores. When the children ask about John's absence, I say, "He is a man with many responsibilities. There is one more task he wants to complete before returning here to stay."

Marie raises her eyebrows. "And he must do that alone?"

"Yes. He has good reasons for what he does."

"Always." She does not look convinced.

Neither is Aubergine fooled. He calls me into John's office, saying he needs my signature on some document. "What happened? Where has John gone? Does his absence involve the red wax-sealed letter you had me send?"

"Why do you ask?"

"Because of the sorrow in your eyes and the firm set of your mouth when you asked me to send it. And the grief in his face last night with it in his pocket. What have you told him?"

I slump against the log wall. "That I've come to my senses. He is impossibly accomplished, so far above my station. I cannot stand by his side in the future the Company gives him now. We are unequally matched. I should have seen that before and not hindered his future. He deserves a helpmeet equal to his opportunities.

He will easily find one. Many women will be interested. Society will easily provide him a new wife."

"Marguerite!" Aubergine's face shows horror. "You told him all that? But you both signed a *façon du nord* that many witnessed, and he added extra vows."

"So do most couples here, but he has not kept the additions." I shrug as if it doesn't matter but bitterness floods my tongue. "These days, such contracts mean little and are easily discarded. It is not a legalized church union and certainly not recognized in Montréal." I taste tears.

"Dear God!" Aubergine's eyebrows knit together. "John provided the best he could. Nothing more was available."

"You are his good friend. Long ago he promised a church marriage but has not taken steps to arrange one. Nor should I have expected. Yet there have been times when clergymen or priests passed through. John could have done something to heal my heart."

"The clergymen passing through here were usually on their way to something urgent. Father Mathieu was the only exception, and John was not here then."

"That I know, but I could have accompanied John to a place with a church or mission. We are not Catholic, but a man of any persuasion would do."

“Marguerite, I see you feel strongly, yet going east would have been difficult when you both were busy with children and also Company demands. Where would you have gone, and how?” He shakes his head. “You have been happy. Still, I ache seeing your heartache.”

“Thank you. Instead of being home when any churchman visited here, John had to cross the ocean twice with worsening pneumonia. I have considered our present reality and released him from our contract.”

He moans. “That is what I feared from your faces last night. My poor friend, John, to lose the treasure you are.”

“He will receive other rewards.”

Aubergine studies me. “You are sure, Marguerite?”

“Dissolving our union is the realistic choice.”

“And you think John can endure that loss after all else?”

“He has survived life-threatening challenges. He’ll see the wisdom of this and be grateful.”

“I doubt that.” Aubergine stares from beneath his bushy brows. “And you? And the children? Will you stay? Or go?”

“I . . . I’m not sure yet. John asked me to wait for his return. I agreed but can’t see beyond that.” I lift a hand to my aching head. “My thoughts tumble and roar like the foaming waterfall on the river west of here. My life needs to flow calmly from this place to more peaceful shores. No more roaring cataracts."

Aubergine nods. "I understand. You've had little peace for some time."

"The girls will stay with me until they marry. Our sons will remain while young. They'll probably join John later for advanced opportunities. Whether I go or stay, I am strong and capable. The same God who helped me until now will help me in the future."

"I'm sure." His mouth works silently. He extends his hands, almost in supplication, and says, "John is my stalwart friend. It is terribly soon, but if your heart is set—If great sorrow means your life with him is over, perhaps one day? I could dare to hope. I am a far less worthy man, but I would forever be the happiest of all if you—"

I draw back. "What? Aubergine! You are dear and sweet, but I cannot get involved with anyone ever again."

"But if you change your mind—if there could be any chance you might care for me, foolish, clumsy bear that I am—" He draws a deep breath, his eyes afire. "I have always loved you, even though you only tolerate me."

"Dear friend, don't be foolish." I touch his arm. "I more than tolerate you. You are resourceful and loyal, funny and kind. But I am without feeling and cannot think. I may never be able to think clearly again. My life is a rushing stream seeking its true stream bed."

"That may be so. Time will tell." He pauses. "I simply ask that in the future when you think of me, you will think kindly. You require time. And yet—" He rocks forward on the balls of his feet.

"Yet what?"

"There is some warmth in your eyes that promises you may care for me a little."

"Of course—a little." I brush his arm again. "How can I not after all the trials and tears we've all shared through the years?"

He huffs out a relieved breath. "We've survived much and built enduring memories, but this I know." His lips curve upward. "In time, with care, the smallest spark can become a blaze large enough to light and warm a home."

"Aubergine, you become poetic."

"Perhaps." He glows like a wood stove giving off radiant heat. I have felt achingly cold for a long time. When he steps forward and encircles me with his strong arms, I relax slightly against him. His voice quivers as he murmurs my name. His hug tightens. My arms entwine around his comfortable frame and I rest my weary head on his shoulder. It seems a good fit.

"Aubergine. Dear Eggplant. Through these long hard years, you have been so dear to us. We all feel your love—especially John."

"Yes, I know. It is fully returned." His big

hands roam my back. "I doubt you know your own heart. You're less resolute than you think, but I choose to have a bit of hope."

After we release each other, he stretches and smooths the wrinkles from his shirt. "I shall do all I can to become a man to deserve you."

I laugh. "Don't speak nonsense. That is easily done. I will never again let myself be loved by any eminent man, for they tower above me in all ways and then go away. It is better to trust someone jolly and gentle, like a friendly bear."

His chuckle rumbles. "That gives me greater hope, for I am gentle, except when I must be a fierce growling bear."

My over-taxed heart steadies, sensing a bit more peace than I've felt for a while.

Dear Lord, thank You for this kind faithful friend. Why is it so hard for me to love and be loved? Perhaps I must live alone like a nun, rather than ever risk my heart being broken again—or breaking someone else's.

I return to our home, but my head pounds. After lunch, I ask Marie to manage dispensary tasks and Catherine to care for the younger children, while I go to the woods to gather herbs. I collect enough in my basket to justify my pleasant walk.

The white eagle still rules his nest. I reach the lakeshore, to the path John took. I see traces of his footsteps, and I hear my father's favorite verse ring in my heart. *I will never leave thee, nor forsake thee . . .*

God have mercy. I'm not sure what those words mean for me or our family now. I believe they are true, but we have been sorely tested. Still, I wrap that promise around me like a cloak and return home.

Aubergine checks on us daily and works at being a polished gentleman. "You know my coat you patched?" he says. "I snagged it again. Could you or Marie please mend it? As I perform John's duties, I must look presentable. Not haphazard."

Looking unpresentable would not have troubled our old friend at all. He looks so serious now, I almost laugh, except it would pain him. He considers his roughhewn words quite carefully before speaking, like tempering iron by passing it through alternating fire and water after hammer blows.

Through the next eight weeks, as trading ships arrive, Aubergine asks for news of John and shares the reports with me. John has been south to Grand Portage, that post now at peace with us again but still in American hands. John has visited the rebuilt fort at Sault Sainte Marie and from there gone to smaller outposts. Some say he's conducting secret surveys to choose important new fort sites for after the Company merger.

We're told every person he treats for illness recovers. These stories make him a legend, not a man, and make me ache to assist him again as we used to, or travel together to distant outposts as we did before his fame. Yet those days are gone. He is destined for Europe and Canada's capital cities and international decisions.

Marie says of Aubergine, "He sparkles these days—like a puppy wagging its tail."

"He wishes to be helpful with Father gone, that's all."

She tilts her head. "No. When Father was away before, Aubergine didn't act so fond." She stares. "It's very noticeable when he's around you."

I inhale a sharp breath but stay silent.

"Surely you've noticed," she says. "He was always friendly, but not so caring. It's almost like he hopes to court you. What has happened?"

My face heats. "Is he so obvious?"

"Yes, or I would not ask. Something has taken place between you and Father that Aubergine knows."

I cannot avoid her piercing eyes. "John is prominent and in great demand," I say. "Yet that's nothing compared to more future honors coming. I will always love him but am a simple mixed-blood woman, unable to be his equal. I have released him from our *façon du nord* contract. Aubergine knows since he arranged delivery of that letter."

Her eyes widen in horror. “Mother! Father loves you!”

“And I love him.” Does my own daughter not understand that I do this because I love John? She starts to say more, but I will not listen. “John’s interests must be considered. He cared for us when your father did not. He will see to it that none of you ever lack and will remain a wonderful influence in your lives, but I will not handicap him.”

Tears pool in her eyes. “You are not seeing clearly. Father does not view it that way. He loves you, not fame. You will break his heart.”

Her words stab. “Fame is thrust upon him. My heart is already broken.”

“But this is the wrong answer.”

“You must trust me to decide.”

She’s right. Aubergine tries to be discreet, yet looks at me tenderly when he visits our home, lifting bushy eyebrows above a smile of uncomplicated joy.

“Discourage him more.” Marie is full of concern.

“I am not encouraging him.”

But the smallest kindness from my hand has an effect. I’m flattered, yet see the problem. “Aubergine, I’ve promised you nothing. You are a dear friend. I make no other commitment.”

His smile lingers. “Perhaps in time?”

“You must act normal.”

"I hope never to be normal again."

My next note from Nancy and McCargo says her birthing draws near—*The baby has dropped into position. I have occasional twinges but not severe. Whether this baby is a boy or girl, it's as active as any schooner captain climbing his rigging to hoist sails. That seems most suitable in a boy, but since I am the mother, it might be a girl doing the same. Robert says he will love either. I am nearly ready to pop, so we are heading your way.*

My heart lifts. I begin remembering to smile.

Six more weeks pass without word of John. The weather includes shrieking storms that bend trees double and whip the lake into frenzy. By mid-afternoon when winds lessen slightly, Joseph joins young men in a sheltered cove where big fish swim. I stand at our window watching when rectangular sails slice the horizon. A ship!

I shade my eyes and see a royal blue pennant on top—McCargo's ship. My daughter and her babe are here. I will soon be a grandmother! I call Marie and Catherine, "Come quickly, Nancy is here."

Joseph leaves his pole and basket of fish. He reaches the wharf before us and catches McCargo's ropes to tie them to shore.

"It's Nancy," Robert pants white-faced as I

reach the ship. “The baby is large and stuck. She suffers. Come help.” He extends the gangplank. His long arms pull me on board.

I rush below and am surprised to find a dear, familiar form with hair as snowy white as an eagle’s feathers bending over her, his shoulders hunched in caring.

Groans rise from my brave girl and sweat beads her face. I push past John and press my cheek against hers, smoothing her hair. “I’m here, Nancy.”

“Thank God, Mother. Help. Me.”

I grasp her hand before taking my place next to John by her bent knees.

“Marguerite,” he says without turning, his tone so gentle it shafts my heart. No anger, no blame—just, “Marguerite,” with all the tenderness in the world. I inhale his clean scent of soap and medicine. And when his shoulder brushes mine, my heart cracks open at his nearness. Thank God he concentrates on Nancy, for I could not survive his gaze.

I must focus on my daughter’s birth. God in heaven, I can’t feel emotion now. Make me numb and strong.

I ask, “How long since her pains began?”

He leans close and whispers, “Too long with little progress. This baby is large and stuck in the birth canal. We fight for Nancy’s life, too, with so much blood loss.”

Nancy moans, her eyes glassy, and reaches a hand, "Mother?"

"Yes, love. Father and I are here." In my mind's eye, I see other mothers lost to hemorrhaging births gone wrong. I hear Peter Arndt tell of losing his wife and child and John losing Joseph's mother when he could not reach her in time.

Robert clutches Nancy's other hand tight, his lips moving in prayer.

As do mine. *Lord Jesus in heaven, have mercy!*

John breaks my reverie. "I've done all I can. She needs your skill. I fear the placenta has torn."

I reach instant focus. "Is there time for infusions?"

"I think so. We've heated water. Tell us what you need." He nods as Marie brings my medical bag.

She and I exchange glances, and she blends two strong cathartic brews, blue and black cohosh and shepherd's purse. I staunch bleeding while she lifts Nancy's head and brings the cup to her lips.

"Uhhhh," Nancy complains but swallows.

"The bitter taste proves the brew is powerful," I tell her.

John's breath is soft in my ear. "My hands are too large. I cannot move the child. You must try."

His beautiful large hands, so skilled, yet unable to do this. My smaller hands easily slip inside Nancy but at first make no headway. The infant is wedged tight, its large head blocking the passage. Nancy's contractions become constant. There's a brief pause between two strong spasms, and I struggle to free and guide her baby. Her clamping womb spills crimson blood.

I lower my head. *Lord Jesus, my child and hers. Help us!*

She bites her tongue as the strongest contraction rips through her. Her taut belly rises and undulates.

"Push," I urge.

She groans and bears down, the effort tearing the soft flesh at her body's opening.

Between terrible contractions, my hands grip and turn the baby's head. I guide the slippery shoulders of this beloved child, my flesh and blood, into life. I catch their baby boy in my hands and cry, "You have a son!"

"God be praised!" Robert weeps. "Is Nancy well?"

"She will be. She must drink more concoctions, but God has helped us."

She sinks against her pillow. None of us have dry eyes. I wipe the newborn clean and place my welcoming kiss on the crown of his perfect head. Then John ties and cuts the umbilical cord before placing him in his mother's arms. Robert reaches his arms around both mother and son as I sag against John.

"Marguerite," John says.

My heart remembers all the times, and ways, and reasons I love this man, yet must *not* love him. Must make my heart rigid and closed for his sake. I pull away. "Her blood flow has slowed. I will massage the placenta to help it release and give her more herbs until the bleeding stops."

Marie moves forward. "I'll do it, Mother."

John touches my arm. "Sweetheart, let Marie assist. Take a moment to wash and then come to me. I will do the same. I have a gift for you. And we must talk."

"Now?" Drained by this difficult birth, I cannot think. I'm not capable of anything more.

"Yes. Good news. Meet me in five minutes."

By then, I will have left this ship and gone somewhere. Anywhere. I spread Nancy's hair across her pillow and for a moment soak in the sight of my adorable newborn grandson. He is strong and active, already eager to latch onto his mother's breast.

I hug my son-in-law. "You have a good lad here, Robert."

"And wonderful wife." He radiates joy. "We've named him Robert John McCargo. When our girl is born, she shall bear your name."

"Mine? No. Choose something finer."

He pecks my cheek. "There is no finer name. Thanks for saving Nancy. She is my world."

"And you are hers." I hug him. "Now your

world is larger. Praise God for preserving my daughter and your son."

In the mirror on the wall, I see my long hair has worked loose from its braided crown and my cheeks are rosy. After washing my hands, I tuck in the loose wisps and begin my escape up the stairs. But not soon enough. John already descends from the main deck, and another man follows him.

John stops, blocking my way. "Since we could not easily go to a church, dear love, I've brought the church to you."

Behind him, our friend Father Mathieu, the explorer priest, steps forward. He carries a Bible and wears wedding vestments. Joseph, Catherine, and our little ones are clustered on the stairs above, watching and smiling. But I only have eyes for John.

He drops to one knee, his eyes filled with love. "Marguerite, my bride, you are the only woman in this world who completes me. May we solemnize our vows now?"

I clasp my hands over my aching breast. "John, don't break my heart."

"I'm not. If true love breaks it, our Lord can mend it. I think you've mostly known conditional love until now, but our Lord teaches unconditional love. That's what I will give. Please accept me as your loving, church-sanctioned husband united to live out His love here on earth while guided by the rules of heaven. Marguerite, does your heart hear the cry of mine? What is your answer?"

"I'm unworthy."

"None of us is worthy, but He paid the price to make us so. You are worthy, and I choose you to be my forever beloved wife."

He tries to still my protests with a kiss, but I turn my face as more words rip from me. "I will not destroy your future."

"You could not destroy anything. You complete it. I desire nothing more than life with you. I've arranged new orders with the merged Company that change everything. Will you hear me?"

I'd rather plug my ears, but he keeps speaking.

"They've approved a choice I was too numb to share the first night of my return. Especially since you—" He wipes his brow. "Never mind. At first they suggested we base in Montréal for my frequent trips to London—"

"As I expected."

He lifts a hand. "And which I refused. That is no life for a family. I believe you will like my negotiated alternative. It would take us to Oregon."

"Seriously? To Oregon?" He has my attention. My eyes lock on his.

"Where Tom is. To manage Astor's fort and more. By the laws ending the War of 1812, Astor must transfer power to us. We would govern the vast region from Canada to Mexico and the

Rocky Mountains to the Pacific—an area larger than many nations and rich with resources." His eyes gleam. "Few men get such opportunity."

"And few women." My breath hitches. "What was your answer?"

"I framed the proposal but have not given final answer. I told them I must first talk with my wife and only accept if she agrees to go with me and stand at my side. Otherwise, I'll leave the Company and practice medicine together with you anywhere you and I decide."

His eyes draw me closer.

"It is your choice, Marguerite. What is your answer? Will you agree and sanction our marriage now before this good priest?"

I study him closely. "Could *you* also be content compared to the other large opportunities you have? You have your life and fame before you. You also must be happy and fulfilled."

His smile rivals the sun. "You are my choice. You and Oregon for us, together."

My mind pictures Tom by a distant ocean, beyond snow-capped mountains that shine like the white peaks of my father's homeland. That scene fills my heart, but not as much as the depths of love shining in John's eyes. "You would choose me and that beckoning wilderness over princely prospects?"

"Yes! Apart from you, no other prospect holds attraction. May the Lord help you see the truth of that as I must have now told you a hundred times."

I fling my arms around this loving man and groan as a dreadful weight leaves me. "John, if I am truly your choice, though you could do so much better."

"Dearest, just answer me."

"I am deeply ashamed of the heartache I've caused, of the pain my refusal brought, although I meant it for your good."

He takes my hand and interweaves his fingers with mine. "You are my good. What answer lies in your heart?"

"I am so terribly sorry. How can you forgive me? I couldn't imagine you saddled with—"

"Not saddled with—lovingly joined." He tightens his grip.

"Please understand, I never meant to hurt you, only to free you for the successes you deserve. With your new prospects, I never dreamed you would choose me. In fact, you shouldn't—"

His arm encircles me. "Marguerite, don't listen to darkness. Only to our Lord with no other comparisons. It's true I worked hard to acquire education. But your knowledge of natural things and inner beauty and goodness draw me like the Shulamite bride in the Song of Solomon. You need nothing more. Surely you, who are wiser than most understand this. Let the truth of my love settle deep in your heart, for that truth will never change." He cups my chin. "I love you and only you. Believe me. That's how it will always be."

He kisses me gently to seal his words. The tender overflow of his heart dissolves the last clogging ice restraining my emotions. As sunshine dispels fog, I see my destiny—our destiny—as we face a wonderfully great task together with the strength of united, unconditional love.

"John, I do love you. I've always loved you, maybe since we first helped poor Gaston together." I laugh and cry, both at once, flinging my arms tighter around him to never let him go.

"Although it takes me hearing you a thousand times to believe, I do at last. Life with you in Oregon would be more joy than I dreamed of. I'm grateful you want me after all I have put you through."

Above us, our children cheer.

He caresses my cheek. "These years stretched us to the breaking point. In fact, we both broke. But we both know broken bones heal stronger than they were before."

"Yes. That's true."

He showers me with more kisses. "We're both better-prepared for our future. While on my awful journey to Montréal, the Lord promised that for every heartache, every deep valley of pain and suffering, He would bring me to that same height of joy and gladness. That's His promise for you, too, Marguerite. He will fulfill every plan He has for us." He pulls me tighter in his arms until we are one, two hearts beating together.

I respond with every unlocked emotion I have not let myself feel these last years. Now I fully deliver and receive love. We sigh and drink deeply until he gently releases me and again pulls from his pocket the black velvet bag holding the lustrous pearl and gold wedding band.

"This shining gift represents our love. Accept it as my church-sanctioned, legally wedded bride for all the world to see."

I extend my hand. "Precious John, I am honored to accept with joy."

He slips his magnificent gift onto my finger, then captures my hands in his to rest them against his heart. "Thank God, Marguerite. Your love empowers me."

"And yours me." Now I draw his hands to my breast so he feels my answering heart. "Darling John, I am the most honored of women to share all of life with you in Christian marriage."

A sheen of tears blurs his dear face as he crushes me to him to claim my lips again, expressing enough sweetness to last a lifetime.

Our audience grows impatient. Father Mathieu clears his throat. "Now that you accept each other, shall I perform legal vows here and now, in the presence of most of your children? Or conduct them tomorrow in the fort's great hall in front of everyone? You decide."

John whispers, "If you would prefer a Protestant ceremony, we can also do that later. I will marry you as often and in as many places as you wish."

I love his smile and dry my tears. "Tomorrow at Fort William is perfect. But I don't have a suitable dress."

Just then Marie, who has been helping Nancy, rounds the corner. "The bleeding has stopped, Mother. And I have a perfect unused dress. When the time comes that I need one, I'm sure I will have another."

"I'll see to that myself." John chuckles. "Do you wish to continue wearing my ring now, Marguerite? Or shall I slip it on your finger during tomorrow's ceremony before witnesses?"

His pearl gleams as bright as the blaze warming my heart. "Both, but tomorrow is perfect."

We return the ring to its velvet bag, which he suspends from a cord around his neck.

Somehow Nancy has overheard because she calls out, "Your joy is such strong tonic, I may be well enough to attend."

"No," we hear Robert object. "It's good you heard their words today, because my wife must be completely well before she resumes adventures anywhere."

"If that is what you wish, dear Robert, that is fine."

John and I look at each other. We marvel that lively Nancy answers her husband sweetly in such gentle tones. In fact, we descend several steps to peek into the room and make sure it is Nancy speaking. It's her, all right, hugging her baby, enjoying her husband's embrace, and radiating tranquility.

"After our ceremony, we'll come show you our finery, Nancy," I promise. I bend to touch the golden-red fluff on her infant's head again, so like his Scottish father's, and place more kisses.

As I rise, Marie pulls John and me into an embrace. "It's high time you accepted his proposal, Mother. Now I'll go to the fort to start preparations. You must have a beautiful cake with lovely hall decorations. Catherine, come help me."

Catherine's eyes dance. "If I may decorate the hall."

Marie laughs. "You may *help,* but I make the final decisions."

"I'll help too," Joseph says, "if there's food involved. And if I may lick the frosting bowl?"

"Food is involved, and you may."

Laughing, Joseph and Catherine herd our younger ones from the ship.

The priest approaches John. "Will you join me briefly to review your written vows?"

"Of course. Thank you. Excuse me, Marguerite." He bends over my hand and kisses it like the gentleman he is, his eyes glowing in a face from which care and sorrow have fled. He looks younger. I feel as if dark years have rolled away from me, as well.

Suddenly, I think of Aubergine at the fort working in John's office. He knows that McCargo's ship is here, but not that John is on board. I must speak to him and help him accept that I am forever John's. I will only ever be his friend.

As soon as I enter his office, he stands but doesn't embrace me. "Aubergine, I must tell you—"

"Say nothing. I already know." He lays his finger across my lips. "Your face is sunshine. You mean the world to me, but John is also my dear friend. I wish you both happiness and am thankful you finally know your place and worth." He beams such kindness that I will never again think of him as a clumsy bear, but as a lost prince discovering his true kingdom and parentage. "I will always wish you perfect joy and happiness." Kindly tears fill his eyes.

Later, when John and I come together to greet dear Aubergine, he congratulates us both with a winning smile.

That evening, as Aubergine and Marie arrange reception details, I note her gentleness with him and his desire to please her. I note how much she resembles me. In fact, she is like me in many ways and wise beyond her years. He is older, but I wonder in days to come if these two might ever discover joy together.

It is late when John and I reach home. Despite hardships, he has regained strength during his six weeks away. He scoops me up in his strong arms and carries me across our threshold. "The next time I whisk you across this step, it shall be as the church-blessed wife of John McLoughlin."

"Mrs. Doctor John McLoughlin," I murmur. "I love the sound of that name and my future with my true love, the father of my children. You own my heart, John."

"As you do mine." He gives a lingering kiss. "We have birthed beautiful children." His eyes twinkle. "There may be more."

"We will love them all."

"I include Evangeline, who I treasure."

"She loves you already. But instead of coming to our room tonight, let me stay with the girls so they can fully prepare me to be your glowing bride."

"Of course, dearest." His Adam's apple bobs. "Though in my eyes, you need nothing more. You have always been my cherished bride, no enhancement needed." He gives a boyish grin, and it pleases me how much Joseph and our younger boys take after him.

He brushes a hand through his thick hair. "I must make my own preparations. Perhaps our barber can tame this snowy mane." He strides to the fort with the energy of a younger man.

The girls and I talk and laugh far into the night. Near dawn, when my eyes briefly close, my heart hears a distant river singing. Or a cascading waterfall bubbling music and laughter. For God has guided the tumultuous stream of my life past plunging cataracts, beyond dangerous fields of tumbled boulders, to this deep, wide, peaceful pool where I am calm and whole and loved by the best of men, one who serves God and reflects His glory.

Whatever steps lie ahead, my beloved husband and I will walk across this continent together hand in hand.

About Delores Topliff

In third grade, Delores began composing rhyming stories. Her classmates' approval encouraged her writing. Two of her four award-winning children's books are rhymed adventures.

Delores grew up near Fort Vancouver, Washington, loving its history. Before it was enclosed for safety, she crawled to the original well's edge, appreciating its stone-lined walls built by early hands. To *absorb* history, she's eaten knobby green apples from the Pacific Northwest's oldest apple tree planted by the fort's founder, Dr. John McLoughlin.

Delores married a Canadian so enjoys U.S. and Canadian citizenships. She loves her doctor sons, families, and five grandchildren, and is something she didn't think she'd be—a snowbird dividing her year between Minnesota and Mississippi.

Besides writing, she teaches university classes and enjoys travel, photography, and various hobbies. She also loves connecting with readers and speaking to writing groups and book clubs.

Find her blogs, books, and more at
delorestopliff.com.
Connect on Facebook at Delores Topliff Books.

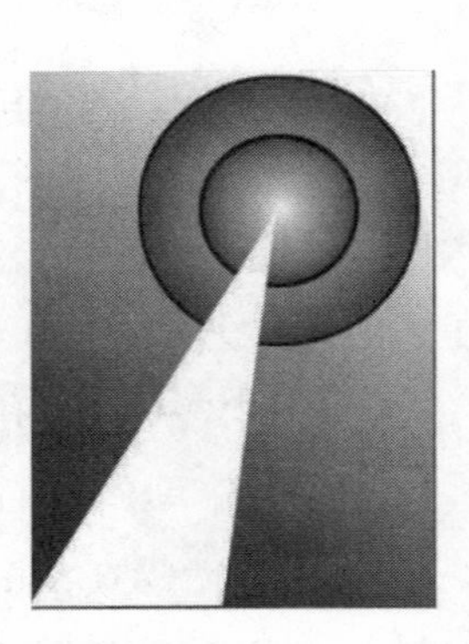

Center Point Large Print
600 Brooks Road / PO Box 1
Thorndike, ME 04986-0001 USA

(207) 568-3717

US & Canada:
1 800 929-9108
www.centerpointlargeprint.com